Latin Lovers
HOT-BLOODED SICILIANS

Three fabulous stories from reader favourites
Lucy Monroe, Sarah Morgan &
Catherine Spencer

LATIN LOVERS COLLECTION

COLLECT ALL SIX!

Latin Lovers

HOT-BLOODED SICILIANS

Lucy
MONROE

Sarah
MORGAN

Catherine
SPENCER

MILLS & BOON

All the characters in this book have no existence outside the imagination
of the author, and have no relation whatsoever to anyone bearing the
same name or names. They are not even distantly inspired by any
individual known or unknown to the author, and all the incidents are
pure invention.

Mills & Boon, an imprint of Harlequin (UK) Limited, Eton House,
18-24 Paradise Road, Richmond, Surrey TW9 1SR

LATIN LOVERS: HOT-BLOODED SICILIANS
© Harlequin Enterprises II B.V./S.à.r.l. 2011

Valentino's Love-Child © Lucy Monroe 2009
The Sicilian Doctor's Proposal © Sarah Morgan 2006
Sicilian Millionaire, Bought Bride © Spencer Books Ltd 2008

ISBN: 978 0 263 88986 4

027-0811

Harlequin (UK) policy is to use papers that are natural, renewable
and recyclable products and made from wood grown in sustainable
forests. The logging and manufacturing processes conform to the
legal environmental regulations of the country of origin.

Printed and bound in Spain
by Blackprint CPI, Barcelona

VALENTINO'S LOVE-CHILD

Lucy Monroe

Lucy Monroe started reading at the age of four. After going through the children's books at home, she was caught by her mother reading adult novels pilfered from the higher shelves on the bookcase… Alas, it was nine years before she got her hands on a Mills & Boon® romance her older sister had brought home. She loves to create the strong alpha males and independent women that people Mills & Boon® books. When she's not immersed in a romance novel (whether reading or writing it), she enjoys travel with her family, having tea with the neighbours, gardening, and visits from her numerous nieces and nephews.

Lucy loves to hear from readers. E-mail her at LucyMonroe@LucyMonroe.com, or visit her website: www.LucyMonroe.com

CHAPTER ONE

VALENTINO GRISAFI brushed a silky auburn curl away from where it blocked his view of his sleeping mistress's face.

Mistress. An old-fashioned word for a very modern woman. Faith Williams would not appreciate the label. Were he to be foolish enough to use it within her hearing, she would no doubt let him know it too. His *carina americana* was no wilting flower.

Pretty American. Now, that suited her. But if he should let on he thought of her like a mistress? *Ai-yi-yi.*

Eyes the blue of a peacock feather would snap with temper while she lectured him on how inappropriate the term was. And he supposed she would have a point. He did not pay her bills. He did not buy her clothes. No matter how many hours they spent together here, she did not live in his Marsala apartment. She did not rely on him for anything but his company.

So, not his mistress. But not his girlfriend, either. Long-term commitment and love had no place between them. Theirs was a purely physical relationship, the duration and depth of which was dictated purely by convenience. Mostly his. Not that Faith had nothing to say in the matter.

She could walk away as easily as he and had no more incentive to make time in her schedule for him than vice versa. Luckily for them both, the relationship— such that it was—worked for each of them.

Perhaps they were friends also and he did not regret it, but that had come after. After he had discovered the way her sweet, curvaceous body responded to the slightest touch of his. After kisses that melted his brain and her resistance. After he had learned how much pleasure he could find basking in her generous sensuality, once unleashed.

The sex between them was phenomenal.

Which was no doubt why he could already feel the loss of the coming weeks.

Tracing her perfect oval features he leaned close to her ear. "*Carina,* you must wake."

Her nose wrinkled and the luscious bow of her mouth twisted into a moue of denial, her exotically colored eyes remaining stubbornly closed. Her recently sated body not moving so much as a centimeter from its usual post-coital curled position.

"Come, *bella mia.* Waken."

"If you'd come to my apartment, I could stay in bed sleeping while you had to get dressed and leave," she grumbled into the pillow.

"Most nights, I leave as well, *carina.* You know this." He liked to have breakfast with Giosuc. His cight-year-old son was the light of Valentino's life. "Besides, I am not waking you up to go. We need to talk."

Faith's eyelids fluttered, but her mouth did not slip from its downward arch.

"You are adorable like this, you know?"

That had her sitting up and staring at him with grumpy startlement, the tangerine, supersilky, Egyptian cotton sheet she'd insisted he use on his bed clutched to her chest. "Sane people do not find cranky attractive, Tino."

Biting back a smile, he shrugged. "What can I say? I am different. Or perhaps it is you. I do not recall finding any of my other *amantes* so cute when they were irritable."

He did not like using the word *lover,* but knew better than to refer to her as the equally ill-fitting title of *mistress*. And she had already cut him off at the knees for referring to her once as a bed partner. She said if he wanted to use such a clinical term, he should consider getting an anatomically accurate blow-up doll.

Why these thoughts were plaguing him tonight, he did not know. Defining her place in his life was not something he spent time doing, nor was he overly fond of labels. So why so preoccupied with them tonight?

"I have no interest in hearing about your past conquests Signor Grisafi." Now she really looked out of sorts, her eyes starting to flash with temper.

"I apologize. But you know I was hardly an untried boy when we met." He had already loved and lost a wife, not to mention the women who had warmed his cold bed after.

He and Faith had been together for a year, longer than he had been with any other woman since the death of his beloved Renata. But that hardly altered his past.

"Neither of us were virgins, but it's bad form to discuss past relationships while in bed with your current lover."

"You are so worried about following protocols, too," he mocked.

He had never known someone less concerned with appearance and social niceties. His *carina americana* was the quintessential free spirit.

A small smile teased her lips at that. "Maybe not, but this is one social norm I'm one hundred percent behind."

"Duly noted."

"Good." She curled up to him, snuggling against his chest, her hand resting casually on his upper thigh and causing no small reaction in his nether regions. "You said you didn't wake me up to send me on my way?"

"No. We need to talk."

She cocked her head to one side. "What about?"

He couldn't help himself. He leaned down and kissed the tip of her straight nose. "You really are adorable when you first wake up."

"I thought it was when I was grumpy."

"Have you ever woken up *not* irritable?"

"I have a perfectly sunny disposition in the morning. Not that you would know that little fact as we've never spent a full night together, but you'll have to take my word on it. It's only when I have to wake up after being sated so gorgeously with your body that I complain."

It was an old argument. She had never taken his refusal to spend the entire night together with full grace. She understood his desire to be home for breakfast with his son, but not his insistence on leaving their shared bed after at most a short nap after their lovemaking.

Her continued pressing the point frustrated him and that leaked out into his voice when he said, "Be that as it may, there is something I have been meaning to tell you."

She stiffened and pulled away, her blue-green gaze reflecting an instant emotional wariness. "What?"

"It is nothing bad. Well, not too bad. It is simply that my parents are going on a trip. They wish to visit friends in Naples."

"Oh, really? I didn't know."

"Naturally, I did not tell you."

"And?"

"And I cannot leave Giosue at night when he does not have his grandparents there to watch over him." Never mind the staff that lived on site at their vineyard, Vigne di Grisafi, much less the housekeeper that had her own room in the house. It was not the same.

"I understand." He could tell from her expression that she really did. "How long will your parents be gone?"

"Two weeks only."

"I won't see you at all?"

"It is unlikely."

She looked like she wanted to say something, but in the end she simply nodded.

"I will miss you," he found himself admitting. Then he scowled. He hadn't wanted to say that. "This." He brushed his hand down her body. "I will miss *this*."

"I heard you the first time, tough guy. You can't take it back now. You may as well admit you like my company as much as me in your bed."

He bore her back to the bed, his mouth hovering above hers. "Maybe almost as much. And speaking of sex. I will have to do without you for two weeks, I think we should take advantage of our time together."

"Have I ever said no to you?" she asked with a husky laugh.

"No and tonight is no time to start."

Faith woke surrounded by warmth and the scent of the man she loved.

Her eyes flew open and a grin split her face. It hadn't been a dream. After making love into the wee hours of the morning, Tino had asked her to spend the night. For the first time ever.

Okay, maybe not asked…more like informed her that she was staying, but it was the same result. She was in his arms, in his bed—the morning after they'd made love.

And it was glorious.

Every bit as delicious a feeling as she had thought it would be.

"Are you awake?" his deep voice rumbled above her.

She lifted her head from its resting place on his hair-covered chest and turned the full wattage of her smile on him. "What does it look like?"

"It looks like you were telling me the truth when you said you had a sunny disposition in the morning. Maybe I will have to start calling you *solare*."

Sunlight? Her heart squeezed. "Tay used to call me Sunshine."

"A past boyfriend?" Tino asked on a growl, the morning whiskers on his face giving him a sexily fierce aspect. "You are right, discussing past *amores* while in bed with your current one is definitely bad taste."

She laughed, not in the least offended. "He was my husband, not a past boyfriend," she said as she scooted out of the bed, intent on making coffee.

"You were married?"

"Yes." Weird that after almost a full year together, she was telling him about having been married before for the first time. But then, that was the nature of their relationship. She and Tino focused on the present when they were together.

She'd learned more about him—and a tragic past similar to her own—from his mother than she'd ever learned from him. Strangely enough, where Tino showed no interest in Faith's art, his mother was a fan. They'd met at one of Faith's showings in Palermo. In spite of the generation difference in their ages, the two women had hit it off immediately and both had been thrilled to discover they lived so close to one another. Vigne di Grisafi was a mere twenty-minute drive from Faith's small apartment in Pizzolato.

Not that she'd ever been there as Tino's guest. She'd been seeing Tino for two months before she realized the Valentino Agata mentioned so frequently was Tino, the man Faith spent her nights making love with. At first, she'd found it disconcerting, but she'd soon adjusted. She hadn't told Agata about the fact she was dating Tino though.

He'd been careful to keep their relationship discreet and she felt it was his prerogative to determine when his family would be told about her.

In another almost unreal twist of fate, Faith was his son Giosue's teacher, too. She taught an art class for primary school children in Marsala once a week. She may have lost her one chance at motherhood, but she still adored kids, and this was her way of spending time with them. Giosue was an absolute doll and she more than understood Tino's desire to be there for him. She applauded it.

"Divorced?" Tino asked, his brown eyes intent on her and apparently not done with the topic of Tay.

"Widowed." She didn't elaborate, knowing Tino wouldn't want the details. He never wanted the details. Not about her personal history.

He said he liked to concentrate on the here and now. Since that was her own personal motto, she didn't balk at the fact he showed no interest in her life before Sicily.

She had to admit, though, that he didn't show much interest in her life here, either.

He knew she was an artist, but she wasn't sure he knew she was a successful one or that she was a clay sculptor. He knew she lived in Pizzolato, a small town a few minutes south of Marsala, but she doubted he knew exactly where her apartment was. In the entire year they'd been together, they had made love in one place only—his apartment.

Not his home, because he didn't live there. He said he kept it for business purposes, but she thought he meant the business of getting sex without falling under the watchful eye of his mother. Tino had been very careful to keep their lives completely separate.

At first, she hadn't minded. She'd been no more interested in a deep emotional connection than he had been. He'd promised her sex and that was all he'd given her.

Only, at some point along the way, she'd realized, she couldn't help giving him love.

Even so, she'd been content to keep their relationship on a shallow level. Or at least convinced herself to be. She'd lost everyone she'd ever loved and had no doubt that one day she would lose him, too. That didn't mean she hadn't loved spending the whole night together—she had. But as for the rest of it, the less entwined in her life he was, the better for her it would be when that time came.

At least, that was how she had thought. She wasn't so sure anymore.

"So, that is all you have to say on the matter?"

She pushed the start button on the coffeemaker and turned to face Tino. "What?"

He'd pulled on a pair of boxers, leaving most of his

tall, chiseled body on mouthwatering display. "Your husband died."

Were they still on that? "Yes."

"How?"

"A car accident."

"When?"

"Six years ago."

He ran his fingers through his morning tousled dark hair. "You never told me."

"Did you want me to?"

"I would think that sometime in a year you would have thought to mention that you were a widow." He came into the kitchen and leaned against the counter near her.

"Why?"

"It is an important piece of information about you."

"About my past."

He frowned at her.

"You prefer to focus on today, not yesterday. You've said so many times, Tino. What's going on?"

"Maybe I'm just curious about the woman I've been bedding for a year."

"Almost a year."

"Do not banter semantics with me."

"I'm glad you're curious."

"I…" For the first time in memory, her lover, the über-cool Valentino Grisafi, looked lost for words.

"Don't worry about it, Tino. It's not a bad thing."

"No, no, of course not. We are friends as well as lovers, *si?*"

"Yes." And she was more relieved than she could say that he saw it that way, too.

"Good. Good." He was silent a second. "Do I get breakfast to go with my coffee?"

"I think that can be arranged."

He got a borderline horrified look on his face. "You do know how to cook, don't you?"

She laughed, truly tickled. "We aren't all filthy rich vintners, Tino. Some of us can't afford a housekeeper or to eat out every meal—thus, knowing how to cook is essential. But I don't mind telling you, I'm pretty good at it as well."

"I'll reserve judgment."

She laughed and launched herself at him to tickle the big man into submission, or at least a lot of laughter before he subdued her wandering fingers.

Faith finished the third form of a pregnant woman she had done in as many days. She hadn't done women *enceinte* since the loss of her baby in the accident that had killed Taylish and any chance Faith would ever have at a family.

Or so she had believed.

Her clay-spattered hand pressed over her still-flat stomach, a sense of awe and wonder infusing her. It had taken her four years and fertility counseling for her to become viably pregnant the first time.

Her first actual pregnancy had occurred a mere two months after she married Taylish at the age of eighteen. They'd been ecstatic when the home pregnancy test showed positive, only to be cast into a pit of despair short weeks later when the ectopic pregnancy had come close to killing her. And of course, there had been no hope of saving the baby with a tubal pregnancy.

Her near death had not stopped her and Tay from trying again. They both wanted children with a deep desperation only those who had no family could appreciate. After a year of trying with no results they'd sought medical help. Tests had revealed that she'd been left with only one working ovary in the aftermath of her ectopic pregnancy.

The fertility specialist she and Tay had sought out had informed them that the single working ovary significantly decreased their chances at getting pregnant. However, she gave them a regime to follow that would hopefully result in conception. It had been grueling and resulted in an already passionless sex life turning flat-out clinical.

But it had worked. When the test strip had turned blue, she'd felt as if it was the greatest blessing of her life. This time she'd felt as if it was a full-on miracle.

Tino was careful to use condoms every time. The number of chances they'd taken by waiting to put the condom on until after some play, and the single time one had broken (Tino had changed where he bought his condoms after that), could be counted on one hand. With fingers left over. However, one of those times of delayed sheathing had occurred a couple of months ago.

With only one working ovary, her menstrual cycles were on an erratic two-month schedule. She hadn't paid any attention when her sporadic period was later than even normal. It wasn't the first time. Pregnancy had never even crossed her mind. Not when her breasts had grown excessively tender. She'd put it up to PMS. Not when the smell of bacon made her nauseous. She wasn't a huge meat eater, anyway.

Not when she got tired in the afternoons. After all, most Sicilian businesses were closed for a couple of hours midday so people could rest. Maybe she was just taking on the habits of her adopted home. She hadn't even clued in she might be pregnant when she burst out crying over a broken glass one morning when she'd been preparing a heavier breakfast than usual. She'd been craving eggs.

The shoe hadn't even dropped when she made her fourth trip to the bathroom before lunchtime one day. She'd made an appointment to see her doctor to test for a suspected bladder infection, only to be stunned with the news she was carrying Tino's child.

She pressed against her hard tummy with a reverent hand. All the symptoms of pregnancy now carried special significance for her. She, a woman who'd had every chance at family she'd ever had ripped from her by death, was expecting. It was almost impossible to believe she'd been so blind to the possibility. With her fertility problems, Faith had assumed there wasn't even a remote chance she could or would ever get pregnant again.

Yet, according to the test her doctor had run, she was. *She was*.

Oh, man.

She hugged herself while looking down at the faceless pregnant figure she'd been working on. The incredible awe and joy she felt at the prospect of having a baby— Tino's baby—could be seen in every line of the figure whose arms were raised above her head in an unmistakable gesture of celebration. Faith turned to look at the first woman she'd done after finding out she was pregnant.

That figure showed the fear that laced her joy. This woman had a face, and her expression was one of trepidation. Her hand rested protectively on her slightly protruding stomach. Faith had done the woman as a native African. Clinging to one side of her traditional dress was another small child, not so thin it was starving, but clearly at risk. The two figures were standing on a base that had been created to look like dry grass.

It was a moving statue, bringing tears to her own eyes. Which wasn't exactly something new. The one place Faith allowed herself to express her inner pain, the feelings of aloneness that she accepted but had never quite learned to live with, was her art. While some pieces were filled with joy and peace, others evoked the kind of emotion few people liked to talk about.

Despite that—or maybe because of it—her art sold well, commanding a high price for each piece. Or at least each one she allowed to leave her workshop. The pregnant woman she'd done yesterday wasn't going anywhere but back into a lump of clay. It was too jumbled a piece. No single emotional connotation strong enough to override the others.

Some work was like that. She accepted it as the cost of her process. She'd spent the entire day on that statue, but not late into the night like she had on the first one. Part of it was probably the fact that Tino had called her.

He rarely called her, except to set up assignations. Even when he traveled out of country and was gone for a week or more, she did not hear from him. But he had called yesterday. For no other reason she could discern other than to talk. Weird.

Really, really.

But good. Any loosening of his strictly sex relationship rule was a blessing. Especially now.

But still. Odd.

She wasn't sure when she was going to tell him about the baby. She had no doubts she would do so, but wanted to time it right. There was always a chance of miscarriage in the first trimester, and with her track record she wasn't going to dismiss that very real possibility. She'd lost every chance she'd had for a family up to now, it was hard to believe that this time would work out any differently.

She could still hope, though.

That didn't mean she was going to share news of the baby before she was sure her pregnancy was viable. She had an appointment with the hospital later in the week. Further tests would determine whether the pregnancy was uteral rather than ectopic. Though her original fertility specialist had told her the chances of having another tubal pregnancy were so slim as to be almost nonexistent, Faith wasn't taking any chances.

And she wasn't telling Tino anything until she was sure.

CHAPTER TWO

THE day before her appointment at the hospital was Faith's day to teach art to the primary schoolers. She'd fallen into the job by accident. Sort of. Faith had told Agata Grisafi how much she loved children and spending time with them, but of course her career did not lend itself to doing so. The older woman had spoken to the principal of her grandson's school and discovered he would be thrilled to have a successful artist come in and teach classes one day a week to his students.

That's how it had begun and how Faith had ended up knowing her lover's mother and son longer than she'd known him. Some people might say Providence had lent a hand, and Faith thought maybe, just maybe they might be right.

Giosue, Tino's darling eight-year-old son, was in the second group she taught for the day.

He was his normal sweet self, shyly asking her opinion of the drawing he had done of Marsala's city hall. They were doing a project combining their writing skills and art to give a picture of their city as eight- and nine-year-olds saw it.

"That's beautiful, Gio."

"Thank you, *signora*."

She moved on to the next child, helping the little girl pick a color for the fish she wanted to draw in the sea so close to Marsala.

It was at the end of class, after all the other children had left, that Giosue came to her desk. "Signora Guglielmo?"

The children called her by the Italian equivalent of William rather than Williams because it was easier for them and she didn't mind a bit.

"Yes, sweetheart?"

He grinned at the endearment, his cheeks pinkening a little, but so obviously pleased that she made a note to use it again. Sparingly.

No matter how special the place in her heart Tino's son had, she would not draw attention to it. To do so would embarrass Giosue, most likely infuriate Tino and compromise Faith's position with the school.

"I would like to invite you to join my family for dinner tonight," he said formally. It was clear he'd practiced the phrase, as well.

"Does your father know you are inviting me to dinner?" she asked, seriously concerned by this turn of events.

"Yes, *signora*. He would be very pleased if you came."

Shock slammed through her. "Did he say that?"

"Oh, yes." Giosue gave her another of his shy smiles. "He is very pleased I like you so well."

Hope bubbled through her like an effervescent spring. Perhaps the black cloud over her life was finally dissipating. Was it possible she had a chance at a real family once again—one that would not be taken away from her? The hope scared her so much it hurt. "I would be honored to join you for dinner."

"Thank you, *signora*." Giosue handed her a folded

sheet of paper. "My father made you directions for coming, in case you need them."

She took the paper. "Thank you, I appreciate that."

She'd been there a few times for lunch with Agata, though the older woman preferred to meet in Pizzolato because she loved visiting Faith's studio. She said she basked in the privilege of seeing the artist's work before it was finished.

"It was my idea to make the map. I helped Papa with it."

That was her cue to open it and marvel over the drawing, which had obviously been done by a child's hand. The detailed written instructions were in Tino's distinctive slashing scrawl, however.

"You did a wonderful job, Gio. I particularly like the grapevines with grapes on them you drew to show me what to expect to see."

"They are ripening on the vines now. Nonno said they will be ready to harvest when he gets back from Naples maybe."

"If your grandfather says it, than I am sure he is right."

"He is a master winemaker," Giosue said proudly.

"Yes. Do you help with the harvest?"

"Some. Nonno takes me into the fields with him. Papa does not work the fields, but that is okay. Nonno says so."

"Your father's gift is for the business side of things, I think."

"Nonno says Papa is very good at making money," Giosue replied artlessly.

Faith laughed. "I'm sure he is."

"He can support a family. Nonna says so."

"I'm sure he can." Was Giosue matchmaking? Faith held in the smile that wanted to break over her features.

She did not want to hurt Giosue by making him think she was laughing at him.

"She thinks he should marry again. She is his mama, he has to listen to her, I think."

It was really hard to bite back the laugh at that, but she did not think Tino would share his son's view on this particular subject. "What do you think, Gio?"

"I think I would like a mother who is not so far away in Heaven."

She couldn't help it. She reached out and touched him. Just a small pat on the shoulder, but she wanted to hug him to her. "I understand, Gio. I really do."

He cocked his head to one side. "You never talk about family."

"I don't have any." Her hand slid down to her stomach. She hadn't. Before. But now, maybe she did.

"You have no mama, either?"

"No. I prayed for one, but it was not God's will." She shrugged.

"Do you think I will have another mother?"

"I hope so, Gio."

"Me, too, but only if I could love her."

Smart boy. "I'm sure your father wouldn't marry a woman you couldn't love as a mama, too."

"She would have to love me also." Giosue looked at her through his lashes, worrying his lower lip with his teeth.

Sweet little boy. "You are very lovable, that would not be a problem, I'm sure."

The next group of children came rushing into the room along with Giosue's teacher, who was apparently looking for her missing lamb.

"I will see you tonight?" he asked as crossed the room to join his teacher at the door.

"Yes."

He was grinning as he exited the room.

So, Tino's son *was* matchmaking. With her. And seemingly, he had Tino's tacit approval. Unbelievable. The prospect terrified her as much as it thrilled her. Had she suffered enough? Was she done being alone?

Somehow, she couldn't quite picture it.

If nothing else, Tino was allowing her into another aspect of his life. The most important one to him. That was so huge, she could barely wrap her mind around it.

The fact that he was doing so without knowing about the baby boggled her mind even more.

He might not love her, but she had a different place in his life than any woman had since the death of his wife six years ago.

Faith concentrated on the strains of classical music filling her Mini. At least, she tried to. She was extremely nervous about this dinner. She shouldn't be. Over the past year, they'd discovered that she and Tino were compatible in and out of bed. She and Giosue got along great in the classroom as well. It should all be good.

Only, telling herself that didn't make the butterflies playing techno music in her stomach go away. This was the two of them together. Tino *and* Giosue. The three of them really.

How they interacted would dictate a big chunk of her future; she was sure of it. Tino had to be testing the waters and, as absolutely inconceivable as she found that, it sort of fit in with his odd behavior lately.

He'd called her again today. She'd missed the call and when she'd tried to return it he'd been in a meeting. His message had simply said he'd been thinking of her.

Seriously strange.

If he'd said he'd been thinking of sex with her, she wouldn't have been surprised at all. The man had the libido of an eighteen-year-old. Sex was a really important part of his life. Important enough that he pursued it even though he had said he never wanted to remarry or get serious with a woman.

But he hadn't said he was missing the sex. He'd said he was missing *her*. Well, they would be together again soon enough. And then they would see what they would see.

Her phone rang, playing his distinctive ring tone. She never answered when she was driving, so she forced herself to ignore it. Besides, she was almost to Grisafi Vineyard. He could say whatever he wanted when she got there. Most likely, he was calling to see where she was.

But she wasn't late.

Well, not much, anyway. Maybe ten minutes. He had to be used to her sketchy time-keeping skills by now. It was one of the reasons that she loved living in Sicily. Tino was very un-Sicilian in his perfect punctuality and rigid schedule keeping. She'd teased him about it more than once.

He'd told her he had no choice, doing business on an international scale. She suspected it was in his nature and that was that.

She couldn't see Tino changing for the convenience of others, not even when it came to making money.

She turned down the long drive that led to Casa di Fede. Faith House. She'd thought it was neat the house shared her name when she'd first come to visit Agata. Later, when she realized Tino lived here, she'd seen it as an indication they were meant to be together. Even if it was temporary.

Thinking about the coincidence sent another bubble of hope fizzing through her. Maybe it meant something more than what she'd thought. He and his family were wrapped around her life, and she was threaded through his, in ways neither had anticipated or even wanted at first.

She pulled up in front of the sprawling farm house. It had been in the family for six generations and been built onto almost that number of times until it had two master suites, one in its own wing with two additional bedrooms. There were four more bedrooms in the rest of the house, a formal salon, a family entertainment room that opened onto the lanai beside the oversize two-tiered pool and spa area, a huge kitchen, a library and two offices.

One was Tino's, and the smaller, less-organized one was his father's. Agata used the library as her office when she was working on her charity work. She had her own sitting room off the master suite, as well.

Faith had learned all of this on her previous visits with the older woman. What she hadn't known was how overwhelming she would find the familiar home now that she was here to share dinner with Tino and his son. She sat in her car, staring at the proof of generations of Grisafis living in the same area. Proof of Tino's roots and his wealth. Proof that he already had what she had most craved her whole life.

A family.

The prospect that he might be willing to share all that with her was almost more than she could take. Terrifying didn't begin to describe it. Because even if Valentino Grisafi wanted her in his life, she of all people knew there was no guarantee she could keep him. No more than she'd kept the father she never knew, or her mother, or the first family that said they would adopt her, or Taylish…or her unborn son, Kaden.

Dwelling on the pain of the past had never helped her before; she knew it wasn't about to start now. She needed to let the past go and hope for the future, or her own fears were going to destroy her chance at happiness.

With that resolved, she opened her car door. Her phone trilled Tino's ringtone again as she stepped out of the car.

She flipped it open. "Wow, I know you're impatient, but this is borderline obsessive, Tino. I'm here already."

"I merely wished to—"

She rang the bell and he stopped talking.

"It is the doorbell. I must let you go."

Shaking her head at that, she shrugged and disconnected the call.

He opened the door and then stood there staring at her as if she was an apparition—of not particularly friendly aspect. In truth, he looked absolutely horrified.

"Faith!"

"The last time I looked, yes."

"What are you doing here?" He shook his head. "It does not matter. You need to leave. Now."

"What? Why?"

"This is my fault." He rubbed his hand over his face. "I can see where my phone calls may have given you the wrong impression."

"That you might be impatient to see me?"

"Yes, I am. I was. But not here. Not now."

"Tino, you aren't making any sense."

"This is not a good time, Faith. I need you to leave now."

"Won't Gio be disappointed?"

"Gio…why would you ask about my son? Look, it doesn't matter, we have a dinner guest coming."

She rolled her eyes. "Yes, I know. I'm here."

"This is no time for jokes, *carina.*"

"Tino, you're starting to worry me." Really. Definitely. Positive that Giosue would not lie and say his father had approved inviting her for dinner, she was flummoxed. Besides, hadn't Tino helped his son make the map? What was going on? "Tino—"

"Signora!" An excited little boy voice broke into the bizarre conversation. "You are here!"

Giosue rushed past his father to throw his arms around Faith in a hug. She returned the embrace with a smile, loving the naturally affectionate nature of most of the Sicilians she had met.

Tino stood there looking at them in abject horror.

Giosue stepped back, self-consciously straightening his button-up shirt. He'd dressed up for the dinner in an outfit close to the uniform he wore to school of obviously higher quality and minus the tie. He looked like a miniature version of his father, who was wearing custom-tailored brown slacks with a champagne colored dress shirt—untucked, the top button undone.

The clothes were absolutely yummy on the father and adorable on the son.

Faith was glad she'd taken the time to change from the clothing she wore to teach in. Her dress was made from yellow silk batiked by a fellow artist with strands of peacock blue, sunset orange and even a metallic dye with a gold cast. Faith had fallen in love with the silk when she'd seen it at an artists' fair and had to buy it. She'd had it made into a dress of simple design with spaghetti straps that highlighted her curves and made her feel deliciously feminine. A new addition to her wardrobe, Tino had not yet seen it.

Regardless of his other reactions to her arrival, that certain gleam she knew so well in her lover's eyes said he approved her choice.

Unaware of the strange overtones to the adults' conversation, Gio took her hand and held it. "Papa, this is Signora Guglielmo." Then the boy smiled up at her with pure innocence. "*Signora,* this is my papa, Signor Valentino Grisafi."

"Your papa and I have met," Faith said, when Tino remained silent and frozen like a statue. An appalled statue.

"You have?" Gio looked confused, maybe even a little hurt. "Papa told me he did not know you. Nonna told him he would like you though."

"I did not realize that Signora Guglielmo was the woman *I* know as Faith Williams." He looked at her accusingly, as if it was her fault.

"You are friends?" Giosue asked.

Faith waited to hear what her lover would say to that.

Tino looked from her to his son, his expression impossible to read. "*Si.* We are friends."

Giosue's face broke out into a grin and he giggled. "You didn't know? Truly?"

"Truly."

"That is a good joke, isn't it, Papa?"

"A good joke indeed," Tino agreed, sounding anything but amused.

Faith wasn't feeling too lighthearted, either. Tino hadn't approved inviting *her* for dinner. He hadn't written those directions out with *her* in mind to use them. He'd had no intention of inviting her into an aspect of his life he had heretofore kept separate from her. In fact, he was clearly dismayed and not at all happy by this evening's turn of events.

He'd approved inviting *his son's teacher*. Another woman. A woman who Tino would have been told by his son and mother was single, near him in age and attractive (or so Agata said every time she lamented Faith's unwed state). If the fact that Giosue had been matchmaking was obvious to Faith, it had to have been just as apparent to his father. Add to that the little detail that Agata had patently put her two cents in, and Faith was painting a picture in her mind that held no gratification for her.

Tino had approved inviting to dinner a woman his son and mother were obviously hoping he would find more than a little interesting.

All of the little pipe dreams Faith had been building since spending the night for the first time at Tino's flat, crashed and burned.

But she wasn't a wimp. Far from it. She'd taken a lot more that life had to dish out without giving up. She was here now. And she had important motivation to make this evening work in spite of her lover's negative reaction to her appearance.

Perhaps if Tino saw how good they could be together around his family, he'd rethink the parameters on their relationship. Then telling him about the baby wouldn't be so hard.

And maybe the Peruvian rain forest would freeze over in a freak weather anomaly tonight, too.

Okay, that kind of negative thinking wasn't going to do her any good. She had to think positive. No matter what, she wasn't about to beg off dinner. That would hurt Giosue, and Faith didn't let children down. Ever.

She'd experienced that particular phenomenon too many times herself to inflict it on the young people in her life.

She gave both males her best winning smile and asked, "May I come in now, or were you planning to have dinner on the front porch?"

Giosue laughed and dragged her over the threshold, forcing his father to move out of the way or get knocked into. "We're eating outside, but in back, silly *signora*."

"And did you cook, Gio?"

"I helped. Ask Papa."

She looked back over her shoulder at the silent man following their progress through the house.

"Indeed he did. He is a favorite with our housekeeper."

"It's easy to understand why. Gio's a little charmer."

"Signora!" Gio exclaimed in the long-suffering tone only an eight-year-old boy could affect so perfectly.

"Do not tell me it embarrasses you to discover your favorite teacher also holds you in high regard," his father teased him.

The boy shrugged, blushing, but said nothing. Faith's heart melted a little more toward him. He would make such a wonderful stepson and big brother. But she was getting ahead of herself. By light-years.

"So, what are we having for dinner?" she asked.

Especially after realizing Tino had not intended to invite her to dinner. That he had, in fact, been wholly ignorant of her relationship with his son and mother.

"Wait until you see. I got to stuff the manicotti. The filling is yummy."

Giosue was right, the manicotti was delicious. As was everything else, and the company wasn't bad, either. Tino started off a little stiff, but being around his son relaxed him. As hard as he so plainly tried to keep things between himself and Faith distant, his usual behavior got the better of him. He touched her when he talked to her, nothing overtly sexual. Just the normal affectionate-Sicilian-nature style, but it felt good—right.

Gio asked tons of questions about her art, questions there wasn't time for during class. Several times she caught Tino looking surprised by her answers. But then, he knew almost nothing about that part of her life. For the first time that really bothered her. Her art made up the biggest part of her life and he was sadly ignorant of it.

That realization, more than anything else, put the nature of their relationship into perspective. While his behavior lately might indicate it was changing, theirs was still primarily a sexually based connection.

"You are asking so many questions, *amorino,* I am beginning to think you wish to grow up to be an artist."

"Oh, no, Papa, I want to be a winemaker like Nonno."

"Not a businessman and vintner like your papa?" Faith asked.

"He will have to have another son to do that. I want to get my hands dirty," Giosue said with absolute certainty.

Rather than take offense, Tino laughed aloud. "He sounds just like my father." He shook his head, the amusement still glittering in his eyes. "However, there will be no brothers, or sisters either. Perhaps Calogero will finally marry and have children, but if not—when I get too old to do my job, we will have to hire a business manager."

"You will never be too old, Papa."

Tino just smiled and ruffled his son's hair. "You know there is nothing to stop you from making art a hobby while you follow in your grandfather's footsteps. Isn't that right, Faith?"

She was still reeling from the dead-on surety in

Tino's tone when he said there would be no sisters or brothers for Giosue, but she managed to nod and smile at the expectant little boy.

CHAPTER THREE

TINO rejoined Faith on the terrace after tucking his son into bed.

Gio had wheedled, pleaded and distracted every time Faith had started making noises about going home. When it was finally time for *him* to go to bed, he had even gone so far as to ask to have her come in and say good-night to him before going to sleep.

She'd done so without the slightest hesitation, kissing Gio's head before wishing him a good sleep and pleasant dreams and then leaving the room. Tino found it disconcerting that she was so relaxed, not to mention good, with his son. Their friendship was of longstanding duration, and he wasn't sure how he felt about that. Except uncomfortable.

He didn't like feeling unsettled. It made him irritable.

And it wasn't at all cute, like his lover when she was woken to go home after an evening of lovemaking.

Faith stood on the edge of the stone terrace, looking out over the vineyard. The green, leafy vines looked black in the moonlight, but she glowed. The cool illumination of the night sky reflected off her porcelain features, lending her a disturbing, ethereal beauty. She looked like an angelic specter that could be snatched to the other realms in the blink of an eye.

It was not a thought he wanted to entertain. Not after that very thing had happened to Maura through her death. The one challenge to their life together that he could not fight.

He was frowning when he laid his hand on Faith's shoulder. "He is on his way to dreamland."

"He's so incredibly sweet. You are a very blessed man, Valentino Grisafi." She turned to face him.

"I know it." He sighed. "But there are times he puts me in an inconvenient situation."

"Like when he invites your current lover to dinner?"

"Yes."

She winced. "You could have said no."

"So could you."

"I thought you wanted me here."

"*I* thought he had invited his teacher from school."

"I am his teacher," she chided. "His art teacher, anyway."

"Why did you never mention this to me?" It seemed almost contrived to him.

"How could you *not* know? I mean, I'm aware you are supremely uninterested in my life outside our time together, but I've mentioned teaching art to primary schoolers in Marsala."

"I thought you did it to support your art *hobby*. My mother told me Gio's teacher was a highly successful artist who donated her time." Realizing how wrong he'd been made him feel like fool.

Another unpleasant and infrequent experience. Grisafi men did not make a habit of ignorance or stupid behavior. His pride stung at the knowledge he was guilty of both. Knowing more about Faith would have saved him the current situation.

"And in your eyes I could not be that woman?" Faith asked in that tone all men knew was very dangerous.

The one that said a husband would be sleeping on the sofa for the foreseeable future. Faith was not his wife, but he didn't want to be cut off from her body, nevertheless. Nor did he wish to offend her in any case.

"In my eyes, that woman, Signora Guglielmo, was Sicilian—and you are not."

"No, I'm not. Is that a problem for you, Tino?"

Where had that question come from? He was no ethnic supremacist. "Patently not. We have been lovers for a year now, Faith."

"Almost a year."

"Near enough."

"I suppose, but I'm trying to understand why my being a Sicilian art teacher would make me an appropriate dinner companion for you and your son, but being your expatriot American lover does not."

"It will not work."

"What?"

"Attempting to use Giosue to insinuate yourself into my life more deeply than I wish you to go."

Hurt sparked in her peacock eyes, and then anger. "Don't be paranoid, not to mention criminally conceited. One, I would never use a child—in any way. Two, I knew your son before I met you. What would you have had me do? Start ignoring him in class once you and I had become lovers?"

"Of course not." He sighed. What a tangle. "But you could have discouraged outright friendship."

"We were already friends. It would never occur to me

to hurt a child with rejection that way. I won't do it now, either, Tino, not even for you."

"That is not what I meant."

"Then what *did* you mean?"

He swore. He wasn't sure, and that was as disturbing as any other revelation from this night. He fell back on what he considered the topic at hand. "Let's not make this more complicated than we need to. You know I do not allow the women I sleep with into my personal life. It would be too messy."

Cocking her head to one side, she gave him a look filled with disbelief. "You don't consider what we do together as personal?"

"You are nit-picking semantics here, Faith. You know what I am meaning here. Why are you being willfully obtuse? You knew the limitations of our relationship from the very beginning." She was not normally so argumentative, and why she had to start being so now was a mystery to him.

Certainly she had strong opinions, but they were not, as a rule, in opposition to his.

"Maybe I'm no longer happy with them." She watched him as if gauging his reaction to that bombshell.

Alarm bells for a five-alarm fire went off in his head. Her words filled him with pure panic—not an emotion he was used to feeling and not one he had predisposed reactions for. "Faith, you must understand something. I have no plans to remarry. Ever."

"I know, but—"

Those three little words sent a shard of apprehension right through him. She could not keep thinking in this manner. "If I did remarry, it would be to a traditional Sicilian woman—like Giosue's mother."

Some Sicilian men married American women, but it was rare. Even rarer still, almost to the point of nonexistent, were Sicilian men who continued to live on the island after marrying them.

Regardless, *were* he to remarry, he felt compelled to provide a female influence as like Giosue's real mother as possible. He owed it to Maura.

Being honest with himself would require he acknowledge that his reasons were not limited to cultural gaps and the obligation he felt to his dead wife, but had as much to do with a promise to keep. Only one woman put his promise to Maura at risk, his promise not to replace his wife, who had died too young in his heart.

And that woman was a smart, sexy American.

Faith crossed her arms, as if protecting herself from a blow. "Is that why you didn't nip your son's obvious attempt at matchmaking in the bud? Because you believed the woman he was trying to fix you up with was Sicilian?"

"Yes." He could not lie, though the temptation was there.

This time Faith didn't just wince, she flinched as if struck. "I see."

"I don't think you do." Needing her understanding—her acceptance—he cupped her face with both hands. "My son is the most important person in my life, I would do anything for him."

"Even remarry."

"If I believed that was what he truly needed for happiness, yes." But not to a woman who would expect access to more than his body and bank account. Not to a woman who already threatened his memories of Maura and his promise to her.

Not Faith.

"Do you?"

Again wishing he could lie, he dropped his hands. "I did not, but after tonight, I am not so sure. He loves his grandmother, but he glowed under your affection in a way that he does not with his nonna."

"He's very special to me."

"If he is so special, why did you not tell me he was your student?"

"You already asked that and the simple truth is that I thought you knew. I assumed he and, well, your mother, talked about me. We are friends. I suppose that's going to send you into another tizzy of paranoia, but please remember, she and I were friends before I even met Gio."

"You and…and…my *mother*?"

"Yes."

Tonight had been one unreal revelation after another. "You did not tell me this."

"I thought you knew," she repeated, sounding exasperated. She turned away from him. "Perhaps Agata and I are not as close as I assumed."

The sad tone in Faith's voice did something strange to Tino's heart. He did not like it. At all. He was used to her being happy most of the time—sometimes cranky but never sad. It did not fit her.

"She did talk about you, but I did not realize it was *you* she was talking about." His mother had mentioned Gio's teacher on occasion. Not often, though, and he too wondered if the two women shared as close a friendship as Faith believed.

His mother was a true patron of the arts. She had many acquaintances in the artistic community. He could easily see her warm nature and natural graciousness being mistaken for friendship. But the only artist she mentioned often was TK.

For a while, Tino had been worried his mother had developed a *tendre* for the male artist. However, when he had mentioned his concern to his father, Rosso Grisafi had laughed until tears came to his eyes. Tino had drawn the conclusion that clearly there was nothing to worry about.

"That's hardly my fault, Tino."

"I did not say it was."

"You implied it by asking why I didn't tell you."

What was it with her tonight and this taking apart everything that he said? "You are apparently very close to both my mother and my son and yet you never once mentioned seeing or talking to them."

"You always discourage me from discussing your family, Tino."

It was true, but for some reason, the reminder bothered him. Probably because everything was leaving him feeling disconcerted tonight. "I did not think they had a place in our combined life."

"We don't have a combined life, do we, Tino?" She was looking at him again and he almost wished she wasn't.

There was such defeat and sadness in her eyes.

"I do not understand what has changed between us?"

"Nothing. Nothing at all has changed between us."

"Then why are you sad?"

"Perhaps because I thought it had."

Why had she believed this?

"You were under the impression I wanted you to come for dinner tonight," he said, understanding beginning to dawn. Clearly she had liked the idea. Learning differently had hurt her. Even though he had not meant for this to happen, he had to take some responsibility for the outcome.

She nodded, silent, her lovely red hair swaying against her shoulders. He had the wholly inappropriate—considering the gravity of their discussion—urge to run his fingers through the familiar silky strands. Worse, he knew he did not want to stop there.

Focus, he must focus.

"It is not good for Giosue to be exposed to my lovers."

"I understand you think that."

"It is the truth."

She said nothing.

He could not leave it there. The compulsion to explain—to make her understand—was too great. "When our relationship ends, he will be disappointed. Already he has expectations that cannot be fulfilled."

"I'm his friend."

"He wants you to be his mother."

"And you don't."

"No." It was a knee-jerk response, the result of ingrained beliefs since his wife's death.

Shocking to realize he wasn't sure he meant it. With that came grief—a sense of loss that made no sense and was something he was not even remotely willing to dwell on.

"Because I'm not Sicilian."

"Because our relationship is not a love affair." But was that true?

How could it be anything else when he *could not* love her? He had promised Maura that he would love her always. Her sudden death had not negated that pledge.

"I thought we were friends, too."

"We are friends." Friendship he could do—was necessary even.

"But not sweethearts."

His heart twinged, making his tone come out more cynical than he meant it to. "What an old-fashioned term."

She shrugged. "It's one Tay used to use." She said the dead man's name with a wistfulness that he did not like.

"I gather he was an unusual man."

"Yes. He was. One of the best, maybe even the best man I ever knew."

"But he is *gone*."

"Yes, just as Gio's mother is gone."

"Maura will never be gone from my heart."

"No, she won't, but are you so sure your heart has no room for anyone else?"

"That is not a discussion you and I should be having." It was one he frankly could not handle.

A Sicilian man should be able to handle anything. Even the death of his wife and raising his child without a mother. But most definitely any conversation with his current mistress. The fact that he could not shamed him.

"Because we agreed that sex and friendship was enough?" she asked in a voice husky with emotion.

"Yes."

"And if it isn't any longer…*for either of us?*"

That could not be true. He would not allow it to be. "Do not presume to speak for me."

"Fine. What if I am only speaking for myself?"

"Then we would need to talk about whether what we have is still working." It was not a discussion he wanted to have. He was far from ready to let her go.

She nodded and turned from him. "I think it's time I was going." She was hurting, for all that she tried to hide it.

"No." He hated the melancholy in her voice.

He hated the sense that somehow it was his fault. He hated thinking of going to bed alone after spending the whole evening in her company. Even worse, he hated feeling as if he might lose her and *really* hated how much that bothered him.

Perhaps he could erase her sorrow while easing his own fears. He was a big proponent of the win-win business proposition. It was even better when applied to personal relationships.

Before she could take more than a couple of steps, he reached out and caught her shoulder.

"Tino, don't."

"You do not mean that, *carina*." He drew her back toward his body. He could not imagine doing the opposite—pushing her away.

Yet he knew he could not hold on to her forever. One day she would tire of life in Sicily—so different from her home—and would return to America. Isn't that what all American women did eventually?

Faith was currently the only single American woman he knew who was making a go of actually living permanently in Sicily. For all its charm, Marsala was a far cry from New York or London.

That only meant they should not waste the time they did have. "We are good together. Do not allow tonight to change that."

"I need more, Tino."

"Then I will give you more." He was very good at that.

"I'm not talking about sex."

He turned her to face him and lowered his head so his lips hovered above hers. "Let's not talk at all."

Then he kissed her. He would show her that they

were too right together to dismiss their relationship because it wasn't packaged in orange blossoms and meters of white tulle.

She fought her own response. He could feel the tension in her, knew she wanted to resist, but though she might want to, she was as much a slave to their mutual attraction as he. Her body knew where it belonged. In his arms.

But her brain was too active and she tore her lips from his. "No, Tino."

"Do not say no. Say rather, 'Make love to me, Tino.' This is what I wish to hear."

"We're supposed to be exclusive."

"We are."

"You were willing to have a blind date with another woman, Tino." She wrenched herself from his arms. "I cannot be okay with that."

"It was not a date."

She glared at him, but it was the light of betrayal in her eyes that cut him to the quick. "As good as."

"I did not consider it a date."

"But you knew your son and mother were match-making."

"I had no intention of being matched."

"But that's changed. You said so. You said you would do anything for Gio, even give him a second mother—*if she's Sicilian*." The tone Faith spoke the last words with said how little she thought of his stance on the matter.

"I said I was considering it, not that I had decided to date other women. You are all the woman I want right now."

"And tomorrow?"

"And tomorrow."

"So, when does my sell-by date come into effect? Next week? Next month? Next year."

He wanted to grab her and hold on tight, but he laid gentle hands on her shoulders instead. "You do not have a sell-by date. Our relationship is not cut-and-dried like that."

"I won't be with you if you're going to date other women," she repeated stubbornly.

"I would not ask you to."

"What does that mean, Tino?"

"It means you can trust me to be faithful while we are together. Just as I trust you."

Her eyes glistened suspiciously, sending shards of pain spiking through his gut. He did not want to see her cry. He kissed her, just once, oh so carefully, trying to put the tenderness and commitment—as limited as it might be—that he felt into the caress.

"Let me make love to you." He was pleading and he did not care.

They needed each other tonight, not empty beds where regrets and memories would haunt the hours that should be for sleep. Or making love.

"No more blind dates."

"It wasn't—"

But she shushed him with a finger to his lips. "It was. Or would have been. Don't do it again."

"You have my word." Then, because he could not help himself; because he needed it more than breathing or thinking or anything else, he once again kissed her.

He poured his passion and his fear out in that kiss, molding their lips together in a primordial dance.

At first she did not respond. She did not try to push

him away, but she did not pull him closer, either. It was the only time in their relationship she had not fallen headfirst into passion with him.

She was still thinking.

He would fix that. Increasing the intensity of their kiss, he stormed her mouth, refusing to allow their mutual desire to remain a prisoner to circumstances that would not…could not…change. Bit by bit her instincts took over.

And once her brain caught up to her body, she melted into him, ending her resistance and giving him access to the interior of her mouth at the same time. She tasted like the coffee laced heavily with rich cream and sweet sugar she had drunk after dinner. It was a flavor he had come to associate only with her.

He drank his own coffee black unless he wanted an erection tenting his slacks—something that was more than inconvenient during his business day, but could be downright embarrassing. This, what they had, was beyond good. It was fantastic, and she *would* not end it. He could not let her.

Tonight, he would remind her how well he knew her body, what he alone could do to it, how much pleasure *he* could give her. Her husband had not elicited those sensations in her, or she would not have acted so shocked by each new one when Tino and Faith had first begun their affair.

She had been almost virginal, many of her reactions belying the existence of previous lovers, much less a husband.

He refused to dwell on the sense of alarm he felt realizing the extent of his ignorance about her life. She'd been his son's art teacher since before they met a year ago, and she had known his mother even longer. Yet Tino had been totally unaware of those facts. As unknowing as he had been about the reality of Faith's widowhood.

How had her husband died? She'd loved him, thought he was a *special* man.

A primal need to erase memories of the other male from her drove Tino to deepen the kiss even further.

Faith made a soft sound against his lips. He loved kissing her. Had from the very first. She was more responsive to his lips claiming hers than any woman he had ever known. And she was far from shyly submissive. She gave as good as she got, with a passion that turned him inside out.

Damn. He wanted her.

But not out here where someone might see what should be entirely private between two people. The temptation to once again make her his, right here under the stars, was strong however. He fought it, sweeping her up into his arms and carrying her inside.

He went directly to his room, no thought of taking Faith anywhere else even entering his mind. This was *his* bedroom. *His* bed. And for now at least, she was his woman.

The huge four-poster with wooden canopy had been used by his family for generations. Though the mattress and box springs were new—a pillow-top with extra coils imported from America on his younger brother's recommendation. It had been a good piece of advice, for more than one reason.

Not only was it incredibly comfortable, but giving up the mattress and even the bed linens he had shared with his wife had been instrumental in Tino finally being able to sleep in his own suite once again.

Pulling back the coverlet, he then laid Faith onto the bed.

She looked around the room, her expression going from curious to surprised. "This is your room."

He locked the door and returned to the bed, unbuttoning his shirt as he went. "Where else would I take you?"

"I don't know." She licked her lips, her focus on his chest as he peeled the shirt from his body. "You're such an incredibly sexy man, you know?"

"You have mentioned believing so before."

She laughed, the sound husky and warm. "I meant it then and I mean it now. I love looking at you."

"I thought it was men who were supposed to be the visual sex."

"Maybe." She shrugged, kicking her sandals off. "Maybe if all women had such yummy eye candy to look at, we'd be considered the visual sex, too."

"So, I am eye candy?"

She licked her lips as if tasting something really sweet and nodded.

His sex jolted at memories of what it felt like to be partaken of by that delectable little tongue. "I think you are a minx."

"You think?"

"I know."

She gave him a saucy wink and stretched her body, putting her curves on sensual display.

He shook his head but knew he had no hope of clearing it. He'd been here before with this woman, so filled with desire that everything else was just a gray fog around them. He unzipped his slacks, hissing as the parting fabric made way for his steel-hard manhood.

This woman affected him like no other.

"I love it when you make that sound."

"You are the only one who has ever heard it." With his admission, he stripped off the remainder of his clothes—the need to deflect automatic.

"Really?" she asked, nevertheless.

"Yes." He joined her on the bed, on all fours above her. "I want you naked."

She brushed her hand down his flank. "I like naked."

He could no more suppress the growl her touch evoked than he could the need to return it. He brought their mouths together again as he reached down and caressed her through the silk of her dress. All evening he had wanted to do this, to feel the curves he knew intimately through the thin fabric. Regardless of how surreal the night had been, his desire for her was as strong as always, building with each minute he was in her company.

She moaned into the kiss, arching into his touch, begging silently for more.

And more was what he was an expert at giving her. He would remind her of that. Show her that each time could be better than the last.

He continued the strokes along her breasts, the dip of her waist and bow of her hips. Over and over again, he touched the places on her body that he knew drove her wild.

Her hands were busy, too, skimming along his heated skin, kneading his chest, but best of all was when she grabbed him—her fingers digging into his shoulders with white-knuckle intensity. When she got to this point—where she could no longer concentrate on pleasuring him—he knew she was past thought. Past control.

Exactly where he wanted her to be.

CHAPTER FOUR

IT WAS time to take her clothes off. He did, using the opportunity to tease and tantalize her further. But revealing her peaches-and-cream body was a double-edged sword. The light smattering of freckles over her shoulders and upper breasts were his downfall. She had none on her face, so the cinnamon dots felt secret—private—for him alone. A special knowledge shared just between them. He was tempted to count them—with kisses—every time he got her disrobed.

This time was no different.

The allure of her body for him never diminished.

He traced the light dots on her skin. "You are so beautiful."

"You've got an unnatural affection for my freckles." It might be a full sentence, but the way she said it, breathless with pauses between words, told him that she was no more in possession of her faculties than she had been a moment before.

"You think?" he asked against her silken skin, tasting the brown sugar dots that his mind told him could not be sweet but his tongue told him they were. But then, everything about her was sweet.

Dangerously so.

Her only answer was a moan as his lips trailed the natural path to one pebbled nipple. She shuddered beneath him, her body translating her every feeling with sexy clarity. She loved nipple play and he loved tasting and touching the turgid buds.

He delicately licked the very tip, then circled the peak with his tongue, moving slowly to lave her aureole despite the need riding him hard enough to make him ache. He refused to rush this. He had something to prove to her.

He kept at it until even the act of huffing a warm breath over her sensitized skin made her tremble and whimper. Then he moved to minister in the same way to its twin.

"What are you doing? Tormenting me?" she cried out as he sucked her nipple gently into his mouth.

He lifted his head and met peacock blue eyes glazed with pleasure. "I am giving you more."

"I don't want more. I want you in me." Then she bit her lip as if realizing what she'd said.

"Trust me, this—" he carefully slid two fingers into her superbly lubricated, swollen channel "—this is where I wish to be also, but only when I have given you *more*." He thrust with his fingers, hitting that interior bundle of nerves some women referred to as their G-spot.

She cried out, the sound adding to his own arousal, making it harder to wait, but he would.

Tonight would be spectacular.

He continued to massage her as he leaned down and once again claimed her mouth as his. Her return kisses were desperate and filled with the feminine fire he found so irresistible.

Her walls clenched around his fingers as he moved

them in and out, stimulating her G-spot with each slow stroke. She undulated, her body straining toward him and moving with those tiny, involuntary jerks that enhanced her pleasure.

He could feel her need to climax rolling off her in palpable waves of sexual energy. Her little whimpers against his lips were an inarticulate form of begging he'd become addicted to their first time together.

His Faith did not play mind games or try to hide her physical needs or desires. She expressed them in a dozen different ways, all of which turned him on. Sex with this woman was volcanically hot, but it was also honest. She amazed and delighted him.

Now it was his turn.

He brushed her clitoris with his thumb, just a light movement back and forth…back and forth, but that was all she needed. Launching upward with her pelvis, she convulsed around his fingers. Her sharp little teeth bit into his lower lip as she made a keening sound in her throat, telling him without words that this was exactly what he wanted it to be.

More.

He kissed her through the orgasm, helping her to come down, but not too far. He was not done with her yet. Not nearly.

When her breathing was less ragged, he gently lifted her legs so they draped over his forearms and he used the position to spread her thighs until she was completely open to his gaze. Her entire body was still flushed from her climax, a beautiful rose red that he could not wait to spear with his own throbbing and as yet unsatisfied flesh. Diamond hard, her nipples poked straight up, pleading for his touch. A soft sheen of perspiration coated her upper chest, attesting to the level of pleasure she had already received.

He started to speak and had to clear his throat.

She smiled at him and the words came out in a masculine growl he wasn't in any way ashamed of. "You are so incredibly beautiful like this."

"Sated from your lovemaking?"

"You are not sated." He tipped his pelvis, brushing her entrance with the tip of his penis, eliciting a second keening sound from her. He smiled. "You still need me."

Something flashed in her eyes, something he could not quite read but that looked a lot like vulnerability. "Yes."

"I need you as well."

"I know." But the words came out sounding bleak.

He did not like it. There was no place for melancholy in their bed.

"You are not my mistress." He didn't know why he said it, but he felt compelled.

Her eyes widened. "What?"

"You are not my mistress. You are *amore mio* and my friend."

"Yes." The smile she gave him was still tinged with sadness, but a glimmer of hope shone in her gaze.

Why it should matter to him that it was there, that he would even desire such a thing, considering what it implied from her earlier words, he did not know. But illogical as it might be, he was glad.

"I am going to give you more now, *carina*. Are you ready for me?"

She nodded, her breath coming out in little pants, but her body did not tense in his hold. She trusted him completely. Amazing. Although she had climaxed, her body was ready for *more*. Ready for *him*.

He pressed forward, allowing the head of his granite-hard penis to brush her opening again, but did not go in, teasing them both. Her lips curved in a familiar smile as she seemed to simply melt against the bed, waiting on him with a sexy expectation he adored. It said she knew he would take care of her wants.

He thrust his hips, allowing his length to slide along her slick folds. It felt so good—so perfect—he groaned, the sound reverberating deep in his chest. With her, he was primal man. "You are so wet."

"You are so earthy, Tino. No one would expect it." Using her lower back muscles, she lifted herself and increased the stimulation, showing the uninhibited aspect of her own nature.

"Only you get to see this side of me." That had to count for something.

"I better be the only one, mister."

He laughed softly as he allowed his thickened member to enter her. "You are like hot silk. I feel like I am going to lose my mind every time I enter you."

"I lost mine a long time ago." She pressed her head back into the pillow, her eyelids going half-mast.

He smiled and shook his head as he moved forward with rocking motions that made it possible for her to take his entire length. He was long and thick, and that had overwhelmed more than one lover. His and Maura's intimacy had been loving and passionate, but nothing like what it was like with Faith.

Maura had never been as comfortable exposing her desire, which was to be expected as she had been raised in the very sheltered environment of a traditional Sicilian household. But he adored that element of Faith's lovemaking. The way his current lover not only *could* take his full length, but *craved* it was something a man like him could and would never take for granted.

He could not help rejoicing in the amount of belief in him that Faith expressed every time they came together.

"You never flinch from me." The wonder that laced his voice embarrassed him a little, but like so many things with this woman—was an uncontrollable response.

In so many ways she was dangerous to him, but he continued to play Russian Roulette with his emotions—risking the promises he had made to his dead wife. His brain told him he should get out before he got in too deep, but everything inside him rebelled at the idea.

"Why would I?" Her brows wrinkled in genuine confusion. "We are a perfect fit."

Perfect only because she relaxed so well for him—for she was tight. Oh, so damn tight. *"So, perfect."*

"Mmmm…" She licked her lips. "You're big, but it's *good*, Tino."

"It is better than good."

"Yessss…" she hissed as he finally sheathed himself to the hilt in her fantastic heat.

He tucked her legs around his hips. "I need to kiss you."

"Please, Tino." She was straining toward him even as he brought their mouths together.

Nothing had ever felt so good.

The part of his brain where guilt resided rejected that thought even as he set a steady, slow rhythm. Kissing, their bodies moved together in a motion filled with tenderness he did not want to examine.

He could feel her desire building as was his. He refused to go over, no matter how much his body clamored for the ultimate release. He was determined to bring her to another shattering peak. Her second climax would be more intense than the first.

It would be *more*.

Of its own volition, his pelvis swiveled on each downward thrust, as if his body had been trained to pleasure this woman exactly as she needed. Pavlov's response. Her pleasure gave him intense satisfaction and pleasure, therefore he did all that he could to bring out every little gasp, each sweet moan, every tightening of her muscles, each shudder she could not control.

Suddenly they were both coming together, his own orgasm taking him over before he could even hope to stop it.

But he did not want to as she contracted around him, her peak lasting seconds that turned into minutes while his body vibrated with matching sensation until his muscles felt like they would collapse.

Their mouths separated, allowing each of them to take in gasps of air and he collapsed, managing only to deflect part of his weight to the side, but maintaining skin contact. From past experience, he knew she preferred that. Thank the Holy Mother because he could not have moved if he tried.

"Thank you."

"No, *cara,* thank you."

She made another sound, but he knew she would slide into sleep soon. People said men fell asleep after sex, but he rarely did. His little American lover, however, experienced orgasm as some kind of somnolence button. He did not mind. He looked forward to these moments when he could cuddle her without having to put up his macho facade.

But tonight he did something he never did. Or at least had not until their last time together in his apartment in Marsala. He let his body relax in preparation for sleep.

Although Giosue woke early, Valentino always woke even earlier. He was not worried about being caught with her. Besides, there just seemed to be something so cold about kicking her out of his bed after such an intense experience. It had been getting harder and harder to do so lately, anyway.

He was going to have to get a handle on this softening of his relationship rules, but not tonight. He wanted to sleep, for just a little while, holding Faith.

Gio would never know and therefore could not be hurt by it. He would no doubt sleep even later than he normally did on a Saturday morning. Valentino had allowed his son to stay up later than usual because of their guest.

Their *guest*.

His lover.

He mentally shook his head at that. He would never have guessed that she was so ingrained in the life of his family. He still was not sure how he felt about that, but he wasn't going to dwell on it tonight. Tomorrow was soon enough to try to figure out how the woman who had shared his bed for almost a year was such an enigma to him.

Just as it would be soon enough to reinstate his necessary rules for the women who shared his bed. Or perhaps he should reconsider those rules for Faith. At least a little.

After all, she was more than a mere bed partner.

She was his friend.

A friend he apparently knew less about than any of

his business rivals. And he trusted her enough to share an intimate side of his life.

For the second time ever, Faith woke in the arms of her lover.

Tino had allowed her to *sleep in his bed? In his family home?*

Maybe he really had given her *more* last night.

Or had that move been an unconscious one? It didn't really matter if he had considered it, or acted on instinct—it had to mean something.

Just as his promise not to go searching for that perfect Sicilian paragon right away meant something. Gio was Tino's heart, but the dedicated father had still reaffirmed his commitment not to date other women while he and Faith were together.

She'd thought her heart was being ripped right out of her chest when he said he thought Gio might need a new mother, but that mother could not be Faith. She'd been angry and hurt and scared and a lot of other emotions that confused her because she couldn't be sure if they were genuine or induced by the pregnancy hormones rampaging through her body.

The two pregnancies she'd had before had sparked serious inner upheavals as well. She and Tay would have argued constantly if he hadn't taken her hormone-driven insecurities in his stride. Would Tino have the same patience? Did she want him to? There had been instances when Tay's tolerance had felt more patronizing than understanding.

Right now she felt she was out of control when it came to her feelings and she didn't enjoy the experience. There had been times the night before she'd been sorely

tempted to sock Tino good and hard, but then the
pendulum that was her emotions had swung to needing
the reassurance that sex provided.

She didn't think Tino was any surer of his feelings
than she was. Because in the same conversation he'd
spoken of getting Gio a Sicilian mother, he'd also
spoken of not wanting to end things with Faith. He
knew she wouldn't be any man's mistress.

Early in their acquaintance, she'd made sure he was
aware of how she felt about those kinds of double standards.

Their intimacy last night had been awesome, she
couldn't deny it. She'd felt more connected to Tino than
ever before. He'd been so intent on giving her pleasure,
but more than that, he'd given her something of himself.
It was in the way he'd moved inside her, with an undis-
putable tenderness that brought tears to her eyes just
before they'd found the ultimate pleasure *together.*

As much as she hated to, she forced herself to slide
from his embrace. Even if she thought Tino could
handle it, she did not want to be caught in his bed by
anyone in his household, but especially by Gio. She
loved the little boy too much to spring such a relationship on him without some sort of leading up to it.

He might be playing matchmaker, but that didn't
mean he was ready for the reality of his father having a
lover, a woman who had taken his mother's place in the
huge four-poster bed. She still could not believe they
had made love in his bedroom. That not only had he initiated the lovemaking, but *he* had *carried* her in here.

She took a quick shower in his en suite, halting
midstep on the way out by the sight of the statue on his
dresser. It was of a faceless woman, her arms out-

stretched to a man holding a baby boy. The man was faceless and so was the baby, but she knew it was male.

How could she not? She'd done the statue. The original, complete with perfect replicas of her own face and that of Taylish holding a little boy whose features were an amalgam of both of them resided in her studio at home.

"My mother bought it for me."

That didn't surprise Faith. Nor did the fact that Tino was awake. He slept too lightly not to have woken to the shower running. "Do you like it?"

"Very much. It reminds me of when Maura was alive."

"Oh." Of course…there was nothing in this statue to show the deep sorrow that etched her face in the original.

"It is as if she has her arms open, welcoming Gio and myself into them."

"Or as if she's letting you go." That's what she'd titled the first one she'd done, but when she created another faceless rendition, she'd simply called it *Family*.

"Is that wishful thinking?" Tino asked, an edge to his voice.

She turned to face him. "What do you mean?"

"Are you hoping my wife has finally let me go so that I might claim someone new in her place?" There was nothing to give away what he was thinking in his face.

It didn't matter. The only course open to her—especially now—was honesty. "If I say yes?"

"I will remind you that if I ever do remarry it will be to a Sicilian woman, someone who can give Gio that little part of his mother at the very least." Pain flashed in his eyes, quickly followed by guilt and then both were gone, leaving only the stoic expression behind.

Promise not to date others notwithstanding, she could really have done without that reminder. The knowledge he was still so adamant about not marrying her hurt. Badly. And she was absolutely certain that pain was not a hormones-gone-wild-induced emotion.

"Why did you let me sleep here last night?" she had to ask as she fought against showing the pain his words had caused.

"I fell asleep."

"You never just fall asleep."

"There is a first time for everything."

So it had been subconscious. She'd wondered and now she knew. He didn't know why he'd brought her to his bed in his family home. And honestly? That didn't matter right now. What did matter was that he regretted it. That much was obvious. Anything else he might be feeling was hidden behind the enigmatic mask he wore.

And she should not be surprised.

She was the first woman to share that bed since the death of his wife. As hard as his regret was for her to bear, the situation was equally difficult for him. Only in a different way.

She'd had her own moments of letting go in the years since Taylish and their unborn son had died. She knew how wrenching they could be. Regardless of her own feelings right now, she could not ignore the pain twisting inside Tino. It was not in her nature to do so, but beyond that—she loved him.

She caressed the statue. It was a beautiful piece. One of her favorites. The one in her studio expressed and brought a measure of peace for an emotional agony she had been unable to give voice to. No one had been there to hear.

She would be there for Tino now, if he wanted her to be. "Tino—"

"I won't be able to see you again until my parents return." The words were clipped, hard.

"I understand." She really did.

He stood there, silent, as if he expected her to say something else.

"It's all right, Tino." She gave one last lingering glance at the statue and then began dressing.

He flinched, as if those were not the words he wanted or expected to hear. "I *will* see you then?"

She paused in the act of slipping on her sandals. "Of course."

"Good." He nodded, looking at a loss. So different from the typical Tino—business tycoon and suave but distant lover.

When she was done dressing she stopped in front of him and leaned up to kiss his cheek. "It really is going to be all right." Letting go was a necessary part of grief.

The fact that Tino was doing so, even if only on a subconscious level, gave her hope.

"No doubt."

"It isn't easy for any of us."

"What do you mean?" he asked, edgy again. Or still. He hadn't relaxed since she came out of the bathroom.

"Letting go."

"I have nothing to let go of."

She didn't argue. There would be no point. And it would only make him more determined to prove himself right. He had enough to overcome in moving forward, without adding another dose of his stubborn will to the mix.

"I'll see you when your parents return from Naples."

* * *

Valentino swore and slammed his hand down beside the statue Faith had admired. His wife letting him go? He did not think so.

Maura would be in his heart forever. He had promised.

The memory was as visceral today as it had been an hour after it happened.

His beautiful young wife had started off not feeling well that morning. He'd had the temerity to hope it meant she was pregnant again.

But that had not been the case.

Ignorant of the tragedy to come, he'd flown out of country for a business meeting in Greece with hope in his heart of increasing his family. He remembered that while his wife's body betrayed her and she slipped further away from him, he had spent the day smiling more than usual, feeling on top of the world. And then his world had come crashing down.

His meeting had been a success, opening the doors for the major expansion of the Grisafi family interests. He would exchange that success and all that had come later for one more lucid day with the mother of his son.

Valentino's mother had called him just before he boarded the jet for home. Papa had taken Maura to the hospital because she had passed out walking up the stairs. By the time Valentino had reached the hospital, his wife was in a coma.

Petrified for the first time in his life, sweating through his expensive shirt, he'd rushed into the room. Maura had been so damn pale and completely motionless. He'd taken her lifeless hand, his heart ceasing at its coolness. He had begged her to wake up, to speak to him, to squeeze his hand—anything.

But nothing. Not then. Not later. No fluttering eyelids. No half-formed words. No goodbyes. Absolutely nothing.

The only sounds had come from him—his desperate pleas and constant talking until his voice was no more than a horse whisper in hopes of sparking a connection to her shut-down brain—and from the machines hooked up to her. Machines and medications that had been unsuccessful at saving her life.

Her first discernable diabetic attack had been her last. Nothing the doctors did brought her blood sugars under control and she died without coming out of the coma.

He'd spent every minute with her, but it had done no good. And when she'd gone into cardiac arrest, the doctors had called security to force him from the room. He'd been in another country when she fell into the coma and out in the hall when she let go of life.

The doctors said her reaction to the disease was extremely rare. But not rare enough, was it? His wife, the mother of his child was dead and nothing would ever change that.

He would never forget the rage, the grief and the utter helplessness he felt holding his small son in his arms as they said goodbye to her. He had promised then, standing over her grave, holding their sobbing son who just wanted his mama. Valentino had promised he would never stop loving her, that he would never replace her in his heart.

Valentino Grisafi had never broken a promise and he wasn't about to start now.

This thing with Faith had to get back on track, or it had to end.

There simply was no other option. No matter what he might want or think he needed.

CHAPTER FIVE

TRUE to his word, Faith did not see Tino again while Agata and Rocco were in Naples. There were no more phone calls, either.

She didn't expect there to be.

Tino wasn't going to accept the change in their relationship gracefully. If he accepted it at all. She had to believe he would though.

Especially after allowing him to make love to her that night. Not that she'd had a lot of choice. Once he set his course on seduction, she was a goner. She loved him. *Needed him*. While that truth scared her to death, she didn't try to deny it. Self-deception was not something she indulged in. She'd accepted the physical intimacy because it substituted for the emotional connection she craved after learning she carried his baby. And sometimes, when he made love to her, she actually felt loved by him—if only for that short while.

It was that simple. And that complicated.

But maybe it was on the way to something better... something truly *more*.

He had initiated the shift in their relationship in the first place. Initially, sleeping all night with her in his apartment in Marsala, and then making love to her in his family home. That reality mitigated her fears for their future, although it did not completely rid her of them.

He might not want to admit it, but he was already thinking about her in broader terms than simply his "current convenient partner." They'd been exclusive from the very beginning—something they had both insisted on. Add that to how well she fit with his family and their friendship and they had a strong basis for a lasting relationship. The fact that she loved him would only make it easier to raise a family with him.

Even if he never came to love her as he'd loved Maura, it would be enough to be his wife and mother of his children. She had never expected to have this much claim to family again. She certainly did not expect it all.

Not after everything she had lost.

Besides, she'd never loved Taylish like she loved Tino, but *he'd* been happy in their marriage. Content to have her loving commitment if not her passion.

There were times she knew he had wanted more, but he'd never regretted their marriage. Only leaving it in death. He'd told her so, just before breathing his last.

But she didn't want to remember that day. It belonged in her past—along with the two families she'd lost. The only real families she'd ever had. Until now.

Her current hopes and dreams were reflected in the series of joy-filled family centric sculptures she did over the next week.

Agata called her when the older couple returned from the continent. Faith did not tell her about having dinner with Tino and Giosue, leaving that bit of information for them to reveal. She also avoided having Agata come to her studio the following week. She did not want Tino's mother to see the revealing pieces of art before Faith had a chance to tell him of his impending fatherhood.

Every day that went by and she did not hear from him, she missed him more. She wanted to share the miracle of her pregnancy with him, but it was important to give him space. He had to come to terms on his own with the new parameters of their relationship.

However, when the silence between them stretched a week beyond his parents' return, she called him. Only to discover he'd had to fly to New York to meet with his brother and a potential client. She tried his cell phone, but the call went straight to voice mail. After that had happened a couple of times, once very late in the evening, she figured out he was avoiding her with diligence.

It bothered her, feeling a lot like rejection. She clung to the knowledge that if he wanted to break it off with her, he would do so definitively. He would not simply begin avoiding her like an adolescent. No, he was just struggling with the changes between them more than she'd anticipated.

It made her nervous about how he might react to the news of her pregnancy. Thankfully, he was as Sicilian as a man could get. Some might think that meant unreconstructed male, but she knew that for Tino that translated into an all-out love for family and children especially. He might not be thrilled about her new role in his life, but he would be happy about the baby. Being the traditional Sicilian that he was, it would never occur to him to seek a relationship with the child that excluded her.

Thank goodness.

His desire to marry a Sicilian woman if he ever did

remarry worried her a little, but he would just have to buck
up and deal with it like a grown-up. It wasn't as if he
objected to her personally. He liked her as much outside
the bedroom as in it. She was sure of it. Even at his apartment they did not spend all their time in bed together.

And when they were in bed, they didn't only have
sex. They talked. Not about anything personal, but about
politics, faith, what they thought of the latest news, his
business—the types of things you didn't talk about with
a bare acquaintance.

He might know much about her art career, but he
knew her stance on environmentalism, government
deficits, latch-key children and his desire to dominate
his own corner of the upscale wine market.

Right now, though, he had to adjust to the fact that
she was a part of his family's life and a bigger part of
his than he had intended when they first got together.

In the meantime, she agreed to join Agata for lunch
at the Vineyard.

A day earlier than he had told his family to expect him,
Valentino pulled his car into his spot in the newer
multicar garage he'd had built to the side of the house
when he married Maura. So she could keep her car
parked inside for her comfort. She'd teased him about
spoiling her, but it had been so easy to do. His dead wife
had been a very sweet woman.

Much like Faith.

He sighed at the thought, frustrated with himself.

The trip to New York had been longer than he wanted
or expected, though it had one side benefit. It had made
it easier to distance himself from Faith. Though for-
warding her calls directly to voice mail had taken a

larger measure of self-control than he would have expected. Much larger.

Which only went to show that he had to become serious about getting their relationship back on track.

Or he would have to let her go, and that was not something he wanted to do.

The craving he felt to hear her voice filled him with anger at himself along with a sense of helplessness he refused to give in to. He had been fighting the urge to sleep all night with her since the beginning. Never before had he been tempted not to be home in the morning for his son to wake up to because of a woman. He'd known giving in would come with a cost, but he had not expected it to be his sanity.

It had felt right taking her to his bed in the family home. Too right. Now he questioned his intelligence in doing so. For that insanely stupid choice had come at an emotional cost, as well, one he had no right to pay.

If he were a truly honorable man, he would let her go completely. He'd told himself so over and over again while in New York. What did it say for his inner strength that he could not do it?

Certainly it was nothing to be proud of.

Physically distancing himself from her was not the same as regrouped emotions, he had learned. His need to see her grew with each day even as he fought it. He might have won, but he hungered for not only the sound of her voice, but the shiver of her laughter and the feel of her skin. He was like a drug addict shaking for his next fix.

It would be a couple of days at least before he could go to her, too. Agonizing days if those in New York were anything to go by. But Gio had missed his papa and had to be Valentino's first consideration.

Of course, if he left when his son was sleeping, Gio would be missing nothing.

The thought derailed from its already shaky tracks as he recognized the melodious laughter mingled with his mother's voice coming from the terrace. He stood frozen, uncharacteristically unsure of what to do. No doubts about what he *wanted* to do. He wanted to see Faith. But what *should* he do?

His decision was taken from him by his mother's voice. "Valentino, *figlio mio,* is that you?"

"*Si,* Mama. It is me."

"Come out here."

He had no choice but to obey. He might be thirty years old, but a Sicilian man knew better than to dismiss a direct command from his mother. It would hurt her and cause her distress. Hurting those he loved was something he avoided at all costs. Even when it was his peace of mind at stake, like now.

Walking out onto the terrace, he found not only his mother and Faith, but his father and Giosue as well.

His son jumped up from where he'd been dangling his feet in the water beside Faith and came running full tilt at Valentino. "Papa, Papa…you are home!"

"*Si,* I am home and glad to be here." He swung his son high into his arms and hugged the wiggling, eight-year-old body to his.

"I missed you, Papa. *Zio* Calogero should not call you to New York."

"Sometimes it is necessary, *cucciola.* You know this."

His son ducked his head. "Papa! Do not call me that. It is a name for little boys, but I am big. I am eight!"

"Ah, but a man's son is always his little one," Rocco Grisafi said as he came and hugged both Valentino and

Giosue. "Welcome home, *piccolo,*" his father said, emphasizing his point with a humorous glint in eyes the same color as Valentino's.

It had been decades since his father had last called him that and Valentino laughed.

Giosue giggled. "Papa is bigger than you Nonno, how can he be your little one?"

Valentino's father, who was in fact a head shorter than he, winked at his grandson. "It is not about size, it is about age, and I will always be older, no?"

"That's right," Valentino agreed. "And I will always be older than you," he said as he tickled his swimsuit-clad son.

Giosue screeched with laughter and squirmed down, running to the pool and jumping in, his head immediately coming up out of the water. "You can't get me now, Papa."

"You think I cannot?"

"I know it. Nonna would be mad if you got your business clothes wet."

That made everyone laugh, including Faith, drawing Valentino's attention like a bee to a rose. *Damn, damn, damn.* She was beautiful, wearing a bright green top and matching pair of Capri pants she had rolled up above her knees so she could dangle her feet in the water of the pool. Her gorgeous red hair fell loose around her shoulders and her sandals were nowhere to be seen.

Even his mother's hug and greeting got only a portion of his attention as the rest of him strained toward the woman he wanted to take into his arms and kiss the daylights out of.

"So, I hear from my grandson that you and my dear friend are well acquainted already," his mother said, finally garnering his whole focus.

Well versed in how his mother's mind worked, he immediately went hyperalert to any nuance and ultracautious in his own reactions. She was on a kick to get him married and fathering more grandbabies for her. His argument that it was time for Calogero to do his duty by the family was met with deaf ears.

His mother wanted more grandchildren from Valentino. Full stop. Period.

And now she'd discovered he was friends with Faith.

He had to be very careful here. If his mother even got a hint of the intimate nature of his relationship with Faith, Agata Grisafi would have her oldest son married off before he could get a word in edgewise. "We'd met before, yes."

"You'd met? I am sure your son said you were friends," his mother chided with a gleam in her eyes, confirming Valentino's worst fears.

He simply shrugged, confirming nothing. Denying nothing. Sometimes that was the only way to deal with his mother and her machinations. Deflection wasn't a bad tactic, either, when he could get away with it.

He'd long ago acknowledged he never wanted to face his mother across a boardroom table. She made his toughest clients and strongest competition look like amateurs.

"More interesting to me is your friendship with her," he said. "You rarely mention Faith."

"You are joking me, my son. I talk about my dear friend TK all of the time."

"Yes, but what has that to do with Faith?"

His mother's eyes widened and she flicked a glance to the woman in question. Faith was not looking at them, but her shoulders were stiff with unmistakable tension. This grilling had to be causing her stress as well.

"You are *not* good friends, are you?" his mother asked, in a tone that said she no longer had any doubts about the superficial nature of their relationship.

Relieved, but unsure what had convinced her, he simply said, "We know each other."

"Not very well."

He shrugged again, but had a strong urge to deny what felt like an accusation. Though the words had been spoken in his mother's normal voice, his own emotions convicted him.

Mama shrugged, looking smug, her expression that of a woman who knew what he did not. "Faith Williams is TK."

"Your artist friend?" he asked in genuine shock. "I thought he was a man!"

"No, she is very much a female, as you can see." The laughter lacing his mother's voice did not faze him.

The memory of Faith saying maybe the woman in the statue on his dresser was letting go did. *She* was the artist of that particular piece of art. When she'd made the comment, she could have been hinting, but more likely she was exposing the true inspiration behind the figure.

Which meant what? That she had a son? "You did not tell me you had a child," he said to her.

She stood up and faced him. "If you will recall, the *father* is holding the child," she said, proving once again that their thoughts traveled similar paths.

"What is that supposed to signify?"

"Figure it out for yourself, Tino. Or better yet, ask your mother. Agata understands far more than you do and knows me much better."

He couldn't believe she was being so argumentative in front of his family. His mother was bound to realize there was more between them than a casual friendship if Faith kept this up. Hell, if he had to explain what they were talking about, things would get dicey. The statue was in his bedroom, after all. How could he explain Faith—his not so good friend—seeing it?

"It's not important," he said, in an attempt to put sand on the fire of his mother's curiosity.

"No, I don't suppose it is." Faith turned to his mother and gave her a strained smile. "It's time for me to be going."

"But I thought you would stay for dinner."

"Yes, do not let my arrival change your plans." He wanted to see Faith, even if it meant being judicious under the watchful eye of his family.

He knew it was not the smartest attitude to take. He was supposed to be cooling down their relationship, but seeing her brought into sharp relief just how hard that had been over the past weeks. How much he had *missed* her.

"I feel the need to create." She hugged his mother. "You know how it is for me when I have a fit of inspiration. You are not offended, are you?"

"Will you let me see the results of this inspiration?" Agata asked. "I am still waiting to see the pieces you made while Rocco and I were in Naples."

Faith's hand dropped to her stomach, like she was nervous. "I'll let you see them all eventually. You know that."

"You promise? I know how you artists are. Especially you. If you think a piece is not up to standards, you will pound it back into clay."

That strained smile crossed Faith's beautiful features again. "I can't promise to keep something I hate, but you should be used to that by now."

His mother gave a long-suffering sigh, but she hugged Faith warmly. "I am. You cannot blame me for trying, though. You have spoiled me, allowing me access to your work before you do others."

Faith's laugh was even more strained than her smile. "You are my friend." Even though he was wet from the pool, she hugged Giosue goodbye, as well. "I will see you next week in school."

Her leave-taking of his father was the usual kisses on both cheeks. But she simply nodded at Tino before turning to go. Though it fit in with the facade of casual friendship he had tried to create, he felt the slight like a blow to his midsection.

He understood being careful in front of his parents, but this went beyond that. Had it been deliberate? Or was she simply doing her part to allay suspicion? Unfortunately, he could not ask her, nor could he request a more warm goodbye without looking suspect himself. They would have to talk about how to act in front of his family, as it was clear that was going to be an issue in the future. He was only surprised it had taken so long for the matter to arise, now that he knew how close she was to his mother and son.

That was secondary as he watched Faith walk away, and he had to fight everything in himself not to go after her.

"And you worried your mother was developing a *tendre* for TK," his father said with a big, amused laugh.

"Never say so!" His mother shook her head. "Sometimes, my son, you are singularly obtuse."

"But he is good at business," Giosue piped in, as if trying to stand up for his deficient father and not knowing exactly what to say.

Apparently everyone else in his family knew Faith's life more intimately than he did.

He was determined to rectify that ignorance. Starting now. "Mama, what did she mean by saying that the father was holding the baby in my statue?"

It was one of the reasons he loved the piece so much. It showed the father having a tender moment with his child as well as his wife.

His mother's pause before answering gave him time to realize what a monumentally stupid question that had been to ask. He had just gotten through admonishing himself regarding this very topic and here he was drawing attention to it.

No doubt about it. Faith Williams messed up his equilibrium and made mush of his usually superior brain function.

There was nothing wrong with the way his mother's brain was working, however. "Do you mean the statue that I bought you? The one that you keep on the bureau in your *bedroom,* Valentino?" she asked delicately like a cat licking at cream.

"Yes, that is the one," he said with as much insouciance as he could muster under his mother's gimlet stare.

He offered no explanation and, surprisingly enough, she did not demand he do so. He could read the speculation in her eyes as easily as a first-year primer.

She looked down at her hands as if examining her manicure, which was incidentally perfect as usual, before looking back at him. "I'm not sure that is something she would care for me to share with you."

He wasn't about to be deterred after the huge gaffe he'd committed to get the information. "Mama," he said with exasperation. "She told me to ask you."

"*Si,* well, I suppose. You know she lost her husband to a car accident six years ago?"

"I know she is a widow, yes."

"She lost her child in the same accident."

"How horrible." It had nearly destroyed him to lose Maura; if he had lost Giosue as well, he did not know how he would have stood it.

"Just so." Mama reached out and hugged her wet grandson to her. "She sells her artwork under TK as a tribute to them. Her husband's name was Taylish and her son would have been named Kaden."

"Would have been?"

"She was pregnant. And from what she said, that was something of a minor miracle. Her life has not been an easy one. She was left an orphan by her mother's death years earlier. She never knew her father—or even who he was, I believe."

"Life has enough pain to make joy all the sweeter," his father said with the same pragmatism he spoke the well-used Sicilian proverb, *cu' avi 'nna bona vigna avi pani, vinu e linga.*

He who owns a good vineyard has bread, wine and wood.

The Sicilian people were a practical lot. The fatalism of their cultural thinking reflected in the fact that Sicilian vernacular had no future tense. Just past and present.

Regardless of his pragmatic heritage, Valentino found it almost debilitatingly painful to discover that his happy-go-lucky Faith had such a sorrow-filled past. Her optimistic nature was one of the things he found most attractive about her. She made him feel good just being around.

To discover that her attitude was in spite of past agonies, not because she had never had any, was so startling as to leave him speechless.

"I think Signora Guglielmo wanted to be a mama very much," Giosue said. "She loves all the children at school, even the bratty ones."

His son's observation made Valentino chuckle even as it made him sad for the woman who had to find an outlet for her nurturing nature with other people's children.

He remembered her once telling him that she believed she was not meant to have a family. He had assumed that meant she thought she was not cut out to be a mother. He had not minded knowing that at all, as it assured him she would not expect marriage and children someday down the road. Now he saw a far more disturbing meaning behind the words.

When Faith had said she wanted more from him, she truly had meant *more*. She wanted what she had thought she could not have. A family.

And the only way he could give it to her was to break a promise that for him was sacred.

It was not an option.

But neither was letting her go so she could find that with someone else.

CHAPTER SIX

FAITH drove like an automaton toward Pizzolato. *They'd met? They knew each other?*

Each word Tino had used to answer his mother's innocent questions had driven into her heart with the precision of an assassin's dagger. And the wounds were still raw and bleeding. As they would be for a very long time.

How could he dismiss her as if she meant *nothing* to him?

But she had the answer to that, an answer she wanted to ignore, to pretend no knowledge of for the sake of her lacerated heart. She only wished she could do it—that she could lie to herself as easily as she had deluded herself into believing things were changing between them.

He could dismiss her as someone of no importance in his life because that was exactly what she was. She was his *convenient sex partner.* Nothing more. Friends? When it was convenient for him to think so, but that clearly did not extend to times with his family.

They'd met. The words reverberated through her mind over and over again. A two-word refrain with the power to torture her emotions as effectively as a rack and bullwhip.

She did not know why he had slept with her that night in Marsala. She had no clue why he had taken her to his bed in his family home, but she knew why he hadn't called her for two weeks and had ignored her calls to him.

Perhaps he regretted that intimacy and was even hoping to end their association.

The pain that thought brought her doubled her over, and she had to pull to the side of the road. Tears came then.

She never cried, but right now she could not stop.

She sobbed, the sounds coming from her mouth like those of a wounded animal, and she had no way of stopping them, of pulling her cheerful covering around her and marching on with a smile on her face. Not now.

She had thought maybe it was her turn for happiness. Maybe this baby heralded a new time in her life, one where she did not lose everyone who she loved.

But she could see already that was not true.

She had lost Tino, or was on the verge of doing so.

Her body racked with sobs, she ached with a physical pain no one was there to assuage.

What if Tino's rejection was merely a harbinger of things to come?

What if she lost this baby, too? She could not stand it.

The first trimester was a risky one, even though her doctor had confirmed her pregnancy was viable and not ectopic. The prospect of miscarriage was a dark, scary shadow over her mind.

Falling apart at the seams like this could not be helping, but she didn't know if she had the strength to rein the tears in. How was she supposed to buck up under this new loss?

The pain did not diminish, but eventually the tears did and she was able to drive home.

She had not lied when she told Agata she felt the need to create, but the piece she did that night was not one she wanted to share with anyone. Especially not a woman as kind as Tino's mother.

Faith could not make herself destroy it, though.

Once again it embodied pain she had been unable to share with anyone else.

It was another pregnant figure, but this woman was starving, her skin stretched taut over bones etched in sharp relief in the clay. Her clothes were worn and clung to the tiny bump that indicated her pregnancy in hopeless poverty. Her hair whipped around her face, raindrops mixed with tears on the visage of a mother-to-be almost certain not to make it another month, much less carry her baby to term.

The figure reflected the emotional starvation that had plagued Faith for so long. She'd tried to feed it like a beggar would her empty belly in the streets. Teaching children art, sharing their lives. Her friendship with Agata. Her intimacy with Tino, but all of it was as precarious as the statue woman's hold on life.

Faith had no one to absolutely call her own and feared that somehow the baby she carried would be lost to her as well.

She could not let that happen.

Valentino called Faith the next day. He'd tried calling the night before several times, after Gio had gone to bed, but she had not answered. He'd hoped to see her, but she had been ignoring the phone.

It was the first time she had done so during their association. He had not liked it one bit and had resolved not to avoid her calls in the future.

This time however, she answered on the third ring, just when he thought it was going to go to voice mail again.

"Hello, Tino."

"Carina."

"Do you need something?"

"No 'How was your trip?' or anything?"

"If you had wanted to tell me about your trip, you would have called while you were away…or answered my calls to you."

Ouch. "I apologize for not doing so. I was busy." Which was the truth, just not the whole truth.

"Too busy for a thirty-second hello? I don't think so."

"I should have called," he admitted.

"It doesn't matter."

"If it offended you, it does." Of course it had offended her.

He would not have cared with any of the other bed partners he had had since Maura's death, but this was Faith. And he cared.

"I guess you didn't have time for phone sex and saw no reason to speak to me otherwise," she said in a loaded tone.

He had already apologized. What more did she want? "Now you are being foolish." They had never engaged in phone sex, though the thought was somewhat intriguing.

"I seem to make a habit of that with you."

"Not that I have noticed."

"Really?" She sighed, the sound coming across the phone line crystal clear. "You must be blind."

Something was going on here. Something bad. Perhaps he owed her more than a verbal apology for avoiding her as he had done. It was imperative they meet. "Can we get together tonight?"

"For sex only or dinner first?"

What the hell? "Is it your monthly?"

She was usually disconcertingly frank about that particular time of month and did not suffer from a big dose of PMS, but there was a first time for everything. Right?

She gasped. There was a few seconds of dead air between them. Then she said, "No, Tino. I can guarantee you it is not that time of month."

Rather than apologize for his error yet again, he said, "It sounds like we would benefit from talking, Faith. Let's meet for dinner."

"Where?"

He named a restaurant and she agreed without her usual enthusiastic approval.

"Would you rather go somewhere else?" he asked.

"No."

"All right, then. Montibello's it is."

She was early, waiting at the table when he arrived. She looked beautiful as usual, but gave a dim facsimile of her normal smile of welcome.

He leaned down and kissed her cheek. "Did you have a good day?"

Looking away, she shrugged.

This was so not like her he really began to worry. Was she ill? Or returning to the States? His stomach plummeted at the thought. "Anything you want to talk about?"

"Not particularly."

Right. He was not buying that, but obviously she was hesitant. Maybe they could ease into whatever was making her behave so strangely by talking about other things. "There is something I think we should discuss."

"Fine." The word came out clipped and infused with attitude.

Okay, then. Reverse was not a gear he used often in his professional or personal life, so he went forward with the original plan. "We need to come up with a strategy for how we behave around my family."

"You really think that's going to become a problem?" she asked in a mocking tone he'd never heard from her. "We've been sleeping together for months and have only been around them together twice in all that time. The first instance would not have occurred if you had known I was your son's teacher, and the second could have been avoided if I had known you were due to return a day earlier than expected."

"Nevertheless, the occasions did happen and I feel we should develop a strategy for dealing with similar ones when they happen again."

"I think you handled it already, Tino. Your family is under the impression we are something between bare acquaintances and casual friends." Her hands clenched tightly in her lap as she spoke.

He wanted to reach out and hold them, but that would be pushing the boundaries of what he considered safe public displays. Both for his sake and hers. He did not hide the fact that they saw each other, but he did not make it easy for others to guess at their relationship, either.

Marsala was a big enough city that he could take her to dinner at restaurants where he was unlikely to run into his business associates. Even less probable was the possibility of being seen by family. However, there were still some small-town ideals in Marsala, and Faith, as a single woman, could not afford to have her reputation tarnished if she wanted to continue teaching art at the elementary school.

"Did my saying that bother you?" Surely she understood the implications if he had reacted differently.

"Does it matter? Our relationship, such that it is, has never been about what I was comfortable with." Her eyes were filled with a hurt anger that shocked him.

"That is not true. You were no more interested in a long-term committed relationship than I was when we first met."

"Things change."

"Some things cannot." He wished that was not the case, but it was. "We do not have to lose what we do have because it cannot be *more*."

"You spent two weeks ignoring me, Tino."

"I was out of country."

It was a lame excuse and her expression said she knew it. "You forwarded my calls to voice mail."

"I needed a breathing space. I had some things to work out," he admitted. "But I have apologized. I will do so again if that will improve things for you."

She flicked her hand as if dismissing his offer. "Did you work out your *problems?*"

"I believe so."

"And it included treating me like a nonentity in your life in front of your family?" she asked with a definite edge to her voice.

"If I had not, my mother would have gotten wind of our relationship. She knows me too well."

At that moment, Faith's eyes reflected pure sorrow. "And that would have been a catastrophe?"

"Yes." He hated giving the confirmation when she looked so unhappy about the truth, but he had no choice.

"It would not be appropriate to have my mistress visiting with my family."

"I am not your mistress."

"True, but were I to try to explain the distinction to Mama, she would have us married faster than the speed of light. She likes you, Faith, and she wants more grandchildren from her oldest son."

"And the thought of marriage to me is a complete anathema to you?"

No, it was not, but that was a large part of the problem. "I do not wish to marry anyone."

"But you would do so."

"If I was absolutely convinced that was what was best for Giosue." Only, he would not marry a woman he could love, a woman who could undermine his honor.

Faith nodded and stood.

"Where are you going? We have not even ordered."

"I'm not hungry, Tino."

He stood as well. "Then we will leave."

"No."

"What do you mean?" Panic made his words come out hard and clipped.

"It's over. I don't want to see you anymore." Tears washed into her peacock-blue eyes.

For a moment they sparkled like grieving sapphires, but she blinked the moisture away along with any semblance of emotion from her face.

He could not believe the words coming out of her mouth, much less the way she seemed to be able to turn off her feelings. It was as if a stranger, not the woman he had been making love to for almost a year, stood across from him. "Because I needed some space and neglected to call you for two weeks?"

"No, though honestly? That would be enough for most women."

"You are not most women."

"No, I've been a very convenient sexual outlet, but that's over, Tino. The well is dried up." A slight hitch in her voice was the only indication she felt anything at all at saying these words.

"What the blazes are you talking about?" The well? What bloody well?

She talked like he'd been using her this past year, but there relationship had been mutual.

"You wanted me just as I wanted you."

She shrugged. *Shrugged,* damn it. Just as if this conversation wasn't of utmost importance.

"Along with agreeing that this thing between us wasn't some serious emotional connection, we also agreed that if it stopped working for either of us, we were completely free to walk away. No harm. No foul. I'm walking." Her voice was even and calm, free of her usual passion and any feeling—either positive or negative.

"How can you go from wanting more to wanting nothing?" he asked, dazed by this turn of events.

"You aren't going to give me more, and nothing is a better option than settling for what we had."

"There was no settling. You wanted me as much as I wanted you," he said again, as if repeating it might make her get the concept.

"Things change."

He cursed loudly, using a word in the Sicilian vernacular rarely heard in polite company.

"You promised."

"What did I promise?"

"To let me walk away without a big scene."

Damn it all to hell. He had, but he had never expected her to want to walk away. "What about my mother?"

"What about her? She's my friend."

"And my son?"

"He is my student."

"You do not intend to ditch either of them?"

"No."

"Only me."

"It's necessary."

"For who?"

"For me."

"Why?"

"What difference does it make? You won't give me more and I can't accept less any longer. The whys don't matter."

"I don't believe that."

"Not my problem."

"I did not know you had this hard side to you."

"I wasn't aware you could be so clingy."

Affronted at the very implication, he ground out, "I am *not* clingy."

"I'm glad to hear it. Goodbye, Tino. I'm sure I'll be seeing you around."

"Wait, Faith…"

But she was gone and the maître d' was apologizing and offering to move their table, asking what they had done to offend. Valentino had no answers for the man. He had no answers for himself.

In a near catatonic state of shock, Faith stood beside her car outside the restaurant. The coldness she had felt toward Tino at the table had permeated her body until she felt incapable of movement.

She had broken up with him.

Really, truly. Not a joke. Not with tears, or hopes he would try to talk her out of it, but with a gut-deep certainty the relationship they had, such as it was, was over.

She hadn't gone to the restaurant with the intention of breaking up. Had she?

She knew her pregnancy hormones had her emotions on a see-saw and she'd been trying to ride them out. She laughed soundlessly, her heart aching. A see-saw? More like an emotional roller coaster of death-defying height, speed and terrifying twists and turns.

She didn't just teeter from one feeling to the next, she swooped without warning.

It hadn't been easy the two weeks he had avoided her calls, but it had been even worse since Tino had denied their friendship to his mother. Faith had realized that what she believed was affection had only been the result of lust on his part. He wanted sex and she gave it to him. Only, she couldn't do that anymore.

She wouldn't risk the baby.

The doctor had said normal sexual activity wouldn't jeopardize her pregnancy, but then he didn't know her past, how easily she lost the people who meant the most to her. She'd known she would have to put Tino off from being physically intimate for at least another few weeks, but she hadn't realized that somewhere deep inside that had meant breaking things off with him completely.

It had all crystallized when he said he wouldn't marry her—at any cost. Once he knew about the baby, that attitude would change, but the underlying reasons for it wouldn't. She knew that. Just as she knew that a marriage made for reasons of duty and responsibility was the last kind she wanted.

It was one thing to marry someone knowing you loved them and they only liked you and found deep satisfaction in your body. But to marry someone you knew did *not* want to marry you and did in fact see something so wrong about you that they would marry someone else over you, that was something else entirely.

She wasn't sure she could do it.

But could she take the baby from Sicily, from its family and raise it alone, knowing it could have a better life in its father's home country? She didn't know. Thankfully, that decision did not have to be made right this second.

She forced her frozen limbs to move, and slid into her car, turning on the ignition.

She drove toward her home while those questions and more plagued her. Plagued by a question she told herself did not need an immediate answer. Her mind refused to let it go, the only eye in the storm of her emotion being that she had no intention of revealing her pregnancy until she was through the more-dangerous first trimester.

At that point she would have to have answers.

Though she normally saw the older woman at least once a week, Faith managed to avoid showing Agata the pregnancy statuary. Faith promised Tino's mother she would be the first to see all the pieces for the new show she was putting together for a New York gallery. Faith had sent pictures of the pieces she'd been doing to a gallery owner on Park Avenue who loved TK's work. The woman had called Faith, practically swooning with delight at the prospect of doing a show for the fertility pieces.

Like her emotions, Faith's work swung between hope

and despair, touching on every emotion in between. It was the most powerful stuff she'd done since the car accident that had stolen her little family. As much pain as some of the pieces caused her, she was proud of them all.

An art teacher had once told Faith's class that pain was a great source of inspiration, as was joy, but that either without the other left an artist's work lacking in some way. Faith was living proof both agony and ecstasy could reside side by side in a person's heart. And she had no doubt her work was all the better for it, even if her heart wasn't.

Tino tried calling Faith several times, but his calls were sent straight to voice mail every time. He left messages but they were ignored. He sent her text messages that received no reply either.

He could not believe his affair with Faith was over.

He wouldn't believe it.

She wasn't acting like herself, and he was going to find out why. And fix it, damn it.

Morning sickness was just that for Faith, with the nausea dissipating by noon. While that did not impact her ability to work much, it did make it more difficult on the days she taught. She'd considered canceling her classes for the first trimester, or withdrawing all together. She doubted they would want an unwed pregnant woman teaching art to their children; it was a traditional village. However, she saw little Gio only on the days she taught and she could not make herself give up those visits, brief though they were.

She loved the little boy. A lot. She hadn't realized how much she had come to see him as something more than a pupil, something like family—until she broke things off with his father and contemplated not seeing the precious boy again. She simply could not do it.

He was as sweet as ever, showing he had no idea she was now persona non grata in his papa's life. He hung back after class to talk to her and she enjoyed that. Today, though, he was fidgeting.

"Is something the matter, sweetheart?"

He grinned. "I like it when you call me that. It's like a mama would do, you know?"

Suppressing the stab of pain at his words, she reached out and brushed his hair back from his face. "I'm glad. Now, tell me if something is wrong."

"Nonna said I could invite you for dinner."

"That is very kind of her."

"Only, Papa said you probably wouldn't come."

"He did?"

Gio looked at her with pleading eyes only a heart of stone could ignore. "Why won't you come again? I thought you and Papa were friends."

"I didn't say I wouldn't come."

"So, you will?" Giosue asked, his little-boy face transforming with the light of hope.

"When does your *nonna* want me to come?"

"She said this Friday would be good."

"It just so happens I am free this Friday."

Gio grinned with delight and gave her a spontaneous hug that went straight to her heart.

Perhaps it was foolish to agree, but she couldn't stand to see the hurt of disappointment come into Giosue's eyes. Besides, Faith had told Tino that she had no intention of giving up her friendship with his mother and son. And she'd meant it.

Being pregnant with Giosue's sibling and Agata's grandchild only made those two relationships more important. Tino wasn't going away and she needed to work on her ability to be around him and remain unaffected. The dinner invitation was an opportunity to do just that.

Her unborn baby deserved to know his or her family and Faith would not allow her own feelings to stand in the way of that.

Besides there was a tiny part of her that wanted to show Tino he was wrong and that she could handle being around him just fine.

Just a small part. Really.

CHAPTER SEVEN

LESS CERTAIN OF HER ABILITY to withstand Tino's company unscathed than she had been in the safety of her art classroom, Faith rang the doorbell of the big villa.

The door opened almost immediately, making her heart skip a beat. However, it was only Giosue on the other side.

Relief flooded her, making her smile genuine. "Good evening, Gio."

"Bueno sera, signora."

She handed him a small gift.

"What is this?" he asked, his voice tinged with anticipation mixed with confusion.

"It is traditional to give one's dinner host a gift. I forgot yours when you invited me before, so I've brought it tonight along with one for your grandmother."

"Because this time she invited you?"

"Exactly."

Gio looked at the present and then up at her, his eyes shining. "Wow. Can I open it now?"

She nodded.

He ripped the package apart with the enthusiasm usually reserved for the young and sucked in a breath as he saw what was inside. They were leather gardening gloves made to fit a child's hands.

"I didn't know if you already had a pair…"

"I do, but they are made of cloth and not nearly so nice. Come, I want to show Nonno."

She smiled, glad her gift had gone over so well, and followed Gio to the lanai, Agata's favorite place to entertain. When they arrived, she saw both Agata and Rocco, but no Tino.

Relieved at what she was sure would be only a temporary respite, Faith watched Gio run to his grandfather to show him the new gloves.

Agata smiled in welcome and hugged Faith, kissing both her cheeks. "It is good to see you."

"Come, Mama, you speak as if it had been weeks rather than a few days since the last time you saw your friend." There was an edge to Tino's voice that Faith could not miss.

She wondered if Agata noticed, but the older woman seemed to be oblivious.

Shaking her head at her son, who had just arrived, she said, "Faith is a dear friend I would see every day if I could. She is good for Gio too."

"Save your matchmaking attempts for someone susceptible, Mama. I do not believe Faith likes me at all."

Oh, he was in fine form tonight. Faith refused to rise to the bait and show her chagrin at his words.

"Nonsense. You're my son, what is not to like?" Agata demanded.

Faith could make a list, but she forebore doing so for Agata's sake. See? She could handle this. She *would* handle this.

Her desire to strangle Tino for his leading comment

morphed to unwilling concern as she saw how haggard he looked. Oh, he was his usual gorgeous self, but there was a certain cast to his skin and lines around his eyes that were not usually there—all of it bespeaking a bone-deep exhaustion.

"You look tired," she blurted out.

"*Si,* this one has been working too many hours. Like a man possessed, he returns to his office after our little Gio goes to sleep and works into the early hours before returning home."

"I told you, I have some things going on that require extra attention right now."

Agata frowned. "You say that to your father and maybe he will believe you. Men! But I am your mother and you are behaving much the same as you did after Maura's death. I do not understand it."

"There is nothing to understand. I am not grieving, I am working." He said it with so much force, Faith couldn't help believing.

Agata did not look so convinced. But then, she was a mother and tended to see the softer side of her child, even if such a side did not exist.

"Is the new venture going well?"

"Yes." Tino's voice was clipped and the look he threw his mother was filled with frustration. "Regardless of what my family thinks, I am damn good at my job."

Rocco had joined them and was shaking his head. "Of course we know you are a success. How could you be anything else? You are my son, no? And I am the greatest vintner in Sicily. Why should you not be a businessman of equal talent? You are a Grisafi."

Faith was tempted to laugh, but knew Rocco would

not take it well. He was serious. Of course. But Faith had no problem seeing where Tino got his arrogance from.

"He is that," Agata said with asperity. "Which means that in this home, he is my son, not some bigshot businessman. And you are my husband, not the maker of the best wines in the country."

"Yes, of course." Rocco did not look the least cowed, but sounded more than willing to be compliant.

Agata shook her head. "Men!"

It was a word she said often over the next few hours, with the same slightly exasperated and amused tone. Faith was gratified that despite the stress of being around Tino, she found the evening highly entertaining and surprisingly comfortable.

So long as she avoided direct contact with her former lover, that is. It wasn't easy in such a small group.

And Tino wasn't helping. He had to know she found being around him difficult, but he engaged her in conversation, and she barely avoided sitting beside him at dinner. In that, Gio was her unwitting accomplice.

However, once dinner had been eaten, it was clear that Gio and Agata both intended to see that Faith and Tino spend as much time together as possible.

Right now she was being given a tour of the vineyard, ostensibly by Rocco. Only, the old man and Gio often moved ahead, or lingered behind, leaving her alone with Tino for brief spurts of time.

"You never answered my mother's question," Tino said during one of those moments.

"I don't know what you mean."

"She asked what there was about me not to like."

"She's biased. She's your mother."

"*Si,* but that's not the point."

"And what is the point?"

"That you never answered her question."

"She didn't seem bothered by that." The older woman had not brought it up again.

"Perhaps not, but I am."

"That's too bad. I'm not here to visit with you, Tino."

"My family will be disappointed. They are matchmaking."

"In vain."

"Yes, but won't you tell me why?"

He was insane. He was the one who refused to consider marriage. Ultimately, wasn't that a far more effective deterrent to his family's attempts at matchmaking than her supposed dislike of him?

"You're arrogant."

"I am a Grisafi."

"So, it comes with the territory?"

"Definitely."

She rolled her eyes.

"What else?"

"I never said I didn't like you, Tino." And she couldn't do so now in honesty. He'd hurt her, but she did like him. She loved the callous lout, but yes, she liked him, too. Just not some of his attitudes.

"You said you never wanted to see me again."

"I said our affair was over."

"And yet here you are."

"Visiting your family, Tino. Not you!"

"You could have arranged to come a different night."

"Why should I?"

He laughed, the sound too sexy for her peace of mind. And highly annoying. "Ah, proving me wrong,

Faith? Making sure that I know I don't matter enough for you to avoid dinner in my home?"

"I told you I wouldn't give up my friendship with your mother or son."

"You wanted to see me, or you would not have come tonight." He brushed her cheek with his hand. "Admit it."

She jumped back from the gentle touch that felt like a brand. "If I hadn't come, your parents would have suspected something was wrong between us. I would think *you* would have realized that and tried to avoid it. You could have made arrangements to be gone tonight without causing suspicion."

"I had no desire to do so." He shrugged, looking scarily determined.

"I don't see why."

"You have refused to answer my calls for the past week."

"That should have given you a message."

"It did. Something is wrong and I want to know what."

"I told you."

"You want more or nothing at all."

"Yes."

"I cannot give you marriage, Faith."

"You would be surprised at what you are capable of giving in the right circumstances, Tino." Why she said it, she didn't know.

The need to challenge him?

"What circumstances would those be?"

She shook her head, absolutely not going there right now. "Just leave it alone."

"I cannot."

"You have to."

"I know about your lost husband and child. I am sorry.

If I could take that old pain away, I would. But I cannot fill the gap they left in your life. That is not in my power."

Did he really believe that? And here she'd thought he was smart. "You have your own past tragedies to deal with," was all she said.

He did not get a chance to answer because they caught up with Gio and Rocco. Faith was given a fascinating description of what happened to the grapes once they were picked. She found it difficult to focus on, however with Tino a brooding presence beside her.

They were once again on their own as Gio and his grandfather had hurried back to the house much too quickly for Faith to keep up in her high-heeled sandals. "How did you find out about Taylish and Kaden?" she asked, posing the question to Tino she could not get out of her mind.

"My mother."

Stunned, Faith stopped walking altogether. She could not imagine Agata sharing Faith's confidences without a prompting to do so. Not even in the effort to matchmake. "You asked her?"

"Yes." Tino stood only a couple of feet away, but the moonlight was not strong enough to illuminate the expression in his eyes.

She could feel its intensity though.

"Wasn't that dangerous?"

"In what way?"

She rolled her eyes, though she doubted he could see it. "Don't play dumb. It showed a more-than-passing interest in me."

Something he'd said he didn't want his mother to get wind of.

"It was worse than that, even," he said, sounding

rueful, but not particularly bothered. "I allowed it to slip that we had discussed the statue in my bedroom."

Did he have any idea what he was revealing of his inner thoughts? Tino—Mr. Certainty, the man who never changed his mind and always knew best—was acting as if he did not know his own mind. Acting in direct opposition to his stated purpose. Maybe he had a deeper insight into the long-term effect of his words than she did.

She shook her head. "You're kidding."

"Sometimes my curiosity gets the better of me." He did not shrug, but the negligent movement was there in his voice.

"I guess," she said with emphasis. "I don't see your mother making a list of wedding guests as you feared."

"She is matchmaking, but being surprisingly low-key about it."

"And that doesn't bother you?"

"That she is matchmaking?"

"Yes." What the heck did he think she meant?

"So long as she maintains subtlety and does not make it into a family argument of dramatic proportions, no."

Maybe she understood his insouciance better now. "In other words, as long as it's easy for you to avoid the outcome she is looking for."

"You could put it that way."

"I just did."

"Si."

"Don't play with me, Tino."

He closed the distance between them but did not touch her. "I am not playing. I want you back."

"As your mistress."

"And my friend."

"That's not what you told your mother."

"I explained that."

"And I found your explanation lacking."

"Faith—"

Lucky for her, because she really didn't want to get into this right now—or ever really—Giosue came running up. "You two are too slow. Nonna said we could swim if you wanted, *signora*."

Faith moved toward Gio, putting distance between herself and his father once again. "Actually, I think it is time I returned home."

There was that look, the disappointment Faith hated to see, but Gio did not attempt to cajole her. He simply nodded and looked down at the ground.

And it was more effective than any type of whining might have been.

She grabbed his hand and said, "Maybe just a short swim. All right?"

He looked up at her, eyes shining. "Really, *signora?*"

"Yes."

"We can play water ball. *Zio* Calogero sent me a new net."

Faith had seen the basketball net attached to the side of the pool on a short pole. "That sounds like fun."

"Yes, it does." Tino took Gio's other hand. "Your papa will join you as well. Provided I am invited?"

"Of course, Papa." Gio's voice rang with joy.

And why shouldn't it? This was exactly what her favorite pupil wanted—the three of them together. Faith had wanted it, too, but she couldn't fight a ghost.

Tension filled her as she contemplated the next thirty minutes. She hadn't counted on Tino joining them in the pool, but she would have to deal with it. She wasn't about to renege on her promise to Gio. Though, for the first time in her life she was seriously tempted to back out on a commitment she'd made to a child.

Fifteen minutes later she was desperate enough to do so.

Tino had been teasing her, touching her under the guise of the game. A caress down her arm. A hand cupped over her hip. An arm around her waist, ostensibly to stop her from going under. But the final straw was when he brushed his lips over the sensitive spot behind her ear and whispered that he wanted her.

She shoved herself away from him and climbed out of the pool in the space of a couple seconds.

"*Signora,* where are you going?"

"It is time for me to leave." She tried to keep the frustration and anger she felt from her voice. It was not Gio's fault his father was a fiend.

"But why?" The little boy's eyes widened with confusion. "We were having fun."

"*Si.* I thought we were having a great deal of fun," Tino said with a purr.

"Really?" she asked—this time making no effort to hide her displeasure. "I'll leave it to you to explain to your son why I need to leave, then."

It was Tino's turn to look confused and he was the mirror image of his son in that moment, only older. Would their child take after him or her? What was she thinking about? This was not the time to consider whether the baby in her womb would resemble its father. Not when she wanted to bean the man.

Without another word, she spun on her heel and stormed to the cabana where she changed back into her clothes. A shower would have to wait until she got home.

She left moments later after hugging Agata and a hastily dried Gio. Rocco had gone to check on something in the wine cellars.

Her goodbye to Tino was perfunctory and verbal only.

Valentino stood outside Faith's apartment in Pizzolato, uncharacteristically hesitant to knock. The evening before had been an exercise in frustration for him. Every time he got a step closer to Faith, she took two backward. And he did not understand why.

He'd used their time in the pool to remind her of what they were both missing. Valentino was sure it had been working, too. Faith's breath had shortened, her nipples growing hard under her one-piece swimsuit. Heaven above knew he'd been hard enough to drill through cement. But then she had pushed away from him with the clear intent to reject and climbed from the pool, saying she had to go. She didn't back down, either, not even when Gio looked heartbroken.

She'd left him there to explain her precipitous departure to his upset son.

What the hell was going on with her?

It was not like her to be so unfeeling. But the look she'd given him could have stripped paint.

It had been weeks since they made love in his family home, but it was not merely her body he craved. He missed her. Like an ache in his gut that no medication could take away. Which was why he was here right now, ready to make it right.

Whatever *it* was.

He gave the closed door a glare. What was he? A wimp? He did not think so. Not Valentino Grisafi.

He knocked on the door. Loudly.

His mother had told him that Faith got caught up in her work and didn't hear the door lots of times. That she worked whenever the mood struck her, the hour of the day not a deterrent no matter how late or early. She'd said a lot more about Faith.

Add this knowledge to everything she'd told him previously about TK, and Valentino had a completely new picture of his lover, an image that convicted him about how little he'd known before. Not that it should have mattered, but with Faith it did. Their relationship would be a year old in two more weeks, and he didn't want to spend the anniversary of their first date grieving her loss.

Taking a deep breath, he knocked again.

"Coming," came from inside.

A few seconds later the door swung open. "Agata, I wasn't expect—"

"My mother is at a fundraising meeting for Giosue's school, I believe."

Faith looked at him with something like resignation and sighed. "Yes. That's what I thought she was doing."

"Are you going to invite me in?"

"Will you go away if I don't?"

"No."

"Why do you want to come in? You've never stepped foot in my building, much less my apartment. I didn't think you even knew where I lived."

He hadn't. He'd had to ask his mother, but Faith didn't need to know that. "I want to see where you work."

She grimaced, but stepped back. He followed her into the apartment. It wasn't huge, but it wasn't small, either. She'd converted the main living area, which opened to a glassed-in balcony, into her studio. The half-glass ceiling bathed the room in the glow of natural light, and he could easily see why she'd picked this location to work.

Although the area was clearly a working studio, she had created a conversation area in one corner with a love seat and two chairs around a low table decorated with traditional Sicilian tiles.

He settled into one of the chairs after declining a drink. "Is my mother the only person who visits you here?"

"No, a couple of the teachers from the school have been by, as well, but since the school day is not yet over…" She let her explanation trail off.

"What about other artists?" He was trying to get a picture of her life, but it was still pretty fuzzy and that bothered him.

She gave a half shrug. "I'm a private person."

"You always came off as friendly and outgoing to me."

She wiped at a spot of clay on her hand with the rag she held as she took the seat farthest from his. "Yes, well, maybe I should say that TK is a private person. I have some friends in the artistic community, but none of them live close enough to drop in during the middle of the day."

He considered this and what she had said about other teachers coming over sometimes, which he read to mean rarely. "You're a very solitary person, aren't you?"

She shook her head, not in negation, but as if she couldn't think what to say. "Why are you here, Tino?"

After last night she could ask that?

"I miss you." There. The bald-faced truth.

"I don't see why you should." She stiffened, drawing herself up into a ramrod sitting posture. "You still have your hand."

Shock struck him like a bolt of lightning, making it hard to breathe for just a second. "That is crude, and implies our relationship is nothing but mechanical sex."

"We no longer have a relationship."

He did not accept that, but to say so would violate their initial agreement. He decided to change the subject instead.

"Are those the pieces my mother is salivating to see?" he asked, referring to several cloth-covered shapes around the room.

"Yes. I told her she could see them when they are finished."

Sharp curiosity filled him. "She likes to see your work in progress." *He* wanted to see Faith's work.

"Not this time."

"Why not?"

"I don't want her to see them before they are cast and glazed."

"You are using the clay as models?"

"For some. There will be a numbered series cast before I break the mold for several, but some will be fired as is and be one-of-a-kind pieces."

"I know very little about your process." Even less than he knew about her.

"True." She didn't look inclined to elaborate.

But didn't most people enjoy rhapsodizing about their passions? From the way her work took over her home, he assumed her art was Faith's biggest passion. "Perhaps you would care to change that now?"

"I don't think so."

Her negative response stunned him. Though why it should, in the face of the way she'd been behaving, he didn't know. He kept expecting her to go back to acting the way she had until a few short weeks ago. "You don't feel like talking about your work?"

"I don't feel like talking to you."

"Don't be like that, *carina.*" He didn't want to examine the way that made him feel, but it was not good. "We are friends."

"That's not what you told your mother."

Must she keep harping on that one moment in time, an answer to his mother's questioning he was past regretting and into mentally banging his head against a wall? "I was protecting myself, I admit it. But I was trying to protect us too, Faith. What would you have had me tell her?"

"The truth?"

"That we are lovers?" He did not think so.

She glared, her eyes snapping with anger and something akin to disgust. "That wouldn't be true, though, would it?"

"We are lovers, perhaps on hiatus, but still together."

"You are delusional. We are not and never were lovers."

"*Now* who is being delusional?"

She stood up, her hands fisted at her sides. "You have to give more than sex to be considered someone's lover. We were *sex partners*. Now we are past acquaintances."

"That is not true. We have more than sex between us." After all, that "more" had cost him the sleep of several nights.

"Oh, really?"

"Yes, *our friendship.*"

"Again, let me refer you to that afternoon by the pool at your family home. You told your mother we were not friends."

"I made a mistake." There, he had said it. "I am sorry," he gritted.

"That was really hard for you, wasn't it?"

He just looked at her.

"Admitting you were wrong isn't your thing."

"It doesn't happen very often."

"Being wrong or admitting it?" she asked with dark amusement.

"Both."

"I don't suppose it does."

He too stood, taking her by the arms and standing close. "Let me back in, Faith. I need you." Those last three words were said even less frequently than an apology by him.

Tears filled her eyes. "I can't, Tino."

"Why not?"

She just shook her head.

"Tell me what is wrong. Let me make it right." He felt like he was drowning, but that wasn't right. He did not want this thing between them to end, but if it did, it shouldn't be *this* wrenching.

"You can't make it right."

"I can try."

"Can you love *me?* Can you make me your wife?"

Something inside him shattered. "No."

"Then you can't fix it."

CHAPTER EIGHT

FAITH spent the next few days in a borderline state where the numbness of loss fought the tendrils of hope each day her pregnancy continued. She missed Tino. She wanted him—both emotionally and physically. She craved his touch, but not in a sexual way, and he didn't want her to give him anything else. She wanted to be held, cuddled and comforted as her body went through the changes pregnancy brought. She wanted someone to talk to in the evenings when she found herself too tired to create but too restless to sleep.

She had not realized how much his presence in her life staved off the loneliness, until he was gone. She found herself in a pathetic state of anticipation every time she spoke to Agata, hoping the Sicilian woman would drop news about her oldest son.

Faith's morning sickness had gotten worse the past few days, but she was more adamant than ever she would not give up her job teaching. She'd lost Tino. She didn't think she could stand to lose her only contact with his son, as well. When had the little boy become so important to her? She didn't know, but she could not deny that the love she felt for the child growing inside her was in equal intensity for the emotion she felt toward her former lover's son.

One evening, almost a week after Tino had left her apartment, she got a phone call from Agata.

"*Ciao, bella.* How are you?"

"Fine."

"You were not home today."

"No, I went shopping in Marsala." She'd needed to get out. To be around other people. There were moments when she felt she was going mad from loneliness.

"I stopped by hoping to have lunch."

"Oh," Faith said with genuine regret. "I'm so sorry I missed you."

"Yes, well, I would only have begged you to show me your work."

Faith laughed. "Soon." She knew just how she was going to announce her pregnancy to her dear friend, but not until the risky first trimester was past.

How she was going to tell Agata that the baby was Tino's was less clear however.

"I would like that." There was an emotional note in Agata's tone that surprised Faith, but maybe it shouldn't have.

She'd never known another human being as connected to her art as the older woman. Not even Taylish had understood the emotion behind the pieces the way Agata did.

"So, how about lunch tomorrow?" Agata asked.

"That would be lovely."

They rang off and Faith turned to face her empty apartment, wondering if her newfound evening nausea would allow her to eat an evening meal.

* * *

Valentino's mother took the seat beside where he watched his son frolic in the pool with his papa.

The worried expression on her face concerned Valentino. He knew she had planned to call Faith. "Mama, what is the matter?"

His mother twisted her hands in an uncharacteristic display of nerves but did not answer.

"Mama."

She looked up as if just realizing he was sitting there. "Oh, did you say something, son?"

"I asked if there was anything the matter."

"Nothing bad. Well, there may well be ramifications, but I'm in a quandary and do not know what to do."

"About what?" he asked with some impatience. Was this about Faith?

His mother sighed heavily. "I did something I should not have."

"What?"

"I do not think I should say."

Valentino waited patiently. He knew his mother. She would not have said anything if she did not want to confess to someone. Apparently, he was that someone. And if it was related to Faith in any way, he was glad.

Not that he should be pining over the woman who dumped him like yesterday's garbage. She'd thrown down her ultimatum and he had refused terms. She'd been unwilling to negotiate—that should be the end of it.

Still, he waited with uncomfortable anticipation for his mother to speak.

She sighed again. Fidgeted some more and then sighed a third time. "I have a key to Faith's apartment."

"Ah." But he didn't feel nearly as insouciant as he sounded. His mother had a key to his lover's apartment, but he did not. Nor did Faith have a key to his apartment in Marsala. Why not? Why was it that his mother had spent more time in Faith's studio than he had?

They were friends. They did not limit their time together to sex. So, why had he never seen any of her works in progress? Why had he not known she was the highly successful sculptor TK?

"I stopped by today. Unannounced."

"I see." Though he didn't.

"I let myself in, you know, thinking she might be back soon." Mama shuddered. "I did a terrible thing."

"You are not the criminal type. I doubt what you did was *terrible*."

"But it *was,* my son. I wanted so badly to see Faith's newest work."

"You peeked."

"Yes, and that is bad enough—but in looking at her work, I revealed a secret she is clearly not ready to share."

"A secret?" What kind of secret? Had Faith been making clay tiles of the fifty states because she missed her homeland? What?

"*Si.* A secret. I have betrayed my friend."

"Mama, whatever it is, I am sure it will be fine. Faith loves you. She will forgive you." If only Faith was as tolerant of her lover.

"But a woman has the right to determine the timing of when she will share such news with others. I have, what is that saying your brother uses—oh, yes—I have stolen her thunder. I cannot pretend not to know when she tells me, for that would be a lie. I cannot lie to my friend." She grimaced. "I did tell her I still wanted to see her work and I do. I stopped looking after the first one because I knew. I knew what it meant."

Valentino ground his teeth and tried not to glare at his mother with impatience. "What *what* meant?"

"The statue. It is so clear to see. You could not miss it," she said, as if trying to convince Valentino.

"I am sure you are right. What was the statue of?" he asked without being able to help himself.

"It is just that I am so worried. If it means what I think, and I'm sure it does—and there is no father in sight. Things are going to get difficult for my friend."

"What does a priest have to do with Faith?"

"A priest? Who said anything about a priest? Faith is Lutheran. They have pastors, I believe."

"Mama, I don't understand. You said 'father.'"

"Yes, the father of her child."

"Child? Faith has no children. Her unborn baby died in the accident with her husband."

"The baby inside her now, Valentino."

Valentino's chest grew tight. Although he knew he was breathing, it felt like all the oxygen had disappeared from the air. "Are you saying you believe Faith is pregnant?"

"Of course that is what I have been saying. Weren't you listening? I should never have snooped. Now when she tells me, I will have to admit I already guessed. She will be let down."

His mother continued to talk, but Valentino did not hear what she said. He had surged to his feet and was trying to rush across the brickwork of the patio. But his movements were uncoordinated and jerky as his mother's words reverberated inside his head like clanging cymbals in a discordant rhythm.

Faith was pregnant?

His Faith? The woman who said she did not want to

see him anymore. The one who had ended their relationship, such as it was.

He shook his head, but the blanket of shock refused to be dislodged.

He was going to be a father again? Now? When he had thought never to remarry, when he had believed Giosue would be his only child. It was unreal but not. Part of him accepted the news with an atavistic instinct of rightness. He had no doubt the baby was his. Dismiss him though she had tried to do, Faith was his. She had been since the moment they met. Hell, a primal part of him claimed she always had been—even before they knew each other.

Even the most rational part of his mind accepted that she was his *now*. She had been with no one else since their first time together, and probably for a long time before that.

He yanked open the door of his Jaguar and climbed inside, slamming it again as he started the car with a loud roar of the engine, and then tearing out of the drive.

How was she pregnant?

They used birth control. Religiously. Rather, he did. Still, there had only been a handful of times that their protection had not been one hundred percent. After each slip, he would be beset by guilt, and work extrahard in future to make sure they were covered.

With a sense of inevitability, he realized one of those times had not been too long ago.

He'd taken Faith to dinner at a favorite trattoria. Instead of sitting outside, so they could watch people on the street—as Faith was wont to do—Valentino had asked for some privacy. They had been given a table in the back corner, the restaurant lighting barely reaching into the shadows that surrounded it. The light from the single candle in the center of the table set a romantic mood.

At least, he'd thought so.

Faith frowned as he helped her take her seat. "I know our relationship isn't common knowledge, but do we have to hide in the dark?"

He leaned down and whispered in her ear. "I thought we could entertain ourselves over dinner, rather than finding our amusement in watching other people."

The embarrassing truth was that Faith liked people-watching—sometimes too much. She paid more attention to the ones surrounding them than to him, and he did not like that. Tonight he was determined to have her entire focus. If it took seducing her publicly, so be it.

And that is exactly what he did, starting with a kiss just below the shell of her ear, using both teeth and tongue as well as his lips.

She was shivering and had made a small whimpering sound by the time he finished and took his own seat across the small table from her.

"Considering what you apparently have planned for our *entertainment*, I now understand why you asked for a table hidden away from curious eyes." Faith smoothed her top, accentuating the way the silky fabric clung to her breasts and exposing hardened nipples, despite two thin layers of fabric over them.

"You think you can survive one evening without people-watching?" he asked, his voice husky with the desire sparking his senses.

"I have a feeling you can make it worth my while."

"You must be psychic," he teased. "For I plan to."

"Call it an educated guess. I've been at the receiving end of your tender mercies too often to discount their effect."

"Good." He had every intention of lavishing those mercies on her tonight.

They teased each other over dinner, working their desire to a fever pitch. He was tempted to find an even darker corner and bring them both to completion right then and there. He refrained, determined to make the night a memorable one for his beautiful lover.

Her peacock-blue eyes were glazed with passion, her lips swollen as if they'd been kissed, and her breathing was shallow and quick. Her nipples were so hard they created shoals in the fabric over them and she'd squirmed in her seat more than once.

"Having trouble, *carina americana mia?*" He meant his voice to be joking, but it came out deep and sensual instead.

A competitive glint shone in her gaze along with the passion. "I think no more than you."

She'd definitely done her utmost to turn him inside out, and she had succeeded.

He reached across the table and brushed her cheek in a rare public display of affection. "I think it is time to make our way to my apartment."

"Yes."

Back in his apartment, they wasted no time in disposing of their clothing, but once they landed naked on the bed, he forced a slowing of the pace. It wasn't easy, he wanted nothing more than to bury himself in her wet, silken depths, but there was more to making love than reaching an orgasm.

There was the element of driving your partner out of her mind.

Her hands were everywhere in a blatant bid to side-track him from his silently stated intention, and he had to gather both her wrists in one hand and hold them above her head.

She gasped, her body bowing in clear need. "Kinky, Tino."

"Necessary, *tesoro*."

"Why?"

"I want you out of your mind with pleasure."

"I'm already there."

"No." He kissed her, sweeping her mouth with his tongue. He pulled back. "You can still talk."

And then he set about taking care of that. He kissed his way down her throat, sucking up a bruise in the dip right below her clavicle bone. His mark.

She shuddered and cried out, like she always did when his hormones got the best of him and he gave her a hickey like he was still an adolescent learning his way around a woman. Maybe that's why he regressed so often.

He moved to her breasts, taking one in his free hand and laving the other with his tongue. Eventually, after a lot of mewling and half-formed words from the dead-to-rights sexy woman below him, he zeroed in on her nipples. He didn't play. He focused. He plucked. And he pleasured.

She screamed.

She arched.

She came, her body going rigid and then shaking.

He released her hands and rolled on top of her, using the head of his penis to tease the swollen nub of her clitoris. She cried out incoherently and he kept it up. Her legs locked around his and she pressed upward, forcing him inside. He rocked and kissed her until he was on the verge of climaxing himself.

It was only then that he remembered the condom he wasn't wearing.

With more self-control than he thought he had, he pulled out and reached for the bedside drawer where he kept his supplies before surging back inside her.

When he came, she was screaming his name and convulsing around him in a second more-intense orgasm.

Remembering made him harder than a rock and twice as immovable.

That night had happened somewhere between two and three months ago. If he looked at his PDA, he could get an exact date. It was something he'd kept track of as zealously as he had their birth control itself. Only, the timing had never come to anything before. Maybe that was why he hadn't been worried along these lines in this instance?

The possibility that Faith might be carrying his child had not even occurred to him. Why would it? A woman didn't break up with the man whose child she carried.

He spit forth a vicious curse as he yanked the door open on his Jaguar. It was entirely too possible, though.

And rather than tell him, Faith had booted Valentino from her life.

Why? What was she thinking? Did she believe he would allow her to take his child back to America and raise it, ignorant of its Sicilian family?

Did she think he would not find out? That he would disappear from her life as easily as she dismissed him from hers?

She did not know him very well, if that was the case. It seemed they both had a great deal to learn about each other.

Something didn't make any sense, though. If she had wanted to marry him as she had hinted, why had she kept this a secret? Surely she knew he would never deny his child the right to his name and heritage. What was the matter with her?

Then he remembered how irrational Maura had gotten on a few occasions while she was pregnant with Giosue.

Faith was no doubt suffering the same emotional fragility. He would have to get himself under control. He could not allow the fury coursing through him a vent. Not in her current condition. He would have to remain calm.

And he would have to remember she was not thinking clearly.

It was his responsibility to make things right and that was something he was good at. Fixing things for others. Had he not taken a slowly sinking vineyard, at risk of closing its doors before the next generation was old enough to take over, and made it a diversified, multinational company?

He had saved the Grisafi heritage and when his younger brother and their father were at loggerheads, Valentino had salvaged the relationship by sending his brother across the ocean to run their offices in New York. The two strong-headed men spoke on the phone weekly and rarely argued any longer.

The only thing he had failed to fix was his wife's illness. He had not been able to save Maura, and he had paid the price for his inability, but he wasn't going to lose another woman who depended on him.

Loud knocking startled Faith from a fitful doze. She sat up, looking around her small apartment in disoriented semiwakefulness.

The pounding sounded again and she realized it was coming from her door. She stumbled to her feet and made her way toward it, swinging the door open just as Tino raised his hand to knock again.

He dropped his arm immediately, a look of relief disparate to the situation crossing his handsome features. "Thank the *madre vergine*. I tried knocking quietly, but you did not hear me." He reached out as if to touch her, but didn't—letting his hand drop to his side once again. "Were you working? Is that safe now? Do the clay or glazes have dangerous fumes? This is something we need to look into. I do not wish to demand you give up your passion, but it may be necessary for these final months."

"Tino?" Was she still too groggy to make sense of his words, or had her former lover lost his mind?

"Si?"

"You're babbling." She'd never heard him say so many words without taking a breath. And none of them made any sense. "You sound like your mother when she gets a bee in her bonnet."

"Mama does not keep insects in her wardrobe and she would not thank you for implying otherwise."

"It's an expression, for Heaven's sake. What is the matter with you tonight?"

"You need to ask me this?" he demanded in a highly censorious voice. His eyes closed and he groaned, just a little, but it was definitely a groan. "Excuse me, Faith."

"Uh, okay?" she asked, rather than said.

He took three deep breaths, letting each one out slower than the one before. Then he opened his eyes and looked at her with this Zen-like expression that was almost as weird as his babbling. "May I come in?"

"You're asking me?" Not demanding she invite him in. Not just forging ahead, assuming he was welcome? "What's going on, Tino?"

He didn't answer, simply giving the room behind her a significant look.

"Oh, all right. Come in." She stepped back.

It wasn't the most gracious invitation she had ever extended, but she was still disoriented from falling asleep after speaking to Agata on the phone. And Tino was acting strange.

Really. Really.

"Can I get you something to drink?"

"I could use a whiskey," he said in an odd tone. "But I will get it. You sit down."

"You've only been here once before, Tino. You don't know where I keep anything."

His hands fisted at his sides, but then the Zen thing was back and he said in a very patient tone, "So tell me."

She knew he wanted her back, but enough to sublimate his usually passionate nature? She would never have guessed.

"Why don't I just get us our drinks instead?"

"You aren't having whiskey, are you?"

She rolled her eyes. "I never drink hard spirits. You know that."

But he'd never acted as if he thought she shouldn't before. Though, considering how tipsy she got on a single glass of wine, perhaps his concern made a certain kind of sense. And honestly, she'd never implied she wanted to drink hard liquor before. But still. "What's the matter with you tonight?"

"We have things to discuss."

"We've done all the talking that needs doing." For right now, anyway. She was frankly too tired and too nauseous to rehash their breakup. She was feeling week and wishing he would just hold her.

She had to get a handle on these cravings. Or she was going to do something stupid, like ask him to fulfill them.

He didn't bother answering. He simply guided her back to the small love seat she'd been dozing on and pressed her to sit down. Bemused by his insistence on getting their beverages, she did. He then picked up her feet and turned her so that they rested on the love seat as well.

Apparently not content with that level of coddling, he tucked the throw she'd been sleeping under around her legs.

He nodded, as if in approval. "I will get our drinks now."

He was seriously working on getting back in her good graces. But no amount of tender care could make up for his refusal to see her as nothing more than a casual lover. Why couldn't he see that?

"If you insist on serving, I'd like a cup of tea." Something that hopefully would settle her tummy. "There is some ginger tea in the cupboard above the kettle. That's where you'll find the whiskey, as well."

An unopened bottle she had purchased in the hope that one day he would break his pattern and show enough interest in her life outside their sexual trysts to come see her.

He went to the kitchen area, nothing more than an alcove off the main living area, really. She watched him fill the kettle and flip the switch to heat the water. The domesticity of the scene tugged at her helter-skelter emotions. It was so much like something she wanted to experience all the time—for the right reasons—that stupid tears burned her eyes before she resolutely blinked them away.

He pulled down the box of tea and the bottle of whiskey from the cupboard. "I've never had ginger tea before."

She had. When she'd been pregnant before. And she was one of the lucky women it helped. "It's not something I drink often."

He gave her an enigmatic look but said nothing as he poured his own drink and waited for her water to boil.

She didn't ask him why he was there or what he wanted to talk about, because the answer was obvious. He wanted her back in his bed, but she'd do her best to avoid that particular conversation. "How is Gio?"

"You saw him only three days ago."

She shrugged. "I wish I taught more days a week," she admitted, before her brain caught up with her mouth.

"I understand."

"You do?"

"You hold my son in deep affection."

"He's easy to love."

"I agree."

"Um…"

"He wishes he could see you more often, as well."

"I know." Only, his father did not want them to grow closer. He'd made that clear.

"I think we can rectify that problem soon enough."

How? Was he going to up the ante of getting her back in bed by offering time with his family on a regular basis? Her rather creative and active imagination offered up a second option. One a lot less palatable.

Maybe he had decided to remarry after all. To find the paragon of Sicilian virtue he thought Gio deserved as a stepmother. Someone who would eradicate the child's fantasies about being his favorite teacher's son.

Faith went from weepy to annoyed in the space of a heartbeat. "I wouldn't rush into anything if I were you."

"And yet some things require quick action."

"Marriage isn't one of them."

Surprise showed clearly on Tino's face. "You believe I plan to marry?"

"Isn't that the way you plan to fix your son's desire to see me more?" Provide the little boy with a mother so he wouldn't miss the teacher he had decided he wanted in that capacity.

"It is, in fact."

Despite everything—knowing how he felt, knowing that he did not want her in his life like that—at Tino's words, unpleasant shock coursed through Faith. Somewhere deep inside, she had believed he would not go that far.

Her stomach tightened in a now familiar warning and she shot to her feet, kicking the lap blanket away. When she reached the commode, she retched. Though, since she had not been hungry earlier, she did nothing but dry heave. It hurt and it scared her. Though she knew that the cramps were in her stomach and not her womb, a tiny part of her brain kept saying it was one and the same.

Tino had come into the small room with her and she could hear water running, but she couldn't look up long enough to see what he was doing. Then a cold, damp cloth draped the nape of her neck while another one was pressed gently to her forehead. Tino rubbed her back in a soothing circular motion, crooning to her in Italian.

The heaving stopped and she found herself leaning sideways into his strength. He said nothing, just let her draw heat and comfort from his touch. She didn't know how long they remained like that—him crouching around her like a protective angel—her kneeling on the floor, but eventually she moved to stand.

He helped her, gently wiping her face with one damp cloth before tossing them both in her small sink. "Better?"

She nodded. "I don't like being sick."

"I do not imagine you do." He handed her a glass of water.

She rinsed her mouth before drinking some down. Placing the glass down by the sink, she turned to leave and weaved a bit.

Suddenly she found herself lifted in the strong arms she had been craving earlier. There was no thought to protest. She needed this. Even if it was a moment of fantasy in her rapidly failing reality.

He carried her to her minuscule bedroom, barely big enough for the double-size bed—another purchase made with hope for something that had never developed between them—and single bedside table that occupied it.

He sat her on the bed, reaching around her to arrange her pillows into a support for her back. Then he helped her to settle against them. It was all too much, too like what she secretly craved that she felt those stupid tears burning her eyes again.

Ignoring the overwrought emotions she knew were a result of pregnancy hormones, she teased, "How did you know where my bedroom was?"

"Instinct?"

She forced a laugh that came out sounding hollow rather than amused, but it was better than crying like a weakling. "Are you saying you have a homing device for beds?"

"Maybe beds belonging to you." He brushed her hair

back from one side of her temple and smiled, the look almost tender.

But she knew better. "This is the only one I have."

"For the last year, almost, you have been sharing the bed in my apartment in Marsala and you have shared my bed in my family home."

"Are you trying to say those beds belong to me in some way now?" she asked, unable to completely quell her sarcasm at such a thought.

"Yes."

She gasped but could think of nothing to say in reply until she spluttered, "That's— It's *ridiculous.*"

He shrugged. "We will agree to disagree."

After everything he had said? She didn't think so. "We will?" she asked in a tone she used so rarely he'd probably never heard it.

He gave her that Zen look again and nodded, as if he had no idea he was in imminent danger of being beaned upside the head with a pillow. "It is the only rational thing to do. You clearly do not need to upset yourself."

"I…" She wanted to tell him he was wrong, but she couldn't. She didn't relish the thought of more dry heaves at all. She wanted to say she didn't know what was wrong, or that she had a touch of the flu or some-thing…anything but the truth. Only, she could not, *would* not lie.

He patted her arm. "Rest here. I will get your tea."

"Fine, but your beds don't belong to me in any way, Tino. You made that clear."

Not a single spark of irritation fluctuated his features. What in the world was going on?

CHAPTER NINE

VALENTINO slammed back the scotch whiskey. It was his favorite brand. An unopened bottle before tonight. There was a message there he did not have time to contemplate.

Faith needed him.

It was worse than he had expected. She was obviously suffering from uncommonly bad morning sickness. After all, it was no longer *morning,* but she was definitely sick.

Maura had been lucky. She had only experienced the lightest amount. However Tino's mother had regaled him with stories of her own debilitating morning sickness when he had become worried during Maura's pregnancy. She'd said over and over again how relieved she was Maura's pregnancy nausea was so light and confined itself to mornings.

Faith's did not.

And that made Valentino feel guilty. After all, she was pregnant with *his* child. He did not want his *carina americana* to be sick.

He would not allow it.

There was only one thing to do.

* * *

Faith could hear Tino's voice, but couldn't imagine who he was talking to. She hadn't heard a phone ring.

Was he muttering to himself? He did that sometimes when he worked at his state-of-the-art laptop when they were together. Only he didn't have his computer and she had a hard time imagining him working instead of bringing her tea. Nor could she imagine him making a business call. He might not love her, but he was not heartless.

He'd actually proven himself to be a more than adequate nurse the one time she'd caught a cold the previous winter. Her illness had brought out a soft side to her stoic, businessman lover. Not quite as concerned as the one now, but then she hadn't been puking then, either.

He'd gotten plenty upset over her stuffy nose, fever and headache.

So, where the heck was he with her tea?

She was on the verge of going after it herself when he walked into the small room, filling it with his presence. Why had he decided to come see her *after* they'd broken up? Even this brief visit was going to haunt her when she tried to sleep in her lonely bed at night.

He placed a steaming mug and a small plate with crackers and mild cheese on it on the table beside her bed. Then he leaned down to adjust the pillows so she could sit up more fully.

"I'm not an invalid, you know." She winced at the crabby tone to her own voice. Ashamed, she laid her hand on his wrist as he reached for the tea again. "I'm sorry. Thank you for getting my tea."

"Do not worry about it. Moodiness is to be expected." He spoke with all the patience of a man bent on humoring the woman in his life.

Only she wasn't in his life. Was she? Right now, it sure didn't feel like they'd broken up.

And she *had* been moody when she'd been sick before. And he'd been patient. She was sure he had been the ideal husband during Maura's pregnancy. And even though he was only being so nice because he thought she was ill, she would take what she could get. "Thanks for being so understanding."

He settled onto the bed beside her, careful not to jostle and handed her the mug. "Drink."

"Bossy."

He shrugged.

She took a sip. "It's sweet." Very.

"The doctor said sugar might help with the nausea. He said the crackers and a nonpungent cheese might also help."

"What doctor?"

"The one I called."

"Overkill, Tino." But sweet. Even sweeter than the tea. She took another sip. The well-sugared beverage did seem to be helping with her upset stomach.

"Not at all. When in doubt, go to an expert."

She shook her head. "You're too funny sometimes."

"Right now I am not laughing."

No, he wasn't. He looked genuinely worried and *guilty*. "It's not your fault I got sick."

"I think it was."

"No. I…it's been like this for the past few days." That at least was pure truth, if not the entire truth.

"Only a few days. It was better before?"

"Naturally."

He examined her, as if he was trying to decide if he believed her or not. She ignored him and took a bite of cheese and cracker. Oh, that did hit the spot. Her empty stomach began to rumble for more sustenance.

"You have not eaten?"

"I wasn't hungry."

"You must take care of yourself. You cannot skip meals."

He was right, even if he didn't know how much. "I'll do better in future."

"I will see that you do."

"Right, because we spend so much time together. I mean before we broke up."

"I do not consider us broken up."

"Don't be arrogant."

"I cannot force you to stay with me, but surely circumstances dictate a certain level of leniency on your part?"

The admission shocked her. She'd always gotten the impression that Tino thought he could make anything happen if he worked at it hard enough. She supposed his words indicated a necessary level of respect for her. But she did not get where he expected tolerance from her.

If he knew she was pregnant, that would be one thing, but there was no way he could know. She didn't show any physical signs and she hadn't told anyone but her doctor. Even if by some weird stroke of coincidence, Tino and her doctor were friends, the older man was hardly likely to chat about his patients.

No, there was no way Tino could know, but he was acting very strangely.

"Uh, Tino, you're being really odd tonight."

"You think so?" he asked.

"Yes, but, uh…that's okay. No need to explain."

"You think not?"

"No, really. We all have our moments."

"Funny, I have never been accused of having *mine* before."

"You're serious?"

"Definitely."

"You need to get out more."

"Lately I have had little excuse for getting out."

"You mean you haven't started shopping for that new wife yet?" The words came rolling off her tongue, a ball of bitterness landing between them.

"I do not need to shop."

"You already know her?" Who was it? Faith tried to think of the women Agata had mentioned, but no one came forth as a potential candidate for Tino's new wife.

"Intimately."

"You bastard." Her hand shot out in an involuntary arc that ended in a crack against his cheek. Shocked at her own actions, she nevertheless cried, "We promised each other exclusivity!"

He grabbed her hand—and examined it for damage. "Did you hurt yourself? You should not get so worked up. You are going to be sick again."

"And whose fault is that?" She meant to sound accusing, but the words came out sounding weak. Bewildered.

Because that was what she felt.

Why wasn't he furious with her?

She'd slapped him. A lump lodged in her throat, and she did her best to swallow it down without giving vent to the emotions roiling through her. She wasn't a violent person. He knew that, but she'd broken her own personal code without thought. She would have imagined he would be spitting nails in anger right now, but he was looking at her with a peculiar expression of indulgence.

"Do you know my doctor?" she asked suspiciously.

"Not that I am aware of, no."

"You don't have psychic tendencies I don't know about?"

"Definitely not."

Okay, so he couldn't possibly know about the baby. "You just admitted to cheating on me," she said, her words laced with pain she couldn't begin to suppress in her current state.

His expression zoomed to total affront in less than a second and was tempered by concern only a half a second later. "I did no such thing. I am no liar. I do not cheat."

"You lied to your mom, about us being friends." She tugged her hand out of his grip.

"I have come to realize I know too little about you to call you a true friend. I will be rectifying this in the future, however. I have already taken some steps to do so."

"You expect me to be your friend when you marry another woman?" None of this was making any sense. He could not be so cruel.

"You are being irrational. This is to be expected, but please remember what kind of man I am before you start flinging such offensive accusations."

She stared at him, totally at a loss as to what to say.

"I did not say I was going to marry another woman."

"Yes, you did." Did he think she would ever have made something so painful up in her own mind?

"I did not."

"I'm nauseous, not nuts. I know what I heard you say." And it had hurt.

"I said I planned to marry."

"Exactly."

"I did not say I planned to marry *someone else*."

He could not mean it. She shook her head. "You don't... You won't... I'm not..."

It was his turn to roll his eyes. "I do. I will. You are."

"Are you asking me to marry you?" In what she might describe as the least-romantic proposal ever. Getting her so upset she had been sick was not the way to a woman's heart.

He flinched, just slightly, but she saw it. "More informing you that I am willing to meet your terms."

Terms. A sinking feeling drained the energy from her and she fell back against the pillows. "You want me in your bed so much you are willing to marry me?"

He didn't answer.

"No. I don't believe that."

"Does it matter what my reasons are?"

"Yes."

"You need me. I need you. We need to marry." He shrugged. "My family loves you already."

She ignored the bit about his family. He hadn't been so quiescent about their affection for her before. "You need my body, not me."

"Stop overanalyzing this."

"Then tell me why. The truth."

He sighed, looking away. "You did not ask me how my mother is."

"I spoke to her on the phone tonight. I know how she is."

"You noticed her upset?"

"She's upset?" No, Faith hadn't noticed. Had she gotten so wrapped up in her own challenges, she ignored a friend in need?

"Very. She feels she betrayed you."

What? Could this night get any more unreal? "How?"

"She came by to see you today at lunch."

"I know. I wasn't home."

"She has a key to your apartment."

"Yes." She'd given it to Agata in case of an emergency. It had made Faith feel like she had someone in the world who cared enough to check on her.

"She used it."

"So?"

"Her curiosity got the better of her."

Understanding washed over Faith in a wave of despair. He *did* know she was pregnant. Everything he had done and said in the last hour now made complete and total sense. Even that bit of tenderness she'd thought she'd seen in his eyes. It had been for the flicker of life within her womb.

"You know." Her voice came out a whisper, but it was the best she could do as those pesky tears she'd been fighting since his arrival redoubled their efforts to expose her weakness.

"I do." He laid his hand on her stomach, leaving no doubt about exactly what they were discussing.

"She guessed."

"Yes."

"I knew she would if she saw the statues."

"She saw only one, but it was enough."

"And she told you?"

"When Mama is upset, she vents. My father was swimming with Giosue."

"So, she vented to you."

"Si."

"And you assumed you were the father."

"As you said, we promised exclusivity."

"You had no doubts about my integrity."

"No."

"And now you want to marry me."

"I have no choice." He took Faith's hand between both of his much larger ones. "*We* have no choice."

She shook her head.

"Be reasonable, Faith. It is the only way."

"No. It… We… There are other options."

Acute horror darkened his eyes to near black. "You would not abort our child."

"No, I wouldn't, and if you really knew me at all, *you* would know that."

"I told you that was something I planned to correct."

"Be still my heart."

"Do not mock me, Faith."

She took a fortifying sip of tea. "I don't have to marry you."

"You would deny my child his father?"

"Sheesh, Tino, you are so all or nothing. First you think I'm going to have an abortion and now you think I'm going to refuse you parental rights."

"Are you?"

So much for his trust in her integrity. "No."

"So, marry me."

"There are other choices."

"None that are as good."

"Right, because marriage for the sake of a baby is going to create a family that baby is going to love being raised in."

"We are compatible—there is nothing wrong with this picture."

"You left out one little aspect that is supposed to exist in marriage."

"What?"

Could he really be that dense? "Love, Tino. I'm talking about love."

"We care for each other."

So much that this was only the second time he had ever been to her apartment. "It's not enough."

"It is. Many people marry with less."

"I loved Taylish and he loved me." Maybe they hadn't felt the same kind of love for each other, but the love had been there.

Tino's jaw hardened. "I loved Maura, but she is gone as is your Taylish. *We* are here now. That is all that matters."

"Not even. You were completely unwilling to entertain the idea of marriage before."

"I did not know you carried my child."

Did he have any concept of the kind of damage his words were doing to her heart? Of course not. Love had not come up between them until she asked for it. He couldn't begin to understand how much his attitude hurt.

She hunched her shoulders, hugging herself, but the cold was seeping into her heart, anyway. "I knew it."

"Knew what?"

"That if I told you I was pregnant, you would insist on marriage. Do you even begin to see how feudal-lord your thinking is?"

"I am a Grisafi." As if that said it all.

"Well, I'm not and I'm not sure I want to be one, either."

His already-tense jaw developed a tic, but his voice remained even. "My mother's heart would be broken to hear you say that."

"I wouldn't be marrying your mother."

"I should hope not." He laughed, the sound low and sexy despite the topic of their conversation—or maybe because of it.

Marriage to Tino. A dream come true for all the wrong reasons.

He put his arm over her thighs in a proprietary gesture she did not miss the meaning of. "You say there are other options."

"There are."

"Name them."

"I didn't say you were going to like them," she felt the need to warn.

"If they do not include marriage between us, I think that is safe to assume." The Zen tone of ultimate patience was back.

"They don't."

He just waited.

"Fine, but I want to point out that I'm in no condition to argue."

Amusement flickered in his dark gaze. "I did not notice you having any trouble doing so up to this point."

"I mean it, Tino. I've had my limit of upset for the evening."

His expression went ultraserious. "I will not distress you again."

She nodded, knowing full well she was taking advantage. But the truth was? She *didn't* want to argue. Her emotional reserves had been in the negative totals for weeks now.

"I could go back to America and raise the baby there. You could visit."

She waited for the explosion, but it never came. He simply sat there staring at her.

"Nothing to say?" she had to ask.

He shook his head, and it was then she realized his jaw was clenched tight.

"I don't want to do that."

"Good." He bit the word out, but the sense of relief he felt was palpable.

"I was just pointing out that it was an option." And trying to hurt him back a little for the pain he had dealt her? The thought mortified her. She was not that kind of person.

"Noted."

"I want to stay in Sicily," she said quickly, wanting him to know right away she wasn't going to hurt him with the baby. "I love it here and I want our child to grow up knowing its family. The Grisafis are all he or she has in the way of extended relatives, and they're wonderful people to boot." She tried a tentative smile.

He did not return it. "So, marry me."

She wanted to, badly, but not merely for the sake of the baby. "I could stay here."

Appalled was the only word to describe his look. "In *this* apartment?"

"It is kind of small for a baby." She bit her lip, wincing when it drew blood. "I could find a bigger place."

"You can move into the family home."

"I considered that." She had, after examining every other alternative—living with the Grisafis was the only way she could give the baby the life it deserved. Not monetarily—she was set in that regard—but the daily access to people who would love the baby and the baby would grow to love. Including its father.

That didn't mean he would have access to her. That point was not negotiable. But she wanted her baby to have a family. The pain of growing up without her parents had dulled with time, but never disappeared. She wanted her baby to have its grandparents, its brother, its father close by—to live in a home filled with love and people who would enrich the baby's life.

The Grisafi home was big enough to accommodate her and the baby in a set of rooms that would be much like having her own apartment. And yet there would be easy and consistent access to familial ties important to the baby's well-being.

"So, you will marry me."

"That's not what I said. I can live in your family home without being your wife. It's definitely big enough."

"Why would you deny me my rightful place in my child's life?"

"I will not do that. You will be named on the birth certificate, the baby can have the Grisafi name."

"But you do not want it."

She was about to say no, but she could not force the word from her mouth. So she shook her head.

"Why, Faith? When you wanted marriage before I knew?"

"That's exactly why."

"I do not understand."

"I think you do."

"You feel slighted because I will marry you for the baby's sake and not your own."

"Yes."

"That is childish thinking, Faith." Not, *I care about you, too*. Not, *It's not the way it looks*. No, just an accusation of immaturity.

Faith's resolve not to be pressured into anything doubled. "Believe what you like, but I am not running to the courthouse for a quickie marriage."

His bark of laughter was mocking. "As if my mother would allow such a thing."

Faith just glared at him.

"You will move in, though?"

"I said it was something I was considering. That it was an option."

"It is the best option you have suggested so far."

"Actually, you suggested it."

"But you had considered it?"

"Yes."

"Favorably?"

"Yes."

"So, what is stopping you from agreeing?"

"I'm not sure I want to live in the same house as you," she answered honestly.

He reeled back as if struck. "You hate me so much."

"I don't hate you at all, but I'm not sure this is what is best for us."

"It is best for the baby and that is all that matters."

"On that point we agree."

"So, you will move in."

"You're stubborn."

"Very."

She sighed.

He took it as acquiescence, if the grim satisfaction on his face could be believed. "How soon?"

"I haven't agreed, Tino," she pointed out. "If I decide that's the best course of action, and provided your parents approve the idea, I would move in after the baby is born."

"You need looking after *now*. Tonight proves that."

"Tonight I thought you were telling me that the father of my unborn child wanted to marry another woman. *A suitable Sicilian woman.*"

"Stress induced your stomach upset?"

"Yes, I think so."

"We will have to make sure you are not distressed in any way from this point forward."

"I would appreciate that." If she had known it would be so easy, she would have played the illness card earlier. Exhaustion overcame her, like it did sometimes lately. "I'm tired," she said, knowing he had to be able to see it. "We can talk more about this at a later time."

"Very well."

She reached up and brushed his cheek, needing to say one last thing before he left for the night. "I'm sorry I slapped you."

"I forgive you."

"Thank you," she slurred as sleep overtook her.

CHAPTER TEN

FAITH had fallen asleep. Just like that.

Thirty seconds later and her breathing had already leveled out into true somnolence. It always amazed him how she could do that, though the only other times he'd seen it was after they had made love. They hadn't done so tonight.

Yet, here she was—sleeping. Dark bruises marred the lovely skin below her eyes. Her pregnancy was taking it out of her. It bothered him to see her looking so frail. Was she taking her vitamins? Had she gone to a doctor? There were so many questions he needed answered, but she wasn't going to be satisfying his need to know right now.

It wouldn't be until morning, if he had his way and she slept the night through. He was careful not to jostle her unduly as he removed her clothes to increase her comfort. He could not help but stop and look at the changes her pregnancy had already wrought on her beautiful body.

With near reverence, he cataloged each one. Her breasts were slightly bigger and the aureoles had darkened. She had an exhausted air about her, but she glowed too, her skin reflecting an overall abundance of health. He could see no evidence of the baby within in the curve of her belly. It was no bigger.

The need to touch was intense and he carefully placed his hand over her lower abdomen, a sense of awe permeating him. It might not look different, but although he might be being fanciful, he would swear he could feel the presence of his child in her womb. Usually when he massaged her tummy, the flesh was soft with feminine give. Now below the silken skin, it felt hard, solid. Amazing.

She made a soft noise and turned on her side to curl into her pillow.

He found himself smiling, but then frowned in thought. He knew she expected him to leave, but he wasn't going to. He'd agreed not to argue; he hadn't agreed to vacate her apartment, leaving her alone, with no one to care for her needs.

He flipped out his cell and called home to tell his parents he would not be returning tonight. Thankfully, his father answered, so Tino was not subjected to a barrage of questions when he said he would not be home that night. His mother tried calling ten minutes later, but he let the call go to voice mail. He wasn't ready to speak to her yet.

He and Faith had some explaining to do and Tino was determined to do it on his own agenda and in his own way.

Faith woke up with a sense of well-being that had been missing for the past several weeks. The sense that she had been held in strong arms all night long tickled at her conscience, but she dismissed it as leftover dreams from the night before. Just like so many other mornings.

Her stomach was slightly upset, but nothing like the night before. Memories of Tino's visit beset her, but she wasn't ready to deal with the implications of his discovery. Not if she wanted to keep a handle on the physical side effects of her pregnancy. She would keep her mind blank, and if she moved slowly, hopefully she could avoid anything beyond the mild nausea.

She started with opening her eyes and orienting herself to her surroundings. The first thing she noticed was the mug of tea on her bedside table. Steam was coming from it. The cheese and crackers on the plate beside it looked fresh, as did the grapes accompanying it.

Trying to make sense of the fresh libations, she sat up carefully. No matter how curious she was, she wasn't going to jostle her queasy tummy.

As the sheets slid against her skin, she realized she was naked.

Completely and totally.

"Tino!"

Despite the evidence of his presence, she was still shocked when he came rushing in. And looking too damn good in nothing but his boxers, too. "Are you all right, *piccola madre mia?* Did you try the tea? It should settle your stomach. Do you need help to the bathroom?"

The babbling would be endearing if, well…maybe it was endearing regardless, but still. And calling her his little mother, that was…it was…she didn't know what it was. Cute? Maybe. "What are you doing here?"

"Caring for you, as you can see." He swept his hand out to indicate the mug and plate of food.

"I meant what are you doing here at all?"

"I spent the night."

"In my bed?"

"Your small sofa is much too short. Besides, you might have needed me in the night."

Once she got used to the fact he was there, with her, in her apartment, she had no problem believing he had spent the night in her bed. And while she knew it should bother her, it didn't. It made her feel cared for, darn it. He hadn't made sexual overtures after all, he'd just been there for her.

The sensation of having been held throughout the night was not her imagination, nor had it been yet another hollow dream. The fact that she wanted it so badly made her cranky. "You said you were leaving."

"I did not."

"You—"

"I promised not to argue with you last night."

Right, and she had assumed that meant he would accede to her wishes. "You are sneaky, Tino."

"I prefer to think of it as resourceful." He gave her the smile that had been melting her heart for almost a year. "You should drink your tea and eat. The doctor said it would be most helpful if you partake before getting out of bed."

"Taylish used to have soda crackers and a glass of flat Seven-Up ready for me in the morning." She sighed, looking around her small room. "I'd forgotten."

"Would you prefer that?" Tino asked with a flat voice. "Only the doctor recommended these items."

"This is fine."

He nodded and left the room.

Mentally shrugging at his strange behavior, she drank her tea. She'd eaten the crackers and cheese and several of the grapes as well before Tino returned. They did help. She felt almost normal, certainly not in any risk for a hasty trip to the bathroom to void her stomach.

Tino was still wearing nothing more than his boxer

shorts, a luxurious emerald-green silk she wanted to touch. Which was really, really stupid, but true all the same.

Her nipples tightened—aching a little because they were tender from the hormonal changes in her body—and reminding her of her total nudity beneath the sheet and blanket. "You undressed me last night. While I was sleeping."

"If I had done it while you were awake, I am sure the outcome would have been quite different." He gave her a heavy-lidded look that sent sparks of arousal straight to her core.

"No." She shook her head in further denial, trying to convince them both that what he was suggesting was not an option.

He sat beside her and cupped her nape, his hand warm and big against her neck. "Are you sure about that?"

"We can't. Tino, no sex." Though her body was aching for the feel of his.

"Why?" His expression grew worried and his entire body tensed. "Has your doctor identified a problem with your pregnancy."

"No," she admitted, knowing she was going to sound paranoid. "He says that I'm healthy and so is the baby." He'd also said that the vast majority of miscarriages in the first trimester could not have been avoided. It was simply a matter of an unviable pregnancy ending itself.

She wasn't that clinically detached.

"So, why no sex?"

"Do you know the risk of miscarriage in the first trimester, Tino?"

"No."

"It's 12.5 percent. The number is probably higher because some women miscarry before they even realize they are pregnant, but one in eight known pregnancies end in miscarriage in the first trimester. But even if it was only one in a million, I wouldn't do anything to risk it."

"Certainly, if making love increases the risk, we will not do so. I am surprised Maura's doctor never said anything." Tino sounded angered by that fact.

Faith had to be truthful. "Um, there's actually no evidence to suggest that normal sexual activity increases the risk of an early trimester miscarriage."

"But you are still afraid of taking the risk."

"Yes."

"So, we will abstain," he said with the air of a man making a great sacrifice if not with pleasure, without re-crimination. "It will make for an interesting wedding night, though."

"We aren't getting married." At least not right now.

"We shall see." He stood up. "Now I believe it is time to ready ourselves for the day. Do you need help in the shower?"

"I'm pregnant, not an invalid, Tino. I can bathe myself."

"That is probably for the best. Prolonged exposure to your wet, naked body would not be good for my self-control."

"You always talk like I'm some sort of femme fatale."

"Perhaps that is because you are death to the control I exercise over my libido."

She laughed, feeling pleased when she knew she shouldn't. After all, they were no longer a couple. But, like the night before, she had a hard time remembering that, when it felt so right to be with him.

Tino dressed while Faith was in the shower, and then he made a couple of business calls while she was getting ready. Anything to keep himself from going into her small bedroom and ravishing her body.

For some reason, Faith feared miscarriage. He refused to add to those fears, no matter how difficult it might be to abstain from intimacy with her luscious body. He had to admit, he had no idea that miscarriage was so prevalent in the first trimester.

He did a quick web search on his PDA while he waited for Faith to come out of the bedroom, and discovered some interesting facts.

When she came out, she was wearing a flowing sundress the same peacock blue as her eyes in a halter style that tied around her neck. The deep vee of the neckline accentuated her burgeoning curves, but the dress looked comfortable, as well. Its empire waistline had no binding around her tummy, he noticed.

It would look even more amazing once her stomach started to protrude with the baby. He could not wait.

"Did you know that the risk of miscarriage drops to less than one percent after the first trimester and that there are *no* studies linking normal sexual activity to the loss of the baby at all?"

She stopped and stared at him for a half second and then laughed. "Tino, you are too much. Did you call the doctor again while I was in the shower?"

Chagrined at the thought that doing so might have carried more weight with her, he shook his head. "Web research."

"I didn't realize you knew the password to my computer."

"I don't. I used my PDA."

"Trust you to go right to the heart of the matter, and yes, I did know that. I told you as much, remember?"

"I didn't know if you realized it held true through-out your pregnancy."

"I did."

"Good."

She just shook her head and went to sit on the love seat she'd used the night before. This time he sat down beside her and pulled her legs into his lap, starting to massage one of her feet.

She gave him a shocked little stare. "Why are you doing that?"

"To make you feel good."

"But…I'm not exactly huge with child and have aching feet yet, Tino."

"So, I am getting some practice in. If you do not like it, I will stop."

She glared. "Don't you dare. It feels wonderful."

He smiled, feeling smug. Faith had always loved a good foot rub. "Now, tell me why you are so afraid of losing this baby."

The look of ecstasy on her face changed to one of deep sorrow tinged with very real fear. "I lose the people I love, Tino. Every single one. I'm not taking any risks with this baby."

"You have not lost my mother…or my son." He didn't mention himself, because in truth, he wasn't sure she loved him. Even when she had asked him if he could love her, he hadn't known if she had those kinds of feelings for him, or was asking in the hopes of building something in the future.

"If you had your way, neither of them would be in my life."

"That is not true."

"You were angry when you found out I was Gio's teacher, that your mom is my friend."

"I was shocked—it made me respond badly—but I would not take them from your life. Even if you were not pregnant with my child." And he realized that given the choice, he would not have prevented Faith from forming the attachments with his family that she had.

She needed them.

"I believe you. I don't know why. I shouldn't, but I do."

"I am glad. I have never wished ill on you."

"I know." She reached out and brushed her fingertips down his arm.

It sent chills through him, but he ignored the stirrings of desire and said, "So you have not lost everyone you love."

"Every chance I had at family has been snatched from me, Tino." The remembered agony on her face was enough to unman him. "First my parents, then the one foster home I felt like I belonged. They were hoping to adopt a baby, and when the baby came, they let me go."

"That is terrible."

She shrugged, but her pain was there for him to see. "When I lost Taylish and our baby…" Tears filled her eyes and then slid down her cheeks while she tried to compose herself to continue. Finally she choked out, "I figured I must not be meant to have a family."

"I understand why you might feel that way." And it broke his heart for her. "But you must realize it is an irrational conclusion to draw. Though you have suffered more tragedy than any woman should have to, you are still alive—you have much to give to a family and much to receive from one." He took the hand still resting on his arm and kissed her palm, squeezing her fingers tightly. "You are my family now, Faith."

She pulled her hand away, with apparent reluctance, but did it all the same. "No, I'm not. If I manage to deliver this baby, *then* I'll have a family—someone who belongs to me." More tears and a final choking whisper, "Someone I belong to."

Her words sliced at his heart, leaving wounds he refused to dwell on in the midst of her sharing such a personal pain. "Marry me and you will have a ready-made son, mother, father and assorted aunts, uncles and cousins."

She shook her head, her eyes telling him she did not believe. "I won't have *you,* will I, Tino?"

"Of course you will have me. I will be your husband." He could not understand how that could mean not having him.

She just shook her head.

He couldn't stand it any longer. He pulled her into his lap, wrapping his arms around her. "I cannot imagine how you have survived losing the people you have. You are a strong, beautiful woman, Faith. A woman I would be proud to call my wife."

He could feel the edges cracking around his promise to Maura, but he could not pull back. Not in the face of Faith's sorrow.

"You only want to marry me for the baby's sake."

"And for your sake and yes, for my sake. I want you, Faith, and maybe you don't think that is very impor- tant, but I have never craved a woman physically the way I do you."

"Not even Maura?"

"No." It hurt to admit and shamed him, but Faith deserved the truth. As much as he had loved his wife, she had not elicited the same sense of soul-deep need for physical oneness that the woman in his arms did.

"I don't want to lose any more family," Faith said in a pained undertone.

"You will not lose this baby. You will not lose me."

"You can't know that."

"And you are not a person who gives up on life because of fear, or you would have given up already." He held her tightly to him. "There is also the baby to consider. We can give her more stability as a married couple, *cara,* than simply living as house mates."

"Her?"

"I can think of nothing I would like better than a daughter who takes after her spirited and beautiful mama."

"Don't say things like that."

"I cannot help it."

"But…"

"I am not only thinking of the baby." He had to convince Faith to marry him.

"Who else?"

"My mother. You carry her grandbaby inside you. She will not be happy if you do not marry me."

"Your mother knows you better than I do, she will understand."

Tino managed a laugh at the implied insult, despite the heavy emotions surrounding them. "No, she will take it quite personally and will be heartbroken if you refuse to make yourself her daughter-in-law."

"I cannot marry you because it will make Agata happy."

"What about Giosue?"

Faith flinched, her beautiful blue eyes clouding. "You said he deserves someone better than me."

"I did not."

"You did. You want to give him a *Sicilian* step-mother, so he will have someone at least that much like his real mother."

Hearing his own reasoning quoted back to him was not pleasant in this instance. How could he have said that to Faith, even if he had believed it at the time? Once again that morning, he felt shame. "My son does not agree. He does not want a traditional Sicilian woman for a stepmother. He wants a free-spirited artist who loves children enough to teach them though it is a mixed blessing for her because being around those children reminds her of what she has lost."

Faith buried her face in his chest. "You said you do not know me."

"Maybe I know you better than either of us thinks." That thought was *not* an unpleasant one. "Can you do it?"

She did not ask what he meant, but he explained anyway. "Can you marry for the sake of our child, for the sake of my mother and your dear friend, for the sake of Giosue's happiness, a little boy you already love? For the sake of your own inner strength that sees beauty and joy in a world that has already taken so much from you? Can you marry me because it is the right thing to do?"

She swallowed and spoke. "Ask me again in two weeks." Her voice was barely above a whisper, as if forcing the words out had been difficult.

"Why two weeks?" he asked, rubbing her back and marveling anew at her resiliency.

He had never known another person like Faith. She amazed him, never more so than today after he heard the short version of her life story.

"My first trimester will be over."

"What has that got to do with anything?"

She sat up and looked away from him, her gaze going to the view out the sunroom's floor-to-ceiling windows. "You only want to marry me because I am pregnant with your child. If that pregnancy ends, you would resent the fact we had married because of it."

"What is all this negative talk? You are not going to lose our baby. If you want to go without sex until you feel it is safe, I will not argue. But I refuse to consider the possibility of future miscarriage in making the decision about marriage. You are not going to lose us."

She was looking at him now, her eyes wide but no longer spilling over with tears. "You can't promise that."

"I can promise that baby, or no baby, I expect to marry you."

"No."

"Yes."

"That makes no sense."

"It does to me."

"It's an obligation thing." Horror cascaded over her features. "You pity me."

He laughed. He could not help it. It was not a sound of happy amusement, but a grim one. "You are too strong to pity."

"I'm not. I'm scared to death. That makes me a coward. I don't want to tempt fate."

"You are no coward."

"I don't know how we jumped to talk of marriage. Last night we were negotiating whether or not I'm going to move into the Grisafi villa."

"I go after what I want."

"And what you want is me to marry you?" She sounded disbelieving.

"Believe it." He tilted her chin with the edge of his hand, so their eyes continued to meet. "You are living scared and that is no way to live."

"Says you."

Instead of continuing to argue with her, he kissed her. It wasn't a passionate, let's-make-love kiss, but a tender salute of comfort. Then, leaning his head against hers, he spoke. "Faith, I want you to live up to your name. I want you to have hope in the future. I want you believe in the family we can make together."

"I don't know if I can."

"I believe in you."

She took a shuddering breath. "I want to show you something."

"Whatever you need."

She stood and he did, as well, wondering what she felt he needed to see. She was his, even if she did not yet acknowledge that fact. And the presence of their baby in her womb meant that no matter what promises he had made, the need to make her a permanent part of his life superseded them now.

He would not break the final promise and allow Faith to replace Maura in his heart, but he would spend the rest of his life proving to Faith that marriage to him was not a mistake. He had no doubts he would convince her of it.

She might not be in love with him, but she loved his mother and his son. And she loved teaching at the primary school. She would not be able to keep that job if she insisted on keeping a single status while pregnant. This was Sicily, not the more liberal UK or America.

He might not agree with all the cultural norms of his country, but he wasn't above taking advantage of them when he needed to.

Faith would marry him.

She stopped in front of a covered statue and met his eyes with hers. "You didn't look."

"No."

"Weren't you curious?"

"Very."

"But you respected my privacy."

"*Si.*" Unlike his mother. But this one time he could give thanks for her excessive curiosity. With her pessimistic views regarding her pregnancy, she would probably have waited to tell him until she was inches from giving birth—if then.

Faith's fingers were on the cloth, but she had not lifted it, though he assumed that was her plan. "You didn't think undressing me compromised that?"

"I have mapped every centimeter of your naked body with my eyes, my fingers…my tongue. There are no secrets between us in that regard."

"And if I did not want you undressing me?"

"It has never bothered you before."

"But we broke up, Tino."

"Did we?" He stepped closer until they were sharing breathing space. "Or were we on hiatus while you worked out best when and how to tell me of our child?"

For he had no doubt she had planned to do so. He remembered comments she had made when they spoke of commitment that had made no sense at the time, but looking back had ominous import.

She looked chagrined, but did not answer.

"Even if I had been looking to marry again—which I was not—you would not have allowed me to do so without informing me of our child's existence, would you?"

"No."

"Nor would I have ever let you walk away, but admit it—you were biding your time before we reconciled."

"I wasn't." She bit her lip and sighed, her blue eyes troubled. "You seem to forget you were the one who was so adamantly opposed to marriage *to me*."

"If I could go back and change my responses to you in that regard, I would." Because even without the baby, he now admitted he could never have let Faith walk out of his life. He wasn't proud of his weakness, but he would not lie to himself about it, either.

"I am arrogant. I admit it, but truth is truth. You have never stopped belonging to me and vice versa."

"We were casual lovers, Tino. Bed partners. Not a couple." Bitterness and confusion laced her voice in equal measure. "We didn't belong to each other."

"That is not how I see it."

"Oh, really? That's why you refused my calls for two weeks while you were in New York." That was his Faith, still fragile from her admissions, but ready to speak her mind regardless.

"Yes."

Blue eyes went wide in shock. "What?"

"I was not comfortable with the depth our relationship had attained, and I attempted to retrench to a less emotionally intimate position." He took a deep breath and prepared to speak words that rarely passed his lips. "I am truly sorry that hurt you."

"I…" She looked lost for words, but then visibly regrouped. "It must have worked, or you would not have denied our friendship to your mother."

"You know that is not true." They would lay this to rest once and for all. "I explained why I said what I did, and if it makes you feel any better, I learned to regret it." Deeply.

"The big bad, business tycoon was afraid of his mother. Very convincing, Tino."

Just about as convincing as his Faith giving in to sarcasm. "Mocking me will not change the truth of our circumstances."

She sighed, as if her anger was deflating. "I know that."

"We belong to each other. My idiocy and your intransigency cannot change that. Admit it."

CHAPTER ELEVEN

FAITH shook her head. "You never give up, do you?"

"No."

"You are a piece of work, Valentino Grisafi."

"If you mean 'a piece of work' like those you create, I will take that as a compliment."

"Thank you."

"You are a very talented artist."

"I hope you continue to think so after seeing these pieces."

And then she showed him, one after another. Each one was a pregnant woman in a different situation and varying stages of pregnancy, from barely pregnant to one where the woman looked as if she was ready to give imminent birth to twins.

The most striking thing about the collection was the wealth of emotion it expressed—and elicited. There was one woman in a state of misery, clearly on the edge of losing her child. There was another who glowed with such joy it choked him. Another was a grouping, a man, a woman and a child. The man and child had their hands on the protruding belly of the mother-to-be. One of her more abstract pieces, their features were blank and the

162   VALENTINO'S LOVE-CHILD

sex of the child was not clear. But Tino was sure it was a little boy and that both man and boy wore grins on their faces.

He was certain the statue represented something Faith hoped for, something Tino was determined he and Giosue could give her. Acceptance. And family.

He reached out to touch the woman who looked on the verge of final tragedy. "Is this how you feel right now?"

"Sometimes."

He pulled the emotionally fragile woman to him and kissed the top of her silky red curls, inhaling her scent and trying to imbue her with his confidence. "You will not lose this baby."

"I have to believe that, or I would go crazy."

"But you are still afraid." He rubbed her back, loving the feel of her smaller body so close to his.

"Terrified."

"You are also happy."

"Ecstatic."

Something inside him settled when she admitted that. "You want the baby."

"Very, very, *very* much." She hugged him tight as if that was the only way to express the depth of her feelings on the matter.

"Three *very*s. That *is* a lot." And he was glad.

"Yes."

He drew back a little, not pulling from her embrace but far enough that he could tilt her head and let their gazes meet. "But you do not want the father."

"That is not what I said." She pouted, just like she did when he told her it was time to go home after a night of lovemaking.

Remembering those occasions now caused an internal wince. "Certain things can be inferred."

"No, they can't."

He leaned back against her worktable, tugging her with him so she ended up plastered against him. "Oh, really?"

She seemed disinclined to move, snuggling against him trustingly. "Yes. I just…"

"What?"

"I told you…I don't want to tempt fate." She dipped her head, so he could not see her face.

He could not help himself from cupping her bottom and massaging it. Her curves were so damn enticing to him. "Why not try trusting in Providence instead of worrying about fate?"

"I never thought I could lose my parents."

"You did."

"Yes and believe me when I tell you that I was sure Taylish and the baby were my shot at a family. A family I was positive could not be taken from me. I knew he would never leave me."

"Then he did."

"It wasn't his fault, but it wasn't mine either, and I was alone again."

"Look at me."

She tilted her head back, her peacock-blue eyes shiny with emotion.

He felt like he'd been kicked in the gut with that look. "You are not alone now."

"You don't think?"

"I know. And so should you. Even without the baby, you had my mother, my son, your friends…me."

"Did I have you, Tino?"

"More than any other woman since Maura's death."

That fact was not a comfortable one for him, but it was something Faith deserved to know.

"You aren't happy about that," she said perceptively.

"If I could choose any woman on the planet to have awakened such emotions in me, it would have been you." He could wish he had not slighted his own honor, but never that another woman had been the cause.

He did not believe any other woman *could* have been.

"I don't know what to say."

"Say you will marry me." He dropped his hand to palm her hard stomach. "I need you to believe in the future, if not for my sake, then for the baby's."

"But—"

He lifted his other hand and pressed a finger to her lips. "No buts."

"I want to believe."

"Then do."

"It's not that easy."

"I know, but you must try."

"My first pregnancy was ectopic." The words were bald and emotionless, but he could feel more remembered pain radiating from her.

For a moment his vocal chords were paralyzed with grief for her. "You lost your first baby?"

"Yes."

"I had read that a tubal pregnancy could be very dangerous for the mother."

She nodded, her expression matter-of-fact. "I almost died."

"And you still risked pregnancy again." He was not sure that as her husband, he would have had the strength to allow her to do so.

Taylish had either been a saint or an idiot. Tino knew which one he preferred to believe.

"Absolutely."

He gave a hollow, self-deprecating laugh. "Do you know? I thought you did not want children."

"I did not think it would ever be an option. I believed I would not be able to get pregnant again. Tay and I had to resort to a fertility specialist before I could get pregnant the second time."

"So, this baby is a miracle."

"Yes."

Joy settled inside him. "Believe in the strength of that miracle, Faith."

"Meeting you was a miracle, Tino."

"What?" He could not accept she had said that.

"Wanting you shocked me. I had not expected to ever have another intimate relationship with a man." She rubbed her cheek against his chest as if she needed the contact.

She had been that in love with Taylish? Certainly, the couple had not had an intensely satisfying sexual relationship. Not like he and Faith did. Her reaction to the pleasure she felt when they first made love indicated she'd never experienced something like it before. "But you desired me."

"Yes."

He squeezed her close. "I want you, too, *bella mia.*"

"I know." There was a smile in her voice, and she moved a little to let him feel that she could feel the evidence pressing against her belly.

"So marry me."

She laughed softly as if amused, not frustrated, by his persistence. "It's not that simple."

"It can be if you let it."

"You're so stubborn, Tino."

"You love that about me."

She was silent for a count of five full seconds, then she kissed him through his shirt, right over his heart. "Maybe."

Faith spent the morning working, feeling inspired and better than she had in weeks. Every brush with her palette knife was perfect, every gentle manipulation of the clay with her fingers resulting in just the effect she was looking for.

A loud beeping from her small alarm told her it was time to start getting ready for lunch with Agata. She was washing the clay from her hands in the kitchen sink when someone knocked.

Thinking Agata had decided to come by and pick her up instead of meeting at the restaurant as planned, Faith dried her hands and swung the door open.

To a frowning Tino. "You did not ask who it was. There is no peephole on your door. How did you know it was me?"

"Sheesh, arrogant much? I didn't know it was you."

"I believed we already established that that is a Grisafi family trait." He bent down and kissed her, his lips lingering just long enough to make it the kiss of a lover and not a typically warm Sicilian greeting. "If you did not know it was me, why did you open the door?"

"I thought it was your mother."

"I was under the impression your plans were to meet at the restaurant for lunch."

Faith didn't remember telling him the details of her lunch appointment, but just like with her first pregnancies, her short-term memory was just a tad compromised. "I thought she might have arrived in town early and decided to pick me up."

"But you did not know."

"Clearly not. After all, I was wrong, wasn't I?"

"And yet you opened the door."

"Is there a point to this interrogation?"

"A point?" He stepped inside and shut the door. "Yes, there is a point. I could have been anyone."

"But you weren't."

"Nevertheless, such behavior is reckless."

"Reckless? Opening the door?"

"Opening your door when you do not know who is on the other side puts your safety at needless risk."

"What are you? The arbiter of in-home security for pregnant women?"

"This has nothing to do with your pregnancy."

She believed him. "You look so fierce, Tino."

"Do not make fun of my concern for you, Faith. I should have visited you here long before this. No doubt, you have been behaving in a similar fashion all this time."

"This is Sicily, Tino, not New York City. I can open the door without worrying the person on the other side is set on robbing me."

"Or worse? I do not think so. Marsala is not such a small city as all that, and there are plenty of tourists with intentions you cannot begin to be certain of."

"Overprotective alert, Tino."

"I think not. Common sense is not overprotective behavior." But color burnished along his chiseled cheekbones.

"I like this side of you," she decided.

"Good. I am unlikely to change."

"That I believe." She grinned, then frowned. "Um, not that I want to kick you out or anything." She so didn't, no matter how little sense that attitude made. "But I'm supposed to meet your mother for lunch in less than an hour and I need to get ready. Was there something in particular you needed?"

"I am horning in on your lunch with my mother."

"What? Why?"

"You have decided to tell her about the baby, yes?"

"Yes." And she was more than a little nervous about doing so.

"As much as we both adore my mother, I am certain you could use my moral support."

"That's really sweet." Man, when he decided to take down the barriers, they crumbled with a crash. She was still glowing from the things he'd said when he'd been trying to convince her to marry him. Going back over the conversation had filled her with renewed hope and dead certainty that no matter what he had said before, Tino *wanted* to be with *her.*

She already knew she wanted to be with him. But maybe not this afternoon. "Won't your presence be suspect? Your mom isn't dumb, she's bound to guess there's more between us than a casual acquaintance."

"I am sure she drew that conclusion when I ran from the house without a word after she told me she thought you were pregnant."

"You didn't."

"I did."

"Tino!"

"I know. I was not thinking, *bella mia.*"

"I didn't want to tell anyone I was pregnant until my first trimester was over," Faith lamented.

"What is done is done."

"Is that a Sicilian proverb?"

He grinned and kissed the tip of her nose. "I believe it is a universal one."

"I suppose." She headed to her bedroom. "I need to change my clothes."

He followed her.

"Tino, I'm getting dressed."

"So?"

"You really don't recognize personal boundaries, do you?"

"You wish to have a wider personal boundary as my wife than you have had as my lover?" He sounded confused and not a little upset.

"We're not married."

"Not yet, but it will happen."

"I haven't said yes." But she would. She loved him and now that she knew his feelings for her had always run deeper than he'd wanted to admit or acknowledge even to himself, she wasn't going to let him go.

He wasn't the only stubborn, possessive one in their relationship.

"You will."

"You are so sure?"

"I cannot allow myself to consider the alternative." And for just a brief moment, her Sicilian tycoon looked as vulnerable as any male on the planet. "For now I will be happy if you admit we are still a couple."

"Were we ever a *couple?*"

"We had our limits on our relationship, but that does not mean we were not together."

"Limits you set."

"I acknowledge it."

"You seem to have dumped them with efficient speed." And she was loving that reality.

"Circumstances change."

"Like finding out I'm pregnant with your baby."

"Believe it or do not, but the walls I imposed between us would have crumpled when you dumped me, regardless of your reason for doing so."

"I do believe it." Did he love her? She didn't have the guts to ask and risk getting shot down again, but the possibility warmed her heart as surely as her baby did. "So, you do admit that I dumped you, regardless of the reasons why?"

Pain darkened his expression for just a moment. *"Si."*

"Then I can admit that we are a couple."

Gorgeous white teeth flashed in a smile that turned her inside out.

He watched as she pulled off her clay-spattered jeans and top, his gaze going hot and hungry when her almost nude body was revealed.

"You're not wearing a bra." His voice was hoarse and his hand made an abortive move to touch her.

She smiled. "No sex, remember."

"How could I forget?"

"You look like you're in danger of doing so."

"I am not, but you would not deny me what pleasure I can have, would you?"

"You are going to get yourself all revved up with nowhere to go." Though knowing he still wanted her so much was nice. Really nice to know, in fact.

He laughed. "I think a tiny part of you enjoys knowing that."

"I think you may be right."

She turned to grab some clothes from the closet,

bending to get the gold and white Roca Wear sandals she wanted to wear with her white sheath dress.

He groaned.

She let her lips curve in a smile because he could not see. "You sure you're going to survive this."

"If Taylish could stand the abstinence, so can I."

"Ohh, competitive. You don't have to be. Tay and I didn't stop making love during either of my pregnancies."

Silence for a full five seconds. "I'll wait for you in the studio." He turned and left the room without another word.

She blinked, not sure what had happened there. One minute she'd been teasing him with her body, positive they were both enjoying it. And the next, he was gone.

He was quiet on the way to the restaurant to meet his mother, too.

"Tino," she said when they pulled up in front of the trattoria. "Is something wrong?"

"What could be wrong?"

"That's what I want to know."

He simply shrugged and got out of the car, coming around to open her door and help her to her feet. He kept his hand on the small of her back as they walked into the restaurant.

Agata was already seated at a table for four; Rocco was across from her.

She smiled at their approach. "Hello, Faith. My son. Why am I not surprised to see you as well?"

"Because you are intelligent enough to add two and two and get four. I, on the other hand, am a little shocked you brought Papa along without warning Faith first."

"Why, am I some ogre my soon-to-be daughter-in-law should need forewarning of my presence?"

"Do not be melodramatic, Papa."

Tino looked down at her to see how she was taking this development and she gave him and then his parents a reassuring smile. "I'm very happy to see you, Rocco."

"And I am very pleased to be expecting a new grandchild."

Tino didn't give her a chance to answer, but pulled her chair out for her. She sat down, glad there was already water at her place. She took a sip and wondered how best to break it to the older couple that she had not yet agreed to marry Tino.

"Faith has not consented to become my wife," Tino said bluntly, taking care of that little detail for her.

"You have not asked her?" Rocco asked in clear censure.

Tino waited to answer until he had taken his own seat at the table. Then he gave his father a look that would make most cringe. "Naturally, I have asked her. She turned me down."

"Flat?" Agata asked in a faint voice, her shock palpable.

Faith glared at Tino. So much for supporting her during this conversation. "I told him to ask me again in two weeks."

"I will start making plans immediately," Agata said with a smile.

"She did not say she would agree, then."

"But of course she will. You simply have to convince her." Rocco gave his son a significant look. "You've already seduced her into your bed, surely you can induce her to marry you."

Faith felt her cheeks going hot, but Tino did not look in the least bothered. "I intend to try."

"You will succeed," his mother said complacently.

"Will I?" Tino looked at Faith, his gaze trying to decipher something in hers. "That is my hope."

"You know why I want to wait."

"Yes, you do not wish to make the mistake of promising to spend the rest of your life with me in the remote chance it is not a necessary sacrifice."

"It's not me I'm worried about."

"And yet I have made it clear I do not wish to wait to make the commitment."

"You didn't want to marry me before I got pregnant. You didn't even want to be my friend."

"I want to marry you now and I was your friend, if too much of a coward to admit it to my mother." He focused on Agata and Rocco. "I am sorry I was less than truthful with you about my relationship with Faith."

"You lied," Rocco said. No compromise.

Tino nodded, looking pained. *"Si."*

"We forgive you, don't we?" Agata said, giving her husband a transparent look that clearly meant he'd better agree or risk being sent to a guest room for the night.

"Si. You are our son."

And that meant forgiveness. Faith smiled. Maybe Tino had been worried about this. She was glad his parents hadn't drawn it out the way he'd clearly been expecting.

Tino looked no happier, but he said, "Thank you."

"So, do you want a big wedding or something small?" Agata asked.

"I told you—"

Agata cut her son off. "I know what you said, but your father and I have complete faith in you." She looked at Faith expectantly.

"I always dreamed of getting married in a church,

with my family there to witness my happiness." She didn't know why she said it. It was a dream that could never be realized.

"I will talk to the father, unless you wish to be married in your Lutheran church?"

Faith shook her head. "I've been attending the Catholic Mass since coming to Sicily. It just felt right."

Agata's face lit up at that. "How wonderful. The father will be very pleased to hear this."

"No doubt," Tino said.

Faith looked at him, a question in her eyes.

He shrugged. "It is one more thing I did not know about you."

"Tino, you know me more deeply than anyone has since Taylish, maybe even better than he did."

Agata glowed at them, while Tino looked almost speechless.

Rocco nodded his head. "As it should be."

While they ate, Agata quizzed Faith on the progress of her pregnancy, wanting to know everything from what doctor she'd gone to see to what her due date was. Tino and Rocco left the conversation to the women for the most part.

They were finished eating when Tino spoke again. "I will be staying with Faith until she moves home. You will have no problem watching over Giosue for me?"

"Naturally not," Rocco said before Agata could answer.

"But Tino, Gio needs you."

"So do you, even if you will not admit it."

Faith opened her mouth to argue further, but Tino shook his head. "Trust me, I will not neglect my son. I will tuck him in at night and then come to your apartment. If you should be willing to join me in the evenings with Gio, we will both be pleased. I will make sure he knows to invite you."

"You're being sneaky again, Tino." No fair bringing his son into it. "You know I cannot refuse Gio."

"The term is resourceful."

Rocco and Agata laughed.

"I am only relieved my son carried more cache with you than his father."

"That's not true."

"Would you have accepted my invitation so readily?"

She wanted to say yes, if only to prove him wrong, but she couldn't. "We'll discuss this later."

"Already they are talking like an old married couple."

"Don't tease the children, Rocco."

Faith had to laugh at that.

CHAPTER TWELVE

TINO GOT OUT OF THE CAR when they arrived back at Faith's apartment building.

"I don't need an escort to my door, Tino."

"That is no surprise. You do not think you need me for anything."

"I didn't mean that, I just…you don't have to walk me up."

"Perhaps I want to."

She nodded, warmth unfurling through her when he placed his hand on the small of her back even though he was clearly upset with her.

"I do need you, Tino," she said as they climbed the stairs to her second-floor apartment.

"That is good to hear." There was something in his voice that she could not decipher, but he sounded sad…defeated.

Something was definitely wrong.

Hoping to find out what, she offered him a drink when they got upstairs.

But he shook his head. "I must get back to the office if I am going to get out of there at a decent hour tonight."

"Something is bothering you. I want you to tell me what it is."

"It does not matter." He looked away from her. "Life is what it is."

"I don't understand. Are you unhappy I'm pregnant? If you don't want to marry me, I'm not going to make you. And as much as they love you, your parents aren't going to, either."

"I am well aware you are all too ready to walk away from me."

"What? Tino, what has gotten into you? I'm not walking away."

"But you want to."

"No, I don't."

"Oh, you are happy enough to have my baby, but it is clear you would have chosen another father for your child. Only the man you would have chosen is dead."

"I don't want this baby to be Taylish's."

"I do not believe you."

"You are being ridiculous, Tino."

He simply shrugged. "I will see you tonight."

"You do not have to stay with me." She knew he would ignore her, but she had to say it.

"So long as you stubbornly refuse to move home, I do."

"Grisafi Vineyards is not my home."

"It became your home the moment you conceived my child and will remain that way until the day you die, should you wish it. Even if you can never bring yourself to marry me."

"You have no idea how much I want that."

"But not enough to commit to taking me along with it, unless it is proven necessary. Right?"

"Tino, what is going on with you today? That is not what I said and you know it. That is so far from what I feel, it isn't even funny."

"I know that I want you to marry me and that you will not do so."

"You're like a single-track CD programmed to repeat."

He didn't respond.

She had to take a deep breath so she would not yell. He could be so irritating. "Tell me something, Tino."

"*Si?*"

"If I miscarried tomorrow, would you still want to marry me?"

"Yes." His dark eyes gleamed with sincerity and something else. Oh, gosh…it looked like love. He meant it.

Really. Truly.

Her knees went weak, but she could not trust what her brain was telling her heart her eyes were seeing. "You don't mean it."

"I do."

"I…"

"Give us a chance, Faith. You may not love me like you did your precious Taylish, but I can make you happy. You said your attraction to me was a miracle to you."

"It was…it is."

"Marry me, *cuore mio*."

My heart. He'd called her his heart. Was it a misspoken word, an attempt at manipulation…or did he mean it? "You…I…"

"Please."

She could not deny him. "Promise me something."

"What?"

"You will not regret it."

"This I can easily promise."

"Why?"

"Why would I promise you?"

"Why is it easy?"

"You have not figured it out yet? I have broken my promise to Maura. I love you. You fill my heart. You are my heart."

"You don't. You can't. You said."

"Many things I wished were true, but the only real truth is my love for you."

"But you aren't happy about it."

"I have never before broken a promise. I could not save Maura and now I cannot keep my last promise to her."

"She made you promise never to love again?" That didn't sound like the woman Agata had told Faith about.

"I promised her at her grave. I told her I would never replace her in my heart."

Faith felt the most amazing sense of release pour through her. And she laughed, the joy-filled sound stopping Tino's pacing. "You find the compromise of my honor amusing?"

Instead of answering, she said, "You're being all-or-nothing again. Loving me doesn't mean that Maura no longer has a place in your heart. She has a place in mine, too, because she loved you and because she gave birth to a little boy that I love very much."

"But not his father. I understand. You loved Taylish too much to love another. I should be grateful for what I have. You carry my child and that is a great gift."

"I loved Taylish, but nothing like I love you."

"What do you mean?"

"I loved Taylish, but I was never in love with him. I have been in love with you since the first night we made love."

"You mean that?"

"More than anything."

"I...this is hard."

She grinned. "Talking about your feelings?"

"*Si*. It is not something I like to do."

"You told me you loved me, that's all you needed to say."

"No. You deserve all of the truth."

"What did you leave out?"

"Maura was the love of my youth, you are the love of my life. It hurt when she died. I grieved a long time, but if I lost you, it would kill me."

Faith threw herself at Tino and he caught her, just as she knew he would. They kissed until they were both breathing hard. He pulled his head back, protecting them both from going too far.

She snuggled her head into his neck. "Just one thing, Tino."

"*Si?*"

"Promises made to dead people don't count. They're a way of dealing with our own grief, but when they cause more sadness than consolation, you have to let them go."

"You sound like you know what you are talking about."

"I do. I made a promise to Tay after he died."

"What was it?"

"That I wouldn't try to make a family with someone else." She sighed and kissed the underside of Tino's jaw. "The promise was for my protection, not his. I made it so I couldn't be hurt again, and when I realized that, I let it go."

"I am glad you were wiser than I."

"I'll remind you that the next time we argue you said that."

"You have my permission, just never remind me what a selfish bastard I was when we were lovers only. I will never forget. But I do not know if I could stand the thought that you won't."

"Tino, we all make mistakes, but real love forgives and forgets."

"You are more than I deserve."

"You just keep believing that, but remember, you are my miracle."

"I love you, *cuore mio*."

"I love you, Tino, more than life."

They married on their one-year anniversary.

Agata had managed to pull together an amazing church wedding and fill said church with family and friends. Faith didn't realize how many friends she'd made in the artistic community and at Gio's school until she saw them all sitting in the pews as she walked up the aisle.

Once her gaze locked on Tino, though, she looked neither to the right nor the left. His expression was filled with love and joy and peace.

It was the peace that made her feel so good. So right.

He was happy to be marrying her, and the guilt he'd felt at loving her was gone now. They'd visited Maura's grave together along with Gio. The trip had seemed to give both males a sense of closure.

Gio was his father's best man, and Agata was Faith's matron of honor. Rocco was giving her away, and the wedding was what she'd always dreamed of and had been sure she could never have. A ceremony celebrating the love and commitment between her and Tino, witnessed by their family.

He had been right about one thing—maybe more than one, but she wasn't telling him that and letting him get a swelled head—that she did have a family now. The Grisafis accepted her as one of their own and unconditionally. Even his brother who lived in New York came home to make her feel welcome and witness his brother's second marriage.

Calogero had insisted on helping Tino by overseeing the transformation of a first-floor room with lots of windows into Faith's new studio. Thereby managing to avoid the brunt of his mother's attempts at changing his single status since returning to Italy. Faith could only be happy that Agata had not made that effort with Tino. Perhaps the older woman had known instinctively her eldest son had already found his second love.

That was all before, though.

Right now Faith hesitated with her hand on the door between the en suite and Tino's—their—bedroom. They had not made love, even when her first trimester had officially ended two weeks before.

Tino had said he wanted to wait for their wedding night. He wanted it to be right. His patience despite his obvious arousal every night when they went to sleep had forever cemented Faith's trust and appreciation for this amazing man she now called husband.

She opened the door and stepped into the bedroom.

Tino stood beside the bed wearing a pair of white silk pajama bottoms.

"White?" she asked with a smile, even though her own lace peignoir was the color of fresh snow.

"It is our first time."

"As husband and wife."

"As a man and a woman who have admitted their love and promised to hold each other in their hearts for a lifetime."

Oh. "I'm going to cry."

"No…you are going to love."

She nodded, too choked up to speak.

He put his arms out. "Come here, *cuore mio*."

She went to him, straight into his arms. He held her there for the longest time, saying nothing. Doing nothing.

Except looking into her eyes, his that dark Hershey-brown that meant his emotions were close to the surface. Finally he said, "Thank you."

"For what?"

"For being mine. For putting up with me. For falling in love with me and not walking away with my baby. For being just who you are, you incredibly precious woman."

The tears rolled then, but they were filled with joy and she made no effort to stop them. "Thank you, Tino, for being mine. For giving me a family again. For being you, but mostly for loving me."

"I will always love you."

"I believe you."

Her fear that she could never have a family was almost completely gone now. His love had given her hope unlike any she'd known since the death of her parents. She'd loved Tay, but she was in love with Tino, and she couldn't help feeling Heaven blessed their union.

His mouth came down on hers, the kiss so incredibly tender and yet sensual, too.

Their tongues played a lazy dance together, getting reacquainted after so much time apart. Their bodies strained together of their own accord as if the very molecules that made up their skin and nerve endings could no longer stand any sort of separation.

Although they had slept curled together for the past few weeks, she felt the need to relearn his body. She let her hands roam freely over hot, silky flesh covering defined muscles. The hair on his chest rubbed her through her lacey peignoir, reminding her just how susceptible she was to the barest touch by this man.

His rapid heartbeat and heavy breathing said he was equally impacted.

He was no slouch in the caressing department, either, his big hands mapping her body in a way that made her ache deep in her core. She needed him.

He cupped the barely there bump in her stomach. "I have this image of you rounded with my baby, wearing one of my shirts and nothing else while you work on your art."

"Fantasizing, Tino?" she asked with a husky laugh.

"Prophesying, I hope."

"You are silly."

"Because I crave seeing you large with child?"

"It's not exactly sexy."

"So, this is not the time to tell you that the image makes my knees weak with lust."

"Are you serious?"

"I love you, Faith. Seeing you that way, seeing the evidence of our love changing your body—it's the biggest turn-on I've ever known."

"I'll remind you of that when I look like a balloon."

"Trust me, I'm not likely to forget."

"I do trust you, Tino."

"Thank you." Then he kissed her again.

They undressed each other slowly, each treating the other like a treasure to be unwrapped.

Then Tino carried her to the bed and laid her down with tender care. He kissed and caressed her body, gently manipulating her breasts since they were sensitive. She returned the favor, holding the velvet hardness of his arousal with both hands.

"I want you," she whispered.

He nodded, the moment profound as he gave in to her desire.

He made love to her slowly, pleasuring her body and building to the peak of perfect oneness with a measured rhythm that drove her insane and made her feel incredibly cherished all at the same time.

Despite the slow build, her climax surprised her, tightening her body and sending convulsions of pleasure through her. He came a second later, calling out his love.

It was the most perfect moment of Faith's life.

She belonged to him completely, just as he belonged to her.

"I love you, Tino. With all my heart and soul."

"*Ti amo,* Faith, who is my heart and reminds me I have a soul."

EPILOGUE

RAFAELLA AGATA GRISAFI was born six months to the day after her parents' marriage. A healthy eight pounds, four ounces, she caused her mother a bit of a problem in the delivery room. Faith was so happy her daughter was healthy and strong, she didn't care how hard the delivery of her precious child had been.

Giosue adored his younger sister and his new mother, often telling anyone who would listen that God must love him an awful lot to give him the best mommy and little sister in the world. Valentino couldn't help agreeing.

He'd lost his first love, but reveled in his second chance at happiness with a woman he looked forward to spending the rest of his life loving.

They were what Faith had always craved—a family.

THE SICILIAN
DOCTOR'S PROPOSAL

Sarah Morgan

Sarah Morgan trained as a nurse and has since worked in a variety of health-related jobs. Married to a gorgeous businessman, who still makes her knees knock, she spends most of her time trying to keep up with their two little boys, but manages to sneak off occasionally to indulge her passion for writing romance. Sarah loves outdoor life and is an enthusiastic skier and walker. Whatever she is doing, her head is always full of new characters and she is addicted to happy endings.

PROLOGUE

'I DON'T believe in love. And neither do you.' Alice put her pen down and stared in bemusement at her colleague of five years. Had he gone mad?

'That was before I met Trish.' His expression was soft and far-away, his smile bordering on the idiotic. 'It's finally happened. Just like the fairy-tales.'

She wanted to ask if he'd been drinking, but didn't want to offend him. 'This isn't like you at all, David. You're an intelligent, hard-working doctor and at the moment you're talking like a—like a...' *A seven-year-old girl?* No, she couldn't possibly say that. 'You're not sounding like yourself,' she finished lamely.

'I don't care. She's the one. And I have to be with her. Nothing else matters.'

'Nothing else matters?' On the desk next to her the phone suddenly rang, but for once Alice ignored it. 'It's the start of the summer season, the village is already filling with tourists, most of the locals are struck down by that horrid virus, you're telling me you're leaving and you don't think it matters? Please, tell me this is a joke, David, please tell me that.'

Even with David working alongside her she was

working flat out to cope with the demand for medical care at the moment. It wasn't that she didn't like hard work. Work was her life. *Work had saved her.* But she knew her limits.

David dragged both hands through his already untidy hair. 'Not leaving exactly, Alice. I just need the summer off. To be with Trish. We need to decide on our future. We're in love!'

Love. Alice stifled a sigh of exasperation. Behind every stupid action was a relationship, she mused silently. She should know that by now. She'd seen it often enough. Why should David be different? Just because he'd *appeared* to be a sane, rational human being—

'You'll hate London.'

'Actually, I find London unbelievably exciting,' David confessed. 'I love the craziness of it all, the crowds of people all intent on getting somewhere yesterday, no one interested in the person next to them—' He broke off with an apologetic wave of his hand. 'I'm getting carried away. But don't you ever feel trapped here, Alice? Don't you ever wish you could do something in this village without the whole place knowing?'

Alice sat back in her chair and studied him carefully. She'd never known David so emotional. 'No,' she said quietly. 'I like knowing people and I like people knowing me. It helps when it comes to understanding their medical needs. They're our responsibility and I take that seriously.'

It was what had drawn her to the little fishing village in the first place. And now it felt like home. And the people felt like family. *More than her own ever had.* Here, she fitted. She'd found her place and she couldn't imagine living anywhere else. She loved the narrow cobbled streets, the busy harbour, the tiny shops selling shells and the trendy store selling surfboards and wetsuits. She loved the summer when the streets were crowded with tourists and she loved the winter when the beaches were empty and lashed by rain. For a moment she thought of London with its muggy, traffic-clogged streets and then she thought of her beautiful house. The house overlooking the broad sweep of the sea. The house she'd lovingly restored in every spare moment she'd had over the past five years.

It had given her sanctuary and a life that suited her. A life that was under her control.

'Since we're being honest here…' David took a deep breath and straightened, his eyes slightly wary. 'I think you should consider leaving, too. You're an attractive, intelligent woman but you're never going to find someone special buried in a place like this. You never meet anyone remotely eligible. All you think about is work, work and work.'

'David, I don't want to meet anyone.' She spoke slowly and clearly so that there could be no misunderstanding. 'I love my life the way it is.'

'Work shouldn't be your life, Alice. You need love.' David stopped pacing and placed a hand on his chest. 'Everyone needs love.'

Something inside her snapped. 'Love is a word used to justify impulsive, irrational and emotional behaviour,' she said tartly, 'and I prefer to take a logical, scientific approach to life.'

David looked a little shocked. 'So, you're basically saying that I'm impulsive, irrational and emotional?'

She sighed. It was unlike her to be so honest. *To reveal so much about herself.* And unlike her to risk hurting someone's feelings. On the other hand, he was behaving very oddly. 'You're giving up a great job on the basis of a feeling that is indefinable, notoriously unpredictable and invariably short-lived so yes, I suppose I am saying that.' She nibbled her lip. 'It's the truth, so you can hardly be offended. You've said it yourself often enough.'

'That was before I met Trish and discovered how wrong I was.' He shook his head and gave a wry smile. 'You just haven't met the right person. When you do, everything will make sense.'

'Everything already makes perfect sense, thank you.' She reached for a piece of paper and a pen. 'If I draft an advert now, I just might find a locum for August.'

If she was lucky.

And if she wasn't lucky, she was in for a busy summer, she thought, her logical brain already involved in making lists. The village with its pretty harbour and quaint shops might not attract the medical profession but it attracted tourists by the busload and her work increased accordingly, especially during the summer months.

David frowned. 'Locum?' His brow cleared. 'You don't need to worry about a locum. I've sorted that out.'

Her pen stilled. 'You've sorted it out?'

'Of course.' He rummaged in his pocket and pulled out several crumpled sheets of paper. 'Did you really think I'd leave you without arranging a replacement?'

Yes, she'd thought exactly that. All the people she'd ever known who'd claimed to be 'in love' had immediately ceased to give any thought or show any care to those around them.

'Who?'

'I have a friend who is eager to work in England. His qualifications are fantastic—he trained as a plastic surgeon but had to switch because he had an accident. Tragedy, actually.' David frowned slightly. 'He was brilliant, by all accounts.'

A plastic surgeon?

Alice reached for the papers and scanned the CV. 'Giovanni Moretti.' She looked up. 'He's Italian?'

'Sicilian.' David grinned. 'Never accuse him of being Italian. He's very proud of his heritage.'

'This man is well qualified.' She put the papers down on her desk. 'Why would he want to come here?'

'You want to work here,' David pointed out logically, 'so perhaps you're just about to meet your soulmate.' He caught her reproving look and shrugged. 'Just joking. Everyone is entitled to a change of pace. He was working in Milan, which might explain it but, to be honest, I don't really know why he wants to come here. You know us men. We don't delve into details.'

Alice sighed and glanced at the CV on her desk. He'd probably only last five minutes, but at least he might fill the gap while she looked for someone to cover the rest of the summer.

'Well, at least you've sorted out a replacement. Thanks for that. And what happens at the end of the summer? Are you coming back?'

David hesitated. 'Can we see how it goes? Trish and I have some big decisions to make.' His eyes gleamed at the prospect. 'But I promise not to leave you in the lurch.'

He looked so happy, Alice couldn't help but smile. 'I wish you luck.'

'But you don't understand, do you?'

She shrugged. 'If you ask me, the ability to be ruled by emotion is the only serious flaw in the human make-up.'

'Oh, for goodness' sake.' Unexpectedly, David reached out and dragged her to her feet. 'It's out there, Alice. Love. You just have to look for it.'

'Why would I want to? If you want my honest opinion, I'd say that love is just a temporary psychiatric condition that passes given sufficient time. Hence the high divorce rate.' She pulled her hands away from his, aware that he was gaping at her.

'*A temporary psychiatric condition?*' He gave a choked laugh and his hands fell to his sides. 'Oh, Alice, you *have* to be joking. That can't really be what you believe.'

Alice tilted her head to one side and mentally reviewed all the people she knew who'd behaved oddly in the name of love. There were all too many of them. Her parents and her sister included. 'Yes, actually.' Her tone was flat as she struggled with feelings that she'd managed to suppress for years. Feeling suddenly agitated, she picked up a medical journal and scanned the contents, trying to focus her mind on fact. Facts were safe and comfortable. Emotions were dangerous and uncomfortable. 'It's exactly what I believe.'

Her heart started to beat faster and she gripped the journal more tightly and reminded herself that her life was under her control now. She was no longer a child at the mercy of other people's emotional transgressions.

David watched her. 'So you still don't believe love exists? Even seeing how happy I am?'

She turned. 'If you're talking about some fuzzy, indefinable emotion that links two people together then, no, I don't think that exists. I don't believe in the existence of an indefinable emotional bond any more than I believe in Father Christmas and the tooth fairy.'

David shook his head in disbelief. 'But I *do* feel a powerful emotion.'

She couldn't bring herself to put a dent in his happiness by saying more, so she stepped towards him and took his face in her hands. 'I'm pleased for you. Really I am.' She reached up and kissed him on the cheek. 'But it isn't "love". She sat back down and David studied her with a knowing, slightly superior smile on his face.

'It's going to happen to you, Alice.' He folded his arms across his chest and his tone rang with conviction. 'One of these days you're going to be swept off your feet.'

'I'm a scientist,' she reminded him, amusement sparkling in her blue eyes as they met the challenge in his. 'I have a logical brain. I don't believe in being swept off my feet.'

He stared at her for a long moment. 'No. Which is why it's likely to happen. Love strikes when you're not looking for it.'

'That's measles,' Alice said dryly, reaching for a pile of results that needed her attention. 'Talking of which, little Fiona Ellis has been terribly poorly since her bout of measles last winter. I'm going to check up on her today. See if there's anything else we can do. And I'm going to speak to Gina, the health visitor, about our MMR rates.'

'They dipped slightly after the last newspaper scare but I thought they were up again. The hospital has been keeping an eye on Fiona's hearing,' David observed, and Alice nodded.

'Yes, and I gather there's been some improvement. All the same, the family need support and we need to make sure that no one else in our practice suffers unnecessarily.' She rose to her feet and smiled at her partner. 'And that's what we give in a small community. Support and individual care. Don't you think you'll miss that? In London you'll end up working in one of those huge health centres with thousands of doctors and you probably won't get to see the same patient twice. You won't know them and they won't know you. It will be completely impersonal. Like seeing medical cases on a production line.'

She knew all the arguments, of course. She understood that a large group of GPs working together could afford a wider variety of services for their patients—psychologists, chiropodists—but she still believed that a good family doctor who knew his patients intimately was able to provide a superior level of care.

'You'll like Gio,' David said, strolling towards the door. 'Women always do.'

'As long as he does his job,' Alice said crisply, 'I'll like him.'

'He's generally considered a heartthrob.' There was a speculative look on his face as he glanced towards her. 'Women go weak at the knees when he walks into a room.'

Great. The last thing she needed was a Romeo who was distracted by everything female.

'Some women are foolish like that.' Alice stood up and reached for her jacket. 'Just as long as he doesn't break more hearts than he heals, then I really don't mind what he does when he isn't working here.'

'There's more to life than work, Alice.'

'Then go out there and enjoy it,' she advised, a smile on her face. 'And leave me to enjoy mine.'

CHAPTER ONE

GIOVANNI MORETTI stood at the top of the narrow cobbled street, flexed his broad shoulders to try and ease the tension from the journey and breathed in the fresh, clean sea air. Above him, seagulls shrieked and swooped in the hope of benefiting from the early morning catch.

Sounds of the sea.

He paused for a moment, his fingers tucked into the pockets of his faded jeans, his dark eyes slightly narrowed as he scanned the pretty painted cottages that led down to the busy harbour. Window-boxes and terracotta pots were crammed full with brightly coloured geraniums and tumbling lobelia and a smile touched his handsome face. Before today he'd thought that places like this existed only in the imagination of artists. It was as far from the dusty, traffic-clogged streets of Milan as it was possible to be, and he felt a welcome feeling of calm wash over him.

He'd been right to agree to take this job, he mused silently, remembering all the arguments he'd been presented with. Right to choose this moment to slow the pace of his life and leave Italy.

It was early in the morning but warm, tempting smells of baking flavoured the air and already the street seemed alive with activity.

A few people in flip-flops and shorts, who he took to be tourists, meandered down towards the harbour in search of early morning entertainment while others jostled each other in their eagerness to join the queue in the bakery and emerged clutching bags of hot, fragrant croissants and rolls.

His own stomach rumbled and he reminded himself that he hadn't eaten anything since he'd left Milan the night before. Fast food had never interested him. He preferred to wait for the real thing. And the bakery looked like the real thing.

He needed a shower and a shave but there was no chance of that until he'd picked up the key to his accommodation and he doubted his new partner was even in the surgery yet. He glanced at his watch and decided that he just about had time to eat something and still time his arrival to see her just before she started work.

He strolled into the bakery and smiled at the pretty girl behind the counter. '*Buongiorno*—good morning.'

She glanced up and caught the smile. Her blue eyes widened in feminine appreciation. 'Hello. What can I offer you?'

It was obvious from the look in those eyes that she was prepared to offer him the moon but Gio ignored the mute invitation he saw in her eyes and studied the pastries on offer, accustomed to keeping women at a polite distance. He'd always been choosy when it came to women. Too choosy, some might say. 'What's good?'

'Oh—well…' The girl lifted a hand to her face, her

cheeks suddenly pink. 'The *pain au chocolat* is my favourite but the almond croissant is our biggest seller.
Take away or eat in?'

For the first time Gio noticed the small round tables
covered in cheerful blue gingham, positioned by the
window at the back of the shop. 'Eat in.' It was still so
early he doubted that his partner had even reached the
surgery yet. 'I'll take an almond croissant and a double
espresso. *Grazie.*'

He selected the table with the best view over the
harbour. The coffee turned out to be exceptionally good,
the croissant wickedly sweet, and by the time he'd
finished the last of his breakfast he'd decided that
spending the summer in this quaint little village was
going to be no hardship at all.

'Are you on holiday?' The girl on the till was putting
croissants into bags faster than the chef could take them
from the oven and still the queue didn't seem to diminish.

Gio dug his hand into his pocket and paid the bill.
'Not on holiday.' Although a holiday would have been
welcome, he mused, his eyes still on the boats bobbing
in the harbour. 'I'm working.'

'Working?' She handed him change. 'Where?'

'Here. I'm a doctor. A GP, to be precise.' It still felt
strange to him to call himself that. For years he'd been
a surgeon and he still considered himself to be a surgeon. But fate had decreed otherwise.

'You're our new doctor?'

He nodded, aware that after driving through the night
he didn't exactly look the part. He could have been
evasive, of course, but his new role in the community
was hardly likely to remain a secret for long in a place

this small. And, anyway, he didn't believe in being evasive. What was the harm in announcing himself? 'Having told you that, I might as well take advantage of your local knowledge. How does Dr Anderson take her coffee?'

All that he knew about his new partner was what David had shared in their brief phone conversation. He knew that she was married to her job, very academic and extremely serious. Already he'd formed an image of her in his mind. Tweed skirt, flat heels, horn-rimmed glasses—he knew the type. Had met plenty like her in medical school.

'Dr Anderson? That's easy.' The girl smiled, her eyes fixed on his face in a kind of trance. 'Same as you. Strong and black.'

'Ah.' His new partner was obviously a woman of taste. 'And what does she eat?'

The girl continued to gaze at him and then seemed to shake herself. 'Eat? Actually, I've never seen her eat anything.' She shrugged. 'Between the tourists and the locals, we probably keep her too busy to give her time to eat. Or maybe she isn't that interested in food.'

Gio winced and hoped it was the former. He couldn't imagine developing a good working partnership with someone who wasn't interested in food. 'In that case, I'll play it safe and take her a large Americano.' Time enough to persuade her of the benefits of eating. 'So the next thing you can do is direct me to the surgery. Or maybe Dr Anderson won't be there yet.'

It wasn't even eight o'clock.

Perhaps she slept late, or maybe—

'Follow the street right down to the harbour and it's

straight in front of you. Blue door. And she'll be there.' The girl pressed a cap onto the coffee-cup. 'She was up half the night with the Bennetts' six-year-old. Asthma attack.'

Gio lifted an eyebrow. 'You know that?'

The girl shrugged and blew a strand of hair out of her eyes. 'Around here, everyone knows everything.' She handed him the coffee and his change. 'Word gets around.'

'So maybe she's having a lie-in.'

The girl looked at the clock. 'I doubt it. Dr Anderson doesn't sleep much and, anyway, surgery starts soon.'

Gio digested that piece of information with interest. If she worked that hard, no wonder she took her coffee strong and black.

With a parting smile at the girl he left the bakery and followed her instructions, enjoying the brief walk down the steep cobbled street, glancing into shop windows as he passed.

The harbour was bigger than he'd expected, crowded with boats that bobbed and danced under the soft seduction of the sea. Tall masts clinked in the soft breeze and across the harbour he saw a row of shops and a blue door with a brass nameplate. The surgery.

A few minutes later he pushed open the surgery door and blinked in surprise. What had promised to be a small, cramped building proved to be light, airy and spacious. Somehow he'd expected something entirely different—somewhere dark and tired, like some of the surgeries he'd visited in London. What he hadn't expected was this bright, calming environment designed to soothe and relax.

Above his head glass panels threw light across a neat waiting room and on the far side of the room a children's corner overflowed with an abundance of toys in bright primary colours. A table in a glaring, cheerful red was laid with pens and sheets of paper to occupy busy hands.

On the walls posters encouraged patients to give up smoking and have their blood pressure checked and there were leaflets on first aid and adverts for various local clinics.

It seemed that nothing had been forgotten.

Gio was just studying a poster in greater depth when he noticed the receptionist.

She was bent over the curved desk, half-hidden from view as she sifted through a pile of results. Her honey blonde hair fell to her shoulders and her skin was creamy smooth and untouched by sun. She was impossibly slim, wore no make-up and the shadows under her eyes suggested that she worked harder than she should. She looked fragile, tired and very young.

Gio's eyes narrowed in an instinctively masculine assessment.

She was beautiful, he decided, and as English as scones and cream. His eyes rested on her cheekbones and then dropped to her perfectly shaped, soft mouth. He found himself thinking of summer fruit—strawberries, raspberries, redcurrants…

Something flickered to life inside him.

The girl was so absorbed in what she was reading that she hadn't even noticed him and he was just about to step forward and introduce himself when the surgery door swung open again and a group of teenage boys stumbled in, swearing and laughing.

They didn't notice him. In fact, they seemed incapable of noticing anyone, they were so drunk.

Gio stood still, sensing trouble. His dark eyes were suddenly watchful and he set the coffee down on the nearest table just in case he was going to need his hands.

One of them swore fluently as he crashed into a low table and sent magazines flying across the floor. 'Where the hell's the doctor in this place? Matt's bleeding.'

The friend in question lurched forward, blood streaming from a cut on his head. His chest was bare and he wore a pair of surf shorts, damp from the sea and bloodstained. 'Went surfing.' He gave a hiccup and tried to stand up without support but failed. Instead he slumped against his friend with a groan, his eyes closed. 'Feel sick.'

'Surfing when you're drunk is never the best idea.' The girl behind the desk straightened and looked them over with weary acceptance. Clearly it wasn't the first time she'd had drunks in the surgery. 'Sit him down over there and I'll take a look at it.'

'You?' The third teenager swaggered across the room, fingers tucked into the pockets of his jeans. He gave a suggestive wink. 'I'm Jack. How about taking a look at me while you're at it?' He leaned across the desk, leering. 'There are bits of me you might be interested in. You a nurse? You ever wear one of those blue outfits with a short skirt and stockings?'

'I'm the doctor.' The girl's eyes were cool as she pulled on a pair of disposable gloves and walked round the desk without giving Jack a second glance. 'Sit your friend down before he falls down and does himself more damage. I'll take a quick look at him before I start surgery.'

Gio didn't know who was more surprised—him or the teenagers.

She was the doctor?

She was Alice Anderson?

He ran a hand over the back of his neck and wondered why David had omitted to mention that his new partner was stunning. He tried to match up David's description of a serious, academic woman with this slender, delicate beauty standing in front of him, and failed dismally. He realised suddenly that he'd taken 'single' to mean 'mature'. And 'academic' to mean 'dowdy'.

'*You're* the doctor?' Jack lurched towards her, his gait so unsteady that he could barely stand. 'Well, that's good news. I love a woman with brains and looks. You and I could make a perfect team, babe.'

She didn't spare him a glance, refusing to respond to the banter. 'Sit your friend down.' Her tone was firm and the injured boy collapsed onto the nearest chair with a groan.

'I'll sit myself down. Oh, man, my head is killing me.'

'That's what happens when you drink all night and then bang your head.' Efficient and businesslike, she pushed up the sleeves of her plain blue top, tilted his head and took a look at the cut. She parted the boy's hair gently and probed with her fingers. Her mouth tightened. 'Well, you've done a good job of that. Were you knocked out?'

Gio cast a professional eye over the cut and saw immediately that it wasn't going to be straightforward. Surely she wasn't planning to stitch that herself? He could see ragged edges and knew it was going to be difficult to get a good cosmetic result, even for someone skilled in that area.

'I wasn't knocked out.' The teenager tried to shake

his head and instantly winced at the pain. 'I swallowed half the ocean, though. Got any aspirin?'

'In a minute. That's a nasty cut you've got there and it's near your eye and down your cheek. It's beyond my skills, I'm afraid.' She ripped off the gloves and took a few steps backwards, a slight frown on her face as she considered the options. 'You need to go to the accident and emergency department up the coast. They'll get a surgeon to stitch you up. I'll call them and let them know that you're coming.'

'No way. We haven't got time for that.' The third teenager, who hadn't spoken up until now, stepped up to her, his expression threatening. 'You're going to do it. And you're going to do it here. Right now.'

She dropped the gloves into a bin and washed her hands. 'I'll put a dressing on it for you, but you need to go to the hospital to get it stitched. They'll do a better job than I ever could. Stitching faces is an art.'

She turned to walk back across the reception area but the teenager called Jack blocked her path.

'I've got news for you, babe.' His tone was low and insulting. 'We're not going anywhere until you've fixed Matt's face. I'm not wasting a whole day of my holiday sitting in some hospital with a load of sickos. He doesn't mind a scar. Scars are sexy. Hard. You know?'

'Whoever does it, he'll be left with a scar,' she said calmly, 'but he'll get a better result at the hospital.'

'No hospital.' The boy took a step closer and stabbed a finger into her chest. 'Are you listening to me?'

'I'm listening to you but I don't think you're listening to me.' The girl didn't flinch. 'Unless he wants to have a significant scar, that cut needs to be stitched by someone with specific skills. It's for his own good.'

It happened so quickly that no one could have anticipated it. The teenager backed her against the wall and put
a hand round her throat. 'I don't think you're listening to
me, babe. It's your bloody job, Doc. Stitch him up! *Do it.*'

Gio crossed the room in two strides, just as the
teenager uttered a howl of pain and collapsed onto the
floor in a foetal position, clutching his groin.

She'd kneed him.

'Don't try and tell me my job.' She lifted her hand to
her reddened throat. Her tone was chilly and composed
and then she glanced up, noticed Gio for the first time
and her face visibly paled. For a moment she just stared
at him and then her gaze flickered towards the door,
measuring the distance. Gio winced inwardly. It was
obvious that she thought he was trouble and he felt
slightly miffed by her reaction.

He liked women. Women liked him. And they usually
responded to him. They chatted, they flirted, they sent
him long looks. The look in Dr Anderson's eyes suggested that she was calculating ways to injure him. All
right, so he hadn't had time to shave and change, but did
he really look that scary?

He was about to introduce himself, about to try and
redeem himself in her eyes, when the third teenager
stepped towards the girl, his expression threatening. Gio
closed a hand over his arm and yanked him backwards.

'I think it's time you left. Both of you.' His tone was
icy cool and he held the boy in an iron grip. 'You can
pick up your friend in an hour.'

The teenager balled his fists, prepared to fight, but
then eyed the width of Gio's shoulders. His hands relaxed
and he gave a slight frown. 'Whazzit to do with you?'

'Everything.' Gio stepped forward so that his body was between them and Dr Anderson. 'I work here.'

'What as?' The boy twisted in his grip and his eyes slid from Gio's shoulders to the hard line of his jaw. 'A bouncer?'

'A doctor. One hour. That's how long I estimate it's going to take to make a decent job of his face. Or you can drive to the hospital.' Gio released him, aware that Alice was staring at him in disbelief. 'Your choice.'

The teenager winced and rubbed his arm. 'She...' he jerked his head towards the doctor '...said he needed a specialist doctor.'

'Well, this is your lucky day, because I am a specialist doctor.'

There was a long pause while the teenager tried to focus. 'You don't look anything like a doctor. Doctors shave and dress smart. You look more like one of those—those...' His words slurred and he swayed and waved a hand vaguely. 'Those Mafia thugs that you see in films.'

'Then you'd better behave yourself,' Gio suggested silkily, casting a glance towards his new partner to check she was all right. Her pallor was worrying him. He hoped she wasn't about to pass out. 'Leave now and come back in an hour for your friend.'

'You're not English.' The boy hiccoughed. 'What are you, then? Italian?'

'I'm Sicilian.' Gio's eyes were cold. '*Never* call me Italian.'

'Sicilian?' A nervous respect entered the teenager's eyes and he licked his lips and eyed the door. 'OK.' He gave a casual shrug. 'So maybe we'll come back later, like you suggested.'

Gio nodded. 'Good decision.'

The boy backed away, still rubbing his arm. 'We're going. C'mon, Rick.' He loped over to the door and left without a backward glance.

'*Dios,* did he hurt you?' Gio walked over to the girl and lifted a hand to her neck. The skin was slightly reddened and he stroked a finger carefully over the bruising with a frown. 'We should call the police now.'

She shook her head and backed away. 'No need. He didn't hurt me.' She glanced towards the teenager who was still sprawled over the seats of her waiting room and gave a wry shake of her head. 'If you're Dr Moretti, we'd better see to him before he's sick on the floor or bleeds to death over my chairs.'

'It won't hurt him to wait for two minutes. You should call the police.' Gio's tone was firm. He didn't want to be too graphic about what might have happened, but it was important that she acknowledge the danger. It hadn't escaped him that if he hadn't decided to arrive at the surgery early, she would have been on her own with them. 'You should call them.'

She rubbed her neck. 'I suppose you're right. All right, I'll do it when I get a minute.'

'Does this happen often? I imagined I was coming to a quiet seaside village. Not some hotbed of violence.'

'There's nothing quiet about this place, at least not in the middle of summer,' she said wearily. 'We're the only doctors' surgery in this part of the town and the nearest A and E is twenty miles down the coast so, yes, we get our fair share of drama. David probably didn't tell you that when he was persuading you to take the job. You can leave now, if you like.'

His eyes rested on her soft mouth. 'I'm not leaving.'

There was a brief silence. A silence during which she stared back at him. Then she licked her lips. 'Well, that's good news for my patients. And good news for me. I'm glad you arrived when you did.'

'You didn't look glad.'

'Well, a girl can't be too careful and you don't exactly look like a doctor.' A hint of a smile touched that perfect mouth. 'Did you see his face when you said you were Sicilian? I think they were expecting you to put a hand in your jacket and shoot them dead any moment.'

'I considered it.' Gio's eyes gleamed with humour. 'But I've only had one cup of coffee so far today. Generally I need at least two before I shoot people dead. And you don't need to apologise for the mistake. I confess that I thought you were the receptionist. If you're Alice Anderson, you're nothing like David's description.'

'I can imagine.' She spoke in a tone of weary acceptance. 'David is seeing the world through a romantic haze at the moment. Be patient with him. It will pass, given time.'

He laughed. 'You think so?'

'Love always does, Dr Moretti. Like many viruses, it's a self-limiting condition. Left alone, the body can cure itself.'

Gio searched her face to see if she was joking and decided that she wasn't. Filing the information away in his brain for later use, he walked over to retrieve the coffee from the window-sill. 'If you're truly Dr Anderson, this is for you. An ice breaker, from me.'

She stared at the coffee with sudden hunger in her eyes and then at him. 'You brought coffee?' Judging from the expression on her face, he might have offered her an expensive bauble from Tiffany's. She lifted a hand and brushed a strand of hair out of her eyes. Tired eyes. 'For me? Is it black?'

'*Si*.' He smiled easily and handed her the coffee, amused by her response. 'You have fans in the bakery who know every detail of your dietary preferences. I was told "just coffee" so I passed on the croissant.'

'There's no such thing as "just coffee". Coffee is wonderful. It's my only vice and currently I'm in desperate need of a caffeine hit.' She prised the lid off the coffee, sniffed and gave a whimper of pleasure. 'Large Americano. Oh, that's just the best smell…'

He watched as she sipped, closed her eyes and savoured the taste. She gave a tiny moan of appreciation that sent a flicker of awareness through his body. He gave a slight frown at the strength of his reaction.

'So…' She studied him for a moment and then took another sip of coffee. Some of the colour returned to her cheeks. 'I wasn't expecting you until tomorrow. Not that I'm complaining, you understand. I'm glad you're early. You were just in time to save me from a nasty situation.'

'I prefer to drive when the roads are clear. I thought you might appreciate the help, given that David has already been gone two days. We haven't been formally introduced. I'm Gio Moretti.' He wanted to hold her until she stopped shaking but he sensed that she wouldn't appreciate the gesture so he kept his distance. 'I'm your new partner.'

She hesitated and then put her free hand in his. 'Alice Anderson.'

'I gathered that. You're really *not* what I expected.'

She tilted her head to one side. 'You're standing in my surgery having frightened off two teenage thugs by your appearance and you're telling me *I'm* not what *you* expected?' There was a hint of humour in her blue eyes and his attention was caught by the length of her lashes.

'So maybe I don't fit anyone's image of a conventional doctor right at this moment…' he dragged his gaze away from her face and glanced down at himself with a rueful smile '…but I've been travelling all night and I'm dressed for comfort. After a shave and a quick change of clothes, I will be ready to impress your patients. But first show me to a room and I'll stitch that boy before his friends return.'

'Are you sure?' She frowned slightly. 'I mean, David told me you didn't operate any more and—'

'I don't operate.' He waited for the usual feelings to rise up inside him. Waited for the frustration and the sick disappointment. Nothing happened. Maybe he was just tired. Or maybe he'd made progress. 'I don't operate, but I can certainly stitch up a face.'

'Then I'm very grateful and I'm certainly not going to argue with you. That wound is beyond my skills and I've got a full surgery starting in ten minutes.' She looked at the teenager who was sprawled across the chairs, eyes closed, and sighed. 'Oh, joy. Is it alcohol or a bang on the head, do you think?'

'Hard to tell.' Gio followed her gaze and shook his head slowly. 'I'll stitch him up, do a neurological assessment and then we'll see. Is there anyone who can help me? Show me around? I can give you a list of what I'll need.'

'Rita, our practice nurse, will be here in a minute. She's very experienced. Her asthma clinic doesn't start until ten so I'll send her in.' Her eyes slid over him. 'Are you sure you're all right with this? We weren't expecting you until tomorrow and if you've been travelling all night you must be tired.'

'I'm fine.' He studied her carefully, noting the dark shadows under her eyes. 'In fact, I'd say that you're the one who's tired, Dr Anderson.'

She gave a dismissive shrug. 'Goes with the job. I'll show you where you can work. We have a separate room for minor surgery. I think you'll find everything you need but I can't be sure. We don't usually stitch faces.'

He followed her down the corridor, his eyes drawn to the gentle swing of her hips. 'Do you have 5/0 Ethilon?'

'Yes.' She pushed open a door and held it open while he walked inside. 'Is that all you need?'

'The really important thing is to debride the wound and align the tissues exactly. And not leave the stitches in for too long.'

Her glance was interested. Intelligent. 'I wish I had time to watch you. Not that I'm about to start suturing faces,' she assured him hastily, and he smiled.

'Like most things, it's just a question of practice.'

She opened a cupboard. 'Stitches are in here. Gloves on the shelf. You're probably about the same size as David. Tetanus et cetera in the fridge.' She waved a hand. 'I'll send Rita in with the patient. I'll get on with surgery. Come and find me when you've finished.'

'Alice.' He stopped her before she walked out of the door. 'Don't forget to call the police.'

She tilted her head back and he sensed that she was wrestling with what seemed like a major inconvenience then she gave a resigned sigh.

'I'll do that.'

CHAPTER TWO

ALICE spoke to Rita, called the police and then worked flat out, seeing patients, with no time to even think about checking on her new partner.

'How long have you had this rash on your eye, Mr Denny?' As she saw her tenth patient of the morning, she thought gratefully of the cup of coffee that Gio Moretti had thought to bring her. It was the only sustenance she'd had all day.

'It started with a bit of pain and tingling. Then it all went numb.' The man sat still as she examined him. 'I suppose all that began on Saturday. My wife noticed the rash yesterday. She was worried because it looks blistered. We wondered if I'd brushed up against something in the garden. You know how it is with some of those plants.'

Alice picked up her ophthalmoscope and examined his eye thoroughly. 'I don't think it's anything to do with the garden, Mr Denny. You've got quite a discharge from your eye.'

'It's very sore.'

'I'm sure it is.' Alice put the ophthalmoscope down on her desk and washed her hands. 'I want to test your vision. Can you read the letters for me?'

The man squinted at the chart on her wall and struggled to recite the letters. 'Not very clear, I'm afraid.' He looked worried. 'My eyes have always been good. Am I losing my sight?'

'You have a virus.' Alice sat down and tapped something into her computer. Then she turned back to the patient. 'I think you have shingles, Mr Denny.'

'Shingles?' He frowned. 'In my eye?'

'Shingles is a virus that affects the nerves,' she explained, 'and one in five cases occur in the eye—to be technical, it's the ophthalmic branch of the trigeminal nerve.'

He pulled a face. 'Never was much good at biology.'

Alice smiled. 'You don't need biology, Mr Denny. But I just wanted you to know it isn't uncommon, unfortunately. I'm going to need to refer you to an ophthalmologist—an eye doctor at the hospital. Is there someone who can take you up there?'

He nodded. 'My daughter's waiting in the car park. She brought me here.'

'Good.' Alice reached for the phone and dialled the clinic number. 'They'll see you within the next couple of days.'

'Do I really need to go there?'

Alice nodded. 'They need to examine your eye with a slit lamp—a special piece of equipment that allows them to look at your eye properly. They need to exclude iritis. In the meantime, I'll give you aciclovir to take five times a day for a week. It should speed up healing time and reduce the incidence of new lesions.' She printed out the prescription on the computer as she waited for the hospital to answer the phone.

Once she'd spoken to the consultant, she quickly

wrote a letter and gave it to the patient. 'They're really nice up there,' she assured him, 'but if you have any worries you're welcome to come back to me.'

He left the room and Alice picked up a set of results. She was studying the numbers with a puzzled frown when Rita walked in. A motherly woman in her early fifties, her navy blue uniform was stretched over her large bosom and there was a far-away expression on her face. 'Pinch me. Go on, pinch me hard. I've died and gone to heaven.'

Alice looked up. 'Rita, have you seen Mrs Frank lately? I ran some tests but the results just don't make sense.' She'd examined the patient carefully and had been expecting something entirely different. She studied the results again. Perhaps she'd missed something.

'Forget Mrs Frank's results for a moment.' Rita closed the door behind her. 'I've got something far more important for you to think about.'

Alice didn't look up. 'I thought she had hypothyroidism. She had all the symptoms.'

'Alice…'

Still absorbed in the problem, Alice shook her head. 'The results are normal.' She checked the results one more time and checked the normal values, just in case she'd missed something. She'd been so *sure*.

'*Alice!*' Rita sounded exasperated. 'Are you even listening to me?'

Alice dragged her eyes away from the piece of paper in her hand, still pondering. Aware that Rita was glaring at her, she gave a faint smile. 'Sorry, I'm still thinking about Mrs Frank,' she admitted apologetically. 'What's the matter?'

'Dr Giovanni Moretti is the matter.'

'Oh, my goodness!' Alice slapped her hand over her mouth and rose to her feet quickly, ridden with guilt. 'I'd *totally* forgotten about him. How could I?'

Rita stared at her. 'How could you, indeed?'

'Don't! I feel terrible about it.' Guilt consumed her. And after he'd been so helpful. 'How could I have done that? I showed him into the room, made sure he had what he needed and I *promised* to look in on him, but I've had streams of patients this morning and I completely forgot his existence.'

'You forgot his existence?' Rita shook her head. 'Alice, how could you *possibly* have forgotten his existence?'

'I know, it's dreadful! I feel terribly rude.' She walked briskly round her desk, determined to make amends. 'I'll go and check on him immediately. Hopefully, if he'd needed any help he would have come and found me.'

'Help?' Rita's tone was dry. 'Trust me, Alice, the guy doesn't need any help from you or anyone else. He's slick. Mr Hotshot. Or I suppose I should call him Dr Hotshot.'

'He's finished stitching the boy?' She glanced at her watch for the first time since she'd started surgery and realised with a shock that almost an hour and a half had passed.

'Just the head, although personally I would have been happy to see him do the mouth as well.' Rita gave a snort of disapproval. 'Never heard such obscenities.'

'Yes, they were pretty drunk, the three of them. How does the head look?'

'Better than that boy deserves. Never seen a job as neat in my life and I've been nursing for thirty years,'

Rita admitted, a dreamy expression on her face. 'Dr Moretti has *amazing* hands.'

'He used to be a surgeon. If he's done a good job and he's finished, why did you come rushing in here telling me he was having problems?'

'I never said he was having problems.'

'You said something was the matter.'

'No.' Rita closed her eyes and sighed. 'At least, not with him. Only with me. I think he's fantastic.'

'Oh.' Alice paused by the door. 'Well, he arrived a day early, brought me coffee first thing, sorted out a bunch of rowdy teenagers and stitched a nasty cut so, yes, I think he's fantastic, too. He's obviously a good doctor.'

'I'm not talking about his medical skills, Alice.'

'What are you talking about, then?'

'Alice, he's *gorgeous*. Don't tell me you haven't noticed!'

'Actually, I thought he looked a mess.' Her hand dropped from the doorhandle and she frowned at the recollection. 'But he'd been travelling all night.'

'A mess?' Rita sounded faint. 'You think he looks a *mess?*'

Alice wondered whether to confess that she'd thought he looked dangerous. Strangely enough, the teenagers hadn't bothered her. They were nothing more than gawky children and she'd had no doubts about her ability to handle them. But when she'd looked up and seen Gio standing there...

'I'm sure he'll look more respectable when he's had a shower and a shave.' Alice frowned. 'And possibly a haircut. The boy was in such a state, I didn't think it mattered.'

'You didn't even notice, did you?' Rita shook her head in disbelief. 'Alice, you need to do something about your life. The man is sex on a stick. He's a walking female fantasy.'

Alice stared at her blankly, struggling to understand. 'Rita, you've been married for twenty years and, anyway, he's far too young for you.'

Rita gave her a suggestive wink. 'Don't you believe it. I like them young and vigorous.'

Alice sighed and wished she didn't feel so completely out of step with the rest of her sex. Was she the only woman in the world who didn't spend her whole life thinking about men? Even Rita was susceptible, even though she'd reached an age where she should have grown out of such stupidity.

'He doesn't look much like a doctor,' she said frankly, 'but I'm sure he'll look better once he's shaved and changed his clothes.'

'He looks every inch a man. And he'd be perfect for you.'

Alice froze. 'I refuse to have this conversation with you again, Rita. And while we're at it, you can tell that receptionist of ours that I'm not having it with her either.'

Rita sniffed. 'Mary worries about you, as I do, and—'

'I'm not interested in men and both of you know that.'

'Well, you should be.' Rita folded her arms and her mouth clamped into a thin line. 'You're thirty years of age and—'

'Rita!' Alice interrupted her sharply. 'This is not a good time.'

'It's never a good time with you. You never talk about it.'

'Because there's nothing to talk about!' Alice took a deep breath. 'I appreciate your concern, really, but—'

'But you're married to your work and that's the way you're staying.' The older woman rose to her feet and Alice sighed.

'I'm happy, Rita.' Her voice softened slightly as she saw the worry in the older woman's face. 'Really I am. I like my life the way it is.'

'Empty, you mean.'

'Empty?' Alice laughed and stroked blonde hair away from her face. 'Rita, I'm so busy I don't have time to turn round. My life certainly isn't empty.'

Rita pursed her lips. 'You're talking about work and work isn't enough for anybody. A woman needs a social life. A man. Sex.'

Alice glanced pointedly at her watch. 'Was there anything else you wanted to talk about? I've got a surgery full of patients, Rita.'

And she was exhausted, hungry and thirsty and fed up with talking about subjects that didn't interest her.

'All right. I can take a hint. But the subject isn't closed.' Rita walked to the door. 'Actually, I did come to ask you something. Although he doesn't need your help, Gio wants two minutes to discuss the boy with you before he sends him out. Oh, and the police are here.'

Alice stood up and removed a bottle of water from the fridge in her consulting room. She couldn't do anything about the hunger, but at least she could drink. 'I don't have time for them right now.'

'If what Gio told me is correct, you're going to make time.' Suddenly Rita was all business. 'They can't go round behaving like that. And you need to lock the door behind you if you come in early in the morning. You might have been the only person in the building. You were careless. Up half the night with the little Bennett girl and not getting enough sleep as usual, no doubt.'

'Rita—'

'You'll tell me I'm nagging but I worry about you, that's all. I care about you.'

'I know you do.' Alice curled her hands into fists, uncomfortable with the conversation. Another person—*a different person to her*—would have swept across to Rita and given her a big hug, but Alice could no more do that than fly. Touching wasn't part of her nature. 'I know you care.'

'Good.' Rita gave a sniff. 'Now, drink your water before you die of dehydration and then go and see Gio. And this time take a closer look. You might like what you see.'

Alice walked back to her desk and poured water into a glass. 'All right, I'll speak to Gio then I'll see the police. Ask Mary to give them a coffee and put them in one of the empty rooms. Then see if she can placate the remaining patients. Tell them I'll be with them as soon as possible.' She paused to drink the water she'd poured and then set the glass on her desk. 'Goodness knows if I'll get through them all in time to do any house calls.'

'Gio is going to help you see the patients once he's discharged the boy. For goodness' sake, don't say no. It's like the first day of the summer sales in the waiting room. If he helps then we might all stand a chance of getting some lunch.'

'The letting agent is dropping the keys to his flat round here. He needs to get settled in. He needs to rest after the journey and shave the designer stubble—'

'Any fool can see he's a man with stamina and I don't see his appearance hampering his ability to see patients,' Rita observed, with impeccable logic. 'We're just ensuring that the surgery is going to be crammed for weeks to come.'

'Why's that?'

'Because he's too gorgeous for his own good and all the women in the practice are going to want to come and stare.'

Alice opened the door. 'What exactly is it about men that turns normally sane women into idiots?' she wondered out loud, and Rita grinned.

'Whoever said I was sane?'

With an exasperated shake of her head, Alice walked along the corridor and pushed open the door of the room they used for minor surgery. 'Dr Moretti, I'm so sorry, I've had a steady stream of patients and I lost track of the time.'

He turned to look at her and for a brief, unsettling moment Alice remembered Rita's comment about him being a walking fantasy. He was handsome, she conceded, in an intelligent, devilish and slightly dangerous way. She could see that some women would find him attractive. Fortunately she wasn't one of them.

'No problem.' His smile came easily. 'I've just finished here. I don't need anyone to hold my hand.'

'Shame,' Rita breathed, and Alice shot her a look designed to silence.

Gio ripped off his gloves and pushed the trolley away from him. 'I think he's safe to discharge. He wasn't knocked out and his consciousness isn't impaired. Fortunately he obviously drank less than his friends. I see no indication for an X-ray or a CT scan at the moment.

He can be discharged with a head injury form.' He turned to the boy, his expression serious. 'I advise you to stay off the alcohol for a few days. If you start vomiting, feel drowsy, confused, have any visual disturbances or experience persistent headache within the next forty-eight hours, you should go to the A and E department at the hospital. Either way, you need those stitches out in four days. Don't forget and don't think it's cool to leave them in.'

The boy gave a nod and slid off the couch, his face ashen. 'Yeah. I hear you. Thanks, Doc. Are the guys outside?'

'They're having a cosy chat with the police,' Rita told him sweetly, and the boy flushed and rubbed a hand over his face.

'Man, I'm sorry about that.' He shook his head and breathed out heavily. 'They were a bit the worse for wear. We were at an all-night beach party.' He glanced sideways at Alice, his expression sheepish. 'You OK?'

She nodded. 'I'm fine.' She was busy looking at the wound. She couldn't believe how neat the sutures were.

The boy left the room, escorted by Rita.

'You did an amazing job, thank you so much.' Alice closed the door behind them and turned to Gio. 'I never would have thought that was possible. That cut looked such a mess. So many ragged edges. I wouldn't have known where to start.'

But obviously he'd known exactly where to start. Despite appearances. If she hadn't seen the results of his handiwork with her own eyes, she would still have struggled to believe that he was a doctor.

When David had described his friend, she'd imagined

a smooth, slick Italian in a designer suit. Someone safe, conservative and conventional in appearance and attitude.

There was nothing safe or conservative about Gio.

He hovered on the wrong side of respectable. His faded T-shirt was stretched over shoulders that were both broad and muscular and a pair of equally faded jeans hugged his legs. His face was deeply tanned, his jaw dark with stubble and his eyes held a hard watchfulness that suggested no small degree of life experience.

She tried to imagine him dressed in a more conventional manner, and failed.

'He'll have a scar.' Gio tipped the remains of his equipment into the nearest sharps bin. 'But some of it will be hidden by his hair. I gather from Rita that you have a very long queue out there.'

Remembering the patients, exhaustion suddenly washed over her and she sucked in a breath, wondering for a moment how she was going to get through the rest of the day. 'I need to talk to the police and then get back to work. I'm sorry I don't have time to give you a proper tour. Hopefully I can do that tomorrow, before you officially start.'

'Forget the tour.' His eyes scanned her face. 'You look done in. The girl who made your coffee told me that you were up in the night, dealing with an asthma attack. You must be ready for a rest yourself. Let's split the rest of the patients.'

She gave a wan smile. 'I can't ask you to do that. You've been travelling all night.' It occurred to her that he was the one who ought to look tired. Instead, his gaze was sharp, assessing.

'You're not asking, I'm offering. In fact, I'm insisting. If you drop dead from overwork before this afternoon, who will show me round?'

His smile had a relaxed, easy charm and she found herself responding. 'Well, if you're sure. I'll ask Mary to send David's patients through to you. If you need any help just buzz me. Lift the receiver and press 3.'

CHAPTER THREE

'WHAT a day!' Seven hours later, Gio rubbed a hand over his aching shoulder and eyed the waiting room warily. Morning surgery had extended into the afternoon well-woman clinic, which had extended into evening surgery. Even now the telephone rang incessantly, two little boys were playing noisily in the play corner and a harassed-looking woman was standing at the reception desk, wiggling a pram in an attempt to soothe a screaming baby. 'I feel as though I have seen the entire population of Cornwall in one surgery. Is it always like this?'

'No, sometimes it's busy.' Mary, the receptionist, replaced the phone once again and gave him a cheerful smile as she flicked through the box of repeat prescriptions for the waiting mother. 'Don't worry, you get used to it after a while. I could try locking the door but it would only postpone the inevitable. They'd all be back tomorrow. There we are, Mrs York.' She handed over a prescription with a flourish and adjusted her glasses more comfortably on her nose. 'How are those twins of yours doing, Harriet? Behaving themselves?'

The young woman glanced towards the boys, her

face pale. 'They're fine.' Her tone had an edge to it as she pushed the prescription into her handbag. 'Thanks.'

The baby's howls intensified and Mary stood up, clucking. She was a plump, motherly woman with curling hair a soft shade of blonde and a smiling face. Gio could see that she was dying to get her hands on the baby. 'There, now. What a fuss. Libby York, what do you think you're doing to our eardrums and your poor mother's sanity?' She walked round the reception desk, glanced at the baby's mother for permission and then scooped the baby out of the pram and rested it on her shoulder, cooing and soothing. 'Is she sleeping for you, dear?' Despite the attention, the baby continued to bawl and howl and Harriet gritted her teeth.

'Not much. She—' The young woman broke off as the boys started to scrap over a toy. 'Stop it, you two!' Her tone was sharp. 'Dan! Robert! Come here, now! Oh, for heaven's sake…' She closed her eyes and swallowed hard.

The baby continued to scream and Gio caught Mary's eye and exchanged a look of mutual understanding. 'Let me have a try.' He took the baby from her, his touch firm and confident, his voice deep and soothing as he switched to Italian. The baby stopped yelling, hiccoughed a few times and then calmed and stared up at his face in fascination.

At least one woman still found him interesting in a dishevelled state, he thought with a flash of amusement as he recalled Alice's reaction to his appearance.

Mary gave a sigh of relief and turned to Harriet. 'There. That's better. She wanted a man's strength.' She put a hand on the young mother's arm. It was a comforting touch. 'It's hard when they're this age. I remember when mine were small, there were days when I thought I'd strangle them all. It gets easier. Before you know it they're grown.'

Harriet looked at her and blinked back tears. Then she covered her mouth with her hand and shook her head. 'Sorry—oh, I'm being so stupid!' Her hand dropped and she sniffed. 'It's just that I don't know what to do with them half the time. Or what to do with me. I'm so tired I can't think straight,' she muttered, glancing towards the baby who was now calm in Gio's arms. 'This one's keeping the whole family awake. It makes us all cranky and those two are so naughty I could—' She broke off and caught her lip between her teeth. 'Anyway, as you say, it's all part of them being small. There's going to come a time when I'll wish they were little again.'

With a forced smile and a nod of thanks, she leaned across and took the baby from Gio.

'How old is the baby?' There was something about the woman that was worrying him. He didn't know her, of course, which didn't help, but still…

'She'll be seven weeks tomorrow.' Harriet jiggled the baby in her arms in an attempt to keep her calm.

'It can be very hard. My sister had her third child two months ago,' Gio said, keeping his tone casual, 'and she's certainly struggling. If the baby keeps crying, bring her to see me. Maybe there's something we can do to help.'

'Dr Moretti has taken over from Dr Watts,' Mary explained, and Harriet nodded.

'OK. Thanks. I'd better be getting back home. She needs feeding.'

'I can make you comfortable in a room here,' Mary

offered, but the woman shook her head and walked towards the door, juggling pram and baby.

'I'd better get home. I've got beds to change and washing to put out.' She called to the boys, who ignored her. 'Come on!' They still ignored her and she gave a growl of exasperation and strapped the baby back in the pram. Libby immediately started crying again. 'Yes, I know, I know! I'm getting you home right now!' She glared at the twins. 'If you don't come now I'm leaving you both here.' Her voice rose slightly and she reached out and grabbed the nearest boy by the arm. 'Do as you're told.'

They left the surgery, boys arguing, baby crying. Mary stared after them, her fingers drumming a steady rhythm on the desk. 'I don't like the look of that.'

'No.' Gio was in full agreement. There had been something about the young mother that had tugged at him. 'She looked stretched out. At her limit.'

Mary looked at him. 'You think there's something wrong with the baby?'

'No. I think there's something wrong with the mother, but I didn't want to get into a conversation that personal with a woman I don't know in the reception area. A conversation like that requires sensitivity. One wrong word and she would have run.'

'Finally. A man who thinks before he speaks...' Mary gave a sigh of approval and glanced up as Alice walked out of her consulting room, juggling two empty coffee-cups and an armful of notes.

She looked even paler than she had that morning, Gio noted, but perhaps that was hardly surprising. She'd been working flat out all day with no break.

'Did I hear a baby screaming?' She deposited the notes on the desk.

'Libby York.' Mary turned her head and stared through the glass door into the street where Harriet was still struggling with the boys. As they disappeared round the corner, she turned back with a sigh. 'You were great, Dr Moretti. Any time you want to soothe my nerves with a short spurt of Italian, don't let me stop you.'

Gio gave an apologetic shrug. 'My English doesn't run to baby talk.'

Alice frowned, her mind focused on the job. 'Why was Harriet in here?'

'Picking up a repeat prescription for her husband.' Mary's mouth tightened and her eyes suddenly clouded with worry. 'I knew that girl when she was in primary school. The smile never left her face. Look at her now and her face is grim. As if she's holding it together by a thread. As if every moment is an effort. If you ask me, she's close to the edge.'

'She has three children under the age of six. Twin boys of five. It's the summer holidays so she has them at home all day.' Alice frowned slightly. Considered. 'That's hard work by anyone's standards. Her husband is a fisherman so he works pretty long hours. Her mother died a month before the baby was born and there's no other family on the scene that I'm aware of. On top of that her delivery was difficult and she had a significant post-partum haemorrhage. She had her postnatal check at the hospital with the consultant.'

She knew her patients well, Gio thought as he watched her sifting through the facts. She was making mental lists. Looking at the evidence in front of her.

'Yes.' Mary glanced at her. 'It might be that.'

'But you don't think so?'

'You want my opinion?' Mary pressed her lips to-gether as the telephone rang yet again. 'I think she's de-pressed. And Dr Moretti agrees with me.'

'A new baby is hard work.'

'That's right. It is.' Mary reached out and picked up the receiver. 'Appointments line, good afternoon.' She listened and consulted the computer for an appointment slot while Alice ran a hand through her hair and turned to Gio.

'Did she seem depressed to you?'

'Hard to be sure. She seemed stressed and tired,' he conceded, wondering whether she gave all her patients this much thought and attention when they hadn't even asked for help. If so, it was no wonder she was tired and overworked.

'I'll talk to the Gina, the health visitor, and maybe I'll call round and see her at home.'

'You haven't got time to call and see everyone at home.' Mary replaced the receiver and rejoined the con-versation. 'She was David's patient, which means she's now Dr Moretti's responsibility. Let him deal with it. Chances are she'll make an appointment with him in the next couple of days. If she doesn't, well, I'll just have to nudge her along.'

To Gio's surprise, Alice nodded. 'All right. But keep an eye on her, Mary.'

'Of course.'

Alice put the cups down and lifted a journal that was lying on the desk.

She had slim hands, he noticed. Delicate. Like the rest of her. It seemed unbelievable that someone so fragile-looking could handle such a punishing workload. She glanced up and caught him looking at her. 'If you want to know anything about this town or the people in it, ask Mary or Rita. They went to school together and they've lived here all their lives. They actually qualify as locals.' She dropped the journal back on the desk and looked at Mary. 'Did the letting agent drop off Dr Moretti's keys?'

'Ah—I was building up to that piece of news.' Mary pulled a face and adjusted her glasses. 'There's a slight problem with the let that David arranged.'

'What problem?'

Mary looked vague. 'They've had a misunderstanding in the office. Some junior girl didn't realise it was being reserved for Dr Moretti and gave it away to a bunch of holidaymakers.' She frowned and waved a hand. 'French, I think.'

Alice tapped her foot on the floor and her mouth tightened. 'Then they'll just have to find him something else. Fast.' She cast an apologetic glance at Gio. 'Sorry about this. You must be exhausted.'

Not as exhausted as she was, Gio mused, wondering whether she'd eaten at all during the day. Whether she ever stopped thinking about work. At some point, Rita had produced a sandwich and an excellent cup of coffee for him but that had been hours earlier and he was ready for something more substantial to eat. And a hot bath. His shoulder was aching again.

'Not that easy.' Mary checked the notes she'd made. 'Nothing is free until September. Schools are back by then. Demand falls a bit.'

'September?' Alice stared. 'But it's still only July.'

Gio studied Mary carefully. Something didn't feel quite right. She was clearly a caring, hospitable woman. Efficient, too. And yet she seemed totally unconcerned about his apparent lack of accommodation. 'You have an alternative plan?'

'Hotels,' Alice said firmly. 'We just need to ring round and see if—'

'No hotels,' Mary said immediately, sitting back in her chair and giving a helpless shrug. 'Full to the brim. We're having a good season, tourist-wise. Betty in the newsagent reckons it's been the best July since she took over from her mother in 1970.'

'Mary.' Alice's voice was exasperated. 'I don't care about the tourists and at the moment I don't care about Betty's sales figures, but I do care about Dr Moretti having somewhere to live while he's working here! You have to do something. And you have to do it right now.'

'I'm trying a few letting agents up the coast,' Mary murmured, peering over the top of her glasses, 'but I'm getting nowhere at the moment. Might need an interim plan. I know.' Her face brightened with inspiration. 'He can stay with you. Just until I find somewhere.'

There was a long silence and something flashed in Alice's eyes. Something dangerous. 'Mary.' There was an unspoken threat in her voice but Mary waved a hand airily.

'You're rattling around in that huge house in the middle of nowhere and it isn't safe at this time of year with all those weirdos on the beach and—'

'Mary!' This time her tone was sharp and she stepped closer to the desk and lowered her voice. 'Mary, don't you dare do this. Don't you *dare.*'

'Do what?'

'Interfere.' Alice gritted her teeth. 'He can't stay with me. That isn't a solution.'

'It's a perfect solution.' Mary smiled up at her innocently and Gio saw the frustration in Alice's face and wondered.

'You've gone too far this time,' she muttered. 'You're embarrassing me and you're embarrassing Dr Moretti.'

Not in the least embarrassed, Gio watched, intrigued. He wouldn't have been at all surprised if she was going to throw a punch. It was clear that she believed that Mary had in some way orchestrated the current problem.

Adding weight to his theory, the older woman looked over the top of her glasses, her gaze innocent. *Far too innocent.* 'It's the perfect solution while I look for somewhere else. Why not?'

'Well, because I…' Alice sucked in a breath and ran a hand over the back of her neck. 'You know I don't—'

'Well, now you do.' Mary beamed, refusing to back down. 'It's temporary, Alice. As a favour to the community. Can't have our new doctor sleeping rough in the gutter, can we? Are you ready to go, Rita?' She stood up as the practice nurse walked into reception. 'What a day. I'm going to pour myself a large glass of wine and put my feet up. Can we call in at Betty's on the way? I need to pick up a local paper. See you in the morning. Oh, and by the way…' She turned to Gio with a wink. 'I suggest you order a take-away for dinner. Our Dr Anderson is a whiz with patients but the kitchen isn't her forte.'

They left with a wave and Gio watched as Alice's hands clenched and unclenched by her sides.

He broke the tense silence. 'You look as though you're looking for someone to thump.'

She turned and blinked, almost as if she'd forgotten his existence. As if he wasn't part of her problem. 'Tell me something.' Her voice was tight. 'Is it really possible to admire and respect someone and yet want to strangle them at the same time?'

He thought of his sisters and nodded. 'Definitely.'

He noticed that she didn't use the word 'love' although it had taken him less than five minutes to detect the warmth and affection running between the three women.

'I want to be so *angry* with the pair of them.' Her hand sliced through the air and the movement encouraged wisps of her hair to drift over her eyes. 'But how can I when I know—' she broke off and let out a long breath, struggling for control. 'This isn't anything to do with you. What I mean is...' Her tone was suddenly tight and formal, her smile forced, 'you must think I'm incredibly rude, but that wasn't my intention. It's just that you've stepped into the middle of something that's been going on for a long time and—'

'And you don't like being set up with the first available guy who happens to walk through the door?'

Her blue eyes flew to his, startled. 'It's that obvious? Oh, this is so embarrassing.'

'Not embarrassing.' He watched as the colour flooded into her cheeks. 'But interesting. Why do your colleagues feel the need to interfere with your love life?'

She was a beautiful woman. He knew enough about men to know that a woman like her could have the male sex swarming around her without any assistance whatsoever.

She paced the length of the waiting room and back again, working off tension. 'Because people have a stereotypical view of life,' she said, her tone ringing with exasperation. 'If you're not with a man, you must want to be. Secretly you must long to be married and have eight children and a dog. And if you're not, you're viewed as some sort of freak.'

Gio winced. 'Eight is definitely too many.' He was pleased to see a glimmer of humour in her eyes.

'You think so?'

'Trust me.' He tried to coax the smile still wider. Suddenly he wanted to see her smile. Really smile. 'I am one of six and the queue for the bathroom was un-believable. And the battle at the meal table was nothing short of ugly.'

The smile was worth waiting for. Dimples winked at the side of her soft mouth and her eyes danced. Captivated by the dimples, Gio felt something clench inside him.

She was beautiful.

And very guarded. He saw something in the depths of her blue eyes that made him wonder about her past.

Still smiling, she gave a shake of her head. 'I know they mean well but they've gone too far this time. It's even worse than that time on the lifeboat.'

'The lifeboat?'

'Believe me, you don't want to know.' She sucked in a breath and raked slim fingers through her silky blonde hair. 'Let's look at this logically. I'm assuming Mary was telling the truth about your flat having fallen through—'

'You think she might have been lying?'

'Not lying, no. But she's manoeuvred it in some way. I don't know how yet, but when I find out she's going to be in trouble. Either way, at the moment, it looks as though you're going to have to stay with me. Aggh!' She tilted her head backwards and made a frustrated sound. 'And I'll never hear the last of it! Every morning they're going to be looking at me, working out whether I've fallen in love with you yet. Nudging. Making comments. I'll kill them.'

He couldn't keep the laughter out of his voice. 'Is that what you're afraid of? Do you think you're going to fall in love with me, Dr Anderson?'

She looked at him and the air snapped tight with tension. 'Don't be ridiculous!' Her voice was slightly husky. 'I don't believe in love.'

Could she feel it? Gio wondered. Could she feel what he was feeling?

'Then where is the problem?' He spread lean, bronzed hands and flashed her a smile. 'There is no risk of you falling in love with me. That makes me no more than a lodger.'

But a lodger with a definite interest.

'You don't know what they're like. Every moment of the day there will be little comments. Little asides. They'll drive us mad.'

'Or we could drive them mad. With a little thought and application, this could work in your favour.'

Her glance was suspicious. 'How?'

'Mary and Rita are determined to set you up, no?'

'Yes, but—'

'Clearly they believe that if they put a man under your nose, you will fall in love with him. So—I move in with you and when they see that you have no trouble at all resisting me, they will give up.'

She stared at him thoughtfully. 'You think that will work?'

'Why wouldn't it?'

'You don't know them. They don't give up easily.' The tension had passed and she was suddenly crisp and businesslike. 'And, to be honest, I don't know if I can share a house with someone. I've lived alone since I was eighteen.'

It sounded lonely to him. 'I can assure you that I'm house trained. I'm very clean and I pick up after myself.'

This time there was no answering smile. 'I'm used to having my own space.'

'Me, too,' Gio said smoothly. Was that what the problem was? She liked her independence? 'But Mary said that your house is large...'

'Yes.'

'Then we need hardly see each other.' In truth he'd made up his mind that he'd be seeing plenty of her but decided that the way to achieve that was a step at a time. He was fascinated by Alice Anderson. She was complex. Interesting. Unpredictable. And he knew instinctively that any show of interest on his part would be met with suspicion and rejection. If he looked relaxed and unconcerned about the whole situation, maybe she would, too. 'And think of it this way—' he was suddenly struck by inspiration '—it will give you a chance to brief me fully on the practice, the patients, everything I need to know.'

She looked suddenly thoughtful and he could see her mentally sifting through what he'd just said. 'Yes.' She gave a sharp nod. 'You're right that it will give us plenty of opportunity to talk about work. All right.' She took a deep breath, as if bracing herself. 'Let's lock up here and make a move. Where did you park?'

'At the top of the hill, in the public car park.'

'There are three spaces outside the surgery. You can

use one of those from now on.' She delved into her bag and removed a set of keys. 'I'll give you a lift to your car. Let's go.'

CHAPTER FOUR

STILL fuming about Mary and Rita, Alice jabbed the key into the ignition and gripped the steering-wheel.

She'd been thoroughly outmanoeuvred.

Why had she been foolish enough to let them arrange accommodation? Why hadn't she anticipated that they'd be up to their usual tricks? Because her mind didn't work like theirs, she thought savagely, that was why.

Vowing to tackle the two of them as soon as Gio wasn't around, Alice drove away from the car park, aware that his low black sports car was following close behind her.

Her mind on Mary and Rita, she changed gear with more anger than care and then winced at the hideous crunch. Reminding herself that her car wasn't up to a large degree of abuse, she forced herself to take a calming breath.

They'd set her up yet again, she knew they had. Rita and Mary. The two mother figures in her life. And they'd done it without even bothering to meet the man in question. Somehow they'd both decided that an attractive single guy was going to be perfect for her. It didn't matter that they'd never even met him, that they knew absolutely nothing about him. He was single and she was single and that was all it should take for the magic to kick in.

Anger spurted inside her and Alice thumped the steering-wheel with the heel of her hand and crunched the gears again. They were a pair of interfering old—old...

She really wanted to stay angry but how could she be when she knew that they were only doing it because they cared? When she remembered just how good they'd been to her since her very first day in the practice?

No, better to go along with their little plan and prove to them once and for all that love just didn't work for her. Gio Moretti was right. If she did this, maybe then they'd finally get the message about the way she wanted to live her life.

Yes, that was it. They obviously believed that Gio Moretti was the answer to any woman's prayers. When they realised that he wasn't the answer to hers, maybe they'd leave her alone. She'd live with him if only to prove that she wasn't interested. Since they considered him irresistible, her ability to resist him with no problem should prove something, shouldn't it?

Satisfied with her plan, she gave a swift nod and a smile as she flicked the indicator and took the narrow, winding road that led down to her house.

Her grip on the steering-wheel relaxed slightly. And living with him wouldn't be so bad. Gio seemed like a perfectly civilised guy. He was intelligent and well qualified. His experience in medicine was clearly very different to hers. She would certainly be able to learn from him.

And as for the logistics of the arrangement, she would put him in the guest room at the top of the house that had an *en suite* bathroom so she need never see him. He could come and go without bothering her. They need never have a conversation that didn't involve a patient. And when Mary and Rita saw how things were, they'd surely give up their quest to find her love.

Having satisfied herself that the situation wasn't irredeemable, she stepped on the brake, pulled in to allow another car to pass on the narrow road and drove the last stretch of road that curved down towards the sea.

The crowds of tourists dwindled and immediately she felt calmer.

This was her life. Her world.

The tide was out, the mudflats stretched in front of her and birds swooped and settled on the sandbanks. Behind her were towering cliffs of jagged rock that led out into the sea, and in front of her was the curving mouth of the river, winding lazily inland.

Cornwall.

Home.

Checking that he was still behind her, she touched the brake with her foot, turned right down the tiny track that led down to the water's edge and turned off the engine.

The throaty roar of the sports car behind her died and immediately peace washed over her. For a moment she was tempted to kick her shoes off and walk barefoot, but, as usual, time pressed against her wishes. She had a new lodger to show round and some reading that she needed to finish. And she was going to have to cook something for dinner.

With a shudder of distaste she stepped out of the car feeling hot, sticky and desperate for a cool shower. Wondering when the weather was finally going to break, she turned and watched as Gio slid out of his car and glanced around him. It was a long moment before he spoke.

'This place is amazing.' His hair gleamed glossy dark in the sunlight and the soft fabric of his T-shirt clung to his broad, powerful shoulders. There was a strength about him, an easy confidence that came with maturity, and Alice was suddenly gripped by a shimmer of something unfamiliar.

'Most people consider it to be lonely and isolated. They lecture me on the evils of burying myself somewhere so remote.'

'Do they?' He stood for a moment, legs planted firmly apart in a totally masculine stance, his gaze fixed on the view before him. 'I suppose that's fortunate. If everyone loved it here, it would cease to be so peaceful. You must see some very rare birds.'

'Over fifty different species.' Surprised by the observation, she leaned into her car to retrieve her bag, wondering whether he was genuinely interested in wildlife or whether he was just humouring her. Probably the latter, she decided. The man needed accommodation.

She slammed her car door without bothering to lock it and glanced at his face again. He looked serious enough.

He removed a suitcase from his boot. 'How long have you lived here?'

'Four years.' She delved in her bag for the keys and walked up the path. 'I found this house on my second day here. I was cycling along and there it was. Uninhabited, dilapidated and set apart from everything and everyone.' *Just like her.* She shook off the thought and wriggled the key into the lock. 'It took me a year to do it up sufficiently to live in it, another two years to get it to the state it's in now.'

He removed his sunglasses and glanced at her in surprise. 'You did the work yourself?'

She caught the look and smiled. 'Never judge by appearances, Dr Moretti. I have hidden muscles.' She pushed open the front door and stooped to pick up the post. 'I'll show you where you're sleeping and then meet you in the kitchen. I can fill you in on everything you need to know while we eat.'

She deposited the post, unopened, on the hall table and made a mental note to water the plants before she went to bed.

'It's beautiful.' His eyes scanned the wooden floors, which she'd sanded herself and then painted white, lifted to the filmy white curtains that framed large, picture windows and took in the touches of blue in the cushions and the artwork on the walls. He stepped forward to take a closer look at a large watercolour she had displayed in the hall. 'It's good. It has real passion. You can feel the power of the sea.' He frowned at the signature and turned to look at her. 'You paint?'

'Not any more.' She strode towards the stairs, eager to end the conversation. It was becoming too personal and she was always careful to avoid the personal. 'No time. Your room is at the top of the house and it has its own bathroom. It should be perfectly possible for us to lead totally separate lives.'

She said it to reassure herself as much to remind him and took the stairs two at a time and flung open a door. 'Here we are. You should be comfortable enough here and, anyway, it's only short term.' She broke off and he gave a smile.

'Of course.'

'Look, I don't mean to be rude and I'm thrilled that you're going to be working here, but I'm just not that great at sharing my living space with anyone, OK?' She shrugged awkwardly, wondering why she felt the need to explain herself. 'I'm selfish. I'm the first to admit it. I've lived on my own for too long to be anything else.'

And it was the way she preferred it. It was just a shame that Rita and Mary couldn't get the message.

He strode over to the huge windows and stared at the view. 'You're not being rude. If I lived here, I'd protect it, too.' He turned to face her. 'And I'm not intending to invade your personal space, Alice. You can relax.'

Relax?

His rich accent turned her name into something exotic and exciting and she gave a slight shiver. There would be no relaxing while he was staying with her.

'Then we won't have a problem.' She backed towards the door. 'Make yourself at home. I'm going to take a shower and change. Come down when you're ready. I'll be in the kitchen. Making supper.'

Her least favourite pastime. She gave a sigh of irritation as she left the room. She considered both cooking and eating to be a monumental waste of time but, with a guest in the house, she could hardly suggest that they skip a meal in favour of a bowl of cereal, which was her usual standby when she couldn't be bothered to cook.

Which meant opening the fridge and creating something out of virtually nothing. She just hoped that Gio Moretti wasn't too discerning when it came to his palate.

Her blue eyes narrowed and she gave a soft smile as she pushed open the door to her own bedroom and made for the shower, stripping off clothes as she walked and flinging them on the bed.

If the way to a man's heart was through his stomach, she was surprised that Mary and Rita had given their plan even the remotest chance of success.

It didn't take a genius to know that it was going to be hard for a man to harbour romantic notions about a woman who had just poisoned him.

When Gio strolled into the kitchen after a shower and a shave, she was grating cheese into a bowl with no apparent signs of either skill or enthusiasm. He watched with amusement and no small degree of interest and wondered who had designed the kitchen.

It was a cook's paradise. White slatted units and lots of glass reflected the light and a huge stainless-steel oven gleamed and winked, its spotless surface suggesting it had never been used. In fact, the whole kitchen looked as though it belonged in a show home and it took him less than five seconds of watching the usually competent Alice wrestle with a lump of cheese to understand why.

At the far end of the room French doors opened onto the pretty garden. Directly in front of the doors, positioned to make the most of the view, was a table covered in medical magazines, a few textbooks and several sheets of paper covered in neat handwriting.

He could picture her there, her face serious as she read her way through all the academic medical journals, checking the facts. He'd seen enough to know that Alice

Anderson was comfortable with facts. Possibly more comfortable with facts than she was with people.

He wondered why.

In his experience, there was usually a reason for the way people chose to live their lives.

'Cheese on toast all right with you?' She turned, still grating, her eyes fixed on his face. 'Oh…'

'Something is wrong?'

She blew a wisp of blonde hair out of her eyes. 'You look…different.'

He smiled and strolled towards her. 'More like a doctor?'

'Maybe. Ow.' She winced as the grater grazed her knuckles and adjusted her grip. 'I wasn't expecting guests, I'm afraid, so I haven't shopped. And I have to confess that I loathe cooking.' Her blonde hair was still damp from the shower and she'd changed into a pair of linen trousers and a pink top. She looked young and feminine and a long way from the brisk, competent professional he'd met earlier. The kitchen obviously flustered her and he found her slightly clumsy approach to cooking surprisingly appealing. In fact, he was fast discovering that there were many parts of Alice Anderson that he found appealing.

'Anything I can do?' Wondering if he should take over or whether that would damage her ego, he strolled over to her, lifted a piece of cheese and sniffed it. 'What is it?'

'The cheese?' She turned on the grill and watched for a moment as if not entirely confident that it would work. 'Goodness knows. The sort that comes wrapped in tight plastic. Cheddar or something, I suppose. Why?'

He tried not to wince at the vision of cheese tightly

wrapped in plastic. 'I'm Italian. We happen to love cheese. Mozzarella, fontina, ricotta, marscapone…'

'This is just something I grabbed from the supermarket a few weeks ago. It was covered with blue bits but I chopped them off. I assumed they weren't supposed to be there. I don't think they were there when I bought it.' She dropped the grater and stared down at the pile of cheese with a distinct lack of enthusiasm. 'There should be some salad in the fridge, if you're interested.'

He opened her fridge and stared. It was virtually empty. Making a mental note to shop at the earliest convenient moment, he reached for a limp, sorry piece of lettuce and examined it thoughtfully. 'I'm not bothered about salad,' he murmured, and she glanced up, her face pink from the heat of the grill, her teeth gritted.

'Fine. Whatever. This is nearly ready.' She pulled out the grill pan and fanned her hand over the contents to stop it smoking. 'I'm not that great a cook but at least it's food, and that's all that matters. Good job I'm not really trying to seduce you, Dr Moretti.' She flashed him a wicked smile as she slid the contents of the grill pan onto two plates. 'If the way to a man's heart is through his stomach, I'm completely safe.'

She wasn't joking about her culinary skills. Gio stared down at the burnt edges of the toast and the patchy mix of melted and unmelted cheese and suddenly realised why she was so slim. It was a good job he was starving and willing to eat virtually anything. Suddenly he understood Mary's suggestion that they get a takeaway. 'Did you eat lunch today?'

She fished knives and forks out of a drawer and sat down at the table, pushing aside the piles of journals and books to make room for the plates. 'I can't remember. I might have had something at some point. So what's your opinion on Harriet?' She pushed cutlery across the table and poured some water. 'Do you think she is depressed?'

He wondered if she even realised that she was talking about work again.

Did she do it on purpose to avoid a conversation of a more personal nature?

He picked up a fork and tried to summon up some enthusiasm for the meal ahead. It was a challenge. For him a meal was supposed to be a total experience. An event. A time to indulge the palate and the senses simultaneously. Clearly, for Alice it was just a means of satisfying the gnawing in her stomach.

Glancing down at his plate, he wondered whether he was going to survive the experience of Alice's cooking or whether he was going to require medical attention.

She definitely needed educating about food.

'Is Harriet depressed? It's possible. I'll certainly follow it up.' He cautiously tasted the burnt offering on his plate and decided that it was the most unappetizing meal he'd eaten for a long time. 'Postnatal depression is a serious condition.'

'And often missed. She was fine after the twins but that's not necessarily significant, of course.' Alice finished her toasted cheese with brisk efficiency and no visible signs of enjoyment and put down her fork with an apologetic glance in his direction. 'Sorry to eat so quickly. I was starving. I don't think I managed to eat at all yesterday.'

'Are you serious?'

'Perfectly. We had a bit of a drama in the bay. The

lifeboat was called out to two children who'd managed to drift out to sea in their inflatable boat.' She broke off and sipped her drink. 'I spent my lunch-hour over with the crew, making sure they were all right. By the time I finished I had a queue of people in the surgery. I forgot to eat.'

To Gio, who had never forgotten to eat in his life, such a situation was incomprehensible. 'You need to seriously rethink your lifestyle.'

'You sound like Mary and Rita. I happen to like my lifestyle. It works for me.' With a fatalistic shrug she finished her water and stood up. 'So, Dr Moretti, what can I tell you about the practice to make your life easier? At this time of year we see a lot of tourists with the usual sorts of problems. Obviously, on top of the locals, it makes us busy, as you discovered today.'

All she thought about was work, he reflected, watching as she lifted a medical journal from the pile on the table and absently scanned the contents. She was driven. Obsessed. 'Do you do a minor accident clinic?'

'No.' She shook her head and dropped the journal back on the pile. 'David and I tried it two years ago but, to be honest, there were days when we were swamped and days when we were sitting around. We decided it was better just to fit them into surgery time. We have a very good relationship with the coastguard and the local paramedics. Sometimes they call on us, sometimes we call on them. We also have a good relationship with the local police.'

'The police?' His attention was caught by the gentle sway of her hips as she walked across the kitchen. Her movements were graceful and utterly feminine and from nowhere he felt a sharp tug of lust.

Gritting his teeth, he tried to talk sense into himself. *They were colleagues.*

He'd known her for less than a day.

'Beach parties.' She lifted the kettle and filled it. 'At this time of year we have a lot of teenagers just hanging out on the beach. Usually the problem's just too much alcohol, as you saw this morning. Sometimes it's drugs.'

To hide the fact that he was studying her, Gio glanced out towards the sea and tried to imagine it crowded with hordes of teenagers. *Tried to drag his mind away from the tempting curve of her hips.* 'Looks peaceful to me. It's hard to imagine it otherwise.'

She rested those same hips against the work surface while she waited for the kettle to boil. 'They don't come down this far. They congregate on the beach beyond the harbour. The surf is good. Too good sometimes, and then we get a fair few surfing accidents, as you also noticed this morning. Coffee?'

Gio opened his mouth to say yes and then winced as he saw her reaching into a cupboard for a jar. 'You are using instant coffee?'

She pulled a face. 'I know. It's not my favourite either, but it's better than nothing and I've run out of fresh. One of the drawbacks of living out here is that both the supermarket and the nearest espresso machine are a car ride away.'

'Not any more.'

'Don't tell me.' She spooned coffee into a mug. 'You've brought your own espresso machine.'

'Of course. It was a key part of my luggage. Along with a large supply of the very best beans.'

She stilled, the spoon still in her hand. 'You're not serious?'

'Coffee is extremely serious,' he said dryly. 'If you expect me to work hard, I need my daily fix, and if today is anything to go by then I'm not going to have time to pop up the hill to that excellent bakery.'

She scooped her hair away from her face and there was longing in her eyes. 'You're planning to make fresh coffee every morning?'

'*Si.*' He wondered why she was even asking the question when it seemed entirely normal to him. 'It is the only way I can get through the day.'

The smile spread across her face. 'Now, if Mary had mentioned that, I would have cancelled your flat with the letting agent myself.' She licked her lips, put down the spoon, a hunger in her eyes. 'Does your fancy machine make enough for two cups?'

He decided that if it guaranteed him one of her smiles, he'd stand over the machine all morning. 'A decent cup of coffee to start your day will be part of my fee for invading your space,' he offered. Along with the cooking, but he decided to wait a while before breaking that to her in case she was offended. 'So tell me about Rita and Mary.' He wanted to know about their relationship with her. Why they felt the need to set her up.

He wanted to know everything there was to know about Alice Anderson.

'They've worked in the practice for ever. Twenty-five years at least. Can you imagine that?' She shook her head. 'It helps, of course, because they know everything about everyone. History is important, don't you think, Dr Moretti?'

He wondered about her history. He wondered what had made a beautiful woman like her choose to bury herself in her work and live apart from others. It felt wrong. Not the setting, he mused as he glanced out of the window. The setting was perfect. But in his opinion it was a setting designed to be shared with someone special.

Realising that she was waiting for an answer, he smiled, amused by her earnest expression. She was delightfully serious. 'I can see that history is important in general practice.'

'It gives you clues. Not knowing a patient's history is often like trying to solve a murder with no access to clues.' Her eyes narrowed. 'I suppose as a surgeon, it's different. It's more task orientated. You get the patient on the operating table and you solve the problem.'

'Not necessarily that simple.' He sat back in his chair, comfortable in her kitchen. *In her company.* The problems of the past year faded. 'In plastic surgery the patient's wishes, hopes, dreams are all an important part of the picture. Appearance can affect people's lives. As a society, we're shallow. We see and we judge. As a surgeon you have to take that into account. You need to understand what's needed and decided whether you can deliver.'

'You did face lifts? Nose jobs?'

He smiled. It was a common misconception and it didn't offend him. 'That wasn't my field of speciality,' he said quietly. 'I did paediatrics. Cleft palates, hare lips. In between running my clinic in Milan, I did volunteer work in developing countries. Children with unrepaired clefts lead very isolated lives. Often they can't go to school—they're ostracised from the community, no chance of employment...'

She was staring at him, a frown in her blue eyes as if she was reassessing him. 'I had no idea.' She picked up her coffee, but her focus was on him, not the mug in her hand. 'That's so interesting. And tough.'

'Tough, rewarding, frustrating.' He gave a shrug. 'All those things. Like every branch of medicine, I suppose. I also did a lot of training. Showing local doctors new techniques.' He waited for the dull ache of disappointment that always came when he was talking about the past, but there was nothing. Instead he felt more relaxed than he could ever recall feeling.

'It must have been hard for you to give it up.'

He shrugged and felt a twinge in his shoulder. 'Life sometimes forces change on us but sometimes it's a change we should have made ourselves if we only had the courage. I was ready for a change.'

He sensed that she was going to ask him more, delve deeper, and then she seemed to withdraw.

'Well, there's certainly variety in our practice. If you're good with babies, you can run the baby clinic. David used to do it.'

She was talking about work again, he mused. 'Immunisations, I assume?' Always, she avoided the personal. *Was she afraid of intimacy?*

'That and other things.' She sipped at her coffee. 'It's a really busy clinic. We expanded its remit a few months ago to encourage mothers to see us with their problems during the clinic rather than making appointments during normal surgery hours. It means that they don't have to make separate appointments for themselves and we reduce the number of toddlers running around the waiting room.' Her fingers tightened on the mug. 'I have to confess it isn't my forte.'

'I've seen enough of your work to know that you're an excellent doctor.' He watched as the colour touched her cheekbones.

'Oh, I can do the practical stuff.' She gave a shrug and turned her back on him, dumping her mug in the sink. 'It's everything that goes with it that I can't handle. All the emotional stuff. I'm terrible at that. How are you with worried mothers, Dr Moretti?' She turned and her blonde hair swung gently round her head.

Was she afraid of other people's emotions or her own? Pondering the question, he flashed her a wicked smile. 'Worried women are my speciality, Dr Anderson.'

She threw back her head and laughed. 'I'll just bet they are, Dr Moretti. I'll just bet they are.'

Alice woke to the delicious smells of freshly ground coffee, rolled over and then remembered Gio Moretti. Living here. In her house.

She sat upright, pushed the heavy cloud of sleep away and checked the clock. 6 a.m. He was obviously an early riser, like her.

Tempted by the smell and the prospect of a good cup of coffee to start her day, she padded into the shower, dressed quickly and followed her nose.

She pushed open the kitchen door, her mind automatically turning to work, and then stopped dead, taken aback by the sight of Gio half-naked in her kitchen.

'Oh!' She'd assumed he was up and dressed, instead of which he was wearing jeans again. This time with nothing else. His chest was bare and the muscles of his shoulders flexed as he reached for the coffee.

He was gorgeous.

The thought stopped her dead and she frowned, surprised at herself for noticing and more than a little irritated. And then she gave a dismissive shrug. So what? Despite what Rita and Mary obviously thought, she was neither blind nor brain dead. And it wasn't as if she hadn't experienced sexual attraction before. She had. The important thing was not to mistake it for 'love'.

He turned to reach for a cup and she saw the harsh, jagged scars running down his back. 'That looks painful.'

The minute she said the words she wished she hadn't. Was he sensitive about it? Perhaps she wasn't supposed to mention it. If he was the type of guy that spent all day staring in the mirror, then perhaps it bothered him.

'Not as painful as it used to. *Buongiorno.*' He flashed her a smile and handed her a cup, totally at ease in her kitchen. 'I wasn't expecting you up this early. I have to have coffee before I can face the shower.'

'I know the feeling.' Wondering how he got the scar, she took the cup with a nod of thanks and wandered over to the table, trying not to look in his direction.

She might not believe in love but she could see when a man was attractive and Gio Moretti was certainly attractive. When she'd said he could have her spare room, she hadn't imagined he'd be walking around her house half-naked. It was unsettling and more than a little distracting.

She sat down. Her body suddenly felt hot and uncomfortable and she slid a finger around the neck of her shirt and glanced at the sun outside. 'It's going to be another scorcher today.' Even though she made a point of not looking in his direction, she sensed his gaze on her.

'You're feeling hot, Alice?'

Something in his voice made her turn her head. Her eyes met hers and an unexpected jolt shook her body. 'It's warm in here, yes.' She caught her breath, broke the eye contact and picked up her coffee, but not before her brain had retained a clear image of a bronzed, muscular chest covered in curling dark hairs. He was all muscle and masculinity and her throat felt suddenly dry. She took a sip of coffee. 'This is delicious. Thank you.'

Still holding her cup, she stared out of the window and tried to erase the memory of his half-naked body. She wasn't used to having a man in her kitchen. It was all too informal. Too intimate.

Everything she avoided.

To take her mind off the problem she did what she always did. She thought about work.

'Rita has a baby clinic this afternoon,' she said brightly, watching as a heron rose from the smooth calm of the estuary that led to sea and flew off with a graceful sweep of its wings. 'Invariably she manages it by herself but sometimes she needs one of us to—'

'Alice, *cara.*' His voice came from behind her, deep and heavily accented. 'I need at least two cups of coffee before I can even think about work, let alone talk about it.' His hands came up and touched her shoulders and she stiffened. She wasn't used to being touched. No one touched her.

'I just thought you should know that—'

'This kitchen has the most beautiful view.' He kept his hands on her shoulders, his touch light and relaxed. 'Enjoy it. It's still early. Leave thoughts of work until later. Look at the mist. Enjoy the silence. It's perfect.'

She sat still, heart pounding, thoroughly unsettled. Usually her kitchen soothed her. Calmed her. But today she could feel the little spurts of tension darting through her shoulders.

It was just having someone else in the house, she told herself. Inevitably it altered her routine.

Abandoning her plan to read some journals while drinking her coffee as she usually did, she stood up and firmly extricated herself from his hold.

'I need to get going.' Annoyed with herself and even more annoyed with him, she walked across the room, taking her cup with her. 'I'll meet you at the surgery later.'

His eyes flickered to the clock on the wall. 'Alice, it's only 6.30.' His voice was a soft, accented drawl. 'And you haven't finished your coffee.'

'There's masses of paperwork to plough through.' She drank the coffee quickly and put the cup on the nearest worktop. 'Thank you. A great improvement on instant.'

His eyes were locked on her face. 'You haven't had breakfast.'

'I don't need breakfast.' What she needed most of all was space. Air to breathe. The safety of her usual routine. She backed out of the door, needing to escape. 'I'll see you later.'

Grabbing her bag and her jacket, she strode out of the house, fumbling for her keys as she let the door swing shut behind her.

Oh, bother and blast.

Instead of starting her day in a calm, organised frame

of mind, as she usually did, she felt unsettled and on edge and the reason why was perfectly obvious.

She didn't need a lodger and she certainly didn't need a lodger that she noticed, she thought to herself as she slid into the sanctuary of her car.

And she was *definitely* going to kill Mary when she saw her.

He made her nervous.

She claimed not to believe in love and yet there was chemistry between them. An elemental attraction that he'd felt from the first moment. And it was growing stronger by the minute.

Gio made himself a second cup of coffee and drank it seated at the little table overlooking the garden and the sea.

She was serious, academic and obviously totally un-accustomed to having a man in her life. He'd felt the sudden tension in her shoulders when he'd touched her. Felt her discomfort and her sudden anxiety.

He frowned and stretched his legs out in front of him.

In his family, touching was part of life. Everyone touched. Hugged. Held. It was what they did. But not everyone was the same, of course.

And, for whatever reason, he sensed that Alice wasn't used to being touched. *Wasn't comfortable being touched.*

The English were generally more reserved and emotionally distant, of course, so it could be that. He drained his coffee-cup. Or it could be something else. Something linked with the reason he was sitting here now instead of in a flat in another part of town.

Why had Mary seen the need to interfere?

Why did she think that Alice needed help finding a man in her life?

And, given his distaste for matchmaking attempts, why wasn't he running fast in the opposite direction?

Why did he suddenly feel comfortable and content?

The question didn't need much answering. Everything about Alice intrigued him. She was complex and unpredictable. She had a beautiful smile but it only appeared after a significant amount of coaxing. She was clever and clearly caring and yet she herself had humbly confessed that she wasn't good with emotions.

And she was uncomfortable with being touched.

Which was a shame, he thought to himself as he finished his coffee. Because he'd made up his mind that he was going to be touching her a lot. So she was going to have to start getting used to it.

CHAPTER FIVE

MARY sailed into the surgery just as Alice scooped the post from the mat. 'You're early.' There was disappointment in her expression, as if she'd expected something different. 'So—did you have a lovely evening?'

'Wonderful. Truly wonderful.' Alice dropped the post onto the reception desk to be sorted and gave a wistful sigh, deriving wicked satisfaction from the look of hope that lit Mary's face. 'I must do it more often.'

'Do what more often?'

'Go home early, of course.' Alice smiled sweetly. 'I caught up on so many things.'

Mary's shoulders sagged. 'Caught up on what? How was your lodger?'

'Who?' Alice adopted a blank expression and then waved a hand vaguely. 'Oh, you mean Dr Moretti? Fine, I think. I wouldn't really know. I hardly saw him.'

Mary dropped her bag with a thump and a scowl. 'You didn't spend the evening together?'

'Not at all. Why would we? He's my lodger, not my date.' Alice leaned forward and picked up the contents of her in tray. 'But he does make tremendous coffee. I suppose I have you to thank for that, given that you arranged it all.'

'You already drink too much coffee,' Mary scolded as they both walked towards the consulting rooms. She caught Alice's arm in a firm grip. 'Are you serious? You didn't spend any time with him at all?'

Alice shrugged her off. 'None.'

'If that's true, you're a sad case.' Her eyes narrowed. 'You're teasing me, aren't you?'

'All right, I'll tell you the truth.' Thoroughly enjoying herself now, Alice threw Mary a saucy wink as she pushed open the door to her room. 'I'm grateful to you, really I am. Even I can see that Gio Moretti is handsome. I don't suppose they come much handsomer. If I have to share my house with someone I'd so much rather it was someone decorative. I could hardly concentrate on my breakfast this morning because he was standing in my kitchen half-naked. *What* a body!' She gave an exaggerated sigh and pressed her palm against her heart. 'I'd have to be a fool not to be interested in a man like him, wouldn't you agree?'

'Alice—'

'And I'm certainly not a fool.' She dropped her bag behind her desk. 'Anyway, I just want you to know that we've been at it all night like rabbits and now I've definitely got him out of my system so you can safely find him somewhere else to live, you interfering old—'

'*Buongiorno.*'

The deep voice came from the doorway and Alice whirled round, her face turning pink with embarrassment. She caught the wicked humour in his dark eyes and cursed inwardly.

Why had he chosen that precise moment to walk down the corridor?

He lounged in her doorway, dressed in tailored trousers and a crisp cotton shirt that looked both expensive and stylish. The sleeves were rolled up to his elbows, revealing bronzed forearms dusted with dark hairs. The laughter in his eyes told her that he'd heard every word. 'You left without breakfast, Dr Anderson. And after such a long, taxing night…' He lingered over each syllable, his rich, Italian accent turning the words into something decadent and sinful '…you need to replenish your energy levels.'

Mary glanced between them, her expression lifting, and Alice suppressed a groan. Friendly banter. Teasing. All designed to give Mary totally the wrong idea. And she'd been the one to start it.

'Finally, someone else to scold you about not eating proper meals.' Mary put her hands on her hips and gave a satisfied nod. 'If Dr Moretti values his stomach lining, he'll take over the cooking.'

'I'm perfectly capable of cooking,' Alice snapped, sitting down at her desk and switching on her computer with a stab of her finger. 'It's just that I don't enjoy it very much and I have so many other more important things to do with my time.'

'Like work.' Mary looked at Gio. 'While you're at it, you might want to reform her on that count, too.' She walked out of the room, leaving Alice glaring after her.

'I've decided that David had the right idea after all. London is looking better all the time. In London, no one cares what the person next to them is doing. No one cares whether they eat breakfast, work or don't work.

And for sure, no one cares about the state of anyone else's love life.' She hit the return key on the keyboard with more force than was necessary, aware that Gio was watching her, a thoughtful expression in his dark eyes. His shoulders were still against the doorframe and he didn't seem in any hurry to go anywhere.

'She really cares about you.'

Alice stilled. He was right, of course. Mary did care about her. And she'd never had that before. Until she'd arrived in Smuggler's Cove, she'd never experienced interference as a result of caring.

'I know she does.' Alice bit her lip. 'I wish I could convince her that I'm fine on my own. That this is what I want. How I want to live my life.'

His gaze was steady. 'Sounds lonely to me, Dr Anderson. And perhaps a bit cowardly.'

'Cowardly?' She forgot about her computer and sat back in her chair, more than a little outraged. 'What's that supposed to mean?'

He walked further into the room, his eyes fixed on her face. 'People who avoid relationships are usually afraid of getting hurt.'

'Or perhaps they're just particularly well adjusted and evolved,' Alice returned sweetly. 'This is the twenty-first century and we no longer all believe that a man is necessary to validate and enhance our lives.'

'Is that so?' His gaze dropped to her mouth and she felt her heart stumble and kick in her chest.

With a frown of irritation she turned her head and concentrated on her computer screen. Why was he looking at her like that? Studying her? As if he was trying to see deep inside her mind? Her fingers drummed a rhythm on the desk. Well, that was a part of herself that she kept private. Like all the other parts.

She looked up, her expression cool and discouraging. 'We don't all have to agree on everything, Dr Moretti. Our differences are what make the world an interesting place to live. And now I'm sure you have patients to see and I know that I certainly do.' To make her point, she reached across her desk and pressed the buzzer to alert her first patient. 'Oh, and please don't give Mary and Rita the impression that we're living a cosy life together. They'll be unbearable.'

'But surely the point is to prove that we can be cosy and yet you can still resist me,' he reminded her in silky tones, and she stared at him, speechless. 'Isn't that the message you want them to receive? Unless, of course, you are having trouble resisting me.'

'Oh, please!' She gave an exclamation of impatience and looked up just as the patient knocked on the door. 'Let's just move on.'

'Yes, let's do that.' He kept his hand on the doorhandle, his eyes glinting darkly, 'but at least try and keep this authentic. For the record, you would not get me out of your system in one night, *cara mia.*'

Her mouth fell open and she searched in vain for a witty reply. And failed.

His smile widened and he wandered out of the room, leaving her fuming.

Alice took refuge in work and fortunately there was plenty of it.

Her first patient was a woman who was worried about a rash on her daughter's mouth.

'She had this itchy, red sore and then suddenly it turned into a blister and it's been oozing.' The mother pulled a face and hugged the child. 'Poor thing. It's really bothering her.'

Alice took one look at the thick, honey-coloured crust that had formed over the lesion and made an instant diagnosis. *Impetigo contagiosa,* she decided, caused by *Staphyloccocus aureus* and possibly group A beta-haemolytic streptococcus. This was one of the things she loved about medicine, she thought as she finished her examination and felt a rush of satisfaction. You were given clues. Signs. And you had to interpret them. Behind everything was a cause. It was just a question of finding it.

In this case she had no doubt. 'She has impetigo, Mrs Wood.' She turned back to her computer, selected a drug and pressed the print key. 'It's a very common skin condition, particularly in children. As it's only in one area I'm going to give you some cream to apply to the affected area. You need to wash the skin several times a day and remove the crusts. Then apply the cream. But make sure you wash your hands carefully because it's highly contagious.'

'Can she go back to nursery?'

Alice shook her head. 'Not until the lesions are cleared. Make sure you don't share towels.'

Mrs Wood sighed. 'That's more holiday I'll have to take, then. Being a working mother is a nightmare. I wonder why I bother sometimes.'

'It must be difficult.' Alice took the prescription from the printer and signed it. 'Here we are. Come back in a week if it isn't better.'

Mrs Wood left the room clutching her prescription and Alice moved on to the next patient. And the next.

She was reading a discharge letter from a surgeon when her door opened and Gio walked in, juggling two coffees and a large paper bag.

'I'm fulfilling my brief from Mary. Breakfast.' He flashed her a smile, kicked the door shut with his foot and placed everything on the desk in front of her. He ripped open the bag and waved a hand. 'Help yourself.'

She sat back in her chair and stared at him in exasperation. She never stopped for a break when she was seeing patients. It threw her concentration and just meant an even longer day. 'I've still got patients to see.'

'Actually, you haven't. At least, not at this exact moment. I checked with Mary.' He sat down in the chair next to her desk. 'Your last patient has cancelled so you've got a break. And so have I. Let's make the most of it.'

She stared at the selection of croissants and muffins. 'I'm not really hungry but now you're here we could quickly run through the referral strategy for—'

'Alice.' He leaned forward, a flash of humour in his dark eyes. 'If you're about to mention work, hold the thought.' He pushed the bag towards her. 'I refuse to discuss anything until I've seen you eat.'

The scent of warm, freshly baked cakes wafted under her nose. 'But I—'

'Didn't eat breakfast,' he reminded her calmly, 'and you've got the whole morning ahead of you. You can't get through that workload on one cup of black coffee, even though it was excellent.'

She sighed and her hand hovered over the bag. Eventually her fingers closed over a muffin. 'Fine. Thanks. If I eat this, will you leave me alone?'

'Possibly.' He waited until she'd taken a bite. 'Now we can talk about work. I'm interested in following up on Harriet. You mentioned that there's a baby clinic this afternoon. Is she likely to attend?'

'Possibly.' The muffin was still warm and tasted delicious. She wondered how she could have thought she wasn't hungry. She was starving. 'Rita would know whether she's down for immunisation. Or she may just come to have the baby weighed. Gina is around this morning, too. It would be worth talking to her. I've got a meeting with her at eleven-fifteen, to talk about our MMR rates.'

'I'll join you. Then I can discuss Harriet.'

'Fine.' Her gaze slid longingly at the remaining muffins. 'Can I have another?'

'Eat.' He pushed them towards her and she gave a guilty smile.

'I'll cook supper tonight in return.' She thought she saw a look of alarm cross his face but then decided she must have imagined it.

'There's no need, I thought we could—'

'I insist.' It was the least she could do, she thought, devouring the muffin and reached for another without even thinking. She loathed cooking, but there were times when it couldn't be avoided. 'Last night's supper of cheese on toast was hardly a gourmet treat. Tonight I'll do a curry.' She'd made one once before and it hadn't turned out too badly.

'Alice, why don't you let me—' He broke off and turned as the door opened and Rita walked in.

'Can you come to the waiting room? Betty needs advice.'

Alice brushed the crumbs from her lap and stood up. 'I'll come now. Nice breakfast. Thanks.'

Dropping the empty bag in the bin on his way past, Gio followed, wondering if she even realised that she'd eaten her way through three muffins.

It was almost eleven o'clock, and she'd been up since dawn and working on an empty stomach until he'd intervened.

Something definitely needed to be done about her lifestyle.

He gave a wry smile. Even more so if he was going to be living with her. After sampling her cheese on toast, he didn't dare imagine what her curry would be like, but he had a suspicion that the after-effects might require medication.

He walked into the reception area and watched while she walked over to the couple standing at the desk.

'Betty? What's happened?'

'Eating too quickly, that's what happened.' Betty scowled at her husband but there was worry in her eyes. 'Thought I'd cook him a nice bit of fish for breakfast, straight from the quay, but he wasn't looking what he was doing and now he's got a bone lodged in his throat. And, of course, it has to be right at peak season when the shop's clogged with people spending money and I can't trust that dizzy girl on her own behind the counter. If we have to go to A and E it will be hours and—'

'Betty.'

Gio watched, fascinated, as Alice put a hand on the woman's arm and interrupted her gently, her voice steady and confident. 'Calm down. I'm sure we'll manage to take the bone out here, but if not—' She broke off as the door opened again and another woman hurried in, her face disturbingly pale, a hand resting on her swollen stomach. 'Cathy? Has something happened?'

'Oh, Dr Anderson, I've had the most awful pains this morning. Ever since I hung out the washing. I didn't know whether I should just drive straight to the hospital but Mick has an interview later this morning and I didn't want to drag him there on a wild-goose chase. I know surgery has finished, but have you got a minute?'

Obviously not for both at the same time, Gio reflected with something close to amusement. No wonder Alice looked tired. She never stopped working. Surgery was finished and still the patients were crowding in. Had he really thought that he was in for a quiet summer?

He glanced towards the door, half expecting someone else to appear, but there was no one. 'Point me in the direction of a pair of Tilley's forceps and I'll deal with the fishbone,' he said calmly, and Alice gave a brief nod, her eyes lingering on Cathy's pale face.

'In your consulting room. Forceps are in the top cupboard above the sink. Thanks.'

Her lack of hesitation impressed him. She might be a workaholic but at least she didn't have trouble delegating, Gio mused as he introduced himself to the couple and ushered them into the consulting room.

'If you'll have a seat, Mr...?' He lifted an eyebrow and the woman gave a stiff smile.

'Norman. Giles and Betty Norman.' Her tone was crisp and more than a little chilly, but he smiled easily.

'You'll have to forgive me for not knowing who you are. This is only my second day here.'

Betty Norman gave a sniff. 'We run the newsagent across the harbour. If you were local, you'd know that. There have been Normans running the newsagent for five generations.' She looked at him suspiciously, her gaze bordering on the unfriendly. 'That's a foreign accent I'm hearing and you certainly don't look English.'

'That's because I'm Italian.' Gio adjusted the angle of the light. 'And I may be new to the village, Mrs Norman, but I'm not new to medicine so you need have no worries on that score.' He opened a cupboard and selected the equipment he was going to need. 'Mr Norman, I just need to shine a light in your mouth so that I can take a better look at the back of your throat.'

Betty dropped her handbag and folded her arms. 'Well, I just hope you can manage to get the wretched thing out. Some surgeries insist you go to A and E for something like this but we have a business to run. A and E is a sixty-minute round trip at the best of times and then there's the waiting. Dr Anderson is good at this sort of thing. Perhaps we ought to wait until she's finished with young Cathy.'

Aware that he was being tested, Gio bit back a smile, not remotely offended. 'I don't think that's a trip you're going to be making today, Mrs Norman,' he said smoothly, raising his head briefly from his examination to acknowledge her concerns. 'And I don't think you need to wait to see Dr Anderson. I can understand that you're wary of a new doctor but I can assure you that I'm more than up to the job. Why don't you let me try and then we'll see what happens?'

She stared at him, her shoulders tense and unyielding, her mouth pursed in readiness to voice further disapproval, and then he smiled at her and the tension seemed to ooze out of her and her mouth relaxed slightly into a smile of her own.

'Stupid of me to cook fish for breakfast,' she muttered weakly, and Gio returned to his examination.

'Cooking is never stupid, Mrs Norman,' he murmured as he depressed her husband's tongue to enable him to visualise the tonsil. 'And fish is the food of the gods, especially when it's eaten fresh from the sea. I see the bone quite clearly. Removing it should present no difficulty whatsoever.'

He reached for the forceps, adjusted the light and removed the fishbone with such speed and skill that his patient barely coughed.

'There.' He placed the offending bone on a piece of gauze. 'There's the culprit. The back of your throat has been slightly scratched, Mr Norman, so I'm going to give you an antibiotic and ask you to come back in a day for me to just check your throat. If necessary I will refer you to the ENT team at the hospital, but I don't think it will come to that.'

Mr Norman stared at the bone and glanced at his wife, an expression of relief on his face.

'Well—thank goodness.'

She picked up her handbag, all her icy reserve melted away. 'Thank the doctor, not goodness.' She gave Gio a nod of approval. 'Welcome to Smuggler's Cove. I think you're going to fit in well.'

'Thank you.' He smiled, his mind on Alice and her soft mouth. 'I think so, too.'

* * *

Alice watched from the doorway, clocked the killer smile, the Latin charm, and noted Betty's response with a sigh of relief and a flicker of exasperation. Why was it that the members of her sex were so predictable?

She'd briefly examined Cathy and what she'd seen had been enough to convince her that a trip to hospital was necessary for a more detailed check-up. Then she'd returned to the consulting room, prepared to help Gio, only to find that her help clearly wasn't required.

Not only had he removed the fishbone, which she knew could often be a tricky procedure, but had obviously succeeded in winning over the most difficult character in the village.

It amused her that even Betty Norman wasn't immune to a handsome Italian with a sexy smile and for a moment she found herself remembering David's comment about women going weak at the knees. Then she allowed herself a smile. *Not every woman.* Her knees were still functioning as expected, despite Mary's interference.

She could see he was handsome, and she was still walking with no problem.

Clearing her throat, she walked into the room. 'Everything OK?'

But she could see that everything was more than OK. Betty had melted like Cornish ice cream left out in the midday sun.

'Everything is fine.' Betty glanced at her watch, all smiles now. She patted her hair and straightened her blouse. 'I can be back behind the counter before that girl has a chance to make a mistake. Nice meeting you Dr...I didn't catch your name.'

'Moretti.' He extended a lean, bronzed hand. 'Gio Moretti.'

His voice was a warm, accented drawl and Betty flushed a deep shade of pink as she shook his hand. 'Well, thank you again. And welcome. If you need any help with anything, just call into the newsagent's.' She waved a hand, flustered now. 'I'd be more than happy to advise you on anything local.'

Gio smiled. 'I'll remember that.'

'By the way…' She turned to Alice. 'Edith doesn't seem herself at the moment. I can't put my finger on it but something isn't right. It may be nothing, but I thought you should know, given what happened to her last month.'

'I'll check on her.' Alice frowned. 'You think she might have fallen again?'

'That's what's worrying me.' Betty reached for her handbag. 'Iris Leek at number thirty-six has a key if you need to let yourself in. I tried ringing her yesterday for a chat, but I think she was away at her sister's.'

'I'll call round there this week,' Alice promised immediately. 'I was going to anyway.'

Betty smiled. 'Thank you, dear. You may not have been born here but you're a good girl and we're lucky to have you.' She turned to Gio with a girlish smile. 'And doubly lucky now, it seems.'

The couple left the surgery and Alice shook her head in disbelief. 'Well, you really charmed her. Congratulations. I've never seen Betty blush before. You've made a conquest.'

His gaze was swift and assessing. 'And that surprises you?'

'Well, let's put it this way—she's not known for her warmth to strangers unless they're spending money in her shop.'

'I thought she was a nice lady.' He switched off the light and tidied up the equipment he'd used. 'A bit cautious, but I suppose that's natural.'

'Welcome to Smuggler's Cove,' Alice said lightly. 'If you can't trace your family back for at least five generations, you're a stranger.'

'And how about you, Alice?' He paused and his dark gold eyes narrowed as they rested on her face. 'From her comments, you obviously aren't a local either. So far we've talked about work and nothing else. Tell me about yourself.'

His slow, seductive masculine tones slid over her taut nerves and soothed her. It was a voice designed to lull an unsuspecting woman into a sensual coma.

'Alice?'

Alice shook herself. She wasn't going to be thrown off her stride just because the man was movie-star handsome. She'd leave that to the rest of the female population of the village. 'There's nothing interesting to say about me. I'm very boring.'

'You mean you don't like talking about yourself.'

He was sharp, she had to give him that. 'I came here after I finished my GP rotation five years ago so, no, I don't qualify as a local,' she said crisply, delivering the facts as succinctly as possible. In her experience, the quickest way to stop someone asking questions was to answer a few. 'But I'm accepted because of the job I do.'

'And it's obviously a job you do very well. So where is home to you? Where are your family?'

Her blood went cold and all her muscles tightened. 'This is my home.'

There was a brief pause and when he spoke again his voice was gentle. 'Then you're lucky, because I can't think of a nicer place to live.' His eyes lingered on her face and then he strolled across the room to wash his hands. 'Do you often do night visits?'

Relieved that he'd changed the subject, some of the tension left her. 'Not since the new GP contract. Why?'

'Because I was told that the other night you were up with a child who had an asthma attack.'

'Chloe Bennett.' She frowned. 'How do you know that?'

He dried his hands. 'I was talking to the girl in the coffee-shop yesterday. Blonde. Nice smile.'

Alice resisted the temptation to roll her eyes. 'Katy Adams.' Obviously another conquest.

'Nice girl.'

Knowing Katy's reputation with men, Alice wondered if she should warn her new partner that he could be in mortal danger. She decided against it. A man who looked like him would have been fending off women from his cradle. He certainly wouldn't need any help from her.

'Chloe Bennett is a special case,' she explained briskly. 'Her mother has been working hard to control her asthma and give her some sort of normal life at school. It's been very difficult. She has my home number and I encourage her to use it when there's a problem, and that's what happened the night before last. I had to admit her in the end but not before she'd given me a few nasty moments.'

'I can't believe you give patients your home number.'

'Not every patient. But when the need is real...' She gave a shrug. 'It makes perfect sense from a management point of view. I'm the one with all the information. It means Chloe gets better care and her mother doesn't have to explain her history all the time.'

'You can't be there for everyone all the time. It isn't possible.'

'But continuity makes sense from a clinical point of view.' She frowned as she thought of it. 'In Chloe's case it means that a doctor unfamiliar with her case doesn't have to waste time taking details from a panicking parent when it's dark outside and the child can't breathe properly.'

'I can clearly see the benefits for your patients.' His eyes, dark and disturbingly intense, searched hers in a way that she found unsettling. 'But the benefits for you are less clear to me. It places an enormous demand on your time. On your life.'

'Yes, well, my job is important to me,' she said quickly, wondering whether there was anyone left in the world who felt the way she did about medicine. 'For me the job isn't about doing as little as possible and going home as early as possible. It's about involving yourself in the health of a community. About making a real difference to people's lives. I don't believe that a supermarket approach to health care is in anyone's interests.' She broke off and gave an awkward shrug, spots of colour touching her cheeks as she reflected on the fact that she was in danger of becoming carried away. 'Sorry. It's just something I feel strongly about. I don't expect you to understand. You probably think I'm totally mad.'

'On the contrary, I think your patients are very fortunate. But in all things there has to be compromise. How can you be awake to see patients—how can you be truly at your best—when you've been up half the night?' He strolled towards her and she felt her whole body tense in a response that she didn't understand.

She'd always considered herself to be taller than average but next to him she felt small. Even in heels she only reached his shoulder. Unable to help herself, she took a step backwards and then immediately wished she hadn't. 'You don't need to worry about me, Dr Moretti,' she said, keeping her tone cool and formal to compensate for her reaction. 'I'm not short of stamina and I really enjoy my life. And my patients certainly aren't suffering.'

'I'm sure they're not.' He gave a slow smile and raised an eyebrow. 'Does it make you feel safer, Alice?'

She took another step backwards. 'Does what make me feel safer?'

'Calling me Dr Moretti.' His expression was thoughtful. 'You do it whenever I get too close. Does it help give you the distance you need?'

She felt her heart pump harder. 'I don't know what you're talking about.'

'Was it a man?' He lifted a hand and tucked a strand of blonde hair behind her ear, his fingers lingering. 'Tell me, Alice. Was it a man who hurt you? Is that why you live alone and bury yourself in work? Is that why you don't believe in love?'

With a subtle movement that was entirely instinctive she moved her head away from his touch. 'You're obviously a romantic, Dr Moretti.'

'You're doing it again, *tesoro*,' he said softly, his hand

suspended in midair as he studied her face. 'Calling me Dr Moretti. It's Gio. And of course I'm romantic.'

'I'm sure you are.' She tilted her head, her smile mocking. 'All men are when it suits their purpose.'

He raised an eyebrow. 'You're suggesting that I use romance as some sort of seduction tool? You're a cynic, Alice, do you know that?'

Was it even worth defending herself? 'I'm a realist.' Her tone was cool. 'And you're clearly an extremely intelligent man. You should know better than to believe in all that woolly, emotional rubbish.'

'Ah, but you've overlooked one important fact about me.' His eyes gleamed dark and dangerous as he slid a hand under her chin and forced her to look at him. 'I'm Sicilian. We're a romantic race. It's in the blood. It has nothing to do with seduction and everything to do with a way of life. And a life is nothing without love in it.'

'Oh, please.' She rolled her eyes. 'I'm a scientist. I prefer to deal with the tangible. I happen to believe that love is a myth and the current divorce statistics would appear to support my view.'

'You think everything in this world can be explained given sufficient time in a laboratory?'

'Yes.' Her tone was cool and she brushed his hand away in a determined gesture. 'If it can't then it probably doesn't exist.'

'Is that right?' He looked at her as if he wanted to say something more but instead he smiled. 'So what do you do to relax around here? Restaurants? Watersports?'

For some reason her heart had set up a rhythmic pounding in her chest. 'I read a lot.'

'That sounds lonely, Dr Anderson,' he said softly. 'Especially for someone as young and beautiful as you.'

Taken aback and totally flustered, she raked a hand through her blonde hair and struggled for words. 'I—If you're flirting with me, Dr Moretti, it's only fair to warn you that you're wasting your time. I don't flirt. I don't play those sorts of games.'

'I wasn't flirting and I certainly wasn't playing games. I was stating a fact.' He said the words thoughtfully, his eyes narrowed as they scanned her face. 'You are beautiful. And very English. In Sicily, you would have to watch that pale skin.'

'Well, since I have no plans to visit Sicily, it isn't a problem that's likely to keep me awake at night.' Her head was buzzing and she felt completely on edge. There was something about him—something about the way he looked at her...

Deciding that the only way to end the conversation was to leave the room, she headed for the door.

'Wait. Don't run,' he said gently, his fingers covering hers before she could open the door.

His hand was hard. Strong. She turned, her heart pounding against her chest when she realised just how close he was.

'We have to meet Gina and—'

'What are you afraid of, Alice?'

'I'm not afraid. I'm just busy.' There was something in those dark eyes that brought a bubble of panic to her throat and her insides knotted with tension.

'You don't have to be guarded around me, Alice.' For a brief moment his fingers tightened on hers and then he let her go and took a step backwards, giving her the distance she craved. 'People interest me. There's often such a gulf between the person on the surface and the person underneath. It's rewarding to discover the real person.'

'Well, in my case there's nothing to discover, so don't waste your time.' She opened the door a crack. 'You're a good-looking guy, Dr Moretti, you don't need me to tell you that. I'm sure you can find no end of women willing to stroll on the beach with you, fall into bed, fall in love or do whatever it is you like to do in your spare time. You certainly don't need me. And now we need to meet Gina. She'll be waiting.'

CHAPTER SIX

GIO spent the rest of the day wondering about Alice. Wondering about her past.

She'd claimed that it hadn't been a man who'd forged her attitude to love, but it had to have been someone. In his experience, no one felt that strongly about relationships unless they'd been badly burned.

He tried to tell himself that it wasn't his business and that he wasn't interested. But he was interested. Very. And she filled his mind as he worked his way through a busy afternoon surgery.

The patients were a mix of locals and tourists and he handled them with ease and skill. Sore throats, arthritis, a diabetic who hadn't brought the right insulin on holiday and a nasty local reaction to an insect bite.

The locals lingered and asked questions. Where had he worked last? Had he bought a wife with him? Was he planning on staying long? The tourists were eager to leave the surgery and get on with their holiday.

Gio saw them all quickly and efficiently and handled the more intrusive questions as tactfully as possible, his mind distracted by thoughts of Alice. She was interesting, he mused as he checked glands and stared into throats. Interesting, beautiful and very serious.

Slightly prickly, wary, definitely putting up barriers. But underneath the front he sensed passion and vulnerability. He sensed that she was afraid.

He frowned slightly as he printed out a prescription for eye drops and handed it to his last patient.

There had been no mention of a social life in her description of relaxation. And David had definitely said that his partner had no time for anything other than work.

'You finished quickly today.' She walked into the room towards the end of the afternoon, just as his patient left. 'Any problems?'

'No. No problems so far.' He shook his head and leaned back in his chair. 'Should I have expected some?'

'People round here are congenitally nosy. You should have already realised that after twenty minutes in the company of the Normans this morning.' This time she stood near the door. Keeping a safe distance. 'This is a small, close-knit community and a new doctor is bound to attract a certain degree of attention. I bet they've been asking you no end of personal questions. Do you answer?'

'When it suits me. And when it doesn't…' he gave a shrug '…let's just say I was evasive. So, Dr Anderson, what next? I've asked about you but you haven't asked anything about me and you're probably the only one entitled to answers, given that we're working closely together.'

Their eyes met briefly and held for a long moment. Then she looked away. 'I've read your CV and that's all that matters. I'm not interested in the personal, Dr Moretti. Your life outside work is of no interest to me whatsoever. I really don't feel the need to know anything about you. You're doing your job. That's all I care about.'

Gio studied her in thoughtful silence. There was chemistry there. He'd felt it and he knew she'd felt it, too. Felt it and rejected it. Her face was shuttered. Closed. As if a protective shield had been drawn across her whole person.

Why?

'Make sure you have your key tonight because I have two house calls to make on the way home, so I'll be a bit late. Then I'm going to call at the supermarket and pick up the ingredients for a curry.' What exactly went into a curry? She knew she'd made it once before but she had no precise recollection of the recipe. 'How was the mother and baby clinic?'

'Fun. Interesting. But no Harriet.'

Alice frowned. 'Did you talk to Gina after our meeting?'

'At length. Interestingly enough, she's found it very hard to see Harriet. Every time she tries to arrange a visit Harriet makes an excuse, but she said that she'd sounded quite happy on the phone so she hasn't pushed. She thinks Harriet is just under a normal amount of strain for a new mother but she's promised to make another attempt at seeing her.'

'And what do you think?'

His gaze lifted to hers. 'After what I saw in the waiting room, I need to talk to her before I can answer that question.'

Alice grabbed her keys and popped her head into the nurse's room to say goodbye to Rita. 'I'm off. If Harriet comes to see you for anything in the next few days, make sure you encourage her to make an appointment with Dr Moretti.'

'I certainly will.' Rita returned a box of vaccines to the fridge and smiled. 'If you ask me, the man is a real find. Caring, warm and yet still incredibly masculine. You two have a nice evening together.'

'Don't you start. It isn't a date, Rita,' Alice said tightly. 'He's my lodger, thanks to Mary.'

Only somewhere along the way he'd forgotten his role. Lodgers weren't supposed to probe and delve and yet, from what she'd seen so far, Gio just couldn't help himself. Probing and delving seemed to be in his blood. Even with Harriet, he'd refused to take her insistence that she was fine at face value. Clearly he didn't intend to let the matter drop until he'd satisfied himself that she wasn't depressed.

Alice watched absently as Rita closed the fridge door. But, of course, at least where the patients were concerned, that was a good thing. It was his job to try and judge what was wrong with them. To pick up signs. Search for clues. To see past the obvious. She just didn't need him doing it with *her*.

'It's not Mary's fault the letting agency made a mess of things,' Rita said airily as she washed her hands. 'And if he were my lodger, I'd be thanking my lucky stars.'

'Well, you and I are different. And we both know that the letting agency wouldn't have made a mess of things without some significant help from certain people around here.' Alice put her hands on her hips and glared. 'And just for the record, in case you didn't get the message the first two hundred times, I don't need you to set me up with a man!'

'Don't you?' Rita dried her hands and dropped the paper towel in the bin. 'Strikes me you're not doing anything about it yourself.'

'Because, believe it or not, being with a man isn't compulsory!'

Reaching the point of explosion, Alice turned on her heel and strode out to her car before Rita had a chance to irritate her further. That day had been one long aggravation, she decided as she delved in her bag for her keys. All she wanted was to be left in peace to live her life the way she wanted to live it. What was so wrong with that?

Climbing into her car, she closed the door and shut her eyes.

Breathe, she told herself firmly, trying to calm herself down. Breathe. In and out. Relax.

Beside her, the door was pulled open. 'Alice, *tesoro,* are you all right?'

Her eyes opened. Gio was leaning into the car, his eyes concerned.

'I'm fine.' Gripping the wheel tightly, she wondered whether the sight of a GP screaming in a public place would attract attention. 'Or at least I will be fine when people stop interfering with my life and leave me alone. At least part of this is your fault.' She glared at him and his eyes narrowed.

'My fault?'

'Well, if you weren't single and good-looking, they wouldn't have been able to move you into my house.'

He rubbed a hand across his jaw and laughter flickered in his eyes. 'You want me to get married or rearrange my features?'

'No point. They'd just find some other poor individual to push my way.' Her tone gloomy, she slumped back in her seat and shook her head. 'Sorry, this really isn't your fault at all. It's just this place. Maybe David was right to get away. Right now I'd pay a lot to live among people who don't know who on earth I am and can't be bothered to find out. I must get going. I've got house calls to make on my way home.'

Unfortunately her car had other ideas. As she turned the key in the ignition the engine struggled and choked and then died.

'Oh, for crying out loud!' In a state of disbelief Alice glared at the car, as if fury alone should be enough to start it. 'What is happening to my life?'

Gio was still leaning on the open door. 'Do you often have problems with it?'

'Never before.' She tried the ignition again. 'My car is the only place I can get peace and quiet these days! The only place I can hide from people trying to pair me off with you! And now even that has died!'

'Shh.' He put a hand over her lips, his eyes amused. 'Calm down.'

'I can't calm down. I've got house calls to make and no transport.'

'I'm leaving now.' His tone was calm and reasonable as he gestured to the low, sleek sports car parked next to hers. 'We'll do the calls together.'

'But—'

'It makes perfect sense. It will help me orientate myself a little.'

'What's happening?' Mary hurried up, a worried expression on her face. 'Is it your car?'

'Yes.' Alice hissed the word through gritted teeth. 'It's my car.'

'Give me the keys and I'll get it taken care of,' Mary said immediately, holding out her hand. 'I'll call Paul at the garage. He's a genius with cars. In the meantime, you go with Dr Moretti.'

A nasty suspicion unfolded like a bud inside her. 'Mary...' Alice shook her head and decided she was becoming paranoid. No matter how much Mary wanted to push her towards Gio, she wasn't capable of tampering with a car. 'All right. Thanks.'

Accepting defeat, she climbed out of her car, handed the keys to Mary and slid into Gio's black sports car.

He pressed a button and the roof above her disappeared in a smooth movement.

She rolled her eyes. 'Show-off.'

He gave her a boyish grin, slid sunglasses over his eyes and reversed out of the parking space.

The last thing she saw as they pulled out of the surgery car park was the smug expression on Mary's face.

He drove up the hill, away from the harbour, with Alice giving directions.

'I'm embarrassed turning up at house calls in this car,' she mumbled as they reached the row of terraced houses where Edith lived. 'It's hardly subtle, is it? Everyone will think I've gone mad.'

'They will be envious and you will give them something interesting to talk about. Is this the lady that Betty was talking about earlier?' Gio brought the car to a halt and switched off the engine.

'Yes. Edith Carne.' Alice reached for her bag. 'She's

one of David's patients but she had a fall a few weeks ago and I just want to check on her because she lives on her own and she's not one to complain. You don't have to come with me. You're welcome to wait in the car. Who knows? Keep the glasses on and you might get lucky with some passing female.'

'But I am already lucky,' he said smoothly, leaning across to open the door for her, 'because you are in my car, *tesoro*.'

She caught the wicked twinkle in his dark eyes and pulled a face. 'Save the charm, Romeo. It's wasted on me.' She climbed out of the car and walked towards the house, her hair swinging around her shoulders, frustration still bubbling inside her.

'If she's David's patient, she's going to be mine,' Gio pointed out as he caught up with her, 'so this is as good a time as any to make her acquaintance. It's logical.'

It was logical, but still she would have rather he'd waited in the car. Having him tailing her flustered her and put her on edge. She needed space to calm herself. Normally she loved her work and found it absorbing and relaxing but today she felt restless and unsettled, as if the door to her tidy, ordered life had been flung wide open.

And it was all thanks to Mary and Rita, she thought angrily, and their interfering ways.

If she hadn't been living with the man, she could have easily avoided him. The surgery was so busy that often their paths didn't often cross during the day.

The evenings were a different matter.

Pushing aside feelings that she didn't understand, she rang the doorbell and waited. 'Her husband died three years ago,' she told Gio, 'and they were married for fifty-two years.'

He raised an eyebrow. 'And you don't believe in love?'

'There are lots of reasons why two people stay together.' She tilted her head back and stared up at the bedroom window through narrowed eyes. 'But love doesn't come into it, in my opinion. Why isn't she answering?'

'Does she have family?'

'No. But she has lots of friends in the village. She's lived here all her life.' Alice rang the bell again, an uneasy feeling spreading through her.

'Why did she fall last time? Does anyone know?'

'I don't think they found anything. The neighbour called an ambulance. She had a few cuts and bruises but nothing broken. But I know David was worried about her.' And now she was worried, too. Why wasn't Edith answering the door? She sighed and jammed her fingers through her hair. 'All right. I suppose I'll have to go next door and get the key, but I hate the thought of doing that.' Hated the thought of invading another person's privacy.

'Could she have gone out?' Gio stepped across the front lawn and glanced in through the front window. 'I can hear voices. A television maybe? But I can't see anyone.'

Alice was on the point of going next door to speak to the neighbour when the door opened.

'Oh, Edith.' She gave a smile of relief as she saw the old lady standing there. 'We were worried about you. We thought you might have fallen again. I wanted to check on how you're feeling.'

'Well, that's kind of you but I'm fine, dear.' Edith was wearing a dressing-gown even though it was late afternoon, and the expression on her face was bemused. 'No problems at all.'

Alice scanned Edith's face, noting that she looked extremely pale and tired. Something wasn't right.

'Can I come in for a minute, Edith? I'd really like to have a chat and check that everything's all right with you. And I need to introduce you to our new doctor.' She flapped a hand towards Gio. 'He's taken over from David. Come all the way from Sicily. Land of *canolli* and volcanoes that misbehave.'

'Sicily? Frank and I went there once. It was beautiful.' Edith's knuckles whitened on the edge of the door. 'I'm fine, Dr Anderson. I don't need to waste your time. There's plenty worse off than me.'

'Consider it a favour to me.' Gio's voice was deep and heavily accented. 'I am new to the area, Mrs Carne. I need inside information and I understand you've lived here all your life.'

'Well, I have, but—'

'Please—I would be so grateful.' He spread his hands, his warm smile irresistible to any female, and Edith looked into his dark eyes and capitulated.

'All right, but I'm fine. Completely fine.'

At least Gio used his charm on the old as well as the young, Alice thought as they followed Edith into the house. Wondering whether she was the only one who felt that something wasn't right, she glanced at Gio but his attention was focused on the old lady.

'This is a lovely room.' His eyes scanned the ancient, rose-coloured sofa and the photographs placed three deep on the window-sill. 'I can see that it is filled with happy memories.'

'I was born in this house.' Edith sat down, folded her hands in her lap and stared at the empty fireplace. 'My parents died in this house and Frank and I carried on living here. I've lived here all my life. I can see the sea from my kitchen window.'

'It's a beautiful position.' Gio leaned towards a photograph displayed on a table next to his right hand. 'This is you? Was it taken in the garden of this house?'

Edith gave a nod and a soft smile. 'With my parents. I was five years old.' She stared wistfully at the photo, her hands clasped in her lap. 'The garden was different then, of course. My Frank loved the garden. I used to joke that he loved his plants more than me.'

Gio lifted the photo and took a closer look. 'It must be lovely to walk in the garden that he planted.'

Alice shifted impatiently in her chair. What was he talking about? And why wasn't he asking Edith questions about her blood pressure and whether she'd felt dizzy lately? What was the relevance of the garden, for goodness' sake?

Edith was staring at him, a strange expression in her eyes. 'Very few people understand how personal a garden can be.'

'A garden tells you so much about a person,' Gio agreed, replacing the photo carefully on the table. 'And being there, you share in their vision.'

Edith twisted her hands in her lap. 'Just walking there makes me feel close to him.'

Alice frowned, wondering where the conversation was leading. True, Edith was much more relaxed than she'd been when they'd arrived and she had to admit that Gio had a way with people, but why were they talking about gardening? She wanted to establish some facts. She wanted to find out whether Edith had suffered another fall but Gio seemed to be going down an entirely different path.

She forced herself to sit quietly and breathed an inaudible sigh of relief when Gio eventually steered the talk round to the topic of Edith's health. It was so skillfully done that it seemed like a natural direction for the conversation.

'I can barely remember the fall now,' Edith said dismissively, 'it was so long ago.'

'A month, Edith,' Alice reminded her, and the old lady sniffed, all the tension suddenly returning to her slim frame.

'I was just clumsy. Not looking where I was going. Tripped over the carpet. It won't happen again—I'm being really careful.'

Alice glanced around the room. The carpet was fitted. There were no rugs. The carpet in the hall and on the stairs had been fitted, too. Her eyes clashed with Gio's and she knew that he'd noticed the same thing.

'Can I just check your pulse and blood pressure?' He opened his bag and removed the necessary equipment. 'Just routine.'

'I suppose so…'

Gio pushed up the sleeve of her dressing-gown and paused. 'That's a nasty bruise on your arm,' he commented as he wrapped the blood-pressure cuff around her arm. 'Did you knock yourself?'

Edith didn't look at him. 'Just being a bit careless walking through the doorway.'

Without further comment Gio checked her pulse, blood

pressure and pulse and then eased the stethoscope out of his ears. 'When you went into hospital after your fall, did anyone say that your blood pressure was on the low side?'

Edith shook her head. 'Not that I remember. They just sent me home and told me they'd set up another appointment in a few months. I'm fine. Really I am. But it was good of you to call in.' She stood up, the movement quite agitated. 'I'll come to the surgery if I need any help. Good of you to introduce yourself.'

Not giving them a chance to linger, she hurried them out of the front door and closed it.

'Well.' Standing on the doorstep, staring at a closed door, Alice blinked in amazement. 'What was all that about? She's normally the most hospitable woman in the community. From her reaction today, you would have thought we were planning to take her away and lock her up.'

'I think that's exactly what she thought.' Gio turned and walked down the path towards his car.

'What do you mean?' She caught up with him in a few strides. 'You're not making sense.'

He unlocked the car doors. 'I think your Mrs Carne has had more falls since David saw her. But she isn't ready to confess.' He slid into the car while Alice gaped at him from the pavement.

'But why?' It seemed simple to Alice. 'If she's falling then she should tell us and we'll try and solve it.'

The engine gave a throaty roar and he drummed long fingers on the steering-wheel while he waited for her to get into the passenger seat. 'Life isn't always that simple, is it?'

She climbed in next to him and fastened her seat belt. 'So why wouldn't she tell us?'

'General practice is very like detective work, don't you think?' He glanced towards her. 'In hospital you see only the patient. At home you have the advantage of seeing the patient in their own environment and that often contains clues about the person they are. About the way they live their lives.'

'And what clues did you see?'

'That her whole life is contained in that house. There were photographs of her parents, her as a child, her husband. There were cushions that she'd knitted on a sofa that I'm willing to bet belonged to her mother. The garden had been planted by her husband.'

Alice tried to grasp the relevance of what he was saying and failed. 'But that's all emotional stuff. What's that got to do with her illness?'

'Not everything about a patient can be explained by science alone, Alice.' He checked the rear-view mirror and pulled out. 'She doesn't want us to know she's falling because she's afraid we're going to insist she leaves her home. And she loves her home. Her home is everything to her. It contains all her memories. Take her from it and you erase part of her life. Probably the only part that matters.'

He was doing it again, Alice mused, delving deep. Refusing to accept people at face value.

She stared ahead as he drove off down the quiet road and back onto the main road. 'Take a left here,' she said absently, her mind still on their conversation. 'Aren't you making it complicated? I mean, if Edith is falling, we need to find the reason. It's that simple. The rest isn't really anything to do with us.'

'The rest is everything to do with us if it affects the patient. You're very afraid of emotions, aren't you, Alice?' His voice was soft and she gave a frown.

'We're not talking about me.'

'Of course we're not.' There was no missing the irony in his tone but she chose to ignore it.

'So now what do we do?'

'I want to check on a couple of things. Look at the correspondence that came out of her last appointment and speak to the doctor who saw her before I go crashing in with my diagnosis.'

'Which is?' The wind picked up a strand of hair and blew it across her face. 'You think you know why she's falling?'

'Not for sure, no. But certainly there are clues.' He eased the car round a tight corner, his strong hands firm on the wheel. 'Her heart rate is on the slow side and her blood pressure is low. What do you know about CSS?'

'Carotid sinus syndrome. I remember reading a UK study on it a few years ago.' Alice sifted through her memory and her brow cleared. 'They linked it to unex-plained falls in the elderly. It can result in syncope—fainting. Are you saying that you think—?' She broke off and Gio gave a shrug that betrayed his Latin heritage.

'I don't know for sure, of course, but it's certainly worth considering. It's important that elderly patients who fall are given cardiovascular assessment. Do you think this happened in her case?'

'Not to my knowledge. We'll check the notes and, if not, we'll refer her immediately.' The wind teased her hair again and Alice slid a hand through the silky strands and tried to anchor them down. 'Well done. That was very smart of you. And all that stuff about her house and the way she was feeling…' She frowned, angry and disappointed with herself. 'I wouldn't have thought of that.'

'That's because you work only with facts and not emotions, but the truth is that the two work together. You can't dissociate them from each other, Alice. Emotions are a part of people's lives.' He gave her a quick glance, a slight smile touching his mouth, a challenge in his dark eyes. 'And she was definitely in love with her husband.'

She tipped her head back against the seat and rolled her eyes upwards. 'Don't let's go there again.'

'You heard the way she talked about him. You saw the look on her face. Do you really think she didn't love him?'

'Well, obviously you're going to miss someone if you've lived with them for over fifty years,' Alice said tetchily, 'and I'm sure they were best friends. I just don't believe in this special, indefinable, woolly emotion that supposedly binds two people together.'

'You don't believe in love at first sight?'

'Nor on second or third sight,' Alice said dryly, letting go of her hair and pointing a finger towards a turning. 'You need to take a right down there so that I can pick up some dinner.'

He followed her instructions and turned into the supermarket car park. 'Listen, about dinner. You cooked last night. Perhaps I ought to—'

'No need. I've got it. Back in five minutes.' She slammed the door and braced herself for her second least favourite pastime after cooking. Shopping for the ingredients.

* * *

Later, wondering whether his taste buds would ever recover, Gio drank yet another glass of water in an attempt to quench the fire burning in his mouth. 'Alice, tomorrow it's my turn to cook.'

'Why would you want to do that?'

Was it all right to be honest? He gave a wry smile and risked it. 'Because I want to live?'

Because he respected his stomach far too much to eat another one of her meals and because he needed to show her that there was more to eating than simply ingesting animal and plant material in any format.

She sighed and dropped her fork. 'All right, it tasted pretty awful but I'm not that great at curry. I think I might have got my tablespoons mixed up with my teaspoons. Does it really matter?'

'When you're measuring chilli powder? Yes,' he replied dryly. 'And, anyway, I'm very happy to cook from now on. I love to cook. I'll do you something Italian. You'll enjoy it.'

She pushed her plate away, the contents only half-eaten. 'We eat to live, Gio, not the other way round. The body needs protein, carbohydrate, fats and all that jazz in order to function the way it should. It doesn't care how you throw them together.'

She was all fact, he thought to himself. All fact and science. As far as she was concerned, if it couldn't be explained by some fancy theory then it didn't exist.

It would be fun to show her just what could be achieved with food, he decided. And atmosphere.

At least she'd stopped jumping every time he walked into the room. It was time to make some changes. Time to push her out of her comfort zone.

He tapped his foot under the table, his mind working. Maybe it was time to show Dr Alice Anderson that there was more to life than scientific theory. That not every-thing could be proven.

Maybe it was time for her to question her firmly held beliefs. But before that he needed to deal with his indigestion.

'Let's go for a walk on the beach.'

She shook her head and dumped the remains of the totally inedible curry in the bin. 'I need to catch up on some reading. You go. Take a left at the bottom of the garden, along the cycle path for about two hundred metres and you reach the harbour. Go to the end and you drop straight down onto the beach. You can walk for miles if the tide is out. Once it comes in you have to scramble up the cliffs to the coast path.'

'I want you to come with me.' Not giving her a chance to shrink away from him, he reached out a hand and dragged her to her feet. 'The reading can wait.'

'I really need to…' Her hand wriggled in his as she tried to pull away, but he kept a tight hold and used his trump card. Work.

'I want to talk about some of David's patients.' He kept his expression serious. Tried to look suitably con-cerned. 'It's obvious to me that the only time we're going to have for discussion is during the evenings. And I have so many questions.'

He struggled to think of a few, just in case he needed to produce one.

'Oh.' She thought for a moment and then gave a shrug. 'Well, I suppose that makes sense, but we don't have to go out. We could do it here and—'

'Alice, we've been trapped inside all day. We both need some air.' Letting go of her hand, he reached out and grabbed her jacket from the back of the door. 'Let's walk.'

'Have you come across a specific problem with a patient? Who is on your mind?'

He racked his brains to find someone to talk about, knowing that if he didn't start talking about work immediately, she'd vanish upstairs and spend the rest of the evening with her journals and textbooks, as she had the previous evening.

'I thought we could talk about the right way to approach Harriet.' He stepped through the back door and waited while she locked it. 'You know her after all.'

'Not that well. She was David's patient. Mary knows her, she might have some ideas.'

She slipped the keys into her pocket and they walked down to the cycle way. Although it was still only early evening, several cyclists sped past them, enjoying the summer weather and the wonderful views.

The tide was far out, leaving sandbanks exposed in the water.

'It's beautiful.' Gio stared at the islands of sand and Alice followed his gaze.

'Yes. And dangerous. The tide comes in so fast, it's lethal.' She stepped to one side to avoid another cyclist. 'There are warnings all over the harbour and the beach, but still some tourists insist on dicing with death. Still, it keeps the lifeboat busy.'

They reached the harbour and weaved a path through the crowds of tourists who were milling around, watching the boats and eating fish and chips on the edge of the quay.

Gio slipped a hand in his pocket. 'Ice cream, Dr Anderson?'

'I don't eat ice cream.' She was looking around her with a frown. 'Bother. We shouldn't have come this way.'

'Why not?'

'Because I've just seen at least half a dozen people who know me.'

'And what's wrong with that?' He strolled over to the nearest ice-cream shop and scanned the menu. Vanilla? Too boring. Strawberry? Too predictable.

'Because if I've seen them, then they've seen me.' She turned her head. 'With you.'

'Ah.' Cappuccino, he decided. 'And surely that's a good thing.'

'Why would fuelling town gossip possibly be a good thing?'

'Because you want to prove that you don't want a re-lationship.' He wandered into the shop and ordered two cones. 'In order to do that, you at least have to be seen to be mixing with members of the opposite sex. If you do that and still don't fall in love then eventually every-one will just give up trying. If you don't, they'll just keep fixing you up.'

She glared at him and he realised that the lady selling the ice creams was listening avidly.

'Perfect evening for a walk, Dr Anderson. We don't see you in here often enough. That will be three pounds forty, please.' The woman took the money with a smile and turned to Gio. 'You must be our new doctor. Betty told me all about you.'

'That's good. Saves me introducing myself.' Gio pocketed the change and picked up the ice creams with a nod of thanks and a few more words of small talk.

Outside he handed a cone to Alice.

'I said I didn't want one.'

'Just try it. One lick.'

'It's—'

'It's protein, Dr Anderson.' He winked at her and she raised an eyebrow.

'How do you work that out?'

'All that clotted cream.' He watched, noting with satisfaction the smile that teased the corners of her mouth. He was going to teach her to relax. To loosen up. To enjoy herself.

'It's a frozen lump of saturated fat designed to occlude arteries,' she said crisply, and he nodded.

'Very possibly. But it's also a mood lifter. An indulgence. A sensory experience. Smooth. Cold. Creamy. Try it.'

She stared at him. 'It's ice cream, Gio. Just ice cream.' She waved a hand dismissively and almost consigned the ice cream to the gutter. 'The body doesn't need ice cream in order to function efficiently.'

'The body may not *need* ice cream,' he conceded, 'but it's extremely grateful to receive it. Try it and find out. Go on—lick.'

With an exaggerated roll of her eyes she licked the cone. And licked again. 'All right, so it tastes good. But that's just because of the coffee. You know I love coffee.' The evening sunlight caught the gold in her hair and her blue eyes were alight with humour. 'It's my only vice.'

Looking at the way her mouth moved over the ice cream, he decided that before the summer was finished Alice would have expanded her repertoire of vices. And he was going to help her do it.

'Lick again and close your eyes,' he urged her, ignoring the fact that his own ice cream was in grave danger of melting.

She stared at him as if he were mad. 'Gio, I'm not closing my eyes with half the town watching! I have to work with these people long after you've gone! I need to retain my credibility. If I stand in the harbour with my eyes closed, licking ice cream, they'll never listen to me again.'

'Stop trying to be so perfect all the time. And stop worrying about other people.' She was delightfully prim, he thought, noticing the tiny freckles on her nose for the first time. He doubted she'd ever let her hair down in her life.

And he was absolutely crazy about her.

The knowledge knocked the breath from his lungs. 'Close your eyes, or I'll throw you in the harbour.' His voice was gruff. 'And that will seriously damage your credibility.'

How could he possibly be in love with a woman he'd only known for a couple of days?

'Oh, fine!' With an exaggerated movement she squeezed her eyes shut and he stepped closer, tempted by the slight pout of her lips.

Suppressing the desire to kiss her until her body melted like the ice cream in her hand, he reminded himself that it was too soon for her.

He was going to take it slowly. Take his time. *Coax her out of her shell.*

'Now lick again and tell me what you taste. Tell me what it makes you feel. What it reminds you of.'

Her lick was most definitely reluctant. 'Ice cream?' Receiving no response to her sarcasm, she licked again and he waited. And waited. But she said nothing.

'Don't you go straight back to your childhood?' He decided that he was going to have to prompt her. Clearly she'd never played this game before. 'Seaside holidays, relaxation? All the fun of being young?'

There was a long silence and then her eyes opened and for a brief moment he saw the real Alice. And what he saw shocked and silenced him. He saw pain and anguish. He saw hurt and disillusionment. But most of all he saw a child who was lost and vulnerable. Alone.

And then she blanked it.

'No, Dr Moretti.' Her voice had a strange, rasping quality, as if talking was suddenly difficult. 'I don't see that. And I'm not that keen on ice cream.' Without giving him time to reply, she tossed it in the nearest bin and made for the beach, virtually breaking into a run in her attempt to put distance between them.

CHAPTER SEVEN

AT THE bottom of the path, Alice slowed her pace and took several gulps of air. Her stomach churned and she felt light-headed and sick but most of all she felt angry with herself for losing control.

Oh, damn, damn damn.

How could she have let that happen? How could she have revealed so much? And because she had, *because she'd been so stupid,* he was going to come after her and demand an explanation. He was that sort of man. The sort of man who always looked beneath the surface. The sort of man who delved and dug until he had access to all parts of a person.

And she didn't want him delving. She didn't want him digging.

She bent down, removed her shoes and stepped onto the sand, intending to walk as far as possible, as fast as possible. *Even though she knew that even if she were to run, it wouldn't make any difference.* The problems were inside her and always would be, and she knew from experience that running couldn't change the past. Couldn't change the feelings that were part of her.

But she'd learned ways to handle them, she reminded

herself firmly as she breathed in deeply and unclenched her hands. Ways that worked for her. It was just a question of getting control back. Of being the person she'd become.

She stared at the sea, watching the yachts streak across the bay, the wind filling their brightly coloured sails. Breathing in the same strong sea breeze, she struggled to find the familiar feeling of calm, but it eluded her.

She was concentrating so hard on breathing that the feel of Gio's hand on her shoulder made her jump, even though she'd been expecting it.

Her instinct was to push him away, but that would draw attention that she didn't want. She could have run but that, she told herself, would just make it even harder later. It would just delay the inevitable conversation. So she decided to stay put and give him enough facts to satisfy him. Just enough and no more.

She turned to face him and dislodged his hand in the process. Immediately she wished she'd thought to wear sunglasses. Or a wide-brimmed hat. Anything to give her some protection from that searching, masculine gaze.

She felt exposed. Naked.

Wishing she'd decided to run, she hugged herself with her arms and looked away, gesturing towards the beach with a quick jerk of her head. 'You can walk along here for about an hour before the tide turns.' The words spilled out like girlish chatter. 'Then you have to climb up to the coast path if you don't want to get cut off.'

'Alice—'

'It's a nice walk and you always lose the crowds about ten minutes out of the harbour.' The wind picked up a strand of her hair and threw it across her face, but she ignored it. 'It will take you about an hour and a half to reach the headland.'

He stepped closer and his hands closed over her arms. 'Alice, don't!' He gave her a little shake. 'Don't shut me out like this. I said something to upset you and for that I'm sorry.'

'You don't need to be sorry. You haven't done anything wrong.' She tilted her head back and risked another glance at his face. And saw kindness. Kindness and sympathy. The combination untwisted something that had been knotted inside her for years and she very nearly let everything spill out. Very nearly told him exactly how she was feeling. But she stopped herself. Reminded herself of how she'd chosen to live her life. 'I just don't happen to like ice cream that much.'

'Alice...' He tried to hold her but she shrugged him off, swamped by feelings that she didn't want to feel.

'I'm sorry, but I need to walk.'

He muttered something in Italian and then switched to English. 'Alice, wait!' With his long stride, he caught up with her easily. 'We need to talk.' His Italian accent was stronger than ever, as if he was struggling with the language.

'We don't need to talk.' She walked briskly along the sand, her shoes in one hand, the other holding her hair out of her eyes. This far up the beach the sand was soft and warm, cushioning the steady rhythm of her feet and causing her to stumble occasionally. 'I don't want to talk! Not everyone wants to talk about everything, Gio.'

'Because you're afraid of your own emotions. Of being hurt. That's why you prefer facts.' He strode next to her, keeping pace. 'You've turned yourself into a machine, Alice, but emotions are the oil that makes the machine work. Human beings can't function without emotions.'

She walked faster in an attempt to escape the conversation. 'You don't need to get into my skin and understand me. And I don't need healing.'

'Most people need healing from something, Alice. It's—*Dios,* can you stop walking for a moment?' Reaching out, he grabbed her shoulders and turned her, his fingers firm on her flesh as he held her still. 'Stop running and have a conversation. Is that really so frightening?'

'You want facts? All right, I'll give you the facts. You and Edith obviously have lots of happy childhood memories. I don't.' Her heart thumped steadily against her chest as her past spilled into her present. 'It's as simple as that. Ice cream doesn't remind me of happy holidays, Gio. It reminds me of bribes. A way of persuading me to like my mother's latest boyfriend. A way of occupying me for ten minutes while my father spent romantic time with his latest girlfriend. Ice cream was a salve to the conscience while they told me I needed to live in a different place for a while because I was getting in the way of *"love"*.' Her heart was beating, her palms were sweaty and feelings of panic bubbled up inside her. Feelings that she hadn't had for a very long time.

Gio sucked in a breath. 'This was your childhood?'

'Sometimes I was a ping-pong ball, occasionally I was a pawn but mostly I was just a nuisance.'

'And now?' He frowned and his grip on her arms tightened. 'Your parents are divorced?'

'Oh, several times. Not just the once.' She knew her tone was sarcastic and brittle but she couldn't do anything about it. Couldn't be bothered to hide it any more. Maybe if he understood the reasons for the way she was, he'd leave her alone. 'You know what they say—practice makes perfect. My parents had plenty of practice. They are quite expert at divorce.'

His eyes were steady on her face. Searching. 'And you?'

'Me? I survived.' She spread her hands. 'Here I am. In one piece.'

He shook his head. 'Not in one piece. Your belief in love has been shattered. They took that from you with their selfish behaviour.' He lifted a hand and touched her cheek. 'My beautiful Alice.'

Her breathing hitched in her throat and her shoulders stiffened. 'Don't feel sorry for me. I like my life. I don't need fairy-tales to be happy.' She tensed still further as he slid a hand over her cheek, his thumb stroking gently. 'What are you doing?'

'Offering you comfort. A hug goes a long way to making things better, don't you think?' His voice was soft. 'Touch is important.'

'I'm not used to being touched.' She stood rigid, not moving a muscle. 'I don't like being touched.'

'Then you need more practice. Everyone likes being touched, as long as it's in the right way.'

He was too close and it made her feel strange. His voice made her feel strange.

'Enough.' Shaken and flustered, she took a step backwards. Broke the contact. 'You just can't help it, can you? I've only known you for a short time but during that time I've seen how you always have to dig and delve into a person's life.'

'Because the answers to questions often lie below the surface.'

She scraped her hair out of her eyes. 'Well, I don't need you to delve and I don't want you to dig. There are no questions about my life that you need to answer. I'm not one of your patients with emotional needs.'

'Everyone has emotional needs, Alice.'

'Well, I don't. And I don't have to explain myself to you! And I don't need you to understand me. I didn't ask to take this walk and I didn't ask for your company. If you don't like the way I am then you can go back to the house.'

'I like the way you are, *cara mia.*' Without warning or hesitation, his hands cupped her face and he brought his mouth down on hers, his kiss warm and purposeful.

Alice stood there, frozen with shock while his mouth moved over hers, coaxing, tempting, growing more demanding, and suddenly a tiny, icy part of herself started to melt. The warmth started to spread and grew in intensity until she felt something explode inside her. Something delicious and exciting that she'd never felt before.

Feeling oddly disconnected, she tried to summon up logic and reason. *Any minute now she was going to pull away.* But his arms slid round her, his hold strong and powerful, and still his mouth plundered and stole the breath from her body. *She was going to punch him somewhere painful.* But his fingers stroked her cheek and his tongue teased and danced and coaxed a response that she'd never given to any man before.

In the end it was Gio who suspended the kiss. 'My Alice.' He lifted his head just enough to breathe the words against her mouth. 'They hurt you badly, *tesoro.*'

She felt dazed. Drugged. Unable to speak or think. She tried to open her eyes but her eyelids felt heavy, and as for her knees—hadn't David said something about knees?

'Dr Anderson!' A sharp young voice from directly behind her succeeded where logic had not. Her eyes opened and she pulled away, heart thumping, cheeks flaming.

'Henry?' Her voice cracked as she turned to acknowledge the ten-year-old boy behind her. Flustered and embarrassed, she stroked a hand over her cheeks in an attempt to calm herself down. 'What's the matter?'

Henry pointed, his expression frantic. 'They're cut off, Dr Anderson. The tide's turning.'

Beside her, Gio ran a hand over the back of his neck and she had the satisfaction of seeing that he was no more composed than she was.

For a brief, intense moment their eyes held and then she turned her attention back to Henry, trying desperately to concentrate on what he was saying.

And it was obviously something important. He was hopping on the spot, his expression frantic, his arms waving wildly towards the sea.

'Who is cut off from what?' She winced inwardly as she listened to herself. Since when had she been unable to form words properly? To focus on a problem in hand?

'The twins. They were playing.'

'Twins?' Alice shielded her eyes from the evening sun and stared out across the beach, her eyes drawn to two tiny figures playing on a small, raised patch of sand. All around them the sea licked and swirled, closing off their route back to the beach. They were on a sand spit and the tide was turning. 'Oh, no…'

Finally she understood what Henry had been trying to tell her and she slid her hand in her pocket and reached for her mobile phone even as she started to run towards the water. 'I'll call the coastguard. Where's their mother, Henry? Have you seen Harriet?' She was dialling as she spoke, her finger shaking as she punched in the numbers, aware that Gio was beside her, stripping off as he ran.

The boy shook his head, breathless. 'They were on their own, I think.'

Alice spoke to the coastguard, her communication brief and succinct, and then broke the connection and glanced around her. They couldn't possibly have been on their own. They were five years old. Harriet was a good mother. She wouldn't have left them.

And then she saw her, carrying the baby and weighed down by paraphernalia, walking along the beach and calling for the twins. Searching. She hadn't seen them. Hadn't seen the danger. And Alice could hear the frantic worry in her voice as she called.

'You go to Harriet, I'll get the twins,' Gio ordered, running towards the sea, his long, muscular legs closing the distance.

The tide was still far out but she knew how fast it came in, how quickly those tempting little sand spits disappeared under volumes of seawater.

She ran with him, aware that Henry was keeping up with them. 'Henry, go to the cliff and get us a line.' She barked out the instruction, her throat dry with fear, her heart pounding. 'You know the line with the lifebuoy.' She knew the dangers of entering the water without a buoyancy aid. 'Gio, wait. You have to wait. You can't just go in there.'

For a moment the kiss was forgotten. The ice cream was forgotten. Nothing mattered except the urgency of the moment. Two little boys in mortal danger. *The weight of responsibility.*

'In a few more minutes those children will be out of reach.'

Alice grabbed his arm as they ran. Tried to slow him. Tried to talk sense into him. The sand was rock hard now as they approached the water's edge and then finally she felt the damp lick of the sea against her toes and stopped. 'You're not going into that water without a line. Do you know how many people drown in these waters, trying to save others?' Her eyes skimmed his body, noticed the hard, well-formed muscles. He had the body of an athlete and at the moment it was clad only in a pair of black boxer shorts.

'Stop giving me facts, Alice.' His expression was grim. 'They're five years old,' he said roughly, 'and they're not going to stand like sensible children on that spit of sand and wait to be rescued. What do you want me to do? Watch while they drown? Watch while they die?' Concern thickened his accent and she shook her head.

'No, but—'

'Get me a buoyancy aid and go to Harriet,' he urged as he stepped into the water. He caught her arm briefly, his eyes on her face. 'And remember emotions when you talk to her, Alice. It isn't always about facts.'

He released her and Alice swallowed and cast a frantic glance up the coast. She knew the lifeboat would come from that direction. Or maybe the coastguard would send the helicopter. Either way, she knew they needed to hurry.

From the moment he plunged into the water she could see that Gio was a strong swimmer, but she knew that the tides in this part of the bay were lethal and she knew that it would only take minutes for the water level to rise. Soon the spit of sand that was providing the twins with sanctuary would vanish from under their feet.

She could hear them screaming and crying and closed her eyes briefly. And then she heard Harriet's cry of horror.

'Oh, my God—my babies.' The young mother covered her mouth with her hand, her breathing so rapid that Alice was afraid she might faint.

'Harriet—try and stay calm.' *What a stupid, useless thing to say to a mother whose two children were in danger of drowning.* She took refuge in facts, as she always did. 'We've called the coastguard and Dr Moretti is going to swim out to them. Henry Fox is getting the buoyancy aid.'

'Neither of them can swim,' Harriet gasped, her eyes wild with panic, and Alice remembered what Gio had said about remembering emotions.

She swallowed and felt helpless. She just wasn't in tune with other people's emotions. She wasn't comfortable. What would Gio say? Certainly not that the ability to swim wouldn't save the twins in the lethal waters of Smuggler's Cove.

'They don't need to swim because the coastguard is going to be here in a moment,' she said finally, jabbing her fingers into her hair and wishing she was better with words. She just didn't know the right things to say. And then she remembered what Gio had said about touch. Hesitantly she stepped closer to Harriet and slipped an arm round her shoulders.

Instantly Harriet turned towards her and clung. 'Oh, Dr Anderson, this is all my fault. I'm a useless mother. Terrible.'

Caught in the full flood of Harriet's emotion, Alice froze and wished for a moment that she'd been the one to go in the water. She would have been much better at dealing with tides than with an emotional torrent.

'You're a brilliant mother, Harriet,' she said firmly. 'The twins are beautifully mannered, tidy, the baby is fed—'

'But that isn't really what being a mother is,' Harriet sniffed, still clinging to Alice. 'A childminder can do any of those things. Being a mother is noticing what your child really needs. It's the fun stuff. The interaction. And I'm so tired, I just can't do any of it. They wanted to go to the beach so I took them, but I was too tired to actually play with them so I sat feeding the baby and then I just lost sight of them and they wandered off.'

Alice watched as Gio climbed onto another sand spit. Between him and the twins was one more strip of water. Treacherous water.

And then she heard the clack, clack, clack of an approaching helicopter and breathed a sigh of relief. Gio didn't even need to cross the water now. The coastguard could—

'No! Oh, no, don't try and get in the water,' Harriet shrieked, moving away from Alice and running towards the water's edge. 'Oh, Dr Anderson, my Dan is trying to get into the water.'

Gio saw it too and shouted something to the boys before diving into the sea to cross the last strip of water. He used a powerful front crawl but even so Alice could see that he was being dragged sideways by the fast current.

It was only after he pulled himself safely onto the strip of sand that Alice realised that her fingernails had cut into her palms.

She saw him lift one of the twins and take the other by the hand, holding them firmly while the coastguard helicopter hovered in position above them.

The sand was gradually disappearing as the tide swirled and reclaimed the land, and a crowd of onlookers had gathered on the beach and were watching the drama unfold.

Alice bit her lip hard. The helicopter crew would rescue them all. Of course they would.

Still with her arm round Harriet, she watched as the winchman was lowered down to the sand to collect the first child.

The baby was screaming in Harriet's arms but she just jiggled it vaguely, all her attention focused on her twins.

'Let me take her.' Alice reached across and took the baby and Harriet walked into the sea, yearning to get to the boys. 'Hold it, Harriet.' With a soft curse Alice held the baby with one arm and used the other to grab Harriet and hold her back. 'Just wait. They're fine now. Nothing's going to happen to them.' Providing the coastguard managed to pick up the second child and Gio before the tide finally closed over the rapidly vanishing sand spit.

Discovering new depths of tension within herself, Alice watched helplessly as the winchman guided the first child safely into the helicopter and then went down for the second.

By now Gio's feet were underwater and he was

holding the child high in his arms, safely away from the dangerous lick of the sea.

The helicopter held its position, the crowd on the beach grew and there was a communal sigh of relief as the winchman picked up the second child, attached the harness and then guided him safely into the helicopter.

'Oh, thank God!' Harriet burst into tears, her hands over her face. 'Now what?' She turned to Alice. 'Where are they taking them?'

'They'll check them over just in case they need medical help,' Alice told her, her eyes fixed on Gio who was now up to mid-thigh in swirling water. She raked fingers through her hair and clamped her teeth on her lower lip to prevent herself from crying out a warning. What was the point of crying out a warning when the guy could see perfectly well for himself what was happening?

'Will they take them to the hospital?' Harriet was staring up at the helicopter but Alice had her gaze fixed firmly on Gio.

There was no way he'd be able to swim safely now. The water was too deep and the current was just too fierce.

The crowd on the beach must have realised it too because a sudden silence fell as they waited for the helicopter to lower the winchman for a third time.

And finally Harriet saw…

'He's risking his life.' She said the words in hushed tones, as if she'd only just realised what was truly happening. 'Oh, my God, he's risking his life for my babies. And now he's going to—'

'No, he isn't.' Alice snapped the words, refusing to allow her to voice what everyone was thinking. 'He's going to be fine, Harriet,' she said, as much to convince

herself as the woman standing next to her in a serious
state of anxiety. 'They're lowering the winchman again.'

What was the Italian for *you stupid, brave idiot?* she
wondered as she watched Gio exchange a few words
with the winchman and then laugh as the harness was
attached. They rose up in the air, swinging slightly as
they approached the hovering helicopter.

Alice closed her eyes briefly as he vanished inside.
For a moment she just felt like sinking onto the sand and
staying there until the panic subsided. Then her mobile
phone rang. She answered it immediately. It was Gio.

'Twins seem fine but they're taking them to hospital
for a quick check.' His voice crackled. 'Tell Harriet I'll
bring them home. It isn't safe for her to drive in a state
of anxiety and shock and by the time she gets up to the
house, picks up the car and drives to the hospital, I'll be
home with them.'

Deciding that it wasn't the right moment to yell at
him, she simply acknowledged what he'd said and
ended the call. 'They seem fine but they're going to take
them to the hospital for a check. Dr Moretti will bring
them home, Harriet,' she said quietly. 'Let's go back to
your house now and make a cup of tea. I don't know
about you, but I need one.'

Gio arrived back at the house three hours later. Three
long hours during which she'd had all too much time to
think about *that kiss* and the fact that she'd told him far
more about herself than she'd intended.

Annoyed with herself, confused, Alice abandoned all
pretence of reading a medical journal and was pacing
backwards and forwards in the kitchen, staring at the

clock, when she finally heard the doorbell. She closed her eyes and breathed a sigh of relief.

She opened the door and lifted an eyebrow, trying to regain some of her old self. Trying to react the way she would have reacted before *that kiss*. 'Forgot your key?'

He was wearing a set of theatre scrubs and he looked broad-shouldered and more handsome than a man had a right to look. She sneaked a look at his firm mouth and immediately felt a sizzle in her veins.

'Careless, I know. I went swimming and I must have them in my trousers.' He strolled past her with a lazy grin and pushed the door closed behind him. Suddenly her hallway seemed small.

'Talking of swimming…' she took a step backwards and kept her tone light '…you certainly go to extreme lengths to pull the women, Dr Moretti. Plunging into the jaws of death and acting like a hero. Does it work for you?'

He paused, his eyes on hers, his expression thoughtful. 'I don't know. Let's find out, shall we?' Without warning, he reached out a hand and jerked her against him, his mouth hovering a mere breath from hers. 'We have unfinished business, Dr Anderson.'

He kissed her hard and she felt her knees go weak but she didn't have the chance to think about the implications of that fact because something hot and dangerous exploded in her body. She wound her arms round his neck for support. *Just for support.*

He gave a low groan and dug his fingers into her hair, tilting her head, changing the angle, helping himself to her mouth.

'You taste good, *cara mia,*' he muttered, trailing kisses

over her jaw and then back to her mouth. He kissed her thoroughly. Skilfully. And then lifted his head, his breathing less than steady. 'I'm addicted to your mouth. It was one of the first things I noticed about you.'

Her head swam dizzily and she tried to focus, but before she could even remember how to regain control he lowered his head again.

With a soft gasp, she tried to speak. 'Stop…' His lips had found a sensitive spot on her neck and she was finding it impossible to think straight. With a determined effort, she pushed at his chest. 'We have to stop this.'

'Why?' His mouth returned to hers, teasing and seducing. 'Why stop something that feels so good?'

Her head was swimming and she couldn't concentrate. 'Because I don't do this.'

'Then it's good to try something new.' He lifted his head, his smile surprisingly gentle. 'Courage, *tesoro*.'

Her fingers were curled into the hard muscle of his shoulders and she remembered the strength he'd shown in the water.

'Talking of courage, you could have drowned out there.'

His eyes searched hers. Questioning. 'You're telling me you were worried, Dr Anderson?' He lifted a hand and gently brushed her cheek. 'Better not let Mary hear you say that. She'll be buying a hat to wear at our wedding.'

'Oh, for goodness' sake.' She knew he was teasing but all the same the words flustered her and she pulled away, trying not to look at his mouth. Trying not to think about the way he kissed. About the fact that she wanted him to go on kissing her. 'What took you so long, anyway? I was beginning to think you'd gone back to Italy.'

'I hurried the twins through A and E, we got a ride home with one of the paramedics and then I dropped them home.'

'And that took three hours? Did you drive via Scotland?'

'You really were worried. Careful, Alice.' His voice was soft, his gaze searching. 'You're showing emotion.'

She flushed and walked past him to the kitchen. 'Given the distance between here and the hospital, with which I'm entirely familiar, I was expecting you back ages ago. And you didn't answer your mobile.'

'I was with Harriet.' He followed her and went straight to the espresso machine. 'She had a nasty shock and she was blaming herself terribly for what happened. She needed TLC.'

And he would have given her the comfort she needed, because he was that sort of man. He was good with people's emotions, she thought to herself. Unlike her.

'I stayed with her for the first two hours,' she muttered, raking fingers through her hair, feeling totally inadequate, 'but she just kept pacing and saying she was a terrible mother. And I didn't know what to say. I'm hopeless at giving emotional comfort. If she'd cut her finger or developed a rash, I would have been fine. But there was nothing to see. She was just hysterical and miserable. I did my best, but it wasn't good enough. I was useless.'

He glanced over his shoulder, his eyes gentle. 'That's not true. You're not hopeless or useless. Just a little afraid, I think. Emotions can be scary things. Not so easily explained as some other things. You'll get better with practice. She's calmer now.' Reaching across the work surface, Gio opened a packet of coffee-beans and tipped them into a grinder. 'And she definitely has post-natal depression.'

Alice stared. 'You're sure?'

'Certain.'

'So what did you do?'

'I listened.' He flicked a switch, paused while the beans were ground and then gave a shrug. 'Sometimes that's all a person needs, although, in Harriet's case, I think she does need something more. Tomorrow she is coming to see me and we are going to put together a plan of action. I think her condition merits drug treatment but, more importantly, we need to get her emotional support. Her husband isn't around much and she needs help. She needs to feel that people love and care for her. She needs to know that people mind how she's feeling. She doesn't have family to do that, so we need to find her the support from elsewhere.'

Alice watched him. He moved around the kitchen the same way he did everything. With strength and confidence. 'You really believe that family holds all the answers, don't you?'

'Yes, I do.' He emptied the grinder and turned to look at her. 'But I realise that you may find that hard to understand, given your experience of family life. You haven't ever seen a decent example, so why would you agree with me?'

She stiffened. 'Look, I wish I'd never mentioned it to you. It isn't important.'

'It's stopped you believing in love, so it's important.'

'I don't want to talk about it.'

'That's just because you're not used to talking about

it. A bit like kissing. You'll be fine once you've had more practice.'

The mere mention of kissing made her body heat. 'I don't want more practice! I hate talking about it!'

'Because it stirs up emotions and you're afraid of emotions. Plenty of people have problems in their past, but it doesn't have to affect the future. Only if you let it. Family is perhaps the most important thing in the world, after good health.' His voice was calm as he started making the coffee, his movements steady and methodical. It seemed to her as she watched that making coffee was almost a form of relaxation for him.

'Is that how it happens in Italy? I mean Sicily?' She corrected herself quickly and saw him smile.

'In Sicily, family is sacred.' He watched as coffee trickled into the cup, dark and fragrant. 'We believe in love, Alice. We believe in a love that is special, unique and lasts for a lifetime. I'm surrounded by generations of my family and extended family who have been in love for ever. Come with me to Sicily and I will prove it to you.'

He was teasing, of course. He had to be teasing. 'Don't be ridiculous.'

'You have been to Sicily?' She shook her head and took the coffee he handed to her.

'No.'

His smile was lazy and impossibly attractive. 'It is a land designed to make people believe in romance and passion. We have the glittering sea to seduce, and the fires of Etna to flame the coldest heart.' He spoke in a soft, accented drawl and she rolled her eyes to hide how strongly his words affected her.

'Drop the sweet talk. It's wasted on me, Dr Moretti. Romance is just a seduction tool.'

And she'd had three long hours to think about seduction.

Three long hours to think about the kiss on the beach.

And the way he'd plunged into the water after two small children in trouble.

And now she also had to think about the way he'd spent his evening with a vulnerable, lonely mother with postnatal depression.

Bother.

She was really starting to like the man. And notice things about him. Things that other women probably noticed immediately. Like his easy, slightly teasing smile and the thick, dark lashes that gave his eyes a sleepy look. A dangerous look. The way, when he talked to a woman, he gave her his whole attention. His rich, sexy accent and the smooth, confident way that he dealt with every problem. And the way he shouldered those problems without walking away.

It was just the kiss, she told herself crossly as she drank her coffee. The kiss had made her loopy. Up until then she really hadn't looked at him in *that way*.

'Did you pick up my clothes?' He strolled over to her and she found herself staring at his shoulders. He had good shoulders.

'Sorry?'

'My clothes.' He lifted an eyebrow, his eyes scanning her face. 'Did you pick them up from the beach?'

'Oh.' She pulled herself together and dragged her eyes away from the tangle of dark hairs at the base of his throat. 'Yes. Yes, I did. I put them on the chair in your room.'

Heat curled low in her pelvis and spread through her limbs. Sexual awareness, she told herself. The attraction of female to male. Without it, the human race would have died out. It was a perfectly normal chemical reaction. *It's just that it wasn't normal for her.* She tried to shut the feeling down. Tried to control it. But it was on the loose.

'Thanks.' He was watching her. 'It would have been hard to explain that to Mary if some helpful bystander had delivered them to the surgery tomorrow.'

She folded her arms across her chest in a defensive gesture. 'It would have made Mary's day.'

'So would this, I suspect.' He lowered his head and kissed her again, his mouth lingering on hers.

This time she didn't even think about resisting. She just closed her eyes and let herself feel. Allowed the heat to spread through her starving body. Her nerves sang and hummed and when he finally lifted his head she felt only disappointment.

It was amazing how quickly a person could adapt to being touched, she thought dizzily.

'I—We…' She lifted a hand to her lips and then let it drop back to her side, suddenly self-conscious. 'You've got to stop doing that.' But even she knew the words were a lie and he gave a smile as he walked towards the door.

'I'm going to keep doing it, *cara mia.*' He turned in the doorway. Paused. His eyes burned into hers. 'So you're just going to have to get used to it.'

CHAPTER EIGHT

Gio looked at Harriet and felt his heart twist. She looked so utterly miserable.

'Crazy, isn't it?' Her voice was little more than a whisper. 'I have this beautiful, perfect baby and I'm not even enjoying having her. I snap at the twins and yesterday I was so miserable I didn't even notice that they'd wandered off.'

'Don't be so hard on yourself and never underestimate a child's capacity for mischief,' Gio said calmly. 'They are young and adventurous, as small boys should be.'

'But I can't cope with them. I'm just so tired.' Her eyes filled. 'I snap at Geoff and he says that suddenly he's married to a witch, and I really can't face sex…' She blushed, her expression embarrassed. 'Sorry, I didn't mean to say that. Geoff would kill me if he thought I was talking about our sex life in the village.'

'This isn't the village,' Gio said gently. 'It's my consulting room and I'm a doctor. And it's important that you tell me everything you are feeling so that I can make an informed judgement on how to help you.'

Her eyes filled and she clamped a hand over her mouth, struggling for control. 'I'm sorry to be so pathetic, it's just that I'm so tired. I'll be fine when I've had some sleep—the trouble is I don't get any. I'm so tired I ought to go out like a light but I can't sleep at all and I'm totally on edge all the time. I'm an absolutely *terrible* mother. And do you know the worst thing?' Giving up her attempts at control, she burst into heart-breaking sobs. Gio reached across his desk for a box of tissues, his eyes never leaving her face.

'Tell me.'

'I'm so useless I don't even know what my own baby wants.' Wrenching a tissue from the box, she blew her nose hard. 'She's my third child and I find myself sitting there, staring at her while she's crying, totally unable to move. And I worry about everything. I worry I'm going to go to her cot in the morning and find she's died in the night, I worry that she's going to catch something awful and I won't notice—'

Gio put his hand over hers. 'You're describing symptoms of anxiety, Harriet, and I think—'

'You think that I'm basically a completely terrible mother and a hideously pathetic blubbery female.' She blew her nose again and he shook his head and tight-ened his grip on her hand.

'On the contrary, I think you are a wonderful mother.' He hesitated, choosing his words carefully. 'But I think it's possible that you could be suffering from depression.'

She frowned. Dropped the tissue into her bag. 'I'm just tired.'

'I don't think so.' He kept his hand on hers and she clamped her lower lip between her teeth, trying not to cry.

'I can't be depressed. Oh, God, I just need to pull my-self together.'

'Depression is an illness. It isn't about pulling your-self together.'

Her eyes filled again and she reached for another tissue. 'Do you mean depressed as in postnatal depression?'

'Yes, that's exactly what I think.'

Tears trickled down her face. 'So maybe this isn't just about me being useless?'

'You're not useless. In fact, I think the opposite.' He shook his head, a look of admiration on his face. 'How you are coping with three children under the age of six and postnatal depression, I just don't know.'

'I'm not coping.'

'Yes, you are. Just not as well as you'd like. And you're not enjoying yourself.' Gio let go of her hand and turned back to his desk, reaching for a pad of paper. 'But that's going to change, Harriet. We're going to sort this out for you.'

She blew her nose. 'My husband will just tell me to pull myself together and snap out of it.'

'He won't say that,' Gio scribbled on a pad, 'because I'm going to talk to him. Many people are ignorant about the true nature of postnatal depression, he isn't alone in that. Once I explain everything to him, he will give you the support you need. I've spoken to Gina, the health visitor, and done some research. This is a group that I think you might find helpful.' He handed her the piece of paper and she looked at it.

'It's only in the next village.'

Gio nodded. 'Will you be able to get there?'

'Oh, yes. I can drive.' She stared at the name. 'Do I have to phone?'

'I've done it. They're expecting you at their next

meeting, which happens to be tomorrow afternoon. You can take the twins and the baby, there'll be someone there to help.'

Harriet looked at him. 'Do I need drugs?'

'I'd like to try talking therapy first and I want to see you regularly. If you don't start to feel better then drug treatment might be appropriate. Let's see how we go.'

Harriet slipped the paper into her bag and gave a feeble smile. 'I feel a bit better already, just knowing that this isn't all my fault.'

'None of it is your fault.' Gio rose to his feet and walked her to the door. 'Go to the meeting and let me know how you get on.'

Alice parked her newly fixed car outside her house and stared at the low black sports car that meant that Gio was already back from his house calls.

Bother. She'd been hoping that he'd work late.

It had been almost a week since the episode on the beach. A week during which she'd virtually lived in the surgery in order to put some distance between her and Gio. A week during which she'd drunk endless cups of black coffee and eaten nothing but sandwiches at her desk. A week during which she'd been cranky and thoroughly unsettled. It was as if her neat, tidy life had been thrown into the air and had landed in a different pattern. And she didn't know how to put it back together.

What she did know was that it was Gio's fault for kissing her.

And Mary's fault for arranging for him to lodge with her.

Pushing open the front door, she was stopped by the smell.

'Well, well. The wanderer returns. I was beginning to think you'd taken root in the surgery.' Gio emerged from the kitchen and her heart stumbled and jerked. A pair of old, faded jeans hugged his hard thighs and his black shirt was open at the neck. 'If you hadn't returned home at a decent hour, I was coming to find you.'

Even dressed so casually he looked handsome and— she searched for the word—exotic?

'I had work to do. And now I'm tired.' She had to escape. Had to get her mind back together. 'I'm going straight up to bed, if you don't mind.'

'Alice.' His tone was gentle and there was humour in his eyes. 'It's not even eight o'clock, *tesoro*. If you are going to try and avoid me, you're going to have to think of a better excuse than that. You've kept your distance for a week. It's long enough, I think.'

Something in his tone stung. He made her feel like a coward. 'Why would I try and avoid you?'

'Because I make you uncomfortable. I make you talk when you'd rather be silent and I make you feel when you'd rather stay numb.'

'I don't—'

'And because I kissed you and made you want something that you've made a point of denying yourself for years.'

'I don't—'

'At least eat with me.' He held out a hand. 'And if after that you want to go to bed, I'll let you go.'

She kept her hands by her sides. 'You've cooked?'

'I like cooking. I've made a Sicilian speciality. It's

too much for one person and, anyway, I need your opinion.' His hand remained outstretched and there was challenge in his dark eyes.

Muttering under her breath about bullying Italian men, she took his hand and felt his strong fingers close firmly over hers.

Instead of leading her into the kitchen, he took her into the dining room. The dining room at the back of the house that she never used. The dining room that was now transformed.

All the clutter was gone and tiny candles flickered on every available surface. The smells of a warm summer evening drifted in through the open French doors.

The atmosphere was intimate. Romantic.

Something flickered inside her. Panic? She turned to him with a shake of her head. 'No, Gio. This isn't what I do, I—'

He covered her lips with his fingers. 'Relax, *tesoro*. It's just dinner. Food is always more enjoyable when the atmosphere is good, and the atmosphere in this room is perfect. Go and take a shower and change. Dinner is in fifteen minutes.'

She stared after him as he strolled back to the kitchen. The guy just couldn't help himself. He'd obviously decided that she needed rescuing from her past and he thought he was the one to do it. The one to show her that romance existed.

She stared at the candles and rolled her eyes. Well, if he thought that a few lumps of burning wax were going to make her fall in love, he was doomed to disappointment.

Telling herself that she was only doing it because she was hot and uncomfortable, she showered and changed into a simple white strap top and a green silk skirt that hugged her hips softly and then fell to mid-thigh.

Staring at her reflection in the mirror, she contemplated make-up and decided against it. She didn't want to look as though she was making an effort. She didn't want him getting the wrong idea.

With that thought on her mind, she walked back into the dining room and came straight to the point.

'I know that some women would just drop to their knees and beg for a man who does all this.' She waved a hand around the room. 'But I'm not one of them. Really. I'm happy with a sandwich eaten under a halogen light bulb. So if you're trying to make me fall in love with you, you're wasting your time. I just thought we ought to get that straight right now, before you go to enormous effort.'

'I'm not trying to make you fall in love with me. True love can't be forced,' he said softly as he pulled the cork out of a bottle of wine, 'and it can't be commanded. True love is a gift, *cara mia*. Freely given by both parties.'

'It's a figment of the imagination. A serious hallucination,' she returned, her tone sharper than she'd intended. 'A justification for wild, impulsive and totally irrational behaviour, usually between two people who are old enough to know better.'

'That isn't love.' He pushed her towards the chair that faced the window. 'From what you've told me, you haven't seen an example of love. But you will do. I intend to show you.'

She rolled her eyes and watched while he filled her glass. 'What are you? My fairy godmother?'

His smile broadened. 'Do I look like a fairy to you?'

She swallowed hard and dragged her eyes away from the laughter in his. No. He looked like a thoroughly gorgeous man. And he was standing in her dining room about to serve her dinner.

'All right.' She gave a shrug that she hoped looked suitably casual. 'I'm hungry. Let's agree to disagree and just eat.'

The food was delicious.

Never in her life had she ever tasted anything so sublime. And through it all Gio topped up her wineglass and kept up a neutral conversation. He was intelligent and entertaining and she forgot her plan to eat as fast as possible and then escape to her room. Instead she ate, savouring every mouthful, and sipped her wine. And all the time she listened as he talked.

He talked about growing up on Sicily and about his life as a surgeon in Milan. He talked about the differences in medicine between the two cultures.

'So…' She reached for more bread. 'Are you going to tell me why you had to give up surgery as a career? Or am I the only one who has to spill about my past?'

'It's not a secret.' He lounged across the table from her, his face bronzed and handsome in the flickering candlelight. 'I was working in Africa. We were attacked by rebels hoping to steal drugs and equipment that they could sell on.' He gave a shrug and lifted his glass. 'Unfortunately the damage was such that I can't operate for any length of time.'

She winced. 'I'm sorry, I shouldn't have asked.'

'It's part of my life and talking about it doesn't make it worse. In a way I was lucky. I took some time off and went home to my family.' He continued to talk, telling her about his sisters and his brother, his parents, his grandparents and numerous aunts, uncles and cousins.

'You were lucky.' She put her glass down on the table. 'Having such good family.'

'Yes, I was.' He passed her more bread. 'Luckier than you.'

'She took me to the park once—my mother.' She stared at her plate, the memory rising into her brain so clearly that her hands curled into fists and her shoulders tensed. 'She was meeting her lover and I was the excuse that enabled her to leave the house without my dad suspecting anything. Although I doubt he would have cared because he was seeing someone, too. Only she didn't know that.'

She looked up, waiting for him to display shock or distaste, but Gio sat still, his eyes on her face. Listening. It occurred to her that he was an excellent listener.

She shrugged. 'Anyway, I was playing on the climbing frame. They were sitting on the seat. Kissing. Wrapped up in each other.' She licked dry lips. 'I remember watching two other children and envying them. Their mothers were both hovering at the bottom of the climbing frame, hands outstretched. They said things like "be careful" and "watch where you put your feet" and "that's too high, come down now". My mother didn't even glance in my direction.' She broke off and ran a hand over the back of her neck, the tension rising inside her. 'Not even when I fell. And in the ambulance she was furious with me and accused me of sabotaging her relationship on purpose.'

Gio reached across the table and took her hand. But still he didn't speak. Just listened, his eyes holding hers.

She chewed her lip and flashed him a smile. 'Anyway, he was husband number two and life just carried on from there, really. She went through two more— Oh, sorry.' She gave a cynical smile that was loaded with pain. 'I should say she "fell in love" twice more before I was finally old enough to leave home.'

'And your sister?'

Alice rubbed her fingers over her forehead. 'She's on her second marriage. She had high hopes of doing everything differently to our parents. She still believed that true love existed. I think she's finally discovering that it doesn't. I've never told anyone any of this before. Not even Rita and Mary. They know I'm not in touch with my parents, but that's all they know.'

It had grown dark while she was talking and through the open doors she could hear the sounds of the night, see the flutter of insects drawn by the flickering candlelight.

Finally Gio spoke. 'It's not surprising that you don't believe that love exists. It's hard to believe in something that you've never seen. You have a logical, scientific brain, Alice. You take a problem-solving approach to life. Love is not easily defined or explained and that makes it easy to dismiss.'

She swallowed. How was it that he seemed to understand her so well? And why had she just told him so much? She looked suspiciously at her wineglass but it was still half-full and her head was clear. She waited for regret to flood through her but instead she felt strangely peaceful for the first time. 'If love really existed then the divorce rate wouldn't be so high.'

'Or maybe love just isn't that easy to find, and that

makes it even more precious. Maybe the divorce rate is testament to the fact that love is so special that people are willing to take a risk in order to find it.'

She shook her head. 'What people feel is sexual chemistry and, if they're lucky, friendship. But there isn't a whole separate emotion called love that binds people together.'

'Because you haven't seen it yet.' He studied her face. 'True love is selfless and yet the emotion you saw was greedy and selfish. They allowed you to fall and they weren't there to catch you.'

Instinctively she knew he wasn't just talking about the incident on the climbing frame.

She lifted her glass. 'So, if you believe in love, Dr Moretti, why aren't you married with eight children?' Her eyes challenged him over the rim of her glass and he smiled.

'Because you don't choose when to love. Or even who to love. You can't just go out and find it in the way that you can find friendship or sex. Love chooses you. And chooses the time. For some people it's early in life. For others...' he gave a shrug that showed his Latin heritage '...it's later.'

She frowned. 'So you're waiting for Signorina Right to just bang on your door?' Her tone had a hint of sarcasm and he smiled.

'No. She gave me a key.' Something in his gaze made her heart stop.

Surely he wasn't saying...

He couldn't be suggesting...

She put her glass down. 'Gio—'

'Go to bed, *tesoro,*' he said softly. 'The other thing

about love is that it can't be controlled. Not the emotion and not the timing. It happens when it happens.'

She stared at him. 'But—'

He rose to his feet and smiled. 'Sleep well, Alice.'

Gio left via the back door, knowing that if he didn't leave the house, he'd join her in her bedroom.

It had taken every ounce of willpower to let her walk away from him.

But he knew instinctively that they'd taken enough steps forward for one night. She'd talked—really talked—perhaps for the first time in her life and he could tell that she was starting to relax around him.

Which was how he wanted it to be.

They'd come a long way in a short time.

He breathed in the warm, evening air and strolled down towards the sea, enjoying the comfort of the semi-darkness.

It felt strange, he thought to himself as he walked, to have fallen in love with a woman who didn't even believe that love existed.

After that night, the evenings developed a pattern and, almost a month after he'd arrived in the surgery, Alice sat staring out of the window of her consulting room, wondering what Gio would be cooking for dinner.

It was so unlike her to dream about food, but since he'd taken over the cooking she found herself looking forward to the evenings.

Sometimes they ate in the dining room, sometimes they ate in her garden and once he'd made a picnic and they'd taken it down to the beach.

Thinking, dreaming, she missed the tap on the door.

It was friendship, she decided, and she liked it.

She could really talk to him and he was an excellent listener. And she enjoyed working with him. He was an excellent doctor.

And, of course, there was sexual chemistry. She wasn't so naïve that she couldn't recognise it. She'd even experienced it before, to a lesser degree, with a man she'd dated a few times at university. Not love, but a chemical reaction between a man and a woman. And it was there, between her and Gio.

But since the incident on the beach, he hadn't kissed her again.

Hadn't made any attempt to touch her.

The door behind her opened. 'Alice?'

Why hadn't he touched her since?

'Dr Anderson?'

Finally she heard her name, and turned to find Mary standing in the doorway. 'Are you on our planet?'

'Just thinking.'

'Dreaming, you mean.' Mary looked at her curiously and then handed her a set of notes. 'You've got one extra. The little Jarrett boy has a high temperature. I don't like the look of him so I squeezed him in.'

'That's fine, Mary.' She took the notes. 'Thanks.'

She pulled herself together, saw Tom Jarrett and then walked through to Reception with the notes just as Gio emerged from his consulting room, with his hand on Edith Carne's shoulder.

He was so tactile, Alice thought to herself, observing the way he guided the woman up the corridor, his head tilted towards her as he listened.

Touching came entirely naturally to him, where-as she—

'The cardiology referral was a good idea,' he said to her as he strolled back from reception and saw her watching him. 'They're treating Edith and it appears that they've found the cause of her falls.'

'You mean, you found the cause. She never would have—'

A series of loud screams from Reception interrupted her and she exchanged a quick glance with Gio before hurrying to the reception area just as a mother came struggled through the door, carrying a sobbing child. He was screaming and crying and holding his foot.

Alice stepped towards them. 'What's happened?'

'I don't know. We were on the beach and then sud-denly he just started screaming for no reason.' The mother was breathless from her sprint from the beach and the child continued to howl noisily. 'His foot is really red and it's swelling up.'

Gio picked up the foot and examined it. 'Erythema. Oedema. A sting of some sort?'

Alice tilted her head and looked. 'Weaver fish,' she said immediately, and glanced towards Mary. 'Get me hot water, please. Fast.'

Mary nodded and Gio frowned. 'What?'

'If you're expecting the Italian translation you're go-ing to be waiting a long time,' Alice drawled, her fingers gentle as she examined the child's foot, 'but basically weaver fish are found in sandy shallows around the beaches down here. It has venomous spines on its dorsal fin and that protrudes out of the sand. If you tread on it, you get stung.'

The mother shook her head. 'I didn't see anything on the sand.'

'It's a good idea to keep something on your feet when you're walking in the shallows at low water,' Alice advised, taking the bucket of water that Mary handed her with a nod of thanks. 'All right, sweetheart, we're going to put your foot in this water and that will help the pain.'

She tested the water quickly to check that it wasn't so hot that it would burn the child and then tried to guide the child's foot into the water. He jerked his leg away and his screams intensified.

'We really have to get this into hot water.' Alice looked at the mother. 'Heat inactivates the venom. After a few minutes in here, the pain will be better. Trust me.'

'Alex, please…' the mother begged, and tried to reason with her son. 'You need to put your foot in the bucket for Mummy. Please, darling, do it for Mummy.'

Alex continued to yell and bawl and wriggle and Gio rubbed a hand over his roughened jaw and crouched down. 'We play a game,' he said firmly, sounding more Italian than ever. He produced a penny from his pocket, held it up and then promptly made it disappear.

Briefly, Alex stopped crying and stared. 'Where?'

Gio looked baffled. 'I don't know. Perhaps if you put your foot in the bucket, it will reappear. Like magic. Let's try it, shall we?'

Alex sniffed, hesitated and then tentatively dipped his foot in the water. 'It's hot.'

'It has to be hot,' Alice said quickly, guiding his foot into the water. 'It will take the pain away.'

She watched gratefully as Gio distracted Alex, producing the coin from behind the child's ear and then from his own ear.

Alex watched, transfixed, and Gio treated him to ten minutes of magic, during which time the child's misery lessened along with the pain.

'Oh, thank goodness,' the mother said, as Alex finally started smiling. 'That was awful. And I had no idea. I've never even heard of a weaver fish.'

'They're not uncommon. There were five hundred cases along the North Devon and Cornwall coast last year,' Alice muttered as she dried her hands on the towel that Mary had thought to provide. 'Keep his foot in the bucket for another ten minutes at least and give him some paracetamol and antihistamine when you get home. He should be fine but if he isn't, give us a call.'

'Thank you so much.' The mother looked at her gratefully. 'What would I have done if you'd been shut?'

'Actually, lots of the cafés and surf shops around here keep a bucket just for this purpose so it's worth remembering that. But the best advice is to avoid walking near the low-water mark in bare feet.'

Alice walked over to the reception desk and Gio followed.

'Weaver fish? What is this weaver fish?' He spoke slowly, as if he wasn't sure he was pronouncing it correctly.

'Nobody knows exactly what is in weaver fish venom but it contains a mixture of biogenous amines and they've identified 5-hydroxytryptamine, epinephrine, norepinephrine and histamine.' She angled her head. 'Alex was probably stung by *Echiichthys vipera*—the lesser weaver fish.'

Gio lifted a brow. 'Implying that there is a greater weaver fish?'

She nodded. '*Trachinus draco*. There are case reports of people being stung. Often fisherman. We've seen one in this practice. It was a few years ago, but we sent him up to the hospital to be treated. The symptoms are severe pain, vomiting, oedema, syncope—in his case, the symptoms lasted for a long time.'

He smiled at her and she frowned, her heart beating faster as she looked into his eyes.

'What? Why are you looking at me like that?'

'Because I love it when you give me facts.' He leaned closer to her, his eyes dancing. 'You are delightfully serious, Dr Anderson, do you know that? And I find you incredibly sexy.'

'Gio, for goodness' sake.' Her eyes slid towards Mary, who was filling out a form with the mother. But she couldn't drench the flame of desire that burned through her body.

And he saw that flame.

'We're finished here.' Gio's voice was low and determined. 'Let's go home, Dr Anderson.'

'But—'

'It's home, or it's your consulting room with the door locked. Take your pick.'

She chose home.

CHAPTER NINE

THEY barely made it through the front door.

The tension that had been building for weeks reached breaking point as she fumbled with her key in the lock, aware that he was right behind her, his hand resting on the small of her back.

Gio's fingers closed over hers and guided. Turned the key. And then he was nudging her inside and shouldering the door closed.

For a moment they both stood, breathing heavily, poised on the edge of something dangerous.

And then they cracked. Both moved at the same time, mouths greedy, hands seeking.

'I need you naked.' He ripped at Alice's shirt, sending buttons flying across the floor, and she reciprocated, fumbling with his buttons while her breath came in tiny pants.

'Me, too. Me, too.' And all the time a tiny voice in her head was telling her that she didn't do this sort of thing.

She ignored it and slipped his shirt from his shoulders, revelling in the feel of warm male flesh under her hands. 'You have a perfect body, Dr Moretti.'

He gave a groan and slid his hands up her back, his

eyes feasting on the swell of her breasts under her simple lacy bra. He spoke softly in Italian and then scooped her into his arms and carried her up the stairs to her bedroom.

'I don't understand a word you're saying, but I suppose it might be better that way. I like it.' With a tiny laugh she buried her head in his neck, breathed in the tantalising scent of aroused male and then murmured in protest as he lowered her onto the bed. 'I want you to carry on holding me. Don't let me go.'

'No chance.' With a swift movement he removed his trousers and came down on top of her, his hands sliding into her hair, his mouth descending to hers. 'And this from the girl who hated being touched.'

He was touching her now. Everywhere. His hands seeking, seducing, soothing all at the same time.

'That was before—' She arched under him, burning to get closer still to his hard, male body while his hands explored ever curve of hers. 'Before…'

'Before?' His hand slid over her breast and she realised in a daze that she hadn't even felt him remove her bra.

'Before you.' The flick of his tongue over her nipple brought a gasp to her throat and she curled a leg around him, the ache in her pelvis intensifying to unbearable proportions. 'Before I met you.' The touch of his mouth was skilful and sinful in equal measures and she closed her eyes and felt the erotic pull deep in her stomach.

'You're beautiful.' His mouth trailed lower and his fingers dragged at her tiny panties, sliding them downwards, leaving her naked.

She slid a hand over the hard planes of his chest, felt his touch grow more intimate. His fingers moved over her, then his mouth, and she offered herself freely, wondering what had happened to her inhibitions.

Drowning in sensation, she shifted and gasped and finally he rose over her and she reached for him, desperate.

'Now.' Her eyes were fevered and her lips were parted. 'I need you now. Now.'

And he gathered her against him and took her, his possessive thrust bringing a gasp to her lips and a flush to her cheeks. For a moment he stilled, his eyes locked on hers, his breathing unsteady. And then he lowered his head and his mouth covered hers in a kiss that was hot and demanding, his powerful body moving against hers in a rhythm that created sensations so exquisitely perfect that she cried out in desperation.

Her skin was damp from the heat and her fingers raked his back as the sensation built and threatened to devour her whole.

She toppled fast, falling into a dark void of ecstasy, and immediately he slowed the pace, changing the rhythm from desperate to measured, always the one in control.

With a low moan she opened her eyes and slid her arms round his neck. 'What are you doing?'

'Making love to you.' He spoke the words against her lips, the hot brand of his mouth sending her senses tumbling in every direction. 'And I don't ever want to stop.'

She didn't want him to stop either and she arched her back and moved her hips until she felt the change in him. Felt his muscles quiver and his skin grow slick, heard the rasp of his breath and the increase in masculine thrust.

And then she felt nothing more because he drove them both forward until they reached oblivion and fell,

tumbling and gasping into a whirlpool of sexual excitement that sucked them both under.

She lay there, eyes closed, struggling for breath and
sanity. His weight should have bothered her, but it didn't.

And she was relieved that he didn't seem able to
move either.

Eventually he lifted his head and nuzzled her neck
gently, his movements slow and languid. 'Are we still
alive?' With a fractured groan he rolled onto his back,
taking her with him. 'You need to wear more clothes
around the house. I find it hard to resist you when
you're naked.'

Her eyes were still closed. 'It's your fault that I'm
naked.'

'It is?' He stroked her hair away from her face and
something about the way he was touching her made her
open her eyes. And she saw.

'Gio—'

'I love you, Alice.'

Her heart jerked. Jumped. Kick-started by pure, blind
panic. 'No need to get all mushy on me, Dr Moretti. You
already scored.'

'That's why I'm saying it now. If I'd said it when we
were making love then you would have thought it was
just the heat of the moment. If I said it over dinner with
candles and wine, you would have said it was the romance of the moment. So I'm saying it now. After we've
made love. Because that's what we just did.'

'I don't need to hear this.' She tried to wriggle away
from him but he held her easily, his powerful body trapping hers.

'Yes, you do. The problem is that you're not used to

hearing it. But that's going to change because I'm going to be saying it to you a lot. A few weeks ago you weren't used to talking or touching but you do both those now.'

'This is different.' Her heart was pounding. 'It was just sex, Gio. Great sex, admittedly, but nothing more.'

His mouth trailed over her breast and she groaned and tried to push him away. 'Stop. You're not playing fair.'

'I'm in love with you. And I'm just reminding you how you feel about me.' He lifted his head, a wicked smile in his eyes, and she ran a hand over her shoulder, trying not to lick her lips. He had an incredible body and every female part of her craved him.

But that was natural, she reminded herself. 'It's sexual attraction,' she said hoarsely, trying to concentrate despite the skilled movement of his mouth and hands. 'If sexual attraction didn't exist then the human race would have died out long ago. It isn't love.' She gave a low moan as his fingers teased her intimately. 'Gio…'

'Not love?' He rolled onto his back and positioned her above him. 'Fine, Dr Anderson. Then let's have sex. At the moment I don't care what you call it as long as you stop talking.'

A week later, Alice walked into work with a smile on her face and a bounce in her step.

And she knew why, of course.

It was her relationship with Gio. And she was totally clear about her feelings. Friendship and sex. It was turning out to be a good combination. In a month or so he'd probably be leaving and that would be fine. Maybe they'd stay in touch. Maybe they wouldn't. Either way, she felt fine about it. She felt fine about everything.

And the fact that he always said 'I love you' and she didn't just didn't seem to matter any more. It didn't change the way things were between them.

The truth was, they were having fun.

Mary caught her as she walked into her consulting room. 'You're looking happy.'

'I am happy.' She dropped her bag behind the desk and turned on her computer. 'I'm enjoying my life.'

'You weren't smiling this much a month ago.'

A month ago Gio hadn't been in her life.

She frowned slightly at the thought and then dismissed it. What was wrong with enjoying a friendship?

'Professor Burrows from the haematology department at the hospital rang.' Mary handed her a piece of paper. 'He wants you to call him back on this number before ten o'clock. And I've slotted in Mrs Bruce because she's in a state. She had a scan at the hospital and they think the baby has a cleft palate. She's crying in Reception.'

Alice looked up in concern. 'Oh, poor thing. Send her straight in.' She flicked on her computer while Mary watched, her eyes searching.

'It's Gio, isn't it?'

'What is?'

'The reason you're smiling. So relaxed. You're in love with him, Alice.'

'I'm not in love.' Alice lifted her head and smiled sweetly. 'And the reason I know that is because there's no such thing. But I'm willing to admit that I like him a lot. I respect and admire him as a doctor. He's a nice man.'

And he was great in bed.

Mary looked at her thoughtfully. 'A nice man? Good, I'm glad you like him.'

Alice felt slightly smug as she buzzed for her first patient. Really, in her opinion, it all went to prove that love just didn't exist. In many ways Gio was perfect. He was intelligent and sharp and yet still managed to be kind and thoughtful. He was a terrific listener, a great conversationalist and a spectacular lover. What more could a girl want in a man?

The answer was nothing. But still she didn't feel anything that could be described as love. And when he left to return to Italy, as he inevitably would, she'd miss him but she wouldn't pine.

Which just went to prove that she'd been right all along.

There was a tap on the door and she looked up as Mrs Bruce entered, her face pale and her eyes tired.

'I'm sorry to bother you, Dr Anderson,' she began, but Alice immediately shook her head.

'Don't apologise. I understand you had a scan.'

Mrs Bruce sank into the chair and started to sob quietly. 'And they think the baby has a cleft palate.' The tears poured down her cheeks and she fumbled in her bag for a tissue. 'There was so much I wanted to ask. I had all these questions…' Her voice cracked. 'But the girl couldn't answer any of them and now I have to wait to see some consultant or other and I can't even remember his name.' The sobs became gulps. 'They don't know what it's like. The waiting.'

'It will be Mr Phillips, the consultant plastic surgeon, I expect.' Alice reached for her phone and pressed the button that connected her to Gio's room. 'Dr Moretti?

If you could come into my room for one moment when you've finished with your patient, I'd be grateful.'

Then she replaced the receiver and stood up. 'You poor thing.' She slipped an arm around the woman's shoulders and gave her a hug without even thinking about it. 'You've had a terrible shock. But there's plenty that can be done, trust me. There's an excellent cleft lip and palate team at the hospital. They serve the whole region and I promise that you won't leave this surgery until you know more about what to expect, even if I have to ring the consultant myself.'

Mrs Bruce blew her nose hard and shook her head. 'She isn't even born yet,' she said in a wavering voice, 'and already I'm worried that she's going to be teased and bullied at school. You know what kids are like. They're cruel. And appearance is everything.'

Alice gave her another squeeze and then looked up as Gio walked into the room.

'Dr Moretti—this is Mrs Bruce. The hospital have told her that her baby has a cleft palate and she's terribly upset, which is totally understandable. They don't seem to have given her much information so I thought you might be able to help reassure her about a few things. Answer some questions for her.'

'It's just a shock, you know?' Mrs Bruce clung to Alice's arm like a lifeline and Gio nodded as he pulled out another chair and sat down next to her.

'First let me tell you that I trained as a plastic surgeon,' he said quietly, 'and I specialised in the repair of cleft lips and palates so I know a lot about it.'

Mrs Bruce crumpled the tissue in her hand. 'Why are you a GP, then?'

Gio pulled a face and spread his hands. 'Unfortunately life does not always turn out the way we intend. I had an accident which meant I could no longer operate for long periods. So I changed direction in my career.'

'So you've operated on children with this? Can you make them look normal?'

'In the hands of a skilled surgeon the results can be excellent but, of course, there are no guarantees and there are many factors involved. A cleft lip can range in severity from a slight notch in the red part of the upper lip…' he gestured with his finger '…to a complete separation of the lip, extending into the nose. The aim of surgery is to close the separation in the first operation and to achieve symmetry, but that isn't always possible.'

He was good, Alice thought to herself as she sat quietly, listening along with the mother. Really good.

Mrs Bruce sniffed. 'Will they do it straight away when she's born?'

'They usually wait until the baby is ten weeks old. The repair of a cleft palate requires more extensive surgery and is usually done when the child is between nine and eighteen months old so that it is better able to tolerate the procedure.'

'Is it a huge operation?'

'In some children a cleft palate may involve only a tiny portion at the back of the roof of the mouth or it might be a complete separation that extends from front to back.' Gio reached for a pad and a pen that was lying on Alice's desk. 'It will make more sense if I draw you a picture.'

Mrs Bruce watched as his pen flew over the page, demonstrating the defect and the repair. 'How will she be able to suck if her mouth is—?' She broke off and gave a sniff. 'If her mouth looks like that?'

'There are special bottles that will help her feed.' Gio put the pad down on the desk. 'Looking after the child with a cleft lip and palate has to be a team approach, Mrs Bruce. She may need help with feeding, with speech and other aspects of her development. The surgeon is really only one member of the team. You will have plenty of support, be assured of that.'

Alice sat patiently while Gio talked, reassuring the mother, answering questions and explaining as best he could.

Finally, when she seemed calmer, he reached for the pad again and scribbled a number on a piece of paper. 'If you have other worries, things you think of later and wish you'd asked, you can call me,' he said gently, handing her the piece of paper.

She stared at it. 'You're giving me your phone number?'

He nodded. 'Use it, if you have questions. If the hospital tells you something you don't understand. Or you can always make an appointment, of course.'

'Thank you.' Mrs Bruce gave him a shaky smile and then turned to Alice and squeezed her hand. 'And thank you, too, Dr Anderson.'

'We'll tackle the problem together, Mrs Bruce,' Alice said firmly. 'She'll be managed by the hospital, but never forget that you're still our patient.' She watched Mrs Bruce—a much happier Mrs Bruce—leave the room and then turned to Gio. 'Thanks for that. I didn't have a clue what to say to her. And I don't know much about cleft palates. Will the baby have long-term problems?'

Gio pulled a face. 'Possibly many. They can be very prone to recurrent middle-ear infections, which can lead to scarring of the ossicular chain in the middle ear, and that can damage hearing or even cause deafness.'

'Why are they susceptible to ear infections?'

'In cleft babies, the muscle sling across the palate is incomplete, divided by the cleft, so they can't pull on the eustachian tube,' he explained. 'Also, scar formation following the postnatal correction of cleft lip and palate can lead to abnormal soft tissue, bone and dental growth. There has been some research looking at the possibilities of operating *in utero* in the hope of achieving healing without scarring.'

This was his area. His speciality. And she was fascinated. 'What else?'

'Sometimes there is a gap in the bone, known as the alveolar defect. Then the maxillary facial surgeon will do an alveolar bone graft.'

There was something in his face that made her reach out and touch his arm. 'Do you miss it, Gio?'

'Sometimes.' He gave a lopsided smile. 'Not always.'

'Well, you were great with her. I knew you would be.'

'You were good with her, too.' He shot her a curious look. 'Do you even realise how much you've changed.'

'Changed? How have I changed?' She went back to her chair and hit a button on her computer.

'You were touching a patient and you were doing it instinctively. You were offering physical comfort and emotional support.'

Alice frowned. 'Well, she was upset.'

'Yes.' Gio's voice was soft. 'She was. And you coped well with it. Emotions, Alice. Emotions.'

'What exactly are you implying?'

'That you're getting used to touching and being touched.' He strolled to the door. 'All I have to do now is persuade you to admit that you love me. Tomorrow I'm taking you out to dinner. Prepare yourself.'

'That's nice.' Her breath caught at the look in his eyes. She didn't love him. *She had absolutely nothing to worry about because she didn't love him.* 'Where are we going?'

'My favourite place to eat in the whole world.'

'Oh.' She felt a flicker of surprise. Knowing Gio's tastes for the spectacular, she was surprised that there was anywhere locally that would satisfy him. Perhaps he'd discovered somewhere new. 'I'll look forward to it.'

It took a considerable amount of planning and a certain amount of deviousness on his part, but finally he had it all arranged.

He was gambling everything on a hunch.

The hunch that she loved him but wasn't even aware of it herself.

She'd lived her whole life convinced that love didn't exist, so persuading her to change her mind at this stage wouldn't be easy.

Words alone had failed and so had sexual intimacy, so for days he'd racked his brains for another way of proving to her that love existed. That she could let herself feel what he already knew that she felt.

And finally he'd come up with a plan.

A plan that had involved a considerable number of other people.

And now all he could do was wait. Wait and hope.

* * *

Alice had just finished morning surgery the following day when Gio strolled into the room.

'Fancy a quick lunch?' His tone was casual and she gave a nod, surprised by how eager she was to leave work and spend time with him.

'Why not?' It was just because she enjoyed his company and was making the most of it while he was here. What was wrong with that?

She followed him out of the surgery, expecting him to turn and walk up the street to the coffee-shop. Instead, he turned left, round the back of the building and towards the surgery car park.

'You're taking the car?' She frowned. 'Where are we going?'

'Wait and see.' He held the door of his car open and she slipped into the passenger seat, a question in her eyes.

'We can't go far. We have to be back for two o'clock.'

He covered his eyes with a pair of sunglasses and gave her a smile. 'Stop thinking about work for five minutes.'

It was on the tip of her tongue to tell him that she hardly thought about work at all these days, but something stopped her. If she made a comment like that, he'd read something into it that wasn't there.

Wondering where he could possibly be taking her and thinking that he was acting very strangely, Alice sat back in her seat and pondered some of the problems that she'd seen that morning. And found she couldn't concentrate on any of them.

It was Gio's fault, she thought crossly. Going out for lunch with him was too distracting. She should have said no.

The wind played with her hair and she caught it and swept it out of her eyes. And noticed where they were.

'This is the airport.' She glanced behind her to check that she wasn't mistaken. 'Gio, this is the road to the airport. Why are we going to the airport?'

He kept driving, his hands steady on the wheel. 'Because I want to.'

'You want to eat plastic sandwiches in an airport?'

'You used to live on plastic sandwiches before you met me,' he reminded her in an amused voice, and she laughed.

'Maybe I did. But you've given me a taste for pasta. Gio, what is going on?' They'd arrived at the small airport and everything seemed to be happening around her.

Before she could catch her breath and form any more questions, she was standing on the runway, at the foot of a set of steps that led into the body of an aircraft.

'Go on. We don't want to miss our slot.' Gio walked up behind her, carrying two cases and she stared at them.

'What are those?'

'Our luggage.'

'I don't have any luggage. I was just coming out for a sandwich.' She brushed the hair out of her eyes, frustrated by the lack of answers she was receiving to her questions. 'Gio, what is going on?'

'I'm taking you to my favourite place to eat.'

'That's this evening. It's only one o'clock in the afternoon.' She watched as a man appeared behind them and took the cases onto the plane. 'Who's he? What's he doing with those?'

'He's putting them on the plane.' Gio took her arm. 'We're leaving at one o'clock because it takes a long time to get there, and we're going by plane because it's the best way to reach Sicily.'

'Sicily?' Her voice skidded and squeaked. 'You're taking me to *Sicily?*'

'You'll love it.'

Had he gone totally mad? 'I'm sure I'll love it and maybe I'll go there one day, but not on a Thursday afternoon when I have a well-woman clinic and a late surgery!' She looked over her shoulder, ready to make a dash back to the car, but he closed a hand over her arm and urged her onto the steps.

'Forget work, *tesoro*. It's all taken care of. David and Trisha are taking over for five days.'

'David?' With him so close behind her, she was forced to climb two more steps. 'What's he got to do with this? He's in London.'

'Not any more. He's currently back in your surgery, preparing for your well-woman clinic.' He brushed her hair away from her face and dropped a gentle kiss on her mouth. 'When did you last have a holiday, Alice?'

'I haven't felt the need for a holiday. I like my life.' She took another step upwards, her expression exasperated. 'Or, rather, I liked my life the way it was before everyone started interfering!'

He urged her up another step. 'I'll do you a deal— if, after this weekend, you want to go back to your old life, I'll let you. No arguments.'

'But I can't just—'

He nudged her forwards. 'Yes, you can.'

'You're kidnapping me in broad daylight!'

'That's right. I am.' His broad shoulders blocked her

exit and she made a frustrated sound in her throat and turned and stomped up the remaining steps.

This was totally ridiculous!

It was—

She stopped dead, her eyes widening as she saw the cabin. It was unlike any plane she'd ever seen before. Two soft creamy leather sofas faced each other across a richly carpeted aisle. A table covered in crisply laundered linen was laid for lunch, the silver cutlery glinting in the light.

Her mouth dropped.

'This isn't a plane. It's a living room.' Glancing over her shoulder, she realised that she'd been so distracted by the fact he was planning to take her away, she hadn't been paying attention. 'We didn't come through the airport the normal way.'

'This is a private plane.' He pushed her forward and nodded to the uniformed flight attendant who was smiling and waiting for them to board.

'Private plane?' Not knowing what else to do, she walked towards the sofas, feeling bemused and more than a little faint. 'Whose private plane?'

He sat down next to her. 'My brother, Marco, has made quite a success of his olive oil business.' Gio's tone was smooth as he leaned across to fasten her seat belt before placing another kiss on her cheek. 'It has certain compensations for the rest of his family. And now, *tesoro*, relax and prepare to be spoiled.'

She wished he'd stop touching her.

She couldn't think or concentrate when he touched her and she had a feeling that she was really, really going to need to concentrate.

CHAPTER TEN

THE moment the plane landed, Alice knew it was possible to fall in love. With a country, at least.

And as they drove away from the airport and along the coast, the heat of the sun warmed her skin and lifted her spirits. It was summer in Cornwall, of course, but somehow it didn't feel the same.

As she relaxed in her seat and watched the country fly past, all she knew was that that she'd never seen a sky more blue or a sea that looked more inviting. As they drove, the coast was a golden blur of orange and lemon orchards and she wanted to beg Gio to stop the car, just so that she could pick the fruit from the tree.

As if sensing the change in her, he reached across and rested a hand on her leg, his other hand steady on the wheel. 'It is beautiful, no?'

'Wonderful.' She turned to look at him. 'Where are we going?'

'Always you ask questions.' With a lazy smile in her direction, he returned his hand to the wheel. 'We are going to dinner, *tesoro*. Just as I promised we would.'

The warmth of the sun and the tantalising glimpses of breathtaking coastline and ancient historical sights distracted her from delving more deeply, and it was early evening when Gio pulled off the main road, drove down a dusty lane and into a large courtyard.

Alice was captivated. 'Is this where we're staying? It's beautiful. Is it a hotel?'

'It has been in my family for at least five generations,' Gio said, opening the boot and removing the cases. 'It's home.'

'Home?' The smile faded and she felt nerves flicker in the pit of her stomach. 'You're taking me to meet your parents.'

'Not just my parents, *tesoro*.' He slammed the boot shut and strolled over to her, sliding a hand into her hair and tilting her head. 'My whole family. Everyone lives in this area. We congregate here. We exchange news. We show interest in each other's lives. We offer support when it's needed and praise when it's deserved and quite often when it isn't. But most of all we offer unconditional love. It's what we do.'

'But I—'

'Hush.' He rested a finger on her lips to prevent her from speaking. 'You don't believe in love, Alice Anderson, because you've never seen it. But after this weekend you will no longer be able to use that excuse. Welcome to Sicily. Welcome to my home.'

She looked a little lost, he thought to himself, seated among his noisy, ebullient family. A little wary. As if she had no idea how to act surrounded by a large group of people who so clearly adored each other.

As his mother piled the table high with Sicilian delicacies, his father recounted the tale of his latest medical drama in his severely restricted English and Gio saw Alice smile. And respond.

She was shy, he noticed. Unsure how to behave in a large group. But they drew her into the conversation in the way that his family always welcomed any guest at their table. The language was a mix of Italian and English. English when they addressed her directly and could find the words, Italian when the levels of excitement bubbled over and they restarted to their native tongue with much hand waving and voice raising, which would have sent a lesser person running for cover. His grandmother spoke only a Sicilian dialect and his younger sister, Lucia, acted as interpreter, her dark eyes sparkling as she was given the opportunity to show off her English in public.

And gradually Alice started to relax. After eating virtually nothing, he saw her finally lift her fork. He intercepted his mother's look of approval and understanding.

And knew that he'd been right to bring her.

The buzz of conversation still ringing in her ears, Alice followed Gio out into the semi-darkness. 'Where are we going?'

'I don't actually live in the house any more.' He took her hand and led her towards a track that wound through a citrus orchard towards the sea. 'Years ago my brother and I built a small villa at the bottom of the orchard. The idea was to let it to tourists but then we decided we wanted to keep it. He's long since moved to something more extravagant but I keep this place as a bolthole. I love my family but even I need space from them.'

'I thought they were lovely.' She couldn't keep the envy out of her voice and suddenly she stopped walking and just stood and stared. Tiny lights illuminated the path that ran all the way to the beach. The air was warm and she could smell the fruit trees and hear the lap of the sea against the sand. 'This whole place is amazing. I just can't imagine it.'

'Can't imagine what?'

'Growing up here. With those people.' She took her hand away from his and reached out to pick a lemon from the nearest tree. It fell into her hand, complete with leaves and stalk, and she stared at it, fascinated. 'It's no wonder you believe in love, Dr Moretti. I think it would be possible to believe in just about anything if you lived here.'

He stepped towards her. Took her face in his hands. 'And do you believe in it, Alice? You met my family this evening. My parents have been together for almost forty years, my grandparents for sixty-two years. I believe that my great-grandparents were married for sixty-five years, although no one can be sure because no one can actually remember a time when they weren't together.' His thumb stroked her cheek. 'What did you see tonight, Alice? Was it convenience? Friendship? Any of those reasons you once gave me for people choosing to spend their lives together?'

Her heart was thumping in her chest and she shook her head slowly. 'No. It was love.' Her voice cracked as she said the words. 'I saw love.'

'Finally.' Gio closed his eyes briefly and murmured something in Italian. 'Let's go—I want to show you how I feel about you.'

* * *

It was tender and loving, slow and drawn out, with none of the fevered desperation of their previous encounters. Flesh slid against flesh, hard male against soft female, whispers and muttered words the only communication between them.

The bedroom of the villa opened directly onto the beach and she could hear the sounds of the sea, feel the night air as it flowed into the room and cooled them.

Long hours passed. Hours during which they feasted and savoured, each reluctant to allow the other to sleep.

And finally, when her body was so languid and sated that she couldn't imagine ever wanting to move again, he rolled onto his side and looked into her eyes.

'I love you, Alice.' His voice was quiet in the semi-darkness. 'I want you to be with me always. For ever. I want you to marry me, *tesoro*.'

'No, Gio.' The word made her shiver and she would have backed away but he held her tightly.

'Tonight you admitted that love exists.'

'For some other people maybe.' She whispered the words, almost as if she was afraid to speak them too loudly. 'But not for me.'

'Why not for you?'

'Because I don't—I can't—'

'Because when you were a child, your mother let you fall.' He lifted a hand and stroked the hair away from her face. 'She let you fall and now you don't trust anyone to be there to catch you. Isn't that right, Alice?'

'It isn't—'

'But you have to learn to trust. For the first time in your life you have to learn.' His mouth hovered a mere breath away from hers. 'You can fall, Alice. You can fall, *tesoro,* and I'll be standing here ready to catch you. Always. That's what love is. It's a promise.'

Tears filled her eyes. 'You make it sound so perfect and simple.'

'Because it is both perfect and simple.'

'No.' She shook her head and let the tears fall. 'That is what my mother thought. Every time she was with a man she had these same feelings and she thought they were love. But they turned out to be something entirely different. Something brittle and destructive. My father was the same. And I have their genes. I believe that *you* can love, but I don't believe the same of myself. I can't do it. I'm not capable of it.'

'You are still afraid.' He brushed the tears away with his thumb. 'You think that you are still that little girl on the climbing frame, but you're not. Over the past few weeks I've watched you and I've seen you learning to touch and be touched. I've seen you becoming comfortable with other people's emotions. All we need to do now is make you comfortable with your own.'

'It won't work, Gio. I'm sorry.'

Their bags were packed and Gio was up at the house having a final meeting with his brother about family business. She hovered in the courtyard, enjoying the peace and tranquillity of the setting.

After four days of lying on the beach and swimming in the pool, she should have felt relaxed and refreshed. Instead, she felt tense and miserable. And the last thing she wanted was to go home.

From the courtyard of the main house she stared down through the citrus orchard to the sea and then glanced behind her, her eyes on the summit of Mount Etna, which dominated the skyline.

'We will miss you when you've gone. You must come again soon, Alice.' Gio's mother walked up behind her and gave her a warm hug.

'Thank you for making me feel so welcome.' The stiffness inside her subsided and she hugged the older woman back, envying Gio his family.

'Anyone who has taught my Gio to smile again will always be welcome here.'

Alice pulled away slightly. 'He always smiles.'

'Not since the accident. He was frustrated. Sad. Grieving for the abilities that he'd lost. His ability to help all those poor little children. You have shown him that a new life is possible. That change can be good. You have given him a great deal. But that is what love is all about. Giving.'

Alice swallowed. 'I haven't—I don't—'

'You will come and see us again soon. You must promise me that.'

'Well, I…' she licked her lips, 'Gio will probably want to bring some other girl—'

His mother frowned. 'I doubt it.' Her voice was quiet. 'You are the first girl he has ever brought home, Alice.'

The first girl?

Alice stared at her and the other woman smiled.

'He has had girlfriends, yes, of course. He is an attractive, healthy young man so that is natural. But love…' She gave a fatalistic shrug. 'That only happens to a man once in a lifetime, and for my Giovanni it is now. Don't take too long to realise that you feel the same way, Alice. To lose something so precious would be nothing short of a tragedy.'

With that she turned and walked back across the courtyard into the house, leaving Alice staring after her.

Gio stood on the beach and stared out to sea, unable to drag himself away. Disappointment sat in his gut like a lead weight that he couldn't shift.

He'd relied on this place, *his home,* to provide the key he needed. To unlock that one remaining part of Alice that was still hidden away. But his plan had failed.

Maybe he'd just underestimated the depth of the damage that her parents had done to her.

Or maybe he was wrong to think that she loved him. Maybe she didn't love him at all.

'Gio?' Her voice sounded tentative, as if she wasn't sure of her welcome, and he turned with a smile. It cost him in terms of effort but he was determined that she shouldn't feel bad. None of this was her fault. None of it.

He glanced at his watch. 'You're right—we should be leaving. Are you ready?'

'No. No, I'm not, actually.' She stepped away from him, a slender figure clothed in a blue dress that dipped at the neck and floated past her knees. Her feet were bare and she was wearing a flower in her hair.

The transformation was complete, he thought to himself sadly. A few weeks ago her wardrobe had all been about work. Practical skirts and comfortable shoes. Neat tops with tailored jackets.

Now she looked relaxed and feminine. Like the exquisitely beautiful woman that she was.

'Well, you have five more minutes before we have to

leave.' He prompted her gently. 'If there are still things you need to fetch, you'd better fetch them fast.'

'There's nothing I need to fetch.' In four days on the beach her pale skin had taken on a soft golden tone and her blonde hair fell silky smooth to her shoulders. 'But there are things that I need to say.'

'Alice—'

'No, I really need to be allowed to speak.' She stood on tiptoe and covered his lips with her fingers, the way he'd done to her so many times. 'I didn't realise. I didn't realise that giving up surgery had meant so much to you. You hid that well.'

He tensed. 'I—'

'It's nice to know that other people hide things, too. That it isn't just me. It makes me realise that everyone has things inside them that they don't necessarily want to share.' She let her fingers drop from his mouth. 'It doesn't stop you from moving forward. It's nice to know that, even though you didn't smile for a while, you're smiling again now. And it's nice to know that I'm the only woman that you've ever brought home.'

'You've been speaking to my mother.'

'Yes.' She glanced down at her feet. Curled her toes into the sand. 'And I want it to stay that way. I want to be the first and last woman that you ever bring here. I should probably tell you that I'm seriously in love with your mother. And your sisters and brother, grandparents, uncles and aunts.'

'You are?' Hope flickered inside him, and the tiny flicker grew as she lifted her head and looked at him, her blue eyes clear and honest.

'You're right that I'm afraid. I'm afraid that everything that's in my past might get in the way of our future. I'm afraid that I might mess everything up.' She swallowed and took a deep breath, her hands clasped in front of her. 'I'm afraid of so many things. But love only happens once in a lifetime and it's taken me this long to find it so I can't let my fear stand in my way.' She held out her hand and lifted her chin. 'I'm ready to climb, Gio, if you promise that you'll be there to catch me. I'm ready to marry you, if you'll still have me.'

He took her hand, closed his eyes briefly and pulled her hard against him. 'I love you and I will always love you, even when you're ninety and you're still trying to talk to me about work when all I want to do is lie in the sun and look at my lemon trees.'

She looked up at him, eyes shining, and he felt his heart tumble. 'I have another confession to make—I haven't actually been thinking about work as much lately.'

'Is that so, Dr Anderson?' His expression was suddenly serious. 'And that's something that we haven't even discussed. What we do about work. Where we are going to live.' Did she want to stay in Cornwall? Was she thinking of moving to Italy?

She shrugged her shoulders. 'It doesn't matter.'

He couldn't hide his surprise. 'Well, I—'

'What matters is us,' she said quietly, her hand still in his. 'You've shown me that. I love you, Gio, and I always will. I believe in love now. A love that can last. This place makes me believe that. You make me believe it.'

For the first time in his adult life words wouldn't come, so he bent his head and kissed her.

SICILIAN MILLIONAIRE, BOUGHT BRIDE

Catherine Spencer

Catherine Spencer, once an English teacher, fell into writing through eavesdropping on a conversation about romances. Within two months she'd changed careers, and sold her first book to Mills & Boon in 1984. She moved to Canada from England thirty years ago, and lives in Vancouver. She is married to a Canadian and has four grown children—two daughters and two sons (and now eight grandchildren)—plus three dogs. In her spare time she plays the piano, collects antiques, and grows tropical shrubs.

You can visit Catherine Spencer's website at www.catherinespencer.com

CHAPTER ONE

TERSE AND ENIGMATIC, the letter sat on Corinne Mallory's dressing table, held in place by a can of hair spray. Hardly a fitting resting place, she supposed, for correspondence written on vellum embossed with an ornate gold family crest. On the other hand, considering her initial response had been to decline its autocratic summons, it was a miracle that she hadn't tossed the whole works in the garbage.

But the name at the end of the typed missive, signed in bold, impatient script, had given her pause. Raffaello Orsini had been married to her dearest friend, and Lindsay had been crazy about him, right up to the day she died. That alone had made Corinne swallow her pride and accede to his wishes. Whatever the reason for his sudden visit to Canada, loyalty to Lindsay's memory demanded Corinne not refuse him.

Now that she was just two short hours away from meeting the man face-to-face for the first time, however, she wasn't so sure she'd made the right decision. What did one wear to an invitation that smacked more of a command performance than a request?

Eyeing the limited contents of her closet, she decided

basic black was probably the most appropriate choice. With pearls. Dinner at the Pan Pacific, Vancouver's most prestigious hotel, called for a touch of elegance, even if the pearls in question weren't the real thing, and the black dress made of faux silk.

At least her black pumps came with a designer emblem on the instep, a reminder of the time when she'd been able to afford a few luxuries.

A reminder, too, of Lindsay, a tiny woman full of big dreams, who hadn't believed in the word "can't."

We'll buy some run-down, flea-bitten old place in the right part of town, and turn it into a boutique hotel, Corinne. I'll take care of housekeeping and decor, and you'll be in charge of the kitchen.

We'll need a fairy godmother to accomplish that.

Not us! We can do anything we set our minds to. Nothing's going to derail us.

What if we fall in love and get married?

It'll have to be to men who share our vision. She'd flashed her dimpled smile. *And it'd help if they were also very, very rich!*

And if they're not?

It won't matter, because we'll make our own luck. We can do this, Corinne. I know we can. We'll call it The Bowman-Raines Hotel, and have a great big old BR emblazoned over the front entrance. By the time we're thirty, we'll be famous for our hospitality and our dining room. People will kill to stay with us….

But all that was before Lindsay went to Sicily on holiday, and fell in love with Raffaello Orsini who was indeed very, very rich, but who had no interest whatsoever in sharing her dreams. Instead he'd converted her to his. Forgetting all about creating the most acclaimed hotel in the Pacific northwest, she'd moved halfway around the world to be his wife and start a family.

And the luck she'd believed in so fiercely? It had turned on her, striking her down at twenty-four with leukemia, and leaving her three-year-old daughter motherless.

Swamped in memories, Corinne blinked back the incipient tears, leaned closer to the mirror to sweep a mascara wand over her lashes and tried to remember the last time she'd worn eye makeup. Far too long ago, judging by the finished effect, but it would have to do, and really, what did it matter? Whatever the reason for his sudden visit, Raffaello Orsini certainly hadn't been inspired by a burning desire to evaluate her artistry with cosmetics.

Downstairs, she heard Mrs. Lehman, her next-door neighbor and baby-sitter, rattling dishes as she served Matthew his supper.

Matthew hadn't been happy that his mother was going out. "I hate it when you go to work," he'd announced, his lower lip trembling ominously.

With good reason, Corinne had to admit. She frequently missed tucking her son into bed, because her work too often involved late nights and time during his school holidays. It was the nature of the beast and much though she'd have preferred it otherwise, there wasn't much she could do about it, not if she wanted to keep a roof over their heads and food on the table.

"I won't be late, and I'll make blueberry pancakes for breakfast," she promised. "Be a good boy for Mrs. Lehman, and don't give her a hard time about going to bed, okay?"

"I might," he warned balefully. Although only four, he'd recently developed an alarming talent for blackmail. He was becoming, in fact, quite a handful. But Corinne hoped tonight wouldn't be one of those nights when she arrived home to find Mrs. Lehman exhausted from fighting to get him to bed, and Matthew still racing up and down the stairs every fifteen minutes and generally raising mayhem.

I should be staying home, Corinne thought, the familiar guilt sweeping over her as smoothly as the black dress slid past her hips. But the letter pulled at her, and even though she could have recited it word for word from memory, she picked it up and scoured it yet again, as if the writer's reason for sending it might be hidden between the lines.

Villa di Cascata
Sicily
January 6, 2008
Signora Mallory:
I shall be in Vancouver later this month on a matter of some urgency recently brought to my attention and which I wish to discuss with you in confidence.

I have reservations at the Pan Pacific Hotel and would appreciate your joining me there for dinner on Friday, January 28, a date I trust you find convenient. Unless I hear otherwise, I shall send a car for you at seven-thirty.
Kindest regards,
Raffaello Orsini

But just as with the first reading, there was nothing. No hint of what she might expect. And if the racket taking place in the kitchen was anything to go by, Matthew was gearing up to give poor Mrs. Lehman another night of grief.

"This had better be good, Mr. Orsini," Corinne muttered, tossing the letter aside, and taking a last glance in the mirror before going downstairs to appease a little boy who had no memory of his father, and whose mother seemed to be making a lousy job of doing double duty as a parent.

The view, Raffaello decided, was impressive. To the north, snowcapped mountains glimmered in carved splendor against the clear night sky. The lights of a bridge spanning the entrance to the harbor looped like so many diamonds above the Narrows. And closer at hand, almost directly below his suite, a yacht some twenty-five meters long or more rocked gently at its moorage.

Not Sicily, by any stretch of the imagination, but arresting nonetheless, as much because it had been Lindsay's home, a setting both wild and sophisticated, beautiful and intriguing, just like her.

Two years ago, one year even, and he could not have come here. The pain had been too raw, his grief too filled with anger. But time had a way of healing even the most savage wounds; of gilding the memories that were his wife's legacy, and turning them into a source of comfort. "I do this for you, *amore mio,*" he murmured, raising his eyes to the heavens.

Somewhere in the city below, a church bell rang out, eight solemn chimes. The woman, Corinne Mallory, was late. Impatient to get down to the business of the evening and be done with it, he paced to the telephone and buzzed the front desk to remind whoever was in charge that she should be directed to his suite when—*if*—she showed up. What he had to propose was not something to be aired in public.

Another ten minutes dragged past before she arrived, her knock so sudden and peremptory that his hackles rose. Curbing his irritation, he shot his cuffs and tugged his lapels into place.

Remember she was Lindsay's best friend. That does not mean she has to be yours, but it will be better for everyone if you can at least establish a sympathetic cordiality, he cautioned himself, striding to the door.

He had seen photographs, of course, and thought he knew what to expect of the woman waiting on the other side. But she was more delicate than he'd anticipated. Like fine lace that had been handled too carelessly, so that her skin was almost transparent and stretched too tightly over her fine bones, leaving her face much too small for her very blue eyes.

Standing back, he waved her across the threshold. "Signora Mallory, thank you for agreeing to see me. Please come in."

She hesitated a moment before complying. "I'm not aware you gave me much choice, Mr. Orsini," she said, her accent so vivid a reminder of Lindsay's that he was momentarily disconcerted. "Nor did I expect our meeting would take place in your room, and I can't say I'm particularly comfortable with that."

What did she think? That he'd traveled halfway around the world to seduce her? "My intentions are entirely honorable," he replied, tempted to tell her that if a romp in bed was all he wanted, he could have found it much closer to home.

She let him take her coat and shrugged, an elegantly

dismissive little gesture that made the pearls nested at her throat slither gently against her skin. "They'd better be," she said.

Suppressing a smile, he motioned to the array of bottles set out on the bar. "Will you join me in a drink before dinner?"

Again, she paused before inclining her head in assent. "A very weak wine spritzer, please."

"So," he said, adding a generous dollop of San Pellegrino to an inch of Pinot Grigio, and pouring a shot of whiskey for himself, "tell me about yourself, *signora*. I know only that you and my late wife were great friends, and that you are widowed, with a young son."

"Which is rather more than I know about you, Mr. Orsini," she replied, with a candor he found rather disarming. "And since I have absolutely no idea what this meeting is all about, I'd just as soon get down to business as waste time regaling you with a life history I'm sure you have no real interest in hearing about."

Joining her on the other side of the room, he handed her the spritzer and raised his own glass in a wordless toast. "That's where you're mistaken. Please understand that I have a most compelling and, indeed, legitimate reason for wanting to learn more about you."

"Fine. Then until you share that reason with me, please understand that I am not about to gratify your curiosity. I don't pretend to know how things are done in Sicily, but in this country, no woman with a grain of sense agrees to meet a strange man alone in his hotel room. Had I known that was your plan, I would most definitely not have come." She set her drink down on the coffee table and glanced very pointedly at her silver wristwatch. "You have exactly five minutes to explain yourself, Mr. Orsini, and then I'm out of here."

He took a sip of his whiskey and eyed her appraisingly. "I can see why you and my wife were such close friends. She, too, drove straight to the heart of a matter. It was one of the many qualities I admired in her."

"Four and a half minutes, Mr. Orsini, and I'm fast losing my patience."

"Very well." He picked up the leather folder he'd left on the coffee table and withdrew the letter. "This is for you. I think you'll find its contents self-explanatory."

She glanced briefly at the handwriting and paled. "It's from Lindsay."

"*Si.*"

"How do you know what it's about?"

"I read it."

A flush chased away her pallor. "Who gave you the right?"

"I did."

"Remind me never to leave private correspondence lying about when you're around," she said, her blue eyes flaring with indignation.

"Read your letter, *signora,* and then I will let you read mine. Perhaps when you've done that, you'll regard me with less hostility, and have a better understanding of why I came all this way to meet you."

She flung him one last doubtful glance, then bent her attention to the contents of the letter. At first, her hand was steady, but as she continued to read, the paper fluttered as if caught in the faintest of breezes, and by the time she reached the end, she was visibly shaking.

"Well, *signora?*"

She raised shocked eyes to his. "This is…ridiculous. She can't have been in her right mind."

"My wife was lucid to the last. Disease might have ravaged her body, but not her mind." He pushed his own letter across the table. "Here is what she asked of me. You'll notice both letters were written on the same day. Mine is a copy of the original. If you wish, you may keep it, to read again at your leisure."

Reluctantly Corinne Mallory took the second letter, scanned it quickly, then handed it back to him and shook her head in further disbelief. "I'm having a hard time accepting that Lindsay knew what she was asking."

"Yet viewed dispassionately, it makes a certain sense."

"Not to me it doesn't," she retorted flatly. "And I can't believe it does to you, either, or you'd have brought it to my attention sooner. These letters were written over three years ago. Why did you wait until now to tell me about them?"

"I accidentally discovered them myself only a few weeks ago. Lindsay had tucked them inside a photograph album, and I admit, on first reading, my reaction was much the same as yours."

"I hope you're not implying you're now in agreement with her wishes?"

"At the very least, they merit serious consideration."

Corinne Mallory rolled her big blue eyes and reached for her wineglass. "I might need something a bit stronger than this, after all."

"I understand the idea takes some getting used to, Signora Mallory, but I hope you won't dismiss it out of hand. From a purely practical standpoint, such an arrangement has much to recommend it."

"I've no wish to offend you, Mr. Orsini, but if you seriously believe that, I can't help thinking you must be a few bricks short of a full load."

"An interesting turn of phrase," he remarked, unable to suppress a smile, "but far from accurate, and I hope to persuade you of that over dinner."

"After reading these letters, I'm no longer sure dinner's such a good idea."

"Why not? Are you afraid I might sway you into changing your mind?"

"No," she said, with utter conviction.

"Then where's the harm in our discussing the matter over a good meal? If, at the end of it all, you're still of a mind to walk away, I certainly won't try to stop you. After all, the doubts cut two ways. At this point, I'm no more persuaded of the viability of my wife's request, than are you. But in honor of her memory, the very least I can do is put it to the test. She would expect no less of me—nor, I venture to point out, of you."

Corinne Mallory wrestled with herself for a moment or two, then heaved a sigh. "All right, I'll stay—for Lindsay's sake, because this meant so much to her. But please don't harbor any hope that I'll go along with her wishes."

He raised his glass again. "For Lindsay's sake," he agreed then, as a knock came at the door, gestured to the dining area situated in the corner. "That'll be our dinner. I ordered it served up here. Now that you realize the delicate nature of our business, I'm sure you agree it's not something to be conducted where others might overhear."

"I suppose not." Her reply signified agreement, but the hunted glance she cast around the suite suggested she was more interested in making a fast escape. "Is there some-place I can freshen up before we sit down?"

"Of course." He indicated the guest powder room at the end of the short hall leading past the kitchen and bedroom. "Take your time, *signora*. I expect the chef and his staff will need a few minutes to set everything up."

She'd need a lot more than a few minutes to pull herself together! Locking the powder room door, Corinne stared in the mirror over the long vanity unit, not surprised to find her cheeks flushed and her eyes feverishly bright. Emotionally she was under siege on all fronts, and had been from the second she'd arrived at Raffaello Orsini's door and come face-to-face with the most beautiful man she'd ever seen.

At the time of her wedding, Lindsay had sent photos, but that was years ago, and even if it had taken place just yesterday, no camera could capture his raw sexual magnetism. A person had to view him in the flesh to appreciate that. For Corinne, the experience had almost put her in a trance.

He did not look the part in which she'd cast him. Yes, he had the smooth olive skin and gleaming black hair typical of someone Mediterranean born and bred, but as she understood it, Sicilian men did not, as a rule, stand over six feet tall, or sport a pair of shoulders that would do a football running back proud.

As for his face, she'd hardly been able to bring herself to look at it, afraid that if she did, she'd focus too intently on his sensuous mouth, rather than the words issuing from it, or lose herself in eyes the color of woodsmoke.

He'd rendered her tongue-tied, and for the first time,

she'd gained a glimmer of understanding for why Lindsay had so readily given up everything to be with him. That chiseled jaw, those exquisitely arrogant cheekbones and mesmerizing voice would have been hard to resist.

His hotel accommodation on the twenty-third floor was equally mind-boggling. A luxury suite, it was larger than most apartments, with a baby grand piano installed in the huge sitting room, seating for six at the round table in the dining alcove, and fabulous artwork on the walls. Not that she could imagine anyone paying much attention to the latter, at least not during the day, with stunning views of Stanley Park, Lions Gate Bridge, Coal Harbour and the North Shore mountains commanding attention beyond the windows.

Finally, and by far the most discombobulating, was the reason he'd asked her to meet him. If she hadn't recognized Lindsay's handwriting, she'd never have believed the letters were authentic. Even accepting that they were, she couldn't wrap her mind around their contents, which was why she'd tucked hers into her purse and brought it with her into the powder room.

Spreading it out on the vanity now, she prepared to read it again, this time without Raffaello Orsini's disturbing gaze tracking her every reaction.

June 12, 2005
Dear Corinne,
I hoped I'd see you one more time, and that we could talk, the way we've always been able to, without holding anything back. I hoped, too, that I'd be around to help Elisabetta celebrate her third birthday.

I know now that I'm not going to be here to do either of those things, and that I have very little time left to put my affairs in order. And so I'm forced to turn to writing, something which was never my strong suit.

Corinne, you've been widowed now for nearly a year, and I know better than anyone how hard it's been for you. I'm learning first-hand how painful grief can be, but to have money troubles on top of sorrow, as you continue to have, is more than anyone should have to put up with. At least I'm spared having to worry about that. But money can't buy health, nor can it compensate a child for losing a parent, something both your son and my daughter have to face. And that brings me to the point of this letter.

All children deserve two parents, Corinne. A mother to kiss away the little hurts, and to teach a daughter how to be a woman, and a son how to be tender. They also deserve a father to stand between them and a world which doesn't seem to differentiate between those able to cope with its senseless cruelties, and those too young to understand why it should be so.

I've known much happiness with Raffaello. He's a wonderful man, a wonderful role model for a young boy growing up without a father. He would be so good for your Matthew. And if I can't be there for my Elisabetta, I can think of no one I'd rather see taking my place than you, Corinne.

I've loved you practically from the day we met in second grade. You are my soul sister. So I'm asking you, please, to bring an open mind to my last wish, which is to see you and Raffaello join forces—and yes, I mean through marriage—and together fill the empty spaces in our children's lives.

You each have so much to bring to the arrangement, and so much to gain. But there's another reason that's not quite so unselfish. Elisabetta's too young to hold on to her memories of me, and I hate that. Raffaello will do his best to keep me alive in her heart, but no one knows me as well as you do. Only you can tell her what I was like as a child and a teenager. About my first big crush, my first heartbreak, my first kiss, my favorite book and movie and song, and so much more that I don't have time to list here.

It's enough to say that you and I share such a long and close history, and have never kept secrets from each other. Having you to turn to would give her the next best thing to me.

I'd trust you with my life, Corinne, but it's not worth anything now, so I'm trusting you with my daughter's instead. I want so badly to live, and I'm so afraid of dying, but I think I could face it more easily if I knew you and Raffaello…

The letter ended there, the handwriting not as sure, as if Lindsay had run out of the strength required to continue. Or perhaps she'd been too blinded by the tears, which had blurred the last few lines and left watery stains on the paper—stains made even larger by Corinne's own tears now.

Desperate to keep her grief private, she flushed the toilet, hoping the sound would disguise the sobs tearing at her, then mopped at her face with a handful of tissues. She didn't need to look in the mirror to know her makeup was ruined. The mascara stung her eyes, adding insult to injury.

"Oh, Lindsay," she mourned softly, "you know I'd do anything for you…anything at all. Except this."

CHAPTER TWO

SHE RETURNED to the main room to find the moon casting an icy swath across the ink-black waters of the harbor. Within the suite, a floor lamp poured a pool of warm yellow light over the love seat next to the window, but at the linen-draped dining table, candles now shimmered over the crystal and silverware, and lent a more subtle blush to a centerpiece of cream roses. She was glad of that. Candlelight was much kinder, its subdued glow helping to disguise her reddened eyes, bereft now of any trace of mascara.

Raffaello Orsini held out her chair before taking a seat opposite, and nodding permission for the hovering waiter to pour the wine, a very fine sparkling white burgundy. Still shaken from rereading Lindsay's letter, Corinne could barely manage a taste, and was sure she'd never be able to swallow a bite of food. She deeply regretted having accepted her host's imperious invitation. Quite apart from the fact that her composure lay in shreds, she knew she looked a mess, and what woman was ever at her sharpest under those circumstances?

At least he had the good grace not to comment on her appearance, or her initial lack of response to his conversation. Instead, as braised endive salad followed a first course of crab and avocado pâté served on toast points, with foie gras-stuffed quail bathed in a sherry vinaigrette as the entrée, he regaled her with an amusing account of his tourist experiences earlier in the day. And almost without her realizing, she was coaxed into doing at least some justice to a meal he'd clearly taken great pains to make as appealing as possible.

By the time dessert arrived, a wonderful silky chocolate mousse she couldn't resist, a good deal of her tension had melted away. The man oozed confidence, and reeked not so much of wealth, although he clearly had money to burn, but of the power that went with it. A heady combination, she had to admit. Watching him, enjoying his dry wit and keen observations, and more than a little dazzled by the smile he allowed so sparingly, she was almost able to push aside the real reason for their meeting and pretend, just for a little while, that they were merely a man and woman enjoying an evening together.

Lulled into a comfortable haze induced by candlelight, and a voice whose exotic cadence suggested an intimacy worth discovering, if only she dared, she almost relaxed. He was a complex man; an intriguing contradiction in terms. His wafer-thin Patek Philippe watch, handmade shoes and flawlessly tailored suit belonged to a CEO, a chairman of the board, a tycoon at his best wheeling and dealing megamillions in the arena of international business. Yet the contained strength of his body suggested he could sling a goat over one shoulder and scale a Sicilian mountainside without breaking a sweat. Despite that, though, there was absolutely nothing of the rustic in him. He was sophistication personified, and much too charming and handsome for his own good.

Or hers. Because, like a hawk luring a mouse into the open, he suddenly struck, diving in for the kill before she realized she'd left herself vulnerable to him. "So far, I've done all the talking, *signora*. Now it's your turn. So tell me, please, what is there about you that I might find noteworthy?"

"Not much, I'm afraid," she said, disconcerted by the question, but not yet suspecting where it would lead. "I'm a single, working parent, with very little time to do anything noteworthy."

"Too occupied with making ends meet, you mean?"

"That about covers it, yes."

"What kind of work do you do?"

"I'm a professional chef."

"Ah, yes. I remember now that my wife once mentioned that. You were snapped up by a five-star restaurant in the city, as I recall."

"Before my marriage, yes. After that, I was a stay-at-home wife and mother. When my husband died, I…needed extra income, so I opened a small catering company."

"You're now self-employed, then?"

"Yes."

"You hire others to help you?"

"Not always. At first, I could handle the entire workload alone. Now that my clientele has increased, I do bring in extra help on occasion, but still do most of the food preparation myself."

"And offer a very exclusive service to your patrons, I'm sure."

"Yes. They expect me to oversee special events in person."

"A demanding business, being one's own boss, don't you find? What prompted you to tackle such an undertaking?"

"It allowed me to be at home with my son when he was a baby."

"Resourceful and enterprising. I admire that in a woman." He steepled his fingers and regarded her sympathetically. "How do you find it, now that your son's older?"

"It's not so easy," she admitted. "He's long past the age where he's content to play quietly in a corner while I create a wedding buffet for sixty people."

He allowed himself a small, sympathetic smile. "I don't doubt it. So who looks after him when you're away taking care of the social needs of strangers?"

"My next-door neighbor," she replied, wincing inwardly at his too-accurate assessment of her clientele. "She's an older woman, a widow and a grandmother, and very reliable."

"But not quite as devoted to him as you are, I'm sure."

"Is anyone ever able to take a mother's place, Mr. Orsini?"

"No, as I have learned to my very great cost." Then switching subjects suddenly, he said, "What sort of place do you live in?"

Bristling, she snapped, "Not a hovel, if that's what you're implying," and wondered how much Lindsay had told him about her straitened circumstances.

"I didn't suggest that it was," he returned mildly. "I'm merely trying to learn more about you. Paint the appropriate background to a very attractive portrait, if you like."

Mollified enough to reply less defensively, she said, "I rent a two-bedroom town house in a gated community several miles south of the city."

"In other words, a safe place where your son can play in the garden without fear that he might wander away."

She thought of the narrow patio outside her kitchen, the strip of lawn not much bigger than a bath towel that lay beyond it and her neighbors on the other side, the Shaws— a crusty old couple in their eighties, who complained constantly that Matthew made too much noise. "Not exactly. I have no garden as such. I take him to play at a nearby park instead, and if I'm not available, my sitter takes him for me."

"But there are other children he can visit in this gated community, boys his own age, with similar interests?"

"Unfortunately not. Most residents are older—many, like my baby-sitter, retired."

"Does he at least have a dog or cat to keep him company?"

"We aren't allowed to own pets."

He raised his elegant black brows. "*Dio,* he might as well be in prison, for all the freedom he enjoys."

In truth, she couldn't refute an opinion which all too closely coincided with her own, but she wasn't about to tell him so. "Nothing's ever perfect, Mr. Orsini. If it were, our children wouldn't be growing up with one parent standing in for two."

"But they are," he replied. "Which brings me to my next question. Now that you've had time to recover from the initial shock, what is your opinion on the content of the letters?"

"What?" She raised startled eyes to his and found herself impaled in a gaze at once penetrating and inscrutable.

"Your opinion," he repeated, a sudden hint of steel threading his words. "Surely, Signora Mallory, you haven't forgotten the real reason you're here?"

"Hardly. I just haven't given the matter…much thought."

"Then I suggest you do so. Enough time has passed since my wife wrote of her last wishes. I do not propose to delay honoring them any longer than I have to."

"Well, I do not propose to be bullied, Mr. Orsini, not by you or anyone else. Since you're so anxious for an answer, though, let me be blunt. I can't see myself ever agreeing to Lindsay's request."

"Her friendship meant so little to you, then?"

"Save the emotional blackmail for someone else," she shot back. "It's not going to work with me."

His smoky-gray eyes darkened. With suppressed anger? Sorrow? Frustration? She couldn't tell. His expression gave away nothing. "Emotion does not play a role in this situation. It is a business proposition, pure and simple, devised solely for the benefit of your child and mine. The most convenient way to implement it is for you and me to join forces in marriage."

"Something I find totally unacceptable. In case you're not aware, marriages of convenience went out of fashion in this country a long time ago. Should I ever decide to marry again, which is doubtful, it will be to someone of my own choosing."

"It seems to me, Signora Mallory, that you're in no position to be so particular. By your own admission, you do not own your own home, which leaves you at the mercy of a landlord, you're overworked and your son spends a great deal of time being cared for by someone other than yourself."

"At least I have my independence."

"For which both you and your boy pay a very high price." He regarded her silently a moment, then in a seductively cajoling tone, went on, "I admire your spirit, *cara mia,* but why are you so set on continuing with your present lifestyle, when I can offer you so much more?"

"For a start, because I don't like having charity forced down my throat." *And calling me* cara mia *isn't going to change that.*

"Is that how you see this? Do you not understand that, in our situation, the favors work both ways—that my daughter stands to gain as much from the arrangement as your son?"

Absently Corinne touched a fingertip to the velvet-soft petals of the nearest rose. They reminded her of Matthew's skin when he was a baby. Before he'd turned into a tyrant.

...Raffaello will do his best to keep me alive in her heart, but having you to turn to would be the next best thing to having me, Lindsay had written, or words to that effect. *I'm entrusting you with my daughter's life, Corinne....*

Seeming to think she was actually considering his proposal, Raffaello Orsini asked, "Are you afraid I'm going to demand my husbandly rights in the bedroom?"

"I don't know. Are you?" Corinne blurted out rashly, too irked by the faint hint of derision in his question to consider how he might interpret her reply.

"Would you like me to?"

She opened her mouth to issue a flat denial, then snapped it closed as an image swam unbidden into her mind, shockingly detailed, shockingly erotic, of how Raffaello Orsini's naked body might look. Her inner response—the jolt of awareness that rocked her body, the sudden flush of heat streaming through her blood—appalled her.

She'd moved through the preceding four years like an automaton, directing all her energies to providing a safe, stable and loving home for her son. As breadwinner, the one responsible for everything from rent to medical insurance to paying off debts incurred by her late husband, she'd had no choice but to put her own needs aside. To be assaulted now by this sudden aberration—for how else could she describe it?—was ridiculous, but also an untimely reminder that she was still a woman whose sexuality might have been relegated to the back burner, but whose flame, it seemed, had not been entirely extinguished.

"Don't feel you have to make up your mind on that point at this very moment," Orsini suggested smoothly. "The welfare of two children is the main issue here, not sexual intercourse between you and me. I shall not press you to consummate the marriage against your will, but you're an attractive woman and as a hot-blooded Sicilian, I would not spurn your overtures, should you feel inclined to make any."

Hot-blooded Sicilian, maybe, she thought, staggered by his arrogance, but it'll be a cold day in hell before I come begging for sexual favors from you. "There's not the slightest chance of that ever happening, for the simple reason that I have no intention at all of agreeing to your proposition. It's a lousy idea."

"Why? What's wrong with two adults uniting to create a semblance of normal family life for their children? Don't you think they deserve it?"

"They deserve the best that we can give them—and that is *not* by having their respective parents marry for all the wrong reasons."

"That would be true only if we were deluding ourselves into believing our hearts are engaged, *signora,* which they most certainly are not. Rather, we're approaching this from a cerebral angle. And that, in my opinion, vastly increases our chances of making the union work."

"Cerebral?" She almost choked on her after-dinner coffee. "Is that how you'd define it?"

"How else? After all, it's not as if either of us is looking for love in a second marriage, both of us having lost our true soul mates, the first time around. We harbor no romantic illusions. We're simply entering into a binding contract to improve our children's lives."

Unnerved as much by his logic as his unremitting gaze, she left the table and went to stand at the window. "You omit to mention the extent to which I would benefit financially from such an arrangement."

"I hardly consider it important enough to merit attention."

"It is to me."

"Why? Because you feel you're being bought?"

"Among other things, yes."

"That's ridiculous."

She shrugged. "Finally we agree on something. In fact, the whole idea's preposterous. People don't get married for such reasons."

"Why do they get married?"

Beleaguered by his relentless inquisition, she floundered for a reply and came up with exactly the wrong one. "Well, as you already made clear. For love."

Yet in the end, at least for her, life had rubbed off all the magic, and what she'd believed was love had turned out to be lust. Infatuation. Make-believe. An illusion. The only good thing to come out of her marriage had been Matthew, and if Joe had lived, she knew with certainty that they'd have ended up in divorce court.

From across the room, Raffaello Orsini's hypnotic voice drifted into the silence, weaving irresistible word pictures. "You would be marrying for love this time, too. For love of your son. Think about him, *cara mia*. Hear his laughter as he runs and plays with a companion, in acres of gardens. Imagine him building sand castles on a safe, secluded beach, or learning to swim in warm, crystal clear waters. See yourself living in a spacious villa, with no monetary cares and all the time in the world to devote to your child. Then tell me, if you dare, that our joining forces is such a bad idea."

He was offering Matthew more than she could ever hope to provide, and although pride urged her not to be swayed by what was, in effect, a blatant bribe, as a mother she had to ask herself if she had the right to deprive her son of a better life. Yet to sell herself to the highest bidder... what kind of woman did that make her?

Torn, confused, she considered her options.

Money could buy just about anything, and it was all very fine for high-minded people to scorn it as the root of all evil, but until they found themselves having to scrape and save every last cent in order to make ends meet, they were in no position to cast judgment on those who faced just such a situation every day.

On the other hand, it was claimed by those who ought to know that there were never any free lunches, and if something seemed too good to be true, it probably was. The kind of lopsided bargain Raffaello Orsini was proposing might well end up costing more than it was worth. Would she really be doing Matthew any favors if she ended up losing her self-respect?

Marshaling her thoughts, she said, "You've gone to

great pains to explain how the arrangement might benefit me, Mr. Orsini, but exactly what's in it for you?"

From the corner of her eye, she saw him go to the bar and pour cognac into two brandy snifters. "When Lindsay died," he replied, joining her at the window and passing one glass to her, "my mother and aunt moved into my house, to take care of Elisabetta and, if I'm to speak with truth, to take care of me, too. It's as well that they did. At the time, I was too angry, too wrapped up in my own grief, to be the kind of father my daughter deserved. These two good women put their own lives on hold and devoted themselves to ours."

"You were very lucky that they were there when you needed them."

He swirled his brandy and warmed the bowl of the glass between his hands. "Very lucky, yes, and very grateful, too."

She heard the reservation in his tone and glanced at him sharply. "But?"

"But they have indulged Elisabetta to the point that she is becoming unmanageable, and I am at a loss to know how to put a stop to that without hurting their feelings. She needs a consistently firm hand, Corinne, and I am not doing such a good job of providing one, in part because the demands of my work take me away from home at times, but also because…" He shrugged ruefully. "I am a man."

His use of her first name left Corinne giddy with such insane pleasure that she lost all control over her tongue. "So I've noticed." Then appalled at how he might interpret her answer, she rushed to explain, "What I mean is, that like most of your breed, you seem to think because you decree something, it shall be done."

He actually laughed at that, the sound as rich and dark as buckwheat honey, then just as suddenly sobered. "You've read Lindsay's letters. You know what she wanted. What you can do for me, Corinne, is carry out her dying wishes. Take her place in Elisabetta's life. Shape my daughter into the kind of woman that would make her mother proud.

"It will be no easy task, I assure you, so if, as I suspect, you think I'm the one doing all the giving, please think again. What I offer to you can, for the most part, be measured in euros. It is impossible to put a price on what you have to offer to me."

"You're very persuasive, Mr. Orsini, but the fact remains, logistics alone make the idea impractical on any number of fronts."

"Name one."

"I signed a three-year lease on my town house."

"I will break it for you."

"I have obligations…debts."

"I will discharge them."

"I don't want your money."

"You need my money."

He had an answer for everything. At her wit's end, she took a different tack. "What if you don't like my son?"

"Are you likely to dislike my daughter?"

"Of course not. She's just a child. An innocent little girl."

His raised hand, palm facing up, spoke more eloquently than words. "Exactly. Our children are the innocents, and we their appointed guardians."

"You'd expect me to disrupt my son's life and move to Sicily."

"What is there to keep you here? Your parents?"

Hardly. Their disenchantment with her had begun when she was still in her teens.

A chef? they'd sneered, when Corinne had shared her ambitions with them. *Is slaving over a hot stove all day the best you can aspire to after the kind of education we've given you? What will people think?*

But that was nothing compared to their reaction when Joe entered the picture. *Marry that fly-boy Joe Mallory, young lady, and you're on your own,* her father had threatened.

Determined to have the last word as usual, her mother had added, *Your father's right. But then, you never did use the brains God gave you, otherwise you'd have chosen that nice accountant you were dating last year, before he got tired of being strung along and ended up marrying someone else.*

That they'd ultimately been proved right about Joe did nothing to lessen Corinne's sense of abandonment. She couldn't imagine ever turning her back on Matthew. Parents just didn't do that to their children. But hers had, and shown not a speck of remorse about it.

"No," she told Raffaello Orsini. "They retired to Arizona and we seldom visit."

"You are estranged?"

"More or less," she admitted, but didn't elaborate.

He closed the small distance between them and with a touch to her shoulder swung her round to face him. "Then all the more reason for you to marry me. I come with instant family."

"I don't speak Italian."

"You will learn, and so will your boy."

"Your mother and aunt might resent a stranger coming into the household and taking over."

"My mother and aunt will accede to my wishes."

Once again, he had an answer for everything. "Stop badgering me!" she cried, desperation lending an edge of hysteria to her voice. No matter how real the obstacles she flung in his path, he steamrolled over it and confronted her with an even better reason why she, too, should *accede to his wishes*. And if she didn't put a stop to him now, she'd end up surrendering to his demands from sheer battle fatigue.

"*Ti prego, pardonami*—forgive me. You're in shock, as was I when I first read my wife's letters, and for me to expect you to reach a decision at once is both unreasonable and inexcusable."

His response, uttered with heartfelt regret, so far undermined her battered defenses that, to her horror, she heard herself say. "Exactly. I need some time to assimilate the benefits and the drawbacks, and I can't do it with you breathing down my neck."

"I absolutely understand." He strode to the desk, returned with an envelope containing several photographs, which he spilled onto the coffee table. "Perhaps these will help clarify matters for you. Would you like me to leave you alone for a few minutes so that you may examine them?"

"No," she said firmly. "I would like to go home and take my time reaching a decision, without the pressure of knowing you're hovering in the background."

"How much time? I must return to Sicily as soon as possible."

"I'll have an answer for you tomorrow." In all truth, she

had an answer for him now, but it wasn't the one he wanted to hear, so she might as well keep it to herself and make her escape while she could. The sooner she put distance between him and her, the less likely she was to find herself agreeing to something she knew was out of the question.

"Fair enough." He slid the photographs back into their envelope, tucked it in the inside pocket of his jacket, then retrieved her coat and, after draping it around her shoulders, picked up the phone. "Give me a moment to alert the driver that we're ready for him."

"You don't need to come down with me," she said, after he'd made the call. "I can find my own way."

"I'm sure you can, Corinne," he replied. "You strike me as a woman who can do just about anything she puts her mind to. But I will accompany you nevertheless."

All the way back to her town house? She sincerely hoped not. Bad enough that his effect on her was such that she hadn't been able to issue an outright refusal to his ludicrous proposition. The enforced intimacy of a forty-minute drive with him in the back of a dark limousine, and there was no telling what she might end up saying.

As it turned out, he had no such intention. He walked her through the lobby and out to where the limousine waited, handed her into the backseat then, at the last minute, withdrew the envelope from his pocket and dropped it in her lap. "*Buena notte,* Corinne," he murmured, pinning her in his mesmerizing gaze. "I look forward to hearing from you tomorrow."

CHAPTER THREE

SHE FLUNG HIM a baleful look and tried to return the envelope to him, but the wretched thing fell open and released its contents, which slithered in disarray over the leather upholstery. By the time she'd scooped them up, the door had clicked shut and the car was moving smoothly into the downtown traffic.

Wearily—she seemed to have been fighting one thing or another ever since the evening began, starting with Matthew's tantrum at once again being left in Mrs. Lehman's care—Corinne stuffed the photographs into her purse. Just because Raffaello Orsini had decreed that she should accept them didn't mean she had to look at them, did it? She'd send them back to him by courier tomorrow, along with her rejection of his proposal.

When the limousine driver at last dropped her off at the entrance to the town house complex, she knew a sense of relief. It might not be much by most people's standards, especially not the obscenely rich Mr. Orsini's, but it was home, and all that mattered most in the world to her lay under its roof. Hugging her coat collar close against the freezing night air, she hurried to her front door, her heels ringing like iron on the concrete driveway she shared with her neighbors.

Once inside the house, she realized at once that it was too quiet. As a rule, Mrs. Lehman watched television in the family room adjoining the kitchen, and being a little hard of hearing, turned up the volume. But tonight, she met Corinne in the tiny entrance hall, her own front door key in her hand, as if she couldn't wait to vacate the premises. In itself, this was unusual enough, but what really dismayed Corinne was the dried blood and ugly bruise already discoloring the baby-sitter's cheekbone, just below her left eye.

Dropping her purse on the floor, Corinne rushed forward for a closer look. "Good heavens, Mrs. Lehman, what happened? And where are your glasses? Did you fall?"

"No, dear." Normally the most forthright of women, she refused to meet Corinne's gaze. "My glasses got broken."

"How? Oh…!" Sudden awful premonition sent Corinne's stomach plummeting. "Oh, please tell me Matthew isn't responsible!"

"Well, yes, I'm afraid he is. We had a bit of a run-in about his bedtime, you see, and…he threw one of his toy trucks at me. It was after ten before he finally settled down."

Corinne felt physically ill. She'd spent the evening being wined and dined with the very best, by a man she'd never met before, and for what? A proposition so absurd it didn't merit a second thought. And meanwhile, her son was abusing the kindness of the one woman she most relied on to help her out when she needed it.

"I hardly know what to say, Mrs. Lehman. An apology

just doesn't cut it." Then, biting her lip at her poor choice of words, she examined the cut more closely. It had stopped bleeding and didn't appear to be deep, but it must be sore. "Is there anything I can get for you? Some ice, perhaps?"

"No, dear, thank you. I'd just like to get to my own bed, if you don't mind."

"Come on, then. I'll walk you home." Taking her arm, Corinne steered her gently to the door.

"Don't trouble yourself, Corinne. It's only a few yards. I can manage by myself."

But Corinne waved aside her objections. Frost sparkled on the path, and she wasn't taking a chance on the poor woman slipping and breaking a hip. Enough damage had been done for one night. "I insist. And tomorrow, Matthew and I will be over to see you—after I've dealt with him, that is."

She barely slept that night for worrying. What if Mrs. Lehman's injury was worse than it looked, and she suffered a concussion? Lapsed into a coma? What if her sight had been damaged? She'd claimed not to have a headache, had seemed steady enough on her feet during the short walk to her front door and had no trouble inserting the key in the lock, but she was well into her seventies and at that age…

Aware she was letting her imagination run riot, Corinne focused on the underlying cause of so much angst. What was happening to her son, that he would behave so badly? A "run-in," Mrs. Lehman had called it, but in Corinne's estimation, broken glasses and a black eye amounted to a lot more than that.

Yet if she was brutally honest with herself, she shouldn't be altogether surprised. Lately she'd come close to a few such "run-ins" herself. How did she put a stop to them before they escalated beyond all control and something *really* serious happened?

Finally, around four in the morning, she fell into an uneasy sleep riddled with dreams in which all the town houses in the complex fell down. Mrs. Lehman rode away in a big black limousine with every stick of her furniture piled next to her on the backseat. Corinne fought her way out of the rubble that she'd once called home, to look for Matthew who was lost, and came face-to-face with Raffaello Orsini shuffling a deck of playing cards. "This is all your house was made of, *signora*," he said, fanning them out for her to see. "You have nothing."

She awoke just after eight, her pulse racing, to find that some time while she slept, Matthew had left his own bed and now lay curled up beside her, safe and sound, and such a picture of innocence that her heart contracted in her breast.

She loved him more than life; too much, she sometimes thought, to be a really effective disciplinarian. When things went horribly wrong, as they had last night, the full brunt of being the only parent weighed heavily on her conscience. Yet she knew that, had he lived, Joe would have sloughed off his share of that responsibility, just as he had every other. He'd been no more cut out for fatherhood than he had for marriage.

Dreading the morning ahead, she inched out of bed, showered and dressed in comfortable fleece sweatpants and top, and went down to the kitchen to prepare breakfast. Should she make her son pancakes, as she'd promised, she wondered, or would that be condoning his bad behavior? Did his transgression justify her breaking her word? Did two wrongs ever make a right?

She was still debating the matter when Matthew came downstairs, trailing his blanket behind him, and climbed up on the stool at the breakfast bar. He looked such a waif, with his hair sticking out every which way, and one side of his face imprinted with the creases in his bedding, that her heart melted.

Okay, pancakes but no blueberries, she decided, pouring him a glass of juice. And for her, coffee, very strong. She needed a jolt of caffeine to drive the gritty residue of too little sleep from her eyes and give her the boost she needed to face what lay ahead.

Overnight, the sky had turned leaden. A persistent drizzle shrouded the trees in mist and reached its damp aura past the ill-fitting window over the sink to infiltrate the house. Next door, Mrs. Shaw screeched for Mr. Shaw to come and get his oatmeal before it grew cold. In Corinne's own kitchen, Matthew, also out of sorts from too little sleep, stabbed his fork into his pancakes and spattered himself with syrup.

Steeling herself to patience, she waited until he'd finished his meal before tackling him about the previous night. As she expected, the conversation did not go well.

"I don't have to," he said, when she scolded him for not obeying Mrs. Lehman. "She's not my mommy. She's silly." Then, sliding down from the stool, he announced, "I'm going to play with my trains and horses now."

Swiftly Corinne corralled him and hauled him back to his seat. "You most certainly are not, young man. You're going to listen to me, then after you're dressed, we're going next door and you're going to tell Mrs. Lehman you're sorry you hurt her."

"No," he said, aiming a kick at her shin. "You're silly, as well."

Barely nine o'clock, and already time-out time, she thought wearily. But when she went to take him back to his room, he turned limp as a piece of spaghetti, slumped on the floor and burst into tears. He was still screaming when the doorbell rang. Leaving him to it, Corinne trudged to answer.

Mrs. Lehman stood outside, her eye almost lost in the swelling around it, her bruise a magnificent shade of purple. "No, dear, I won't come in, thank you," she said in response to Corinne's invitation. "I'm going to stay with my married daughter, to give her a hand with the new baby, and she'll be here any minute to pick me up."

"That's nice," Corinne said, hardly able to look at the poor woman, her face was such a mess. "But you should just have phoned, Mrs. Lehman, instead of coming out in this weather. And if you're worried about looking after Matthew, please don't be. Business is always slow in January, and I'm sure I can—"

"Yes, well, about that. I'm afraid I won't be looking after him anymore, dear, because I'm not going to be living next door much longer. My daughter and her husband have been after me for months to move in with them, and I've decided to take them up on it. That's why I came over. You've always been very kind to me, and I wanted to tell you to your face. And give you back your key."

"I see." And Corinne did, all too clearly. The episode last night had been the last straw. "I'm so sorry, Mrs. Lehman," she said miserably. "I feel as if we're driving you out of your home."

"Oh, rubbish! The plain fact is, there's nothing to keep

me here since I lost my husband, and I've been ready for a move for some time now. And truth to tell, even if I wasn't, I couldn't have continued baby-sitting your boy much longer. He's got more energy than he knows what to do with, and I'm past the age where I can keep up with him." A wry smile crossed her face as Matthew's wails echoed through the house. "Anyway, I'd better let you get back to him. From the sound of it, you've got your hands full this morning."

Just then, a car drew up outside her door. "There's my daughter now, and I've still to pack a few things to see me through the next day or two," she said, and thrust a slip of paper in Corinne's hand. "Here's what you owe me. Just drop a check in my mailbox, and I'll collect it when I come to get the rest of my stuff." She bathed Corinne in a fond, sad smile. "Goodbye, dear, and all the best."

Corinne watched as the daughter climbed out of her car. Heard the younger woman's shocked exclamation at the sight of her mother. Saw the outraged glare she directed at Corinne. Never more ashamed or embarrassed than she was at that moment, Corinne slunk back inside the house, shut her own front door and retraced her steps to the kitchen.

She found Matthew quite recovered from his tantrum and happily playing with his trains and horses. She wished she could leave it at that, let last night's incident go and just move on. But young though he might be, he had to be held accountable for his actions. And if she didn't teach him that, who would?

Sighing, she waded in to what she knew would be a battle royal. Tried reason in the face of defiance; calm in the midst of storm. Nothing worked. He resisted her at every turn, flinging himself on the floor, giving vent to his frustration at the top of his lungs.

He broke her heart with his tears and anger. What had happened to her sunny-tempered little boy, that he was now in his room for a "time-out," when he should have been enjoying himself?

She knew what. He needed a full-time mother, and she couldn't give him one. And the fact that she was doing the best she could under trying circumstances did nothing to ease her conscience. Something had to change, and fast, but what—and how?

Pouring a fresh cup of coffee, she paced the confines of her kitchen and considered her options. She could hire extra staff for her business and spend more time at home with her son. But not only was good help hard to find, it didn't come cheap, and money was a perennial problem. Had been ever since Joe died and her credit rating had hit the skids because of the debts he'd run up on their jointly held accounts.

Shortly after his death, the bank had foreclosed on their mortgage and she'd lost the house. She'd been forced to leave the upscale suburban neighborhood with its acred lots and treed avenues, where Matthew had been born and just about everyone else on the street had young families. Had had to trade in her safe, reliable car for a twelve-year-old van, large enough to hold her catering supplies, certainly, but with such a history of abuse that she never knew when it might let her down. In a bid to avoid bankruptcy, she'd cut all her expenses to the bone, yet had to splurge on supplies to give her fledgling catering company a fighting chance of success.

But although she might be the one caught in a vicious financial bind, in the end, Matthew was the one paying the real price, and how high that price might go didn't bear thinking about.

We don't have fun together anymore, she thought sorrowfully. *I used to play with him. Sing to him. Make him laugh. Now I make him cry, and I can't remember the last time I really laughed until my stomach ached.*

She used to do other things, too, like look forward to tomorrow, and wring every drop of enjoyment out of life. Now she woke up and wondered how she'd get through the day. She was afraid all the time, waiting for the other shoe to drop.

What sort of message did that send to Matthew?

Our children are the innocents, Raffaello Orsini had said last night.

Raffaello Orsini… Even the silent mention of his name was enough for him to fill the house with his invisible presence; his implacable logic.

Think about your boy….

What's wrong with a binding contract to improve our children's lives…don't they deserve it?

Involuntarily her glance swung to the table in the dining nook where she'd tossed the envelope he'd given her. Exercising a mind of their own, her feet followed suit. She sat down. Picked up the envelope. Dared to examine its contents.

She discovered pictures of a villa, its rooms cooled by whirring fans and dressed in soothing shades of oyster-white and dove-gray and soft blue. Original oil paintings hung on its walls, antique rugs covered its pale marble floors, elaborate wrought-iron grilles accented its elegant curved windows, and frescoes its high domed ceilings.

Lindsay's kind of house: spacious, airy and charming. And outside its ancient stone walls, palm trees and flower beds filled with vivid color, and emerald-green lawns as smooth as velvet, and a distant view of turquoise seas.

Slowly Corinne lifted her gaze and looked at her present surroundings, at the place Matthew called home. The town house was too old to be sought after, and not nearly old enough to be chic. The rooms were poky and, on days like today, dark; the walls so paper thin that, at night, she could hear Mr. Shaw snoring in bed, next door.

She thought of Matthew being confined to a square of patio barely large enough to hold a sandbox, and much too small for him to ride his trike. She remembered last summer when Mrs. Shaw had vehemently accused him of kicking his soccer ball and breaking the plastic planter holding her geraniums. "Keep that brat on his own side of the property," she'd snapped.

Corinne thought of his never having play dates because no other children lived close by. Of his constantly being told not to make noise because he might disturb the neighbors. Little boys were supposed to make noise. They were supposed to run and play themselves into happy exhaustion. But his life was bound by other people's rules and expectations to the point that he was like a tender young plant, so deprived of light and water that it couldn't thrive.

Viewed from that perspective, Lindsay's request no longer seemed quite as far-fetched as it had upon first reading. "A business proposition, pure and simple, devised solely for the benefit of your child and mine," Raffaello Orsini had called it.

If, as he'd maintained, emotion wasn't allowed to enter the picture, could they make it work? And if so, what would it be like to look forward to tomorrow, instead of dreading what it might bring? For that matter, when was the last time she'd looked forward to anything except getting through each day the best way she knew how?

The question brought her up short. With an attitude like hers, was it any wonder Matthew misbehaved? Her own disenchantment had spilled over onto him. But now, suddenly, the power to change all that lay within her grasp.

Horrified, she realized her resolve to turn down Raffaello Orsini's proposal was weakening, and as if to drive the final nail in the coffin of her resistance, one last photograph fell out of the envelope and held her transfixed. Unlike the others, it had nothing to do with luxury or locale. This time, the camera had recorded the face of a little girl.

Although the date in the corner showed the picture had been taken within the last six months, the face was Lindsay's all over again. The vivacious smile, the eyes, and the dimples were hers. Only the hair was different; darker, thicker, springier.

I'm trusting you with my daughter's life, Corinne... having you to turn to would give her the next best thing to me....

Corinne traced a fingertip over the delicate features of the girl in the photograph. "Elisabetta," she breathed, on a soft sigh of defeat.

Patience was not his strong suit, at least not when it came to matters of business. And the proposal he'd put before

Corinne Mallory last night was entirely concerned with business. Surely a woman of reason could quickly ascertain that the pros vastly outweighed the cons? Yet here it was, almost four o'clock, and still no response from her.

Deciding he'd waited long enough, he picked up the phone. Then, about to punch in her number, he abruptly changed his mind, called the hotel's front desk instead and ordered a car and driver. Slightly more than an hour later, with daylight fading fast, he was at her town house.

That he was the last person she expected to find on her doorstep became immediately apparent when she answered his ring. "What are you doing here?" she inquired, so flustered she could barely articulate the question.

"I would prefer not to be," he replied. "Indeed, had you seen fit to contact me as you promised, I would have spared myself the trouble. But, they say, do they not, that if the mountain will not come to the man, then the man must come to the mountain? Not," he added, eyeing her too-slender frame judiciously, "that I consider you to match the proportions of such a land mass, but you are, it would seem, equally immovable."

"You've got it backward, Mr. Orsini. It's 'if the man won't come to the mountain, then the mountain must come to him.' And if you'd waited a bit longer, you could have saved yourself the trouble." She waved a large envelope in his face. "I have your answer here. In fact, when I heard someone buzzing to be let through the gates, I assumed it was the courier come to collect it."

"Well, since I have no intention of leaving empty-handed, you'd better call and cancel the pickup," he said.

"I suppose I'd better." She shifted her weight from one

foot to the other. "And I suppose, since you're here anyway, we might as well get this over with. Please come in."

Her demeanor suggested she'd rather invite a plague of rats into her household. *"Grazie tante,"* he said, with more than a touch of irony.

She led the way down a short hall to a kitchen, and went immediately to the telephone, leaving him free to look around. At one end of the room, separated by a high breakfast counter, was a sitting area of sorts, with a glass door looking out on what appeared to be a dismally small area which he supposed comprised her garden. A floor lamp, a television set on a stand, a shelf unit crammed with children's books and puzzles, and a two-seater couch and armchair separated by an occasional table, made up the furnishings, with what he thought might be a toy box in the corner.

Yellow paint on the walls, a rather fine old rug on the floor and a vase of pale daffodils on the counter added bright touches of warmth and comfort, while a cake cooling on a rack beside the stove filled the air with spicy fragrance. But although she was obviously a woman of taste and had made the place as charming as possible, it struck him as barely adequate and a world removed from the comfort he could provide.

Had she looked at the photographs he'd given her, and arrived at the same conclusion? Curious to know, he took a seat on a high stool at the counter and went to pick up the courier envelope she'd left there. But, ending her phone call, she forestalled him and snatched it out of his reach.

"Now that you're here, we can dispense with that and talk face-to-face," she said.

"As you wish."

"I just made tea. Would you like some?"

"I'd prefer to get down to the matter between us. After, if there is occasion to do so, we can linger over tea."

"Very well." She cleared her throat and flung him a harried glance. "After much thought and soul searching, I've decided to accept your offer."

In the business world, he was renowned for his poker face; for his ability to hide his emotions and reactions so proficiently that his associates never could tell where they stood in negotiations with him. But she, in a few succinct words, came close to stripping his inner feelings bare.

Collecting himself with difficulty, he said, "I was expecting a different answer."

"Are you disappointed?"

"Surprised, certainly, but not disappointed, no." He regarded her closely, noting again the fine texture of her skin, the lush fringe of lashes shielding her very blue eyes and the thick, shining mass of her hair, which she wore loosely tied back today. "Last night, you left me with the impression that nothing could persuade you in my favor. What changed your mind?"

"My son." She fixed him in a candid stare. "Let me be very frank with you, Mr. Orsini. If there was any way I could afford to turn you down, I would do so. But I looked through your photographs and have a pretty good idea of your standard of living. And you've seen enough of this house to draw your own conclusions about mine. Last night, you said that this is all about the children, and you were right. If, by selling myself to you, I can provide Matthew with a better life, then that's what I'm willing to do. In return, I will do my utmost to be a mother to your daughter."

"And as my wife?"

She blushed so deeply, she might have been a virgin confronting the prospect of intimacy with a man for the first time, rather than a widow who'd borne a child. "I will honor my vows to the extent that you wish me to."

"In other words, you will be dutiful?"

She looked as if she'd taken a bite out of an apple and found only half a worm left behind in the remainder. "I will do my best. And if you'd like me to sign a prenuptial contract, I'm willing to do that, too."

"Why would I ask such a thing of you?"

"As a token of my good faith. I'm not so mercenary that I'd marry you solely for your money, then seek a divorce as soon as the ink dried on the marriage certificate."

"I'm glad to hear it," he said wryly, "although in all fairness, I must point out that, had you planned to do so, you would most certainly fail. I do not believe in divorce, and those who do strike me as spineless weaklings unwilling to fight for something they presumably once found eminently desirable. I therefore urge you to think very carefully before you sacrifice yourself for your son's sake because, eventually, he will outgrow the need for your protection. Marry me, however, and you will remain my wife as long as we both shall live."

"I understand," she said. "And in the same spirit of full disclosure, I think it only fair to introduce you to my son before you make any further commitment to me."

"He's here?"

"Yes. We had a…trying morning, so I put him down for an afternoon nap, but if I don't wake him soon, I'll have trouble getting him to settle down tonight."

"Then I would very much like to get to know him."

Briefly she held his gaze, and in that moment, he saw the exhausted defeat her eyes could not hide. "Once you do, you might live to regret asking us to share your life."

The boy was in trouble, he realized; and she, at the end of her rope in dealing with him. Stirred to sympathy, because he knew firsthand the pitfalls of single parenthood, he said gently, "If you're trying to warn me off, Corinne, you should know that I never walk away from a challenge."

"You haven't met Matthew," she said, and with a last doubtful glance, she disappeared upstairs.

CHAPTER FOUR

ONCE SAFELY UPSTAIRS, Corinne shut herself in her room and collapsed on the bed, shaking. The shock of finding Raffaello Orsini on her doorstep had robbed her of her faculties. How else could she account for blurting out that she was prepared to marry him?

Agreeing in writing to his proposal had been insanity enough. Going so far as to order a courier to deliver her acceptance, even worse. But always at the back of her mind had been the notion that, before she actually turned the letter over to the messenger, she'd come to her senses. Or Mr. Orsini would come to his, and rescind his offer before any damage was done.

For him to show up out of the blue and leave her with little choice but to tell him her decision to his face was nothing short of emotional blackmail. Nor did it help that her memory hadn't played her false and he was every bit as good-looking as she'd thought on first meeting. No woman could be expected to act rationally when confronted by such a specimen of masculine beauty. Especially not when, as appearances went, hers left much to be desired. Faded blue sweatpants and top, and fuzzy felt slippers hardly showed her at her best. As for her hair, escaping in wild strands from the elastic she'd used to hold it back while she baked a cake…well, if she'd stood in a pail of water and stuffed a steel skewer into the nearest electrical outlet, she couldn't have looked more deranged.

Next door, the sound of Matthew stirring catapulted her off the bed. Shedding the sweatpants, socks and top in record time, she exchanged them for sheer black panty hose, tailored black slacks, a long-sleeved white shirt and flat-heeled black shoes. Yanking her hair free of the elastic, she raked a brush through it until it fell into some sort of reasonable order. One last glance in the mirror told her she looked about as cheerful as a grave digger, so she added a pair of red hoop earrings to the ensemble, a touch of gloss to her lips and a swipe of blusher over her pale cheeks.

Next door, Matthew kicked idly at the wall dividing his room from hers, a sure sign he was growing restless at his confinement. "We have company, sweetie," she told him, as she hastily washed his face and stuffed him into a clean pair of jeans. "Remember your manners, okay?"

Then taking him by the hand, she led him downstairs to meet the man who might become his stepfather.

She found Raffaello Orsini thumbing through the weekend newspaper, but he put it aside at her return. "This is my son," she said. "Say hello to Mr. Orsini, Matthew."

For a moment, she thought he'd balk at the idea, but eventually he peeped out from behind her legs and managed a shy, "Hi."

Raffaello bent down and gravely shook his hand. "*Ciao*, Matthew. It's a pleasure to meet you at last."

Clearly taken with this kind of man-to-man interaction,

Matthew emerged from her protection and offered, "Guess what? I've got a train set."

"Have you?" he replied, looking properly impressed. "Will you show me?"

"Okay."

From her post at the breakfast bar, Corinne watched as the pair of them hauled the various parts out of the toy box, then embarked on a solemn discussion of the best configuration for the railroad tracks. What was it about trains that had grown men and little boys so enraptured, she wondered. Raffaello Orsini's immaculately tailored suit probably cost more than she earned in six months, but he didn't seem to care as he sprawled out on her old rug, engrossed in assembling a plastic bridge while Matthew hooked the engine to a line of carriages.

"How old are you, Matthew?" she heard him ask.

"Four." Matthew stopped what he was doing long enough to hold up four fingers and, to Corinne's horror, went on, "How old are you?"

To his credit, Raffaello didn't so much as blink. "Thirty-five," he said, adjusting a curving length of track to fit under the bridge. "Very old indeed."

Matthew eyed him speculatively. "Are you my new daddy?"

Raffaello spared her an amused glance. "Not quite yet, no."

Dismayed, Corinne realized she should have anticipated something like this. Matthew often asked why he didn't have a daddy like other children they saw at the park, and although she'd explained that Joe had died when Matthew was still a baby, her son had never quite grasped the idea that she couldn't just go out and buy him another.

Blithely unaware of the exchange or the sudden heightened tension in the room, Matthew struck off in a different direction. "I like horses."

"So do I," Raffaello replied, not missing a beat. "Which ones do you like best?"

"Brown ones."

"A very good choice."

"And black ones."

"Big or small?"

"Big."

"Me, too." He offered his palm for a high-five. Matthew burst into a grin and slapped at his hand with four-year-old enthusiasm. And Corinne released the breath she'd been holding, only then acknowledging to herself how relieved she was that the two of them were getting along so famously, not for any other reason than that she so badly wanted someone to see her son in a positive light.

Over Matthew's head, Raffaello glanced her way a second time, his gaze disturbingly intense. "It appears your boy and I have a great deal in common. A cause for celebration, wouldn't you say?"

"I suppose so, yes." Flustered, she hesitated, aware that the next move was up to her. "It's getting a bit late for afternoon tea. Would you…um, care to join us for dinner, instead?"

"I have a better idea." Ruffling Matthew's hair, he hoisted himself to his feet. "Why don't I take us all out for dinner?"

"Oh, I don't think so, thank you. There's not much in

the way of fine dining in this neighborhood, just mostly family places that are child-friendly."

"*I* am child-friendly, Corinne."

So it seemed. But she doubted he'd ever dined in the kind of establishment she had in mind. "I'm talking about a restaurant with high chairs and booster seats, and children's menus and crayons for coloring paper place mats."

"But is it also man-and-woman-friendly?"

"Well, parent-friendly, at any rate."

"Then both you and I also qualify, do we not?"

Was he never at a loss for an answer? "Fine," she said, throwing out her hands in defeat. "Don't say I didn't warn you."

They went to a place just far enough away to warrant riding in the limousine he'd left waiting on the road outside the complex because it was too big to fit in any of the visitor parking stalls. Matthew was in seventh heaven, fascinated by the uniformed driver and luxurious leather built-in child safety seat, and wanted to know everything about the television set and multitude of other gadgets not to be found in her ancient van.

"He is interested in this new experience," Raffaello said, when she apologized for the barrage of questions. "I would find it strange if he was not."

Once seated in the restaurant, she looked around, seeing it as he must. Ketchup bottles, salt and pepper shakers, little packets of sugar and a paper napkin holder, all arranged at one end of a table finished in imitation wood. Plastic-covered menus offering variations on chicken strips, fish and chips and hamburgers. Thick white plates, sturdy enough to withstand clumsy young fingers. Water glasses etched by too many cycles in the dishwasher. Plain stainless steel cutlery. And a motherly server who asked him cheerfully, "What's everyone having tonight, hon?"

Unfazed, he looked inquiringly at Corinne. "Chicken strips for my son, and no sauce, please," she said, mortified by the woman's blithely misplaced familiarity. Couldn't she see he was *different* from everyone else in the place?

"And for you, Corinne?" he inquired.

"I haven't decided," she muttered and made a pretense of studying the menu.

Turning to the server, he said, "What do you recommend, *signora?*"

"The burgers," she replied without hesitation, using her pencil to point out the selection. "Plain, with cheese, mushroom, bacon or any combination of same, all made from scratch, and the best in town."

"Then that's what I'll have. A burger with mushrooms."

"Coffee with that, hon?"

He nodded, causing the overhead light to glint in his dark hair. *"Si, per favore."*

"That's Italian, right? I recognize it from that old Marlon Brando movie, *The Godfather.*" She let out a wheeze of laughter and dug him in the ribs. "Not part of the Mafia, are you, hon?"

"Not that I know of," he said, his grin dazzling enough to light up the night.

"I'll have the same as my friend," Corinne interjected, dying inside. "And a small glass of apple juice for my son."

Until their food arrived—which didn't take long, thank goodness—Raffaello entertained Matthew by helping him color his paper place mat, and engaged Corinne in small talk. Not that she contributed much to the conversation; she was still too rattled.

This was not how she'd foreseen the evening turning out, although she supposed it could have been worse. Matthew was happy enough to divide his time between scribbling in red crayon all over his place mat and devouring his chicken strips. And despite her misgivings, Raffaello seemed perfectly at ease, as if sitting in a vinyl-upholstered booth and dining on a lowly hamburger were normal everyday occurrences for him. From her perspective, however, the scene was too surreal to pass for anything even approaching normal.

What was a sophisticated Italian megamogul in an exquisite custom-tailored suit doing, dipping French fries in ketchup, and apparently enjoying the experience? What was *she* doing, entertaining thoughts of marrying him? And how long before Matthew tired of being on his best behavior and started acting up? Already he was squirming in his seat and asking to be allowed to leave the table.

Noticing, Raffaello said, "He has had enough of this place."

"I'm afraid so, yes."

"Then since we are also finished eating, we will leave."

In short order, he had summoned their server, paid the bill and ushered them through the rain to the waiting limousine. "This weather," he growled, handing her into the warmth and comfort of the car, "is uncivilized."

You probably think we are, too, she almost answered, as Matthew voiced a noisy objection at not being allowed to crawl over to the pane of glass separating driver from passengers, and plant his sticky fingers all over it. "I'm so sorry, Raffaello," she muttered, finally managing to buckle the little rebel into the safety seat.

Raffaello, though, appeared undisturbed and waved aside her apology. "Relax, Corinne. There is no harm done."

"I can't relax," she admitted. "I want you to like him."

"What is there not to like? He has a boy's natural curiosity for the world around him. I would be disturbed if he had not."

But his actions when they reached the town house complex belied his words. Although he escorted them to their front door and even went so far as to carry Matthew, who obstinately refused to walk the short distance, he refused her offer to come inside and sample the cake. "*Grazie*, but no," he said. "I have much to do before returning to Sicilia." And after brushing a kiss on each of her cheeks, he hurried away through the cold wet night as if he couldn't be gone fast enough.

So where does that leave us, she wondered, staring after him, confused. Was the marriage arrangement on, or off? Had she failed some unspoken test? Shown herself to be unsuitable substitute wife and surrogate mother material, after all?

He did not contact her the next day, nor the day after that. Not sure whether she was insulted or relieved, Corinne did her best to put him out of her mind as thoroughly as he appeared to have put her out of his. Viewed rationally, the whole marriage idea had been doomed from the outset. She was lucky he'd recognized that before they took matters to the next level. And if she experienced a certain disappointment at the outcome, it had to do more with the spark of attraction she'd felt for him than it had with any real regret

It had been such a long time since a man had piqued her interest. Too long, apparently. Why else was she finding it so hard to dismiss him from her thoughts?

Then, when she'd almost reconciled herself to never seeing him again, he blew back into her life on the tail end of a late January gale. At least on this occasion, he warned her ahead of time with a phone call, so that she was prepared when he actually arrived at her door, quite late in the evening, three days after his first visit.

"*Ciao,* again," he said, filling her tiny front entrance hall with his windswept presence, and again dusting her cheeks with a cool kiss. "I brought this for later."

"This" was a bottle of Krug, kept properly chilled in a wine saver.

"Why?"

"To seal our contract and celebrate our forthcoming marriage."

Somehow containing the annoying bubble of delight suddenly exploding inside her, she said, "I thought you'd backed out on the deal. Had second thoughts and returned to Sicily."

"Without you and your son?" He appeared perplexed. Amazed even, as though someone present must be a fool and since he wasn't it, that left only her. "Had we not reached an agreement?"

"Yes, but—"

"Then why would you assume I'd changed my mind?"

"Probably because of the way you left things up in the air after your last visit. The way you took off, claiming you had business to take care of, gave me the impression we were no longer part of your plans."

"I have been occupied having a lawyer draw up the terms of our agreement, and arranging for you to be properly welcomed to my home."

Her elation dwindled away as swiftly as it had arisen. "So you've decided to protect yourself with a prenuptial contract, after all."

"No." Following her into the family room, he withdrew a legal-looking document from his inside pocket and slapped it down on the breakfast bar. "I decided I must protect you and your son, in the event that you should find yourself a widow a second time. Take a look for yourself, if you don't believe me."

Swallowing, she said, "I see."

"I hope you do, Corinne." He fixed her in a very direct, smoky-gray gaze. "Ours might not be a conventional marriage by most standards, but it nonetheless requires a mutual investment of trust if it is to succeed. I am not a man to break my word. You may rely on that, no matter what else you might find lacking in me."

His calm logic, the straightforward manner in which he spoke to her, left her feeling both foolish and ashamed. Not everyone was as irresponsible and glib with the truth as her late husband. "I do believe you, Raffaello," she said. "And from everything Lindsay told me about you, I also know I can trust you. I wouldn't contemplate putting Matthew's future in your hands, if I didn't. It's just that, when it comes to him, I'm…fragile. I want what is best for him."

"That is the way of all good mothers."

"I'd like to think so, but lately, I haven't been doing too well in that department. The night we met, though, you said that our children are the innocents and deserved the best we could give them, and the more I thought about it, the more I realized you were right. It's not the only reason I changed my mind about our joining forces, but it's the one that made the deepest impression."

"So why the sudden loss of faith in me?"

"Because when my husband was killed and I found myself a single mother with a baby, I promised myself I was done with relying on other people because the only person I could ever really depend on was myself. I made up my mind that, from there on, it would be just me and my child, and I'd never do anything to jeopardize his happiness or security. Then you came along and almost overnight I decided to throw in my lot with you. But after what seemed to be a promising beginning, two days went by without a word from you, and it struck me how close I might have come to breaking that promise and putting Matthew's future at risk."

"I'm sorry if I caused you unnecessary worry. It was not my intention." He crossed the room to where she stood by the fireplace, and took her hands firmly in his. "Whatever the future holds, I give you my solemn word, neither you nor your boy will suffer as a result of this marriage."

His hands were cold, yet his touch filled her with a subtle warmth. She couldn't recall the last time she'd felt so safe.

"And I'll do my best to see that you never regret making that promise."

"Then we have a deal?"

"We have a deal."

She expected he'd release her then and open the wine, but he didn't. Still holding her hands, he drew her closer and for the first time, placed his mouth on hers in a kiss so fleeting, she wondered if she'd imagined it. But the bolt of heat, streaking to some near-forgotten area below her waist, assured her otherwise.

Shaken, she pulled away and said, "So what's next?"

"For now," he said, the amusement rippling in his voice leaving her aghast at how he might have interpreted her question, "I suggest you read the contract. Then, if it meets with your approval, we'll both sign it and toast to our joint venture with a glass of champagne."

"I don't need to read it. I already told you, I trust you."

"I can't possibly agree to that. Under no circumstances should you ever sign anything, let alone a legal document, without first reading it." He inclined his head to where the contract lay on the breakfast bar. "Go ahead, Corinne. It's brief and to the point and I doubt you'll have any difficulty understanding it, but if you do have any concerns, now's the time to air them."

He was quite right, of course, on all points. Just because he stirred various other body parts to outrageous response was no excuse for her brain to turn to mush. And the contract, all of two pages long, couldn't have been more plainly set out.

She agreed to live with him in Sicily as soon as possible, once the agreement was signed.

They would share parenting responsibility for his daughter and her son.

Should Raffaello predecease her, she would inherit half his estate, the other half being left to Elisabetta. Should Corinne predecease Raffaello, Matthew would inherit her share of the estate.

Should either parent die before the children reached the

age of majority, the remaining parent would undertake to care for both minors in the manner to which they had become accustomed.

Should both parents die before the children achieved the age of majority, the estate would be held in trust and a guardian, to be decided upon mutually by both parties, would be appointed to administer the funds and assume legal custody of the children.

"Well?" he inquired, as she finished reading.

"I'm overwhelmed by your generosity. If I have any reservations at all, it's that I'm not bringing enough to the bargain."

"You are fulfilling my wife's last wishes. That is enough to satisfy me."

My wife, he said, and Corinne's spirits sagged a little at that. *What will he call me, once we're married?* she wondered, signing her name next to his in the space provided at the bottom of the contract. *My substitute spouse? My wife's stand-in?*

"Now that business is taken care of, we can celebrate," he declared, stripping the foil away from the bottle of Krug. "Where do you keep your champagne flutes, Corinne?"

Fortunately she had a couple, though they were neither very fine nor very elegant, but if he noticed, he was kind enough not to comment. Instead he tapped the rim of his against hers and said, "To the future!"

"And to our children. They are, after all, what this is really all about." She ushered him to the couch next to the fireplace. "So what comes next?"

"Tomorrow, I shall obtain a marriage license. The wedding will take place as soon as it can be arranged, but most certainly within the week."

"Don't be ridiculous!" she exclaimed, startled enough to forget about being polite. "A week won't leave me nearly enough time! I have to close my business, pack, speak to my landlord—"

"Mere details, Corinne. Now that you've made your decision, all that remains is for you to decide which items you wish to take with you to Sicily. I will see to the rest."

"But—"

"And you understand, I'm sure, that I prefer not to be away from Elisabetta any longer than is absolutely necessary."

"I do, of course." She lifted her shoulders helplessly, knowing that if the situation were reversed, she'd be hopping with impatience to get back to Matthew. Still, what he proposed struck her as virtually impossible to achieve in a matter of days.

Correctly reading her doubts, he touched her cheek briefly. "Trust me, *cara mia.*"

"I do," she said, and was surprised to realize that it was the truth. "I'm just not used to being taken care of, that's all."

"Get used to it. It will be my wedding gift to you." He fixed her in a smiling glance. "You're frowning. Do you doubt my word?"

"No. I just realized something we've overlooked. Matthew should be starting school in September, but he won't be able to do that in Sicily. He doesn't speak the language."

"You worry for nothing, my dear. Elisabetta has a governess who teaches in English as well as Italian. Matthew will fit in very well, and be fluent in Italian by Christmas

Now, is there any other problem you can think of to delay our wedding?"

"No," she said. "Not a thing."

Events moved quickly after that because, as Corinne quickly learned, Raffaello was not a man to let obstacles stand in his way. In short order, he dealt with her landlord, settled her debts, sent a two-man crew to pack her and Matthew's possessions—mostly photograph albums, toys and a few other treasured mementoes—and arranged for ownership of her catering company to be transferred to three women who'd worked for her occasionally and who, upon hearing she was closing her business, leaped at the chance to run it themselves and bought all her supplies and equipment. The only miracle he didn't pull off was securing passports for her and Matthew, and that was only because she'd already obtained them herself, two years previously, when she'd won a trip to Mexico.

Consequently, exactly ten days after meeting him, she stood before a marriage commissioner in downtown Vancouver, at twenty after ten in the morning, and became Mrs. Raffaello Orsini. At a quarter to three that same afternoon, accompanied by her new husband and her son, she boarded an Air Canada jet bound for Rome and, half an hour later, found herself on the first leg of the journey to her new life.

CHAPTER FIVE

THE PHOTOGRAPHS of his home didn't begin to do justice to the place. Villa di Cascata was, quite simply, breathtaking. Vast, luxurious, it could have passed for a royal residence, and considering the style in which she'd traveled to reach it, Corinne shouldn't have been surprised. First class passage to Rome, followed by corporate jet to a private landing strip carved out of the Sicilian countryside ought to have warned her she was setting foot in a world far removed from what she was used to.

As if to underscore the fact, the message was driven home with a vengeance, the second Raffaello introduced her to his mother and aunt. The last word in dignified elegance, Malvolia Orsini and Leonora Pacenzia stood side by side in the grand entrance hall, their dark eyes wary as they sized up the stranger suddenly thrust into their midst.

"Welcome," and "We are pleased to meet you," they said, their English almost as flawless as Raffaello's. But the words lacked any real warmth, and in all fairness, who could blame them if they thought she was nothing but a fortune hunter, when Corinne had leveled the same accusation at herself a hundred times or more in the last week?

Beside them, she felt inadequate, unsophisticated, her wedding outfit, a pretty dove-gray suit, which had seemed such a good buy two days ago, sadly lacking beside the understated elegance of her mother-in-law's black dress. The woman's nostrils practically twitched with distaste as she surveyed Corinne's skirt where Matthew's sticky fingers had left their mark.

You try keeping stain and wrinkle-free after almost fifteen hours in a confined space with a four-year-old, Corinne thought resentfully.

Finally tearing her gaze away from the offending sight, Malvolia switched her attention to Matthew. "And this, of course must be—?"

"My son," Corinne said, unable to quell her confrontational tone. She wouldn't be responsible for her actions if the woman showed even a smidgeon of disapproval for Matthew.

Whatever her opinion of her son's new wife, however, Malvolia Orsini's response to Matthew couldn't be faulted. Bending her aristocratic spine until she was at eye level with him and holding out her arms, she crooned, "*Ciao,* little one. What a handsome boy you are. Will you come here and tell me your name?"

Wretched traitor that he was, he walked unhesitatingly into her embrace and said, "Matthew. What's yours?"

"I am Signora Orsini."

"Are you my new baby-sitter?"

"No," she said, stroking the hair away from his forehead. 'I am your new grandmother, but you may call me Nonna." Then straightening, she beckoned to her sister. "And this s your new aunt, Zia Leonora."

The sister, a slightly less intimidating woman, gave

him a hug, and shot Corinne a glance. "You have a fine son, *signora*."

"I agree," Corinne said.

"And somewhere in these parts, I have a fine daughter," Raffaello remarked to his mother, slipping a casual arm around Corinne's waist. "How is it that she's not here to meet her new stepbrother?"

"I sent her to the stables with Lucinda. Lorenzo promised to give her a riding lesson."

"Why now, *Madre mia?* You knew when to expect us and surely must be aware how anxious I am to see her and introduce her to our new family members."

Malvolia stiffened imperceptibly. "It was better, I decided, not to overwhelm your...wife with too much, too soon." She laid just enough emphasis on *wife* to make it plain that she in no way considered Corinne to be anything other than an upstart who had no business using the villa's front door, when there was a perfectly good one at the back designed expressly for servants. "She would prefer to freshen up before meeting Elisabetta, would you not, *signora?*"

"Thank you," Corinne returned with equal formality, "I would. Very much."

"A wise decision." Malvolia inclined her head in regal acknowledgment before delivering a final barb. "You have only one chance to make a good first impression, after all."

The subtle insult almost undid Corinne. She'd learned long ago that tears brought nothing but puffy eyes and a red nose, and that the only way to overcome obstacles was to fight them. But at that moment, she had no fight left in her. It was now Saturday and she hadn't slept a wink since Thursday night. Not only that, despite the drawbacks inherent in her old life, cutting all ties with it had turned out to be a lot harder than she'd expected. The town house might not have amounted to much, especially by Malvolia Orsini's exalted standards, but it had been home, whereas this place…

Choking back another threatened meltdown, Corinne took stock of her surroundings. A circular staircase rose in a sweeping curve beneath a high domed ceiling whose stained-glass panes bathed the creamy marble steps in muted rose and mauve, and touched the ornate black iron bannister with gold. Illuminated wall niches displayed various objets d'art: a bronze life-size hawk, wings spread, alighting on a tree branch; an alabaster bust of Napoleon; a priceless Ming vase.

Although indisputably magnificent, the place was foreign territory, and she very much the alien. She couldn't imagine there'd ever come a time when she'd feel comfortable with such grandeur.

Leonora must have seen how close she'd come to losing her composure because she said quite kindly, *"Venite, signora,* and I will show you the way to your suite of rooms."

"Do so, and I will keep this little one amused." Malvolia placed a propriety hand on Matthew's head. "He will be quite happy with me, *signora.*"

At any other time, Corinne might have disputed that, but right then, escaping her mother-in-law's cool, assessing gaze was uppermost in her mind, and she seized on the aunt's invitation with the desperation of a drowning woman clutching a life ring.

Watching them leave, Raffaello noted Corinne's stiff posture, the square set of her slender shoulders, the jerky, marionettelike motion of her legs as she climbed the stairs. He'd witnessed much the same taut apprehension throughout the long flight from Canada, half a world away. Although her son had curled up next to her, a stuffed toy dog she'd taken from his backpack tucked next to his cheek, and slept soundly for eight hours straight, not once in all that time had she relaxed. Instead she'd remained bolt upright in her seat, her gaze empty and every fragile bone strung to its neighbor with tension wire.

Her gaze wasn't empty now, though. As she turned to follow Leonora, he caught the utter desolation in her eyes, and he knew who'd put it there.

Calling on one of the household staff to keep an eye on Matthew, Raffaello waited until they were alone then grasped his mother's elbow and steered her firmly through the anteroom beyond the hall, and into the *soggiorno*. "I hoped this wouldn't be necessary, and that enough time had passed for you to come to terms with my new living arrangements, Mother, but since you clearly have not, we are going to arrive at an understanding of how you treat my family. You might disapprove—"

"Of course I disapprove!" she exclaimed, shaking her arm free. "Your informing us you planned to fly halfway around the world to persuade a woman you've never met to become your wife and a stepmother to your daughter, was shocking enough. But I told myself you acted on the spur of the moment, driven by your lasting devotion to Lindsay, and that you'd come to your senses before any real damage was done."

"Then you underestimated my determination, as you very well knew when I phoned to tell you the wedding was a fait accompli."

"You think confronting me now with this woman—this foreigner who has no more knowledge or understanding than a flea of our way of life—is enough to persuade me you have done the right thing?"

"This *foreigner* you dismiss so contemptuously happens to be my wife, Mother."

"Is that what you call her?" she retaliated. "After little more than a week of shopping, I'd have thought 'souvenir' a more appropriate description."

"Then I suggest you modify your thinking," he said, not even trying to hide his displeasure, "because like it or not, Corinne is here to stay and I will not tolerate your treating her with disrespect."

His mother sniffed disparagingly. "You'll be telling me next that this is a love match."

"Not in the least. It is an arrangement arrived at solely for the benefit of our children."

"And her. Or are you going to pretend she is a woman of independent means, and was not in the least swayed by your wealth and position?"

"No. I'm going to remind you that you took much the same exception to Lindsay when I first brought her here as my wife. Yet, at the end, you mourned her death as deeply as anyone."

"Lindsay adored you, and you, her. She bore you a child, gave me a granddaughter. What is this new wife bringing to the table beyond an appetite for comfort and financial security?"

"That is between me and her."

Malvolia sank into her favorite chair near the fireplace. "If finding a woman to give you comfort mattered so much,

Raffaello, I can name at least a dozen here in Sicily who'd have been more than happy to call themselves Signora Orsini. Women of breeding and background, who'd have shared our customs and language. Instead you come with a stranger. What makes her so special?"

"She shares a knowledge and love of Lindsay, and will be a good mother to Elisabetta."

At that, his mother uttered a yelp of outrage mixed with distress. "And what of me and your aunt? Where do we fit into this new regime? Or have we outlived our usefulness and must now be banished to the dowager house next door?"

"I would resort to such an extreme measure with the utmost reluctance," he said, fixing her in a telling glance. "You are, and always will be Elisabetta's cherished grandmother and Leonora her great-aunt. I'd even go so far as to say that Corinne hopes you'll both eventually find room in your big and loving hearts for her son."

His mother's expression softened at the mention of Matthew. "He is an engaging little thing, that I do admit. So fearless and forthright in the way he looks one in the eye. And I admit it will be good for Elisabetta to have a playmate closer to her own age. I sometimes think she spends too much time with old women."

"Then we understand one another?"

She sighed. "Yes. And I apologize for my earlier remarks. I was too harsh and am, perhaps, too quick to find fault. But I am afraid for you, my son. Granted, this woman seems respectable enough, but how much do you really know of her?"

"As much as I need to know, and I'd have thought you knew *me* well enough to trust my judgment, and that I could count on your support now."

"You can, Raffaello. I am on your side always." She sighed again. "Which means that, ultimately, I'm on hers, too."

"Thank you for that." He dropped a kiss on her cheek and left, anxious to find Corinne and do what he could to reassure her. Theirs might not be a match made in heaven, but nor had it been forged in hell.

He found her standing in the middle of the sitting room in their suite, her face a study in dismay. Joining her, he cupped her jaw and gently tilted her chin so that her gaze met his. "What is it, Corinne?"

"I'm trying to figure out what I'm doing here."

"Where else would you be, *cara mia?* This is your new home."

"No, Raffaello," she said, her eyes glassy with unshed tears. "It's *your* home, but it'll never be mine."

"If you're referring to my mother's less than gracious reception—"

"She was merely stating the obvious, which is that I don't belong here."

"Certainly you do. You are my wife."

"Label me anything you please, but it won't change the fact that I'm as much out of place here as a weed in a rose garden."

"That is not so. I see you as a vital link between the past and the future. Remember, this isn't about you and me, and certainly not about my mother or aunt. We married because of Matthew and Elisabetta."

As if to drive home his point, the faint sound of children's laughter drifted up from the garden. "Who've obviously met and hit it off famously," he added, and taking her by the hand, he opened the French doors at one end of the sitting room and led her to the wide veranda that ran the width of the upper floor of the house.

At the foot of the sloping lawn directly below, the children played with one of the puppies from the litter born ten weeks ago in the stables. Although the sky was clear, the temperature hovered around eight degrees Celsius, but they didn't feel the cold. They were too busy having a good time to notice it was still early February which, even in Sicily, meant that winter wasn't quite over yet.

"You see, Corinne? Already they have become friends. Look at your son, then tell me again that you made a mistake in bringing him here."

She leaned against the iron railing, some of the strain easing from her face as she watched the boy tumbling around on the lawn. He was much like a puppy himself, all high spirits and boundless energy. "I haven't heard him laugh like that in a very long time," she admitted softly.

"Surely that is enough to relieve your doubts? Or am I so repulsive to you as a husband that nothing can make you glad you agreed to our marriage?"

She raised startled eyes to his. "It's not you, Raffaello, it's me. Dress it up any way you like, but there's no question in anyone's mind that, of the two of us, I made the better bargain."

"You're speaking of material advantages, but—"

"Well, yes," she said, with a rueful laugh. "Look around you, for heaven's sake! Both floors of my old town house would fit inside this suite, and still leave room to spare." With a sweeping motion of her arm, she gestured to the chairs and couches in the sitting room; the occasional tables, the writing desk, the lamps, the paintings. Fine quality accessories which, in his world, hardly merited notice. "And never mind the small matter of marble floors and exotic furnishings and priceless art. You've introduced me to a level of luxury beyond anything I knew existed."

"I never made a secret of the fact that I have money, Corinne."

"You didn't spell out exactly how much, either."

"You didn't ask."

She let out a shocked exclamation. "I would never be so crass as to do that!"

"Precisely," he said. "You accepted me on trust, as I accepted you. You can't put a price ticket on that. So let there be no more talk of wealth or assets. They play no part in the equation which brought us to this point, so put them out of your mind and let me introduce you to your new stepdaughter."

After a moment's hesitation, she nodded. "All right, I'd like that. But your mother was right. I need to make myself presentable first—and by the way, thank you."

"For what?"

"Taking the time to make me feel better. Reminding me why we got married yesterday." She offered a brave, tentative smile. "For being you."

She undid him with that smile. Drawing her to him, he said, "Not much about yesterday followed tradition. There was no wedding cake, no first dance, no champagne, nor did I carry you over the threshold of your new home, but this much at least I can do."

And he bent his head to kiss her. Not deeply, or at length, not urgently, or with fire, but simply as a token to seal their union and let her know she could count on him to stand by her.

What he had *not* counted on was the impact of her body imprinted against his. The response it aroused in him shook him to the core. What he'd intended to be tame turned feral. Primitive. Hot and hungry and deeply sensual.

He was no saint. His sex drive hadn't died with Lindsay. He'd known physical need and desire in the years since she'd been gone, and he'd satisfied both with women who asked nothing of him but a night of mutual pleasure. But they never *touched* him, not in any real sense. Not in his heart or his soul. They didn't arouse his tenderness or the urge to protect them. Their memory didn't stay with him. By the time he left them, he'd sometimes forgotten their names, which was quite fine with them. They were experienced enough to know how the game was played. To know the score.

Kissing Corinne shouldn't have been all that much different. Ideally they should both have enjoyed the moment. Perhaps used it as a stepping stone to greater intimacy. They were, after all, husband and wife, and he had no interest in breaking his marriage vows and straying to another woman's bed. But she should not have engaged his heart with her fragility and vulnerability. Even if his body responded with unbridled enthusiasm, his mind should not have grown cloudy with emotion. Theirs was not that kind of marriage.

On the last point, she obviously agreed with him, although her response was more explosive than his, and for reasons a lot less flattering. Choking back a sob, she planted her palms flat against his chest, and pushed him away. "What was that?" she cried thickly, tears streaming down her face.

"An error of judgment, and my fault entirely," he said bleakly. "It meant nothing and was in no way a betrayal of the people we once were married to. You have no reason to feel guilty."

She stared at him, her blue eyes bruised with shock and pain.

"Forget it, Corinne," he urged, taking a linen handkerchief from his breast pocket and drying her tears. "Go about your business as if it never happened. You said something earlier about freshening up before you meet Elisabetta."

"So I did." She stared around the room, her eyes dazed and unfocussed. "Where can I wash my face?"

Don't you mean, rinse out your mouth to rid yourself of the taste of me? he almost said, but there was awkwardness enough between them, without his making matters any worse. "The bathrooms are through there." He pointed out the door on the other side of the small foyer. "Yours is the one on the left. Why don't you enjoy a leisurely bath, then take a nap? You'll have plenty of time to dress for dinner later. We usually meet for cocktails at half-past seven."

"But what about Matthew?"

"Right now, Matthew is in good hands and having too much fun to miss you." Turning her around, he propelled her gently across the room, opened the door to the bedroom end of the suite and steered her through. "You've had an exhausting few days, Corinne. Do yourself a favor and let someone else take over for once. There'll be time enough in the weeks to come, to establish some sort of routine with the children. For the next hour or two, forget everything else and concentrate on you."

* * *

She didn't think it possible. How could any woman concentrate, when her entire world had tilted on its axis in a matter of seconds?

Raffaello might have been gallant enough to take the blame for what had happened between them, but it hadn't been his fault at all. It had been hers, albeit by accident, and while he might be able to forget it, she never would.

Apart from the night they'd signed their marriage agreement and immediately after the wedding ceremony, he'd only ever kissed her on each cheek, in the way that Europeans did. So when he went to kiss her again before leaving her to take her bath, she anticipated it would be more of the same, and lifted her face, angling it toward him just so.

The trouble was, her timing was off and without her knowing quite how it happened, her mouth had blundered against his, briefly and clumsily. But just as a spark could ignite a can of gasoline and turn it into a raging inferno, so it had been with them at that moment.

Their lips clung, fused. The breath locked in her throat, searing her lungs with its heat. Stunned, she swayed against him. His mouth was the stuff women's fantasies were made of. Masterfully seductive; persuasively erotic.

His hands slid from her shoulders to her waist and he pressed her closer. Tightened his hold, trapping her clenched fist between their bodies, against the firm, warm contours of his chest. And what had begun awkwardly transposed itself into something wonderful and unforgettable.

His mouth had lingered. One hand strayed to the curve of her hip and exerted just the slightest pressure. Aware that he'd grown hard against her, she'd felt a shifting inside, as if her body—her feminine, female parts—were awakening from a long winter's sleep and preparing to bask in summer's heat again.

She'd found the sensation at once so powerful and exquisite that her eyes had filled with tears at the miracle of it. A terrible thudding hunger had overtaken her, and she'd ached for him so badly that she'd had to push him away, or risk embarrassing them both by begging him to make love to her.

In a perfect world, that might not have been such a bad thing, but in reality, she knew in his heart, he'd been kissing Lindsay, and had attributed a similarly misplaced response to herself, assuming she'd been thinking of Joe. Why else had he said she had no reason to feel guilty?

But what would he say if she told him he'd been mistaken, and that she'd known very well what she was doing and whose arms were wrapped around her?

What would he think if she confessed that the early passion between her and Joe had soon burned itself out, and left behind a residue of disillusionment, obligation and resentment so bitter, she'd actually felt more relief than sorrow when he was killed?

Would Raffaello then relegate her to the ranks of those he'd so scathingly dismisssed as being too spineless to fix a marriage gone wrong? Decide he'd acted too hastily and settled for someone not nearly good enough to fill Lindsay's hallowed shoes?

She'd burned too many bridges to risk finding out, and so she'd seized on his suggestion that she take extra time for herself, and escaped before she said something she'd regret.

Her bathroom, connected to his by a mirrored dressing

room, was enormous, with a curved window looking out onto a tiny private garden with orchids growing in the niches of an old stone wall, and a miniature waterfall cascading into a black marble bowl. The extensive use of pink-veined ivory marble inside, the array of toiletries set out on the vanity, the thick, velvety bath towels, deep clawfoot tub and glass-enclosed steam shower again all seemed to point to the fact that she was so far out of her element here that, even without her shameful secret, she'd never measure up.

"Oh, snap out of it!" she berated herself, letting the rush of water filling the tub drown out the self-pitying voice whining in her head. "You're here for the children, not the man and definitely not for yourself. And if that means putting up with a suspicious mother-in-law and more luxury than you ever guessed existed under one roof, at least it beats not knowing where next month's rent's coming from. Earn your keep, do well what you've been hired to do and don't ask for the moon on top of it all."

Stripping away her clothes, she sank up to her neck in the warm, scented water and soaked away the ache and dust of travel. Then she climbed into the marriage bed and fell asleep.

When she awoke, darkness had fallen and the ormolu clock on the bedside table showed ten after six. Time to get ready to face her husband again, not to mention his dragon of a mother.

And yet, she thought as she dressed, how fair was she to condemn the woman for reservations she herself would certainly have entertained if Matthew showed up with a complete stranger and introduced her as his wife?

Checking herself one last time in the dressing room mirror, she felt reasonably pleased with what she saw. Her hair gleamed from its recent shampooing, a shimmer of blusher lent color to her pale cheeks, and a touch of concealer disguised the dark shadows under her eyes. As for what she was wearing, if the best she could manage was the black dress, black pumps and fake pearls she'd worn to her first dinner with Raffaello, at least they were presentable.

Reminding herself it was easier to catch flies with honey rather than vinegar, she pinned a smile on her face and went down to face the evening ahead.

CHAPTER SIX

GASTONE, THE BUTLER, whom she later learned was married to Filomena, the cook, met her at the foot of the stairs and directed her to what he called the *soggiorno*. Loosely translated, it meant sitting room, but to Corinne, hovering unnoticed on the threshold, so pedestrian a description hardly fit the elegant scene before her.

Silk-shaded table lamps offset the ink-black night pressing against the tall, curved windows lining one wall. Those set at right angles next to it opened onto a pillared porch which must, during the day, provide lovely views over the coast.

The furniture was classic Italian Provincial, all clean, pure lines enhanced by sublime brocade upholstery. A white grand piano stood in a curved alcove. Deep, intricate moldings framed the arched entrance and windows. Logs burned in the marble fireplace. Jewel-toned paintings graced the walls. Again, Lindsay's kind of room, as tastefully charming as she herself had been. And set squarely in the middle of it all, Matthew, showing terrifying interest in the carved figure of a horse displayed on a glass-topped table.

"Honey, don't touch—" Corinne exclaimed, darting toward him.

Malvolia, imposing in crushed velvet the color of garnets, paused in the act of sipping from an exquisite Waterford sherry glass. "Ah, here you are at last, Corinna. I was beginning to wonder if you were lost."

You wish, Corinne thought, removing Matthew from the site of potential disaster and parking his wriggling little body next to hers on a couch. He was all spruced up in a clean white shirt and black corduroy pants, she noticed, and didn't appear to have missed her at all. "I'm sorry if I've kept you waiting."

"You haven't. My sister and I are enjoying our cocktail hour, as usual."

Nodding her thanks, Corinne accepted a glass of sherry from the butler and took a firmer grip on her squirming son who was bent on returning to the horse. "I thought Raffaello would be here, too."

"He's spending a little quality time with his daughter. She missed him when he was gone. But they'll join us shortly. Let the child go, Corinna. He's up to no harm."

The name's Corinne, and you have no idea how quickly he could turn this room into a disaster zone, she thought, pasting a stiff smile on her face. "He will be, if he knocks over that statue. It'll smash your glass table."

"The Chinese sculpture, you mean?" Malvolia chirped with amusement. "There's no chance of that, dear girl. It's carved from solid jade, and far too heavy for him to move."

"Nevertheless, I'll feel better if he leaves it alone."

"And I insist that you not worry and let the child be."

It was as well that Raffaello showed up just then, or she might have forgotten herself so far as to lean forward and pinch the woman. As it was, he looked so divinely handsome in a silver-gray suit that it was all Corinne could do to tear her glance away from him and concentrate on the girl at his side.

Even though Corinne had seen a photograph and thought herself prepared, Elisabetta in the flesh brought Lindsay alive again in such startling miniature that Corinne choked up at the sight of her.

"You're looking more rested, Corinne," Raffaello remarked, nothing in his manner suggesting he was in any way referring to their encounter in the bedroom.

Pulling herself together, she said, "I'm feeling much better, and so glad to meet your daughter at last. Hello, Elisabetta. I'm Matthew's mommy."

"You're Papa's new wife, as well," the child replied, with disquieting candor. "Nonna told me all about you."

"Which wasn't very much, *tesoro,*" Malvolia amended, shooting a nervous glance at Raffaello. "What could I say, after all, when I myself know almost nothing?"

But the mixture of apprehension and confusion in the little girl's eyes said plainly enough that finding herself saddled with a stepmother she hadn't asked for was difficult enough, without anything her grandmother might or might not have seen fit to add.

"It hardly matters," Corinne said, smiling at the poor little thing. "Now that I'm here, you can learn all about me for yourself."

Elisabetta, though, decided getting to know more about Matthew was a better idea. "Come here," she ordered, crooking an imperious little finger. "Papa brought home a new floor puzzle for me, and he's going to help us put it together, aren't you, Papa?"

"I'll help you get started," he said.

Not needing a second invitation, Matthew charged off to join them. Corinne was just as glad to see him go. Raffaello wouldn't let him run wild, and tomorrow, in private, was soon enough for her to start building a relationship with her self-possessed little stepdaughter. The only immediate drawback was that it now left Corinne at her mother-in-law's inquisitive mercy.

"This is your first visit to Sicily, I understand?" Malvolia said, fixing her in a gimlet-eyed stare.

"Yes. My first visit to Italy, in fact."

"You have not traveled extensively?"

"Not in Europe, no."

"Where were you educated?"

"Mostly in Canada, at the Art Institute of Vancouver, although I did spend three months serving an apprenticeship in New York."

"You are an artist?"

"Of sorts, yes. I studied culinary arts."

"Then you're a cook—or, I suppose, more accurately a chef. How did you manage to juggle such a demanding career with motherhood?"

"It hasn't always been easy."

"I'm sure not." Malvolia regarded her intently a moment. "Raffaello earned his degree in economics in Milano, and a second degree in equine sciences at Colorado State University in America."

"Really? I didn't know he was interested in horses."

"My dear, I suspect you have a great deal to learn about my son. His interest in horse breeding is but one of his passions. But tell us more about your family,

Corinna. Doesn't it upset your parents, to be separated from their grandson?"

"No," she said absently, paying more attention to the trio working on the floor puzzle near the piano, than the woman sitting across from her. Elisabetta was busily fitting pieces of the puzzle together, but Matthew wilted visibly against Raffaello's knee, his lashes drooping as the excitement of the day finally caught up with him.

Then, belatedly aware of the thundering silence her reply had created, Corinne dragged her attention back to the women staring at her in open dismay. "What I mean is, they live in Arizona and barely know him."

"Then you are not close," Malvolia pursued, "in the way that families usually are, that is?"

"No," Corinne said baldly. Why bother pretending, when the truth was bound to come out, sooner or later? "My parents never wanted children. I was an unexpected and unwelcome midlife baby. They were glad when I grew old enough to look out for myself, and showed absolutely no interest in being grandparents."

To give her her due, Malvolia looked quite stricken. "How very sad for you, Corinna. I cannot imagine such a situation. Can you, Leonora?"

"Not at all." Leonora turned pitying eyes on Corinne. "We have always been a close-knit family. And now that you're married to Raffaello, we hope you'll feel part of it, *cara*. You and your son both."

"I hope so, too," she said, "but speaking of my son, he's practically falling asleep on his feet. Is it possible for me to give him his dinner early, and put him to bed before the rest of us sit down to eat?"

"He's already eaten, child," Malvolia said, her tone warmer than it had been hitherto. "Over an hour ago. We don't expect him or Elisabetta to sit through a late adult meal when they're still both so young. As for seeing him to bed, his nanny will do that."

"Nanny?"

"Lucinda. I'd forgotten you've yet to meet her, but you need have no worries. She's been with us since Elisabetta was born, and is very good with children."

"I'm sure she is, but I prefer to take care of him myself, especially tonight. He will be in a strange bed, after all, and he is only four."

After a pause, Malvolia nodded. "You're quite right. We'll hold dinner until he's asleep and you feel comfortable leaving him. I'll have Lucinda show you to the nursery wing."

Overhearing, Raffaello scooped Matthew into his arms and climbed to his feet. "I'll do that. It's time both children went down for the night anyway, and I haven't read my daughter a bedtime story in nearly two weeks. Come on, Elisabetta. You go first and show Corinne which room is Matthew's."

The nursery wing—a term which initially struck horror in Corinne with its Victorian connotations of grim-faced nannies and barred windows—turned out to be three adjoining rooms directly across the hall from the master suite. Already, Matthew's collection of plastic boats were lined up next to the tub in his bathroom, and Doggy-dog, his favorite stuffed toy, lay on the pillow in his bedroom. Not that he noticed. He was asleep even before she had him into his pajamas. Even so, she lingered by his bed for a while.

This, she thought, watching the even rise and fall of his chest by the dim light of a bedside lamp, was what her marriage was really all about. Not the absurd jolt of awareness every time she looked at her husband, or the electric shock of his touch, but the simple pleasure of watching her son sleep and the knowledge that his future was secure at last.

Almost nodding off herself, she didn't realize she was no longer alone until a hand closed over her shoulder. "How's he doing?" Raffaello asked in a low voice.

"Fell asleep without a murmur."

"Same with Elisabetta. She didn't last past the first page of her bedtime story. How are you holding up?"

"Pretty well, all things considered." She ventured a glance at him. The lamplight played over his beautiful face, highlighting his classic cheekbones but leaving his eyes shadowed. "I learned more about you in ten minutes' conversation with your mother, than I did in the entire time I've spent alone with you."

"Anything you wanted to know, you only had to ask. I have no secrets."

She shrugged, the weight of his hand on her shoulder oddly comforting. "The opportunity never arose. We rushed from one thing to another with scarcely enough time in between to breathe, never mind get better acquainted."

"Now that you're more fully informed, have you decided you made a mistake in marrying me?"

"No," she said, too weary to feign indifference. "I just hope *you* don't live to regret marrying *me*."

"Why would I, Corinne? You're a level-headed woman, a devoted mother and exactly the sort of maternal influence Elisabetta needs in her life."

"What about what you need, Raffaello?"

The words swam out into the room so unexpectedly that she almost looked around to see who'd spoken them. But he never entertained a moment's doubt as to their origin. "What are you really saying, Corinne?" he inquired, tugging her to her feet so that she stood facing him. "That you'd like to renegotiate the fine print of our marriage agreement—which is to say, that part that has nothing to do with our children and applies only to you and me?"

"No, of course not," she muttered, stumbling over her answer and desperately hoping the lamplight was dim enough to hide the furious blush flooding her face. "I just want you to get fair value for your money…if you know what I mean."

"I'm not sure I do," he said, drawing her into the equally dimly lit dayroom connecting the two bedrooms. "Why don't you try spelling it out for me?"

Even though she felt hot all over, she was trembling like a leaf. "You're doing all the giving," she whispered. "I want to give a little, too."

"How? Like this?" He dipped his head and once again touched his mouth to hers. "Or had you something more intimate in mind…like this?" He slid his finger in a straight, sure line past the pearls at her throat, and cupping a brazen palm over her breast, teased her nipple with his thumb.

A sharp, sweet arrow of sensation speared the length of her and found its target between her legs, leaving her embarrassingly damp. Aghast, she stammered, "Only if it's what you want."

He put her from him as if he suddenly found her repugnant. "Sorry, Corinne, that's not a good enough reason. The day—or night—has yet to come that I take a woman to my bed because she feels she owes me her body."

She recoiled as if she thought he might hit something, and she wasn't too far off the mark. The urge to smash his fist against the wall rose in him strong and violent. Not that he'd make much impression on the wall, but the pain he inflicted on himself would at least put paid to the erection he couldn't control.

Touching her soft, warm curves, even so briefly, had left him half-blind with frustrated desire. But it was what *she'd* touched that inflamed him to anger. She'd touched his heart, making inroads where she had no business being, and *that* he found insupportable.

Brusquely he said, "It's past the dinner hour and we've kept my mother and aunt waiting long enough, so pull yourself together and get rid of the wounded deer look. Can you do that, do you think?"

She lifted her head and stared him straight in the eye. "I can do just about anything I put my mind to. I married you, didn't I?"

He'd have laughed if he hadn't been so incensed. "Yes, you did," he said. "Fine print notwithstanding."

Nose in the air, she swept past him and down the stairs with an hauteur that would have done a duchess proud, reaching the hall just as Malvolia and Leonora were making their way into the dining room.

"So sorry to have kept you waiting," he heard her say, joining them and leaving him to trail three paces behind like a mere consort.

He had to hand it to her. Whatever her private thoughts on him and what had transpired between them, not a hint of it showed on her face or in her manner during the meal. She sat opposite him at the long table, composedly sipped her wine, displayed a professional appreciation for the soup and excellent swordfish *involtini* which followed, admitted she had a sweet tooth and somehow managed to avoid addressing a single word directly to him, leaving Malvolia and Leonora none the wiser.

"I find her rather engaging," his gentle aunt declared, after Corinne had begged off joining them for coffee and gone to bed. "She has manners and a quiet self-assurance which is very becoming."

His mother nodded. "Nor is she afraid of hard work, and that speaks well of her."

"She's not overly impressed with my assets, either," Raffaello said, smiling grimly at the irony only he knew lay in his reply. Not only did Corinne appear indifferent to him as a man, but she'd shown remarkably little curiosity about his material wealth, which probably explained her almost fearful reaction when he'd shown her aboard the corporate jet that afternoon.

"This is *yours?*" she'd whispered.

"Yes," he said, and left it at that. She'd eyed the Gulfstream's plush interior so nervously that he hadn't had the heart to tell her he owned another jet, even larger.

"So your work involves a lot of travel?"

"Quite often, yes."

"If you don't mind my asking, exactly what is it that you do? Beyond the fact that you were married to my best friend and fathered a daughter with her, and have shown incredible generosity to me and my son, I know next to nothing about you."

"I have a few real estate investments," he said offhand-edly, seeing no reason to mention that they were scattered over most of Europe. "I also have agricultural holdings in Sicily, and I like to keep my finger on the pulse of our chocolate factory."

"Chocolate factory?"

"That's right. It's been in my family since the early twentieth century. Sicilian chocolate is among the best to be found anywhere. We export ours all over the world."

"Chocolate's one of my secret indulgences," she con-fessed. "But then, you probably already figured that out, when I practically attacked that divine chocolate mousse you served me in your hotel suite in Vancouver."

He'd smiled. "I remember."

"Were you shocked?"

"Why would I be?"

"It's not fashionable for women to wallow in dessert. We're supposed to care more about being thin."

Considering she probably didn't weigh more than fifty-five kilos at the most, she could afford to wallow. "I've never been particularly taken with bone racks," he said. "Women were designed to have curves."

"How very nice of you to say so. You're a born diplomat."

She'd obviously changed her mind on that score. The cool glance she'd sent his way as she'd said good-night had made it clear she found him little more than a barbarian. It was enough to goad him into climbing into the big bec in the master suite, just to rattle her composure and show her who really had the upper hand.

But he wasn't willing to risk doing so. One rejection a night was enough.

Not about to give Raffaello the chance to snub her a second time, Corinne prepared for bed, then crossed the hall to the nursery wing. Despite her earlier nap, she was so tired she could have slept standing up if she had to, but a leather recliner in the corner of Matthew's room offered more comfort. With the blanket and pillow she found on the top shelf of his closet, she'd manage well enough spending the night in the chair.

She was just drifting off when *he* showed up, opening the door just wide enough for the light from next door to slice across her face and make her blink.

"What the devil do you think you're doing in here, Corinne?"

"I'd have thought it was obvious that I'm trying to sleep," she hissed, shading her eyes with one hand. "And avoiding you," she added for good measure. "Now go away and leave me alone. I'm in no mood to argue with you."

"Nor I with you," he said snottily. "It's not my style to waste breath trying to reason with an adult bent on behaving like a child."

And before she could drum up a quelling response, he tugged the blanket away and hauled her over his shoulder with about as much dignity as he'd afford a sack of potatoes.

Outraged, she squeaked, "Put me down this instant—"

He pinned his forearm across the back of her knees and maneuvered the pair of them out of the room. "Stop screeching, unless you want to wake the boy and have half the household coming to investigate," he advised.

If the prospect, particularly of the latter, wasn't enough to rob her of a coherent reply, the scent and feel and upside-down view of him certainly were. Not that he allowed her much time to enjoy the ride. Scarcely were they inside the master suite than he dumped her on the floor and impaled her in a glare that might have had her quaking in her shoes if she'd been wearing any.

"Let me make clear my expectations of you," he said, spitting the words out like bullets. "No matter how annoyed with me you might be, you will not make a public spectacle of our marriage in front of my family or my household staff."

"If that's what I'd had in mind, I'd have done something about it at dinner."

"That you chose not to was a very wise decision."

His ominous tone chilled her. "Is this what our so-called marriage is all about?" she asked, almost managing to keep her voice steady. "Your issuing orders and my meekly accepting them?"

"No," he said. "It's about a man and a woman working together for the good of their children. For that reason alone, I expect us to present a united front during the day."

"What about at night?"

"At the end, when Lindsay needed professional care, I turned my upstairs study into an extra bedroom for a nurse. I shall sleep there."

"Won't that give the household staff something to talk about?"

"No. It connects to this suite directly from the outside hall and opens into my bathroom. Only Patrizio, my valet, has access to it and his discretion is absolute." He brushed one hand against the other. "So you see, *cara mia,* your little drama was quite unnecessary. You may sleep in the master bed secure in the knowledge that your virtue is safe."

Swallowing what tasted horribly like disappointment, she said airily, "Well, that's a relief."

He headed for the dressing room door, then turned at the last minute and, with deadly accuracy, fired a final shot. "For both of us, I assure you. *Buona notte,* Corinne."

She really didn't expect they'd smooth over their disagreement as easily as he seemed to believe, but when she and Matthew came into the sun-filled breakfast room the next morning, Raffaello looked up from his newspaper and greeted her as if nothing untoward had occurred the night before.

"I'll introduce you to the staff and show you around the neighborhood later on, if you feel up to it," he offered her, as she fixed fresh fruit and cereal for Matthew at the buffet on the sideboard, and helped herself to coffee and yogurt. "The sooner you know your way around, the sooner you'll feel at home."

"What about your work? Surely you must be anxious to get back to it, after being away for so long?"

"It's Sunday, Corinne," he said, lifting Matthew onto a chair. "And I always reserve my weekends for my wife and children."

She glanced at her son busily devouring his cereal. "Well, speaking of feeling at home, I'd like to unpack the cartons you shipped over for us. Can we perhaps leave meeting the staff until this afternoon?"

"Of course." He eyed her appraisingly. "But give some thought to how you want things done around here. As mistress of my house, these are now your decisions to make."

"I'm in no hurry to make any changes, Raffaello. My being here at all is enough of an adjustment for your mother. Where are she and your aunt, by the way?"

"At the stables, with Elisabetta."

"Already? It's barely eight o'clock."

"They're early risers." He snapped his newspaper shut and refilled his coffee cup from the silver urn on the sideboard. "On weekdays, Elisabetta has classes from nine o'clock until two, so she has to be up early if she wants to spend time with her pony."

Matthew looked up from his cereal. "I want a pony, as well."

"Matthew, that's not polite," Corinne scolded.

Raffaello, though, shrugged off her reproach. "Every boy should have a pony, *figlio mio.* Your mother and I will see what we can arrange."

"You're going to end up spoiling him if you keep this up," she said quietly.

"He deserves a little spoiling. You both do. And if I can provide it, I see it as my duty to do so."

Later, as she was on her hands and knees arranging Matthew's favorite books on the shelf in his room, she glanced over her shoulder and found Elisabetta hovering in the open doorway. Again, the child's face told all, but if it wasn't exactly beaming with pleasure, Corinne, who'd been wondering how she could finagle some time alone with her without being too obvious about it, wasn't about to turn down a heaven-sent opportunity when it landed in her lap.

Smiling, she said, "Hi, sweetie."

"What are you doing?" Elisabetta asked mistrustfully.

"Just putting some of Matthew's books and toys away. Want to have a look?"

"No. I've got my own books and toys."

Oh dear, talk about getting off to a roaring start. "What if I told you I brought something for you, too. Would you like to see that?"

A flicker of curiosity flared in her stepdaughter's eyes. "I guess."

Standing up, Corinne brushed her palms together, and resisted the urge to take the child's hand. No point in pushing too hard, too soon. "Come on, then. It's in my room."

She led the way across the wide hall and into the sitting room of the master suite, where contents from half a dozen cardboard cartons were strewn about. "Here it is," she said, taking a flat box about the size of a paperback from the coffee table.

Elisabetta dropped down onto the sofa, opened the box and stared at the silver-framed photograph inside. "Who is it?"

"Your mother, Elisabetta, when she was just a few years older than you are now."

"Is it yours?"

"Yes. But I thought you might like to have it."

The girl traced her finger over the laughing face in the photograph. "She was pretty."

"Just like you, sweetie. You look a lot like her, you know."

"That's what Papa always says, but he doesn't have any pictures of her when she was little."

"I know. That's why I also brought lots of other photographs with me. They're in those albums over there. You can look at them any time you want, and if there are some you'd like to have for yourself, I'll get prints made for you."

"How come you have so many pictures of my mama?"

"She was my best friend, Elisabetta. We were like sisters. We did everything together, and I loved her very much."

"That's why Papa brought you here, isn't it?" Elisabetta cast her a sideways glance. "Because Mama wanted him to."

Corinne nodded. "Yes."

"But not because you wanted to."

"That's not true. I wanted very much to get to know my best friend's little girl."

"Maybe…but that doesn't mean you can be my mother."

"I know that, sweetheart. In fact, another reason I came here is to tell you everything I know about your real mama and make sure you never forget her. But even though I can never take her place, I want *you* to know that you can always come to me if something's troubling you, or if you want to talk about your mama. I have so many stories to tell you, when you're ready to hear them."

"And you'll let me look at your photographs whenever I want?"

"Absolutely. Just ask, and I'll get them out for you."

Elisabetta chewed her lip thoughtfully. "Matthew calls my father Papa. What am I supposed to call you?"

"Why don't we start with Corinne, and see where we go from there?"

"Okay." She picked up her framed photograph and with stilted formality said, "*Grazie* for the present. I'm going to show it to Papa now, then put it beside my bed."

Winning this little one over wasn't going to be easy, Corinne realized, watching as the child made her sedate way from the room. Unlike Matthew, who had no memories whatsoever of his father, Elisabetta remembered her mother all too well, and Lindsay was a hard act to follow, as Corinne very well knew. But at least she'd made a start, and that was something. As for what came next, she could only hope patience and affection would work in her favor.

Raffaello was as good as his word when it came to doing his duty by his new family. In fact, Corinne grew quite tired of hearing about duty in all its many applications. He made it his duty to familiarize Corinne with the outlying areas of his land which covered several hundred acres. Considered it his duty to show her the most pleasant places to walk, the path at the southeast corner of the property that led to the village, the steps descending to the beach.

Over her objections, he gave her a car, a dark blue Porsche Cayenne SUV, small enough to navigate the narrow streets of the nearby towns, and sturdy enough that she didn't have to worry about taking the children out in it.

"This is your home now," he told her, dropping the keys into her hand. "Yours to explore as you please. One thing I caution you against, however. Do not venture off-road behind the stables. This is not Vancouver, with its wide, well-lit streets and avenues. The land to the north of us is wild and treacherous."

"For heaven's sake, Raffaello!" she exclaimed in horror. "Matthew and Elisabetta roam all over the place unsupervised."

"But always on fenced Orsini land, and always within sight of someone who works for me. No harm can come to them here."

He introduced her to the stable hands, in particular Lorenzo, his head groom, a friendly, capable man who was married to Lucinda, the nanny. "What he doesn't know about horses isn't worth knowing in the first place," Raffaello said. "He'll choose the right pony for Matthew and teach him to ride."

One day, about three weeks after her arrival on the island, he took her to Modica, a beautiful old town originally dating back to medieval times, which was destroyed by an earthquake at the end of the seventeenth century and rebuilt over the next several years. After touring the chocolate factory, they climbed one of the many flights of steps connecting the lower and upper parts of the town, and stopped in a tiny family-style restaurant where he ordered mouthmelting *mpanatigghi*, a pastry turnover filled with minced meat mixed with cacao, "to satisfy your chocolate craving," he said.

"Considering how much I already sampled at the factory, I'll have put on ten pounds by the time we get home," she protested.

But he dismissed her concern. "You'll work it off this afternoon. You can't come to Modica and not see the churches of San Pietro and San Giorgio, or the Castle of the Counts."

The churches were magnificent; opulent and imposing, with their intricate carvings and gold-painted interiors. And although the climb to the ruined medieval castle just about killed her, it was worth the effort for the stunning view of the town itself, nestled on the slopes of the Iblei mountains.

"I want to come back another day and explore the shops," she sighed, when at last they headed home.

"Get my mother and aunt to bring you. They know the best boutiques, and you could use some new clothes."

"I can't afford them," she said, flushing. She knew well enough that, compared to Malvolia and Leonora, her wardrobe was inadequate, but the little money she'd made when she sold her business, she'd put aside for emergencies.

"*Dio,* Corinne, how often do you need to be reminded that you can now afford whatever your heart desires?" he said irritably.

"I don't feel comfortable taking your money."

"Why ever not? You're certainly earning it."

That much, at least, was true. Elisabetta had bonded quickly with Matthew, but was less easily inclined to allow Corinne to grow closer. As for Malvolia, she was a pain in the neck, forever undermining Corinne's authority with the children. Until the day she went too far.

"They are *bambini,*" she insisted, upon hearing Corinne had banished both children to their rooms for trampling a flower bed to ruin. "God's little miracles and *perfecto.* You're too hard on them, Corinna."

"They're little miracles with more mischief between them than a wagonload of monkeys, Malvolia."

"They have spirit."

"They have ears, too, and it's not good for them to hear us disagreeing about how to handle them. We should present a united front."

"*Si, si!*" Malvolia sighed and flung out her hands. "You are right, *cara,* and I am an opinionated old woman who must learn to keep silent."

"That's not what I meant at all," Corinne said hastily. "Really, Malvolia, you have every right to your opinion and

I don't expect you always to agree with me, but please, let's not sort out our differences in front of the children."

"It won't happen again. You have difficulties enough as it is with my granddaughter who is not making things easy for you. I'm afraid my son expected a very great deal when he brought you here to stand in for Lindsay. I could hardly blame you if you've since come to regret marrying him."

"I have no regrets," Corinne replied fervently. "Raffaello is the finest man I have ever known, and nothing will ever make me go back on my promises to him."

"*Santo cielo!*" Malvolia regarded her with something approaching wonder. "I begin to think you care more for my son than you'd like him to know."

She was right. Without ever intending to do so, Corinne had started to fall in love with him. What had begun as sheer physical attraction had deepened to a more simmering passion, to a richer appreciation that went far beyond his startling good looks.

Raffaello Orsini was a man of many layers; of principle and intellect and an abiding respect for all living creatures. Considerate employer, charming host, devoted son and nephew, loving father, he assumed all roles with consummate ease, comfortable in his own skin, tolerant of those less capable, and indefatigable in the face of adversity.

Yet, it wasn't enough for her. For all they made a show of going upstairs and into the master suite together, she might as well have been living in a nunnery. And if truth be told, she was tired of it.

She was married in name only to this beautiful, sexy man who treated her with faultless courtesy, was wonderful with her son and who, with little more than the stroke of a pen, had elevated her overnight from exhausted, under-paid drudge to lady of leisure. And that's as far as it went. He didn't try to kiss her and he didn't touch her. Not by accident, not in the casual way that ordinary people touched one another—on the hand or the arm, in passing. He was simply there, and the distance he maintained between them tormented her as she lay alone in her big lonely bed every night.

He was her husband, yes. But not really. Not in the way she most wanted him to be.

CHAPTER SEVEN

"I HAVE TO GO away next week," Raffaello announced at dinner one night, toward the middle of March.

Corinne wasn't particularly surprised. He quite often went off on business, bearing out what he'd told her early on, that he traveled a fair bit.

"Where to, this time?" his mother inquired.

"Firenze." Then, with a glance at Corinne, "Florence, to you."

"Firenze, city of art and all things romantic." Leonora sighed dreamily. "Alphonso and I honeymooned there."

Across the table, Malvolia paused in the act of scooping a fat prawn from the excellent Sicilian fish stew Filomena had prepared, a little smile curling her mouth. "Now's your chance to do the same, Raffaello. Take Corinna with you and spend a few extra days showing her the city. You'd like that, wouldn't you, Corinna?"

Forestalling Corinne's reply, he said in a tone suggesting he'd rather undergo root canal therapy than be saddled with his wife's undiluted company, "Not possible. I'll be gone only two days, and in meetings most of that time."

"Even if you weren't, I wouldn't leave the children," Corinne said, cut to the quick by his rejection.

Malvolia pursed her lips and puffed out a dismissive little breath. Ever since their dust-up, she'd been much more cordial with Corinne, even though she did still spoil the children, every chance she got. *"Non dire sciocchezze!"* she said. "Such rubbish I never before heard. Leonora and I will look after the children, meetings don't last all night and Corinne's seen nothing of Italy. Firenze would be a wonderful place for her to start."

He heaved a defeated breath. "Would you like to go with me, Corinne?"

"No," she said, meeting his gaze and thinking he looked positively hunted. "I'd rather stay here with Matthew. It's not as if you and I would see much of each other."

"True, but you'd have no trouble keeping yourself entertained. Quite apart from the museums and churches, which would take years to explore in depth, you could go shopping for clothes." His glance skimmed over the black dress she regularly wore to dinner. "Perhaps you'll find something more to your taste in Firenze than you have in Modica."

Pride ought to have made her refuse. But where he was concerned, her pride more often than not took a beating. A smile, a conversation lasting more than a few minutes, a word of thanks for her continued efforts with Elisabetta, standing with his shoulder brushing hers as her son had his first riding lesson—such ordinary, everyday incidents were all it took to make her heart soar with hope that perhaps, in time, she and Raffaello would grow closer as husband and wife. Foolish hope because, despite his unfailing courtesy and remote kindness, he gave no indication he saw her as anything other than another addition to his stables. Her pedigree just wasn't quite up to the standard of his other horses.

"If you're sure I won't be in the way, then yes, I'd like to come with you. And," she added, flinging Malvolia and Leonora a quick glance, "if you're sure about looking after Matthew. I've never spent a night away from him before, so I don't know how he'll react."

"Matthew will be perfectly fine," her mother-in-law declared. "*You're* the one who'll fret about being away from *him,* but you may phone home whenever you please, just to reassure yourself that he's coping."

And so, on a warm, sunny morning, she found herself once again aboard the corporate jet as it headed northwest to Florence. Spring had come to the island. Although the mountains still had snow, wildflowers carpeted the valleys. The almond trees were in blossom, the vineyards being readied for the coming grape harvest.

From his seat beside her, Raffaello said, "Was leaving Matthew as difficult as you expected?"

"For me," she admitted ruefully, "but not for him. He's taken to the Sicilian way of life with a vengeance."

"And you, Corinne? How's it going for you and Elisabetta."

"Much better. She warmed up to me quite a bit after I showed her all the photographs of Lindsay and me, and really seems to enjoy hearing stories about when we were young. I think she's decided that if her mother liked me, I can't be all bad."

He shifted in his seat and, for a moment, she thought he was going to put his hand over hers. At the last minute though, he merely rearranged his long limbs more comfortably, and tugged at the knife-crease in his gray linen trousers. "You've been very patient with her. Don't think I haven't noticed, or that I don't appreciate it."

"It's the least I can do, Raffaello, considering everything you've done for Matthew. He's never been happier."

"He's a good kid, and easy to love. Just ask my mother and aunt, if you don't believe me."

"Tell me about your meetings," she said, changing the subject in a hurry. As far as she was concerned, love—paternal, fraternal or in any other form—wasn't something she wanted to talk about with Raffaello. In her mind, her heart, the man and the emotion were too volatile a mix. "Are they about the chocolate factory?"

He shook his head. "No. They're to do with a breeding program I started several years back. I've always been interested in the Sanfratellani, a Sicilian horse whose history goes back centuries."

"Thoroughbreds?"

"Not in the usual sense, despite their distant Arabian and Thoroughbred bloodlines. They once roamed the northern slopes of the Nebrodi Mountains, but their numbers have greatly decreased so that, worldwide today, only a few hundred are alive, including eight in my stables."

"And you want to preserve the breed?"

He nodded. "I'm meeting with a consortium from Argentina who share my passion. Hopefully we can strike a deal that will benefit both horse and man."

"I don't know much about horses," she said. "I wouldn't recognize a Sanfratellani if I fell over one."

"You'd recognize mine. They're the black ones you admired, the first time I took you to the stables."

"Oh, *those!*" she exclaimed, thinking how long ago it seemed that she'd leaned against the fence beside him in the bright winter sunshine, impressed by the horses' graceful conformation and the satin shine of their coats. "I remember commenting on how handsome they were."

"Possessed of great stamina, too. With careful breeding, their numbers can be increased without sacrificing the qualities that make them so sought after."

"Are your colleagues already in Florence?"

"I hope so. Our first meeting is scheduled for this afternoon. I'll have time to check us into the hotel, then you'll be on your own until this evening." He reached into his briefcase and took out a handful of English language tourist pamphlets and a street map. "You might find these useful. They'll help you get oriented and give you some ideas of what there is to see and do."

"I appreciate your going to so much trouble," she said, touched by his thoughtfulness.

He shrugged. "I didn't," he said dampeningly. "They were my wife's."

And what does that make me? Corinne wondered miserably, as the jet began its descent over the Tuscan countryside. *An accessory after the fact?*

Oblivious to her distress, he pointed out the famous landmarks in the ancient city below. "...the Duomo... Giotto's bell tower....the Palazzo Vecchio..."

They could have been landing in Siberia, for all she cared. With just four words, he'd erased any magic the place might have held.

"Corinne?"

She looked up to find him watching her, the corners of his beautiful, sexy mouth twitching with amusement. "Hmm?"

"Did you hear a word I just said?"

"Yes." *As well as those you didn't say, such as I'll never amount to anything but a poor imitation of Lindsay.*

"So we'll meet back at the hotel around six?"

"Fine."

He unbuckled his seat belt as the jet cruised to a stop on the tarmac. "If anything changes before then, I'll leave a message."

Their suite, on the top floor of a hotel set in private gardens, which screened it from the city bustle outside its gates, offered a step back in history, and whatever else Corinne might think of Raffaello, she couldn't fault him on his choice of accommodation.

High eighteenth-century frescoed ceilings, period furniture and extravagantly swagged silk draperies all contributed to an air of refined elegance, but it was the attention to small details that made it all special. The bouquets of jasmine and roses that perfumed the parlor and bedroom; the toiletries and robes in the double en suite bathrooms; the bowl of fresh fruit on an inlaid rosewood side table; a sterling silver tray bearing champagne chilling in a sterling silver ice bucket. And from every window, breathtaking views of the city and the blue hills of Tuscany beyond.

And if all that wasn't luxury enough, their own private butler was on call, twenty-four hours a day. No question that as honeymoon locations went, the place took some beating. The only thing missing was the bridegroom.

"You can't have lunch before you leave?" she'd asked, trying very hard not to whine with disappointment when she saw Raffaello stuffing papers into his briefcase and heading for the door before the butler had finished unpacking their suitcases.

"Afraid not, but you'll be fine on your own. Pretty much everyone speaks English, Firenze's an easy city to discover on foot, and the hotel's close to the major art centers and shopping areas." He'd stopped just long enough to drop a brotherly kiss on her head. "Have fun, enjoy the afternoon and I'll catch up with you later."

The next moment, he was gone, only the faintest smell of expensive leather mingling with the scent of the flowers to signal that he'd ever been there. She was starving, but since eating alone under the vigilant eye of the butler held no appeal, she collected her purse and the tourist pamphlets and took the private elevator down to the lobby.

Leaving the hotel gardens by a side gate, she immediately found herself swept up in the ambience of the famous city. Its noisy, cheerful crowds, its colors and scents and stunning architecture, lent enchantment to her explorations as she wandered the narrow streets and sun-drenched piazzas.

She visited the souvenir shops along the Ponte Vecchio and bought T-shirts and painted wooden pencil boxes for both children, as well as a model of the Duomo for Matthew, and a little gold bracelet hung with dainty filigree charms for Elisabetta.

Just before two in the afternoon, Corinne made her way to the Mercato Centrale, a huge indoor market housed under a nineteenth century glass and iron roof. In chef heaven, she browsed the array of multicolored pasta cheeses, olive oils, balsamic vinegars and other gourmet foods displayed on the stalls. Finally she found an empty table at an outdoor coffee bar in a quiet square, and ordered a cappuccino.

She was pleased with her purchases, especially the charm bracelet, because she'd wanted to take something special home for Elisabetta. She hadn't exaggerated when she told Raffaello that her relationship with his daughter had improved. Lately, when Matthew climbed on her lap for storytime, Elisabetta inched closer, too, and leaned against Corinne, something she'd never done in the early days.

What he didn't know, because talking about it reduced Corinne to tears, was that she still had a long way to go in erasing the loneliness of a little girl who traced her finger over pictures of her dead mother, and whispered, "Mama was pretty, wasn't she?"

"Yes, she was," Corinne always replied, her heart aching for the child. "Just like you, sweetheart."

She'd finished her coffee and was debating making a quick visit to the Uffizi Gallery when Raffaello called her on her cell phone. "Glad you picked up," he began, sounding harried. "I've only got a couple of minutes, but wanted to let you know we're invited out tonight. Dinner with the Argentines at a restaurant in the country. Probably a high-end affair. Thought you might like advance warning."

Although the stone walls of the surrounding buildings glowed ochre in the afternoon light, at his words it seemed to her that a cloud had passed over the face of the sun. "Thanks for the heads-up," she said coldly. "I'll do my best not to embarrass you."

"*Dio,* Corinne!" His irritation fairly exploded in her ear.

"Give me a break, will you? I'm keeping you informed, that's all, not trying to insult you."

But trying to or not, he had. She didn't need to be reminded that the few dressy clothes she'd brought with her to Sicily were inadequate, and that it was past time she invested in a wardrobe more suited to the social circles in which she now moved. But when it came right down to spending his money on herself, she still hadn't been able to bring herself to do it. So she'd turned a deaf ear to his mother and aunt's offer to introduce her to their couturiers, and obstinately refused to use the credit cards he'd given her.

Until now, that was. *I'll fix him,* she thought, seething inside as she consulted her tourist pamphlets, paid for her coffee, gathered up her parcels and took a taxi to the city's fashion mecca, the chic Via Tornabuoni and Via della Vigna. She wouldn't give him cause to question her appearance again.

They were there in all their exclusive, ruinously expensive glory: Versace, Prada, Armani, Dolce & Gabbana, Bulgari. And somewhere amidst their dazzling one-of-a-kind display, she'd find something to make her reluctant husband sit up and take notice.

Three hours and thousands of euros she spent, selecting outfits for every conceivable occasion. With every stop, the number of purchases grew: smartly casual slacks and shirts, sportswear, afternoon dresses, glove-soft walking shoes and silk pumps with narrow, elegant heels. A floor-length silver-threaded dark red skirt and matching shawl for evenings at home. A gorgeously sophisticated sapphire blue dinner gown to impress the Argentines. Purely for he own enjoyment, exquisite lingerie the color of whipped cream and peaches and midnight. And finally, for the sheer indulgence of it, a black velvet opera cape trimmed with Swarovski crystals.

She loved the feel of the lush fabrics against her skin, and how just the right cut and color turned her into someone she barely recognized. She'd knock Raffaello's socks off, or die trying.

She didn't try to delude herself, though. No amount of fancy window dressing could change the basic model. A natural blond, too tall and curvy to pass for petite, she might at best be considered nice looking, unlike Lindsay who'd been beautiful.

But for once, Raffaello would look at Corinne and see not the person he'd chosen to stand in for his dead wife, or the devoted mother working so hard to fill the empty place in his daughter's heart, but a woman in her own right.

"Hell hath no fury, and all that," she muttered, swanning out of the last atelier and stepping into the taxi the zealous doorman had hailed for her.

Once back in the suite, she stashed her purchases, then phoned the hotel beauty spa. The day had left her looking a little ragged around the edges, and the works was in order: body, face, fingers, toes and hair, she needed it all, and such was the clout of the Orsini name that she had no trouble securing an immediate appointment.

Raffaello paced the parlor, nursing a single malt scotch and trying to rein in his impatience. It was twenty after eight already, and the front desk had phoned to say the driver and car he'd ordered to deliver them to the country inn for nine, were waiting at the curb. Not that anyone would be too upset if they arrived a few minutes late, but he'd hoped he and Corinne would have time to smooth over their earlier spat before leaving. She, though, wasn't cooperating, and when she finally did put in an appearance, he was so stunned by her appearance that he could barely string two words together.

She'd done something different with her hair. Piled it on top of her head in a shining silver-blond coil. Painted her fingernails, which she no longer kept cut short, a rich, dark red. Applied something glossy to her mouth that made him want to kiss it. And she'd hit the boutiques with a vengeance. Long platinum earrings dangled from her ears. She wore heels. Very high heels, so that she stood only seven or eight centimeters shorter than him. Whatever dress she had on was hidden under a voluminous cloak of some sort that, if he hadn't known better, he might have thought was studded with diamonds.

"Er," he said, swallowing. "Um…I phoned the children. They're fine."

"I know," she said, sweeping past him, regal as a queen. "I spoke to them myself, not ten minutes ago. Come along, Raffaello. I'm sure you don't want to keep your important friends waiting."

So much for effecting a truce!

"You look nice," he said, eyeing her during the short ride down in the elevator.

"Do I?" she said snootily. "How kind of you to say so."

It took a lot to provoke him into cursing but, at that moment, he came close to uttering a few choice profanities She quelled the urge with one forbidding blue-eyed glare

During the drive to the restaurant, she sat as far away from him as possible—not exactly difficult, considering the limo's backseat was wide enough to accommodate four passengers with ease—her spine ramrod straight.

Willing to make one more effort to melt the ice, he said, "I gather you went shopping this afternoon."

"Very astute of you, Raffaello," she snipped back, and turned her head to watch the rural scenery flashing by, which she must have found riveting considering darkness had fallen hours earlier and the moon had not yet risen.

The last time a woman had left him at a loss for words, he'd been thirteen, and the daughter of one of the farmhands had dragged him behind the stables, lifted her blouse to bare her breasts and offered to let him touch them. He'd been both fascinated and terrified by her audacity.

Corinne just plain irritated him with hers. Not inclined to sugarcoat his annoyance, he said baldly, "It's unlike you to be so out-of-sorts, *cara mia*. Did something you ate not agree with you?"

He'd have done better to keep his mouth shut. Very slowly, she turned her head to look at him, didn't seem to like what she saw, and very slowly turned her head away again. Shortly after, the car turned into the long driveway leading to the country house where they were to have dinner.

Wonderful, he thought. It promised to be a pip of an evening.

Nice. After all the trouble she'd gone to, to impress him, the best he could offer by way of a compliment was that she looked nice. *Nice!*

Well, she'd show him!

Their hosts, four men in all, stood at the window of a private dining room, but turned as one when she and Raffaello were shown in. If they weren't quite as handsome as Raffaello, they were nonetheless charmingly cosmopolitan. They kissed her hand and buzzed around her, plying her with champagne. They told Raffaello he was a lucky man, that his wife was *muy hermosa*—very beautiful.

In short, they did what he had not: they made her feel special, desirable. They flirted harmlessly with her, and she flirted back, lowering her lashes at their compliments and smiling over the rim of her champagne flute.

Across the beautifully dressed table, Raffaello leaned back in his chair and observed, something of a smile on his face, as well. Probably because she wasn't embarrassing him, after all, she thought, sparing him a brief glance before turning her attention back to the other four who seemed bent on learning everything there was to know about her life before she came to live in Sicily.

At first, he joined in the conversation, but as the evening wore on and one delectable course followed another, he grew increasingly grim, speaking only when addressed directly and keeping his replies brief and to the point. By the time the passion fruit gelato dessert arrived, his smile had grown fixed, and although his manner remained coolly and impeccably courteous, the light in his smoky-gray eyes hinted at a fire within.

Not until they returned to the hotel, though, did she learn just how savagely it burned.

CHAPTER EIGHT

THE ARGENTINES rode back to the city with them, dropping them off at the hotel, before going on to their own. Raffaello thanked them, bid them good-night and swiftly escorted her into the lobby. No trace of a smile, wooden or otherwise, remained on his face, nor did he speak during the short time it took the elevator to whisk them to the penthouse level.

"I had a good time tonight," she remarked, as the doors slid open at their floor. "I liked your friends."

He swung around, blocking her entrance to the sitting room and leaned into her, pressing her between him and the wall. His face was pale beneath his tan; the look in his eyes, frightening. "Did you really?" he said with such soft menace that chills raced up her spine. "What would it take to make you see me in the same benevolent light, I wonder? This, perhaps?"

He caught her chin firmly between his thumb and forefinger, abruptly tipped her head back and crushed her mouth with his. He tasted of rage and frustration and something else. Something dark and dangerous and intoxicating.

For a moment she resisted him, clamping her lips shut

against his invasion. A pointless exercise. She'd been yearning for him to pay attention to her for far too long to quibble about finesse when opportunity finally struck.

What counted was that he'd noticed her. Seen past the surrogate mother to discover the woman, and that was enough for her senses to swim. For her blood to churn. She went so weak at the knees that she had to clutch the satin lapels of his black dinner jacket to keep herself upright.

Then, as suddenly as it had started, it was over. He thrust her away and stepped back. Bosom heaving, she stared at him. Her lungs were seizing up, but he wasn't even breathing hard. "Or is that too crude for your sensibilities, Corinne?" he inquired icily. "Would I have more success if I kissed your hand instead? Would you then giggle, and lead me to believe you found me irresistible, the way you did with them?"

Incensed, she said, *"I did not giggle!"*

"You most certainly did." He inhaled a furious breath. "You giggled, and you simpered, and you hung onto their every word as if you couldn't get enough of their foolishness."

She shrugged flippantly. Better that, than let him know how badly she wanted to feel his mouth on hers again. "So what if other men find me attractive and I like it? Why do you care?"

"Because *I* do not like it," he said ominously. "I do not like it one little bit."

"Why not?"

"Because you're married to me, that's why."

She'd been baiting him all evening and knew her defiance now was pushing him to the limits of his patience. But she didn't give a damn. She was tired of living in limbo.

Either she was his wife in every sense of the word, or she wasn't. And tonight, she'd make him decide which it was to be.

"I'd never know it," she said.

"I could change your mind about that very easily."

Her pulse quickened. "I don't see how."

"By doing something I should have done weeks ago, *cara mia*. By reminding you whose ring you wear on your finger," he said, and cupping one hand at the back of her head, he kissed her again. A hot, openmouthed kiss that slid with devastating intent from her lips to the corner of her jaw, and from there to her throat.

Her hair came loose, tumbling around her shoulders, and then his fingers were at the closure on her cape. He yanked the garment free and let it slither in a whisper around her feet, then brought his gaze to dwell on the upper curve of her breasts, visible above the low-cut neckline of her gown.

"Now what?" she taunted. "Are you going to tear my dress away, too?"

"Would you like me to?"

"You wouldn't dare."

He made a sound low in his throat. A feral sound that should have terrified her, but thrilled her instead. "Try me," he ground out tightly.

He was beautiful in his raw anger, the most beautiful man she'd ever known, and she went at him like a starving woman, clawing at his fine dinner jacket, ripping at his bow tie, craving everything about him. Dying for him.

In a flash, he had her pinned against the marble wall of the tiny foyer once again. "This time, you push me too far, *streghetta,*" he hissed, and yanked the skirt of her gown up around her waist. The rasp of his zipper opening drowned out the faint screech of her panties as he ripped them away, and then he was between her thighs, probing at her flesh until, at last, he was where she'd wanted him to be almost from the first. Thrusting deep inside her, hot and silken and desperately trying to outrace the devils chasing him.

She whimpered and dragged his mouth back to hers again. Tasted the passion consuming him and responded to him with everything she had to give. Convulsing around him as he climaxed. Clinging to him as if she'd never let him go.

The aftermath made her heart bleed. Withdrawing, he rested his forehead against hers, and a tear leaked between the lashes of his closed eyes. "*Dio,* Corinne, I'm sorry...."

"No," she whispered, stroking his face. "Don't be sorry. I wanted this. You have to know I did."

He looked at her, and she saw the hell in his eyes, the self-loathing. "Never like that," he said. "Never in anger."

"How, then? Like this?" She took his hands and pressed them against her breasts so that he could feel how her nipples surged at his touch. "Or like this?" And she lifted her mouth to his and kissed him softly, deeply, the way a woman kisses the man she loves.

"You don't know what you're asking for," he groaned.

"Oh, but I do. I want to lie beside you at night. I want to hear you breathing and feel your warmth next to me. I want to be more than a mother to our children, Raffaello. More than your wife in name only."

He winced, his face the picture of a man in torment. "Corinne...!"

"Please." Her voice broke, her pride no match for the urgent, visceral ache of wanting him.

For a long minute, he stared at her, searching to find the truth of her words.

"*Please,* Raffaello!" she begged again. "Just for tonight, be my husband. You want to. I know you do."

She touched him. Cradled the weight of him. Felt his flesh stir again.

He cursed under his breath, then lifting her into his arms, he strode through the suite, and by the light of the moon riding high above the Tuscan hills, he took her to the bedroom, undressed her and did as she asked. Not hastily this time, but with dedication and a sort of despair, as if serving penance to some unholy god.

His mouth danced over her skin, discovering every inch with meticulous dedication. His touch left her floating in sensation. Ecstasy beyond description washed over her, wave after wave, each more tumultuous than the one before. She sobbed mindlessly, afraid she might die from the divine torture he inflicted. Wishing she would, because she was splintering apart, shards of her flying into orbit, and without him, she'd never be whole again.

Finally he possessed her a second time, so heavy and silken and potent that she shuddered. She raked her fingernails down his back, marking him hers, at least for that night. Locked her legs around his waist. Felt his muscles tense, and the tremors overtaking him. Heard his agonized breaths. Saw the sweat glistening on his shoulders. Felt him flooding into her, hot and powerful.

Then there was nothing but the calm hush of the night and the silent beat of their hearts.

Finally he rolled onto his side and lay on his back, his arm beneath her shoulder. She stole a glance at him and saw that his eyes shone like rain-washed stones in the moonlight, and his mouth was curved in unutterable misery.

If she had dared, she'd have told him he was wonderful, that he consumed her thoughts and filled her heart more than she'd ever dreamed possible. But then again, perhaps it was better that she did not, because where were the words to do justice to the enormity of all she felt?

There weren't any. They'd never before been spoken, or written, or thought. Nothing man had invented could come close to expressing the aching depth of her love for him.

He waited an eternity for her to fall asleep. At last, when her breathing had been deep and regular for nearly half an hour, he inched out of bed. Stealthily, like the thief in the night that he was, he left her. He had stolen her trust in him, betrayed his own code of decency and needed to cleanse himself of the guilt.

He dressed in the bathroom, then went from the suite, using the fire stairs rather than risk the discreet tone of the elevator wakening her. Once he gained the street, he turned at the corner, crossed the piazza and headed south to the river.

Firenze was as familiar to him as the back of his hand. He could have found his way in the dark anywhere in the city, but the sky to the east was touched with dawn when at last he reached the Ponte delle Grazie, to him the most beautiful of the bridges spanning the Arno.

At that hour, he had it to himself. A good thing. He wasn't fit company for man or beast.

How was he to face her again? How justify his behavior?

Mi scusi, Corinne, for yet another error of judgment. My fault. Too much champagne, I'm afraid, and not enough decent restraint....

The thing was, he'd taken no more than a glass or two of wine and couldn't blame his actions on inebriation. They'd arisen from something much more lethal. He'd been drunk on jealousy and rage, a combination more deadly than anything alcohol could induce.

This is my wife you're ogling, he'd wanted to bellow to the Argentines. *Get the hell away from her and find some other woman to drool and slobber over!*

That he hadn't, that he'd contained his fury with them, shamed him only a little less than that he'd vented it on her. He should have flattened the first man to step out of line and pinned him to the ground with a foot across the throat. Maybe that would have relieved the pressure building in him. Instead he'd waited until he was alone with her, then behaved abominably. Inexcusably. And, if he was honest, because he hadn't been able to help himself.

He'd believed Lindsay had been the love of his life and had neither wanted nor expected to feel that way again about another woman. Yet despite his most stringent efforts to deny it, with each passing day, each passing hour, his attraction to his new wife had grown.

At first, he'd put it down to proximity and tried avoiding her, hoping that, like a bothersome head cold, he'd eventually get over her. Instead he found himself more drawn to her, despite her letting him know in a dozen subtle ways that she wasn't interested in another husband. Why else had she spurned his generosity and persisted in wearing the plain, if not downright drab wardrobe she'd brought with her to Sicily? What other reason was there for her to hide her luscious body under clothes better suited to a nun, if not to remind him that she was Joe Mallory's widow far more than she'd ever be Raffaello Orsini's wife?

For weeks now, she'd used clothes to keep him at arm's length. Why last night had been different, he couldn't begin to fathom. Still, he'd curbed the hunger gnawing at him. Retained the upper hand over his libido—until the urge to brand her as his alone had driven him to near-madness.

He'd wanted to drown in her; to give her everything of himself. Instead he'd coerced her without mercy, over-powering her with brute force until she acquiesced instead of resisted, because compliance was preferable to stoking the rage he hadn't been able to control.

And now he had to live with the knowledge of what he'd done.

Close by, a church bell rang just as the sun rose high enough to bathe the skyline in golden light and glint on the restless water flowing beneath the bridge. No matter how much he wished it was otherwise, morning had come, and with it, the unenviable task of facing Corinne again.

She awoke to sunlight streaming through the window, and the delicious lassitude of a woman who, the night before, had been well and truly loved by the man of her dreams. Her body ached in places not mentioned in polite society, her skin burned slightly from the rasp of his jaw, her mouth felt swollen as a ripe strawberry. The scent of him lingered on the pillow next to her, on the bed linen and most of all, on her. She would never bathe again!

Nor would she ever forget how he'd looked, standing

proud and naked in the dim lamplit glow of midnight. Every sleek, sculpted curve and angle, from his broad shoulders to his long, powerful legs were forever etched in her memory, all elegantly gift-wrapped in dusky golden skin touched with dark, tempting shadows.

Reliving the sequence of events, her flesh pulsed again with echoes of rapture. The terrible risk she'd taken in stirring him to anger had paid off. The fire in his eyes had transmuted into a white-hot passion that refused to be satisfied. She couldn't wait for him to come back from wherever he'd gone so early in the day, so that they could do it all over again.

Stretching languidly, she drifted in a fantasy world. She'd open her arms and offer herself to him. They'd make love again, this time learning in the bright light of day the secrets the night had kept hidden. And in the sweet aftermath, she'd tell him the truth about everything: that her first marriage had been built on a foundation of infatuation and ultimately ended in disaster, but that she'd fallen irrevocably in love with him, Raffaello.

In turn, he'd admit that against all odds, he'd come to love her, too. That he couldn't imagine his life without her. That he was reborn, a whole man again, because of her.

The sound of the elevator doors whispering open sent her pulse roaring into overdrive. The moment was at hand.

He came directly to the bedroom and filled the doorway, a tall, well-dressed stranger regarding her as if he'd found an alien species in his bed, and she knew before he even opened his mouth that her happy ending wasn't going to happen.

"I'm glad you're awake," he said. "Corinne, we need to talk."

She cringed, all the stardust of the night before tainted by what she saw. No inner hell darkened his eyes. No tortured guilt, or bitter remorse touched his features, and certainly no eager pleasure. Rather, he remained so immune to emotion in any shape or form that she wondered how she'd ever managed to break through his defenses last night.

He dropped his leather jacket over the back of a chair, hooked his thumbs in the side pockets of his wheat-colored linen pants and came to stand at the foot of the bed. She knew what was coming next, could have recited the words for him before he even opened his mouth.

...terrible mistake last night...all my fault...can't be what you want me to be...wish I didn't have to hurt you...

She couldn't bear the indignity of it; the absolute humiliation of lying there naked beneath his cool, remote gaze. The only thing worse would have been his pity. She might have been swept off her feet by the events of last night, but his clearly had remained firmly planted on the ground.

Strike first and get it over with, the inner voice of self-preservation urged, and she seized on it as if it were all that stood between her and annihilation. Better a swift end, than a lingering death.

"If you're here to talk about last night," she said, dragging the shredded remnants of her pride around her, along with the bed sheet, "I'd just as soon not."

"At the very least, allow me to apologize."

"No need. I think it best we both forget whatever happened and move on."

"Can we do that, Corinne? Is it possible?"

Suddenly he looked haunted, and just as suddenly, she

was overcome with guilt. She'd pushed him into having sex with her. The least she could do was push him out and spare him flagellating himself for something that was entirely her fault.

"Certainly," she said, and steeled herself to degrade the most wonderful night of her life with a monstrous lie. "I wasn't myself and don't remember much of anything. Did we actually…?"

"Yes," he said grimly. "Twice."

"Really? I don't know what got into me."

A glimmer of bitter amusement flared briefly in his eyes. "I believe I did," he said. "I can only hope there'll be no lasting repercussions." He flicked a glance at his watch. "How soon can you be ready to leave?"

"For breakfast?"

"For the flight home."

"Don't you have more meetings scheduled for today?"

"My business here is concluded," he said grimly, "but if you wish to stay a few days longer, you're welcome to do so."

"That wouldn't say much for our so-called honeymoon, would it?" she said, amazed that she could sound so utterly in control when she was falling apart inside.

"Ours has never been your standard marriage. We each brought complications to the arrangement, some of which I don't anticipate we'll ever resolve."

"You mean, I don't fit your idea of the model wife. I'm not glamorous enough."

"You're a beautiful woman. But that you normally choose to hide behind nondescript clothing indicates to me, at least, that you don't wish to draw attention to the fact. You might as well have been wearing widow's weeds all this time—until last night when, for reasons known only to you, you decided to cast off your dowdy image. And look what happened as a result."

"It's a bit late in the day for regrets, Raffaello."

"Isn't it, though!" He stared bleakly around the room. "Well, do I instruct the butler to pack your bags, too, or are you staying on?"

"No. I've seen the sights and shopped till I dropped. Besides, I'm anxious to get back to Matthew."

"Then I'll meet you downstairs in an hour."

He flicked a disapproving glance to the floor, at the crumpled heap of sapphire-blue silk that was her gown, at her gorgeous French lingerie scattered like careless petals in a trail from the door to the bed and finally at one of her high-heeled shoes, sprawled indecently on its side, as wantonly depraved as its owner. Then without another word, he turned and left.

It was all she could do not to leap out of bed and fling herself at him. To hang on to his leg and beg him not to go. And knew that she could not, because nothing she did would change the facts.

The sad truth was, he didn't care about her, and he never would, at least not in the way she wanted him to. Not with gut-wrenching obsession and sleepless nights and endless mind games of "what if?" What if they'd met under different circumstances? What if he'd never known Lindsay?

She felt disloyal even entertaining such a thought.

When he'd first proposed marriage, she'd been afraid it might end up costing her more than it was worth. But she'd been thinking along the lines of self-respect and selling herself to a man willing to offer her more than she could afford to turn down. Certainly she'd found him attractive, irresistibly so. Any woman with half a brain would have. But there was a world of difference between that, and falling so deeply in love with him that she'd crave whatever attention he cared to toss her way.

She'd never dreamed she'd physically ache for him, morning, noon and night, so acutely that she'd cast aside every shred of pride and resort to entrapment to gain her ends. Never thought she'd beg him to take her to bed at any price.

In retrospect, of course, that was all he'd done. She had wanted him to make love to her, but for him, it had been sex, pure and simple. She'd been crazy to imagine, even for a moment, it could ever be otherwise when he'd made it clear from the outset that his heart belonged only to Lindsay.

The smartest thing she could do now was climb in the shower, and scrub away every lingering trace of him from her skin. The pity of it was, she couldn't erase him from her mind and heart, as well.

CHAPTER NINE

THERE WERE REPERCUSSIONS. Even though she tried to ignore them in the weeks following the aborted honeymoon, Corinne had been through it all before and recognized the symptoms too well to be fooled into thinking she had the "flu"—or any of the other myriad ailments desperate women clung to when an unplanned baby was on the way.

Early pregnancy did not agree with her. She was tired, couldn't stand the smell of food and looked like hell. Morning sickness was an unkind myth perpetuated by men who thought having M.D. behind their names made them experts on all things female—or by women who'd never conceived a child. In reality, the nausea lasted all day long, sneaking up at a moment's notice and sending her scurrying for the nearest bathroom where she'd try to retch quietly, so as not to alert anyone else in the house to the true state of affairs.

Not that she needed to worry that Raffaello would notice anything out of the ordinary, because she wasn't the only one burgeoning with new life. Heavily involved in every aspect of organic agriculture, he was often gone from dawn to dusk, overseeing operations. The fields hummed with activity as vegetables of every size, shape and color ripened by the truckload. Although a year-round undertaking, most of the citrus harvesting took place between February and June. The Orsini vineyards, on the southernmost eastern tip of the island and lower slopes of Mount Etna, grew heavy with fruit, as did the olive groves, closer to home.

And if all that wasn't enough to keep him occupied, he spent days, and sometimes nights, at the stables, monitoring the health of his prize mare as she approached the end of a difficult pregnancy.

By comparison, Corinne didn't rate a second glance, and even if she had, he probably wouldn't have noticed anything amiss. In fact, no one did, because she did such a good job of hiding the evidence. Putting away all the pretty clothes she'd acquired in Florence, she reverted to the T-shirts and over blouses she'd brought with her from Canada. Supplemented by a couple of Muumuu-style sundresses that floated around her in loose folds, and a dinner dress with a dropped waist, she was able to disguise her condition well into her fourth month.

Part of the reason was that life in the house became more informal with the onset of hot weather. In June, the governess was sent home to her family in Calabria until September. At least once a week, Raffaello would steal a few hours away from other things to take the children to the stables and supervise their riding lessons. The rest of the time, Corinne organized picnics on the beach with them. She felt safe from prying eyes there, knowing that Raffaello was off taking care of business and that neither Malvolia nor Leonora would dream of tackling the steep steps leading down the cliff.

She'd strip down to the black bathing suit she wore under her concealing shirt and shorts, and wade into the limpid water next to Matthew as he dog-paddled in the shallows, or toss a ball to Elisabetta, who swam like a fish. They'd eat lunch in the shade of a big umbrella, and stay there until the worst of the day's heat had passed. Often, Matthew napped for an hour or two, worn out from all the activity of the morning, leaving Corinne free to work on cementing her bond with her stepdaughter.

Those were special times. Elisabetta would curl up next to her on the blanket and beg, "Tell me again about Mama when she was little."

"Which story today, sweetie?"

"The time that she cut her hair with the kitchen scissors," she'd say, or "When she fell in the goldfish pond," or "At the school Christmas play when she forgot her lines."

No matter how often Corinne repeated the stories, Elisabetta never tired of hearing them.

They also had many a solemn discussion about heaven and angels, and if Lindsay could see Elisabetta and knew that her hair had grown into pigtails, and that she could read.

"I'm sure she does," Corinne always replied because, accurate or not, it was the best comfort she could offer a child much too young to have lost one of the two most important people in her life. "Your mama is always watching over you."

Once the children were in bed, the adults usually ate dinner by candlelight on the bougainvillea-draped terrace. Raffaello was unfailingly polite on those occasions, dutifully asking Corinne about her day and commending her on her improved relationship with Elisabetta. In turn, she inquired after the new foal or, if he'd been away on business elsewhere, if he was pleased with the outcome. He'd made several trips overseas, once to finalize the purchase of a hotel in Paris, and another time to inspect a stallion on a horse ranch outside Buenos Aires.

"For stud purposes," he'd explained.

"You're thinking of shipping the poor creature all the way here just for that?" she'd asked, scandalized.

He'd burst out laughing, a rare occurrence ever since the trip to Florence. "No, Corinne, it'll be a long-distance love affair. In other words, by artificial insemination."

She both dreaded and loved those evenings. Dreaded them because she was terrified someone would make an issue of the fact that she hadn't touched her wine, or comment that she seemed to be putting on weight. And loved them because, for a few short hours, she could drink in the sight and sound of him, and pretend they were just like any other husband and wife. But the pleasure always ended up being tainted by the pain of knowing that when he looked at her, he saw only the woman who'd stepped into Lindsay's shoes.

The master suite was her sanctuary during those difficult weeks, the one place in the house where she didn't have to pretend about anything. She didn't have to hide her thickening middle. She didn't have to water the closest plant with her wine when no one was looking. She didn't have to put on a happy face and smile until her jaw ached.

She couldn't have what she really wanted, either, and sometimes wished she'd never agreed to her bogus marriage. But Matthew had taken to his new life like a bud opening in the warmth of the summer sun. He thrived on the organized routine, on the people who'd become constants in his life.

He and Elisabetta were inseparable, sharing everything: toys, people, animals, and until recently, even lessons in the little schoolroom at the back of the house.

Lucinda, Filomena and the rest of the household staff doted on him, sneaking him into the kitchen to eat cookies still warm from the oven. They taught him Italian, sang to him, called him their little prince. As for Malvolia and Leonora, he'd always had them wound around his little finger.

And Raffaello? However far he fell short of her hopes as a husband, Corinne couldn't fault him as a father. Although Joe had failed miserably in the role, she always tried to present him in a positive light to Matthew. After all, no child should have to grow up feeling ashamed of his roots. But when it came to a role model for her boy, she couldn't ask for a better man than Raffaello. From the first, he'd treated her son as his own, and Matthew idolized him, following him around the stables like an adoring puppy, every chance that came his way.

How could all that not be enough for her? How could she ask for more?

She knew how. Raffaello had reminded her that she was a woman still in her prime. He'd awoken her from the long, cold sleep of widowhood, and the memories of that one magnificent night in Florence haunted her.

Sometimes, she awoke in the night, crying. Sometimes she closed her eyes, hugged her pillow and pretended she was hugging him. And sometimes, she simply remembered. Remembered how he felt inside her; how he'd held her face between his hands and buried hi mouth against hers. Remembered the sweat gleaming on his olive skin, and the passion in his beautiful gray eyes, and the frantic bursts of his heart beating against hers.

Sometimes, she thought he remembered, too. She'd catch him watching her, his expression veiled, and the atmosphere would sizzle with sudden awareness. Goose bumps would chase over her skin, her stomach would turn over, and a distant throb of awareness would settle between her thighs. But then, at other times, his gaze was oddly indignant, as if she'd offended him simply by breathing, and the thought of telling him she was pregnant horrified her.

She knew she was running out of time; that sooner rather than later, he'd have to know. But when he eventually did find out, it was in a way she'd never anticipated, and the fallout was about as bad as that following the night she'd conceived.

Sagra di metà, or high summer festival, was a local tradition somewhat similar to Thanksgiving. Since there was never a time that something or other wasn't being harvested on Orsini land, though, the celebration took place on a Saturday at the end of July, instead of in October.

The first Corinne heard about it was when Raffaello announced earlier in the week that she'd be attending it with him. The event, a night of music, dancing and feasting, was held in the village square, and considering that just about everyone living in the area worked for the Orsinis in one capacity or another, she figured there'd be quite a crowd.

"We'll be expected to put in an appearance, stay long enough to be seen enjoying ourselves and leave early enough that everyone can cut loose without the boss watching," he told her.

She understood exactly what he meant. The real Sicily was all about its people. About men and women who lived and breathed its fertile valleys and wild mountain terrain. About customs and superstitions going back hundreds of years. But even in the twenty-first century, a pronounced class distinction still existed. Raffaello might be highly respected by those he employed, but he played a very limited role in their personal lives.

Saturday night was hot, the air still and the sky a bolt of black velvet studded with stars, except where the reflection of lights from the festivities hung in the air like pearl-tinted clouds. She and Raffaello arrived at the party shortly after nine, walking along the gravel lane that began just past the boundary of his land and ended at a stile, about half a mile from the village.

When they finally reached the square, the scene reminded her of something taken from a movie. At one end stood the church, its stone facade washed with gold from the many lanterns hanging in the gnarled old olive trees. Huge vats of seafood stew flavored with garlic and capers simmered over a fire pit. Long tables covered in oilcloth groaned under the weight of other foods. Bread, something normally served only with the midday meal, spilled warm and fragrant from wicker baskets. Bowls of pasta vied for space with trays of roasted peppers, tomatoes, zucchini and eggplant.

Men playing accordions and tambourines filled the night with sound. At smaller tables placed randomly under the trees, people poured wine from painted stone pitchers and thumped their fists in time to the music, while in the middle of the square, couples of all ages danced a wild tarantella, the women wearing long, full skirts in vibrant shades of red and purple and green. Children and dogs darted among the shadows under the benevolent watch of grandmothers and great-grandmothers soberly clad in black.

For almost an hour, Raffaello mingled with the villagers, introducing Corinne as he worked his way from one group to the next. They sampled a little food, he drank a little wine and she did as usual, discreetly disposing of hers on the dusty ground.

Then, as the musicians struck up again, he took her by the hand and drew her into the crowd milling around the impromptu dance floor.

He hadn't touched her with any sort of familiarity since that night in Florence. To have him slide his arm around her now, over four months later, and smile down at her as if he was proud to call her his wife, filled her with such profound happiness that, even knowing it was an act put on for the benefit of those watching, she welcomed it. Was so desperate for him that she forgot to be careful, and went willingly into his embrace.

He spun her around, led her sure-footedly through some complicated country dance, laughingly pulled her close when she almost tripped over an uneven flagstone. And suddenly, with everyone else twirling madly around them in the flickering lantern-light, he stopped dead.

His smile faded. Very cautiously, he lowered his hands to the front of what had once been her waist and rested them there. As if he knew his father's touch, her baby moved for the first time with just the faintest flutter of acknowledgment. Raffaello couldn't possibly have felt it, but Corinne knew from the look on his face that she didn't have to worry about when or how to tell him she was expecting a baby. Her body had spoken for her. Very plainly.

"Raffaello—" she began.

"Do not say another word," he warned her, his lips barely moving. "Not now, and not here."

Then taking her wrist in an unforgiving grip, he wove a path through the other dancers, and with a deceptively nonchalant wave here and cheerful nod there, bid everyone good-night and practically frog-marched her back the way they'd come, less than two hours before.

The music and laughter had died to an echo when he stopped at the stile and swung around to confront her. By then, the moon had risen. Its cold light showed his mouth set in a thin, harsh line and turned his eyes black with disgust.

"Is there a reason you haven't shared your news with me before now?" he inquired, his voice a whiplash of contempt.

"I wanted to. I just didn't know how."

"'I'm pregnant' would have sufficed. Or, 'I'm expecting a child.' My English is more than adequate to grasp the import of either statement."

"They aren't words you wanted to hear."

"What I want, Corinne, is the truth. Preferably before I find myself the laughingstock of the whole of Sicily."

"What truth?" she said, bewildered.

"Is it mine?" He fired the question at her, lethal as a bullet aimed straight at her heart.

Reeling from the impact, she grabbed blindly at the stile and stared at him, shell-shocked. "Yes, it's yours," she said with quiet dignity when she could trust herself to speak. "And I will never forgive you for suggesting otherwise."

He had the grace to look ashamed. "What is it abou

you, that makes me want to hurt you?" he muttered, dragging his hand down his face.

"You resent me because I'm not Lindsay."

"I don't expect you to be."

"Yes, you do, and I've had enough of it. I loved Lindsay dearly and still miss her to this day, but I'm really not interested in spending the rest of my life trying to measure up to her."

"Then we are of the same mind, since your closing your beautiful blue eyes and pretending I'm your dead husband when I kiss you, doesn't work for me, either."

"Fine, then! Let's put this farce of a marriage out of its misery, and end it once and for all."

"That is not an option, nor will it ever be, as you have known from the outset. We married for the sake of Matthew and Elisabetta. Now we have a third child on the way. Does this baby not need us just as badly as the other two?"

"What about what you and I need?" she cried. "How long can we go on pretending to the whole world that our marriage is real, when we both know you care more about your blasted horses than you ever will about me? I'm tired of always running second best, Raffaello—almost as tired as I am of living a lie."

"Then we have to try harder. Start over. Make a better beginning."

"How can we, when I know you don't want another child?"

"How do you know that?"

"Because you said, in Florence, after…that night, that you hoped there wouldn't be any repercussions, and…well…there are."

"Indeed." He nodded. "Which leads me to ask, do you regret that you're pregnant?"

"No," she said, and wished she dared tell him that having his baby was the next best thing to having him tell her he loved her.

"Then since we are baring our souls at last, let me tell you that I am tired, too. Tired of fighting the inevitable where you and I are concerned. I am not made of stone, Corinne. You are a beautiful woman, and I'm—"

"A hot-blooded Sicilian who won't spurn my advances," she finished bitterly. "Yes, you made that clear, the first time we met. Unfortunately you were anything but pleased when I took you at your word. Or have you forgotten our blighted attempt at a honeymoon?"

"You caught me by surprise. But I am willing to give us another chance, and so should you be. There are, after all, much less pleasurable obstacles to overcome than physical intimacy, when trying to make a marriage work."

"Are there?"

"I am sure of it."

"Right now, I'm not very sure about anything."

He unclipped his phone from his belt. "Because you are overwrought," he said, in the kind of soothing tone he might use on a highly-strung mare. "The evening has been too much for a woman in your condition. I shall call for a car to take us home."

"No need. I can walk back."

"No, *cara mia,* you cannot. The path is too rough. You must take better care of yourself now. On Monday, I will arrange an appointment for you with a doctor in Modica."

"I already have a doctor in Modica. An obstetrician, in

fact, who assures me I'm as healthy as a horse." *Just not as important as one.*

"I would like to hear that for myself."

"If you must," she said, all at once weary of the whole unhappy mess they called a marriage. Why was it, she wondered, that after weeks of pining for his undivided attention, she found herself so dissatisfied, now that she'd got it?

She knew why. He'd very kindly given her a handful of stars, when what she wanted was the moon. Well, too bad. The moon wasn't to be had, and that was that.

"I must," he said. "As your husband, it is both my right and my duty."

Ah yes, she thought bleakly. *That word "duty" again.*

He punched in a number, relayed his request for a car and during the few minutes it took for it to arrive, tucked his arm around her shoulder and pulled her close.

She sank against him, too exhausted to fight him, or herself, any longer.

Malvolia cornered her the next morning at breakfast. "Raffaello has told me," she said. "It is wonderful news."

"You think?"

A small silence followed then, to her surprise, Malvolia reached across the table and took her hands. "You and I have had our differences, Corinna, and I confess that, in the beginning, I was not in favor of my son's marrying you so hastily. I did not think it fair to you, to him, or to Elisabetta."

"You thought I married him for his money."

"At first, I did, yes. He has so much and you clearly had very little, and I feared you would take advantage of his generosity. But that was in the beginning, and much has changed since then."

She squeezed Corinne's hands gently. "Corinna, I love my son and granddaughter deeply. They both have suffered greatly in the past and their happiness matters more to me than anything else. But you, my dear, have brought a harmony to this house which has been missing for a very long time. You are a wonderful mother who has taken Elisabetta into your heart with all the love and patience anyone could ask of you, and that, I know, has been no easy task. As a mother myself, I applaud you for that. But that you have proved yourself also to be a good and loving wife to my son is more than I ever dared hope to see. So if I haven't told you before how much I admire and care for you, then let my pleasure at your making me a grandmother again speak for me."

This, coming on top of last night's confrontation with Raffaello, was more than Corinne could bear. "Please don't be so nice," she wept, sobbing into her napkin. "I'm enough of an emotional mess, as it is."

"You're supposed to be, *figlia mia.* It's part of the process of cooking a new life."

At that, she choked back a laugh. "Then I should have a perfect baby."

"I'm sure you will." Malvolia tipped her head to one side, her dark eyes filled with concern. "And yet, I detect a sorrow in your heart. Why is that, Corinna? A baby you and my son have created together is a good thing for everybody, surely?"

"But not something we planned."

"What does that matter? Such things happen and you *are* married, after all."

"Raffaello's a very busy man. I'm not sure he really wanted another child."

"Nonsense! He's never too busy for his family, and I can tell you without fear of contradiction that he is overjoyed at becoming a father again."

Which is more than she could say for her late husband, Corinne thought, shuddering at the memory of the day she'd told Joe that Matthew was on the way.

He'd looked as thunderstruck as if she'd admitted to burying a body in the back garden. "What do you mean, *we're* having a baby?" he'd snapped, glowering at her across the dinner table. "How the hell did you let that happen?"

"Well, it takes two," she'd reminded him.

"No, Corinne. It only took you, because you're the one supposed to be on the pill."

"And I was...except for the time I had the stomach flu."

"Well, your mistake, sweet cheeks, not mine."

Stung by his attitude, she said, "What are you implying? That I'm on my own in this and you want no part of our child?"

He'd relented a little at that, and she'd hoped that once he got used to the idea, he'd share her anticipation. And for a while, he had, taking pride in the evidence of his virility. "All I had to do was hang my pants on the back of the bedroom door, and bingo!" he'd boasted to his pilot friends.

Sure she'd give birth to a son, he already had a name picked out. "Matthew, after my dad, and Joseph, after me," he'd declared.

But when he discovered that regardless of its sex, a baby demanded attention almost twenty-four hours a day, fatherhood soon lost its luster. He started staying out late.

Sometimes didn't come home at all. "Mine's a high-stress job," he'd contended. "I need to relax in my off-time, and there's none of that to be found around here with the brat squalling half the night."

And then, suddenly, it was all over. Matthew started sleeping through the night, but it no longer mattered. Joe was dead, killed trying to land a float plane in heavy fog, at a remote fishing camp in northern B.C.

Within the year, Lindsay was dead, too. Which brought Corinne full circle to where she was today: married a second time and pregnant again—this time to a husband man enough to face up to his responsibilities without the need to lay blame on someone else.

If for no other reason than that, she had to agree with Raffaello. They must try harder to make their marriage work. Three innocent lives depended on it.

CHAPTER TEN

IN THE WEEKS FOLLOWING, she could hardly fault him for his efforts. He attended every doctor's appointment with her. Made sure she followed to the letter every instruction regarding vitamins, exercise, rest. Catered to whatever craving happened to be her flavor of the day. Chocolate-covered marzipan and tomatoes, one week; sardines and figs drizzled in balsamic vinegar, the next.

He massaged the small of her back when it ached. Worried if her ankles swelled. Commented if he thought she looked tired, so much so that she took to wearing sunglasses whenever possible, just to shut him up.

He insisted on buying her a maternity wardrobe extensive enough to keep six pregnant women in haute couture sophistication. Fine silk and cashmere skirts and slacks and tunic tops for daytime wear. Lovely flowing dresses in rich, gorgeous velvets for evening, some falling from the shoulder in straight simple lines and others with high empire waists and flattering necklines that dipped to reveal a hint of cleavage. Voluminous nightdresses and peignoirs of soft combed cotton trimmed in satin and French lace, that fell to her ankles and caressed her skin. Beautiful handcrafted suede shoes with heels high enough to be elegant but low enough to be safe.

He slept with her in the big master bed. Put his arms around her and kissed her good-night. Sweetly, softly, on the mouth. Even made love to her occasionally, with great tenderness and attention to her pleasure, rather than his own. But never with the untamed passion, the rampant desire he'd shown in Florence.

In other words, he went through the motions, but his heart wasn't really in it. She knew that because, if she moved too close to him in the middle of the night, he'd turn his back to her and inch to the far side of the mattress. If she reached over in the dark to take his hand and place it on her swollen belly so that he could feel the baby kick, he'd snatch it away again as if she'd burned him.

She could hardly blame him. What man wouldn't be repelled by a wife so bloated, she couldn't see her own toes anymore, and who waddled around like an over-stuffed penguin?

When he wasn't there to monitor her every waking breath, his mother and aunt stepped in, smothering her in affectionate concern.

"Don't go down to the beach anymore, *figlia mia.* You could fall on the steps and hurt the baby."

"Be careful with that heavy picnic basket. We don't want the baby arriving before his time."

"Put your feet up and look after the little one you're carrying, Corinna, and leave the other two children to us."

The baby this, the baby that… And because she was the sacred vessel entrusted to carrying it safely to term, she was treated like spun glass. It irritated her beyond words.

"I won't break," she snapped, when Raffaello suggested she shouldn't be tramping around the garden by herself when she was seven months along. "For heaven's sake, stop fussing and leave me alone!"

She didn't really want him to leave her alone. She wanted him to care about her, not just because she was pregnant, but because she was his wife. Besides, what did he think? That she'd deliberately do anything to endanger their child whom she'd loved desperately from the second she knew she'd conceived?

Then there were Elisabetta and Matthew, and their pointed questions.

"Why are you so fat?"

"Because there's a baby growing inside me."

"Who put it there?"

Not prepared to launch into a graphic explanation of how babies were made, she said, "It grew from a seed."

"How does it get out? Like a balloon bursting if you prick it with a pin?"

Dear God, she hoped not!

She enjoyed a slight reprieve in late autumn, with attention turned to the fall harvest. Nets were spread under the olive trees and as one army of workers hand-picked the crop, another filled baskets with the fruit and took them to the oil press. Orsini olive oil was exported worldwide, and very big business. No sooner was that task completed than it was time to pick the moscato grapes from which the yellow fortified Orsini wine was made. It, too, enjoyed an international reputation.

Glad something else was the chief focus of her husband's attention, even if only temporarily, Corinne devoted those weeks to assembling the baby's layette, making a point of including the children in the preparations whenever possible. Elisabetta and Matthew both had made so many amazing adjustments in their lives, and the last thing she wanted was for either of them, especially Elisabetta, to feel displaced by the new arrival.

She took them shopping when morning classes were over, and let them choose items for the baby's room. A lamp in the shape of a crescent moon, with star-shaped cut-outs where the light showed through. A framed print, a quilt, a musical mobile, a soft, cuddly teddy bear. And always, at the end of the trip, they'd get to choose a little something for themselves. A book, perhaps, or new crayons and thick pads of sturdy construction paper in a rainbow of colors.

Usually they went to nearby Noto, a beautiful little city of churches on the left bank of the River Asinaro, renowned for its eighteenth century baroque architecture. As long as she was home and dressed for dinner in one of her lovely gowns before anyone had time to miss her, no questions were asked about where she and the children had been, or how they'd spent their time.

Once, though, on a cool, overcast afternoon toward the middle of November, she drove as far as Modica. After browsing the boutiques along the main Corso, she treated the children to gelato in a little shop near the Church of Saint Mary of Bethlehem.

Elisabetta had been unusually quiet that day, leaving Corinne to wonder if she was coming down with something

"When the baby comes," the child eventually asked, studiously poking her spoon into her ice cream, "what will it call you, Corinne?"

"Nothing," Corinne said. "Babies don't start talking until they're about a year old, as a rule."

"But when it does start, will it call you Mommy, the way Matthew does?"

"I expect so, yes."

"And Papa will be Papa?"

"Yes."

"So I'll still be the one left out," she said, and plopping down her spoon, burst into tears.

"Oh, sweetheart!" Finally understanding what lay behind the questions, Corinne pulled the little girl onto her lap—or what was left of it, these days. Although Matthew had claimed Raffaello as his own within days of arriving in Sicily, Elisabetta had never been able to bring herself to call Corinne "Mommy" or "Mama."

"I don't want the baby to live with us," she sobbed now. "I want Papa to send it to Canada."

"If he did that, my angel, I'd have to go, as well, and I'd miss you terribly. Not only that, this baby is really looking forward to having you for a big sister, and how could you be that, if we lived so far away?"

"I'm not going with you," Matthew piped up, between shoveling in mouthfuls of gelato. "I like it here with Papa and Nonna and Zia and my pony."

Disloyal little toad!

Not about to be distracted, Elisabetta whimpered, "I won't really be its sister, because you're not really my mother."

"But I love you as much as if I were," Corinne said, stroking her hair. "In my heart, you really are my little girl, just as much as Matthew is my little boy, and I promise you, you're definitely this baby's big sister."

The tears subsided gradually until just one stray was left to roll down the petal-soft cheek. "Really and truly?"

"Cross my heart."

"But how will it know?"

"Well, for a start, because you'll always be there, playing with it, and helping me to look after it. Only very important people like sisters and brothers get to do that. Of course, if you called me Mommy or Mama, then for sure the baby would know we all belong to the same family—but only if you want to."

"If I did, do you think Mama will mind?"

Had it been anyone but Lindsay they were talking about, Corinne might have sunk low enough to be jealous. But she understood all too well how unforgettable Lindsay was, even to the child she'd mothered for only three short years.

Stroking Elisabetta's hair away from her flushed face, she said, "I guarantee that if you're happy, your mama will be happy, too."

Elisabetta considered the matter gravely, then nodded, sending her pigtails flying. "Well then, p'raps I'll call you Mommy, like Matthew does, then it won't hurt Mama's feelings and she won't think I've forgotten about her."

"You're a very smart little cookie, Elisabetta Orsini. You just made your mama and me very happy and proud."

"I know." Confidence restored, she slithered off Corinne's lap and climbed back on her own chair. "I'll finish my gelato now so we can shop for our treats before we go home."

They stayed in town a good bit longer than Corinne intended, and arrived home after dark to find Malvolia and Leonora twittering like distraught sparrows, and a grim-faced Raffaello about ready to call out the equivalent of the national guard.

"Tell me, if you will, Corinne, what purpose there is in carrying a cell phone, if you do not have it turned on?" he exploded, the minute she set foot in the house. "I've been trying to contact you for the last hour or more."

"Why? Did something happen?"

"*Si,* something happened! You and the children went missing."

"Oh, don't be so melodramatic," she scoffed. "We went shopping in Modica, that's all."

"You think it melodramatic that my mother and aunt have been sick with worry? You think it unreasonable for a husband to show concern for a wife who disappears with his children, and says not a word to anyone about where she can be found or when she might return?"

"I'm sorry you're so upset. Time kind of got away from me, but as you can see, we're all perfectly fine, and no harm's been done."

"In your opinion, perhaps, but not in mine. You're thirty-six weeks pregnant, woman—much too far along to be driving such a distance. Look at you, so pale and exhausted. And in case you haven't noticed, it's raining. Hardly ideal driving conditions, especially after dark. What if you'd had an accident?"

"But I didn't," she said calmly. "I'm perfectly capable of looking after myself *and* the children, so please stop treating me as if I'm a half-wit who's never driven in rain before."

Unconvinced, he eyed her severely. "I want your word that you will not put yourself or the baby at risk like this again. If you must go to Modica, I or someone else in the household will take you. Promise me, Corinne."

"Oh, all right," she sighed, secretly quite happy to go along with his request. Contrary to her assertions, driving home along dark, twisting country roads, with the rain slashing across the windshield, had been downright nerve-racking at times, and she was more than ready to play the submissive wife in need of a keeper. "Is that all, *signor,* or may we go upstairs and change for dinner now?"

"I should punish the three of you by making you dine on bread and water in the kitchen," he growled, unable to keep his face as straight as he might have liked. "You've given me gray hairs before my time."

"You shouldn't talk to Mommy like that," Elisabetta scolded, skipping blithely past him. "Not when she's preggernant."

Astonished, he flicked a glance at Corinne and inquired sotto voce, "So it's 'Mommy' now, is it? When did this happen?"

"While we were misbehaving in Modica. You want to spank me for that, as well?"

Again, his mouth twitched in the beginnings of a smile. "An excellent idea, *mia moglie,* and one I'm sorely tempted to act upon."

"In your dreams!"

"You have what they call in America 'a smart mouth,' my dear."

"Just one of my many talents," she said breezily, and gathering up her purchases, trundled her bulk up the stairs after the children.

Later that evening, after Elisabetta and Matthew were in bed, and the adults gathered in the *soggiorno* for after-dinner espresso and brandy—all except Corinne who sipped a caffeine-free latte—he announced, "Tomorrow, I must go to Milano and shall be away for three days."

Disturbed, Malvolia set down her demitasse. "Is that wise, Raffaello, with Corinna so close to confinement?"

"What if the baby comes while you're gone?" Leonora added, making it sound as if a woman giving birth without her husband there to wipe the sweat from her brow was tantamount to treason. "Imagine if you were not here to see your son or daughter born."

"I hardly think that's going to happen. My due date's not for another four weeks," Corinne reminded the room at large.

She might as well have saved her breath. "It's a chance I'm going to have to take," Raffaello said. "I have matters urgently requiring my attention. If I could put them off, I would, but—"

Flaring up, she said, "There's no reason to put anything off. I saw Dr. Sabbatini just yesterday, and he's perfectly satisfied that everything is as it should be, and I'm right on schedule for the delivery."

"Nevertheless, any sign that that might change, and you are to contact me immediately. I can be home in less than two hours." Raffaello touched her hand briefly, making her ashamed of her irritation. "Nothing will keep me from your side when you give birth, Corinne."

He sounded so sincere, so much the devoted husband, she had to remind herself it was the baby he really cared about. Well, better that, than to be like Joe: utterly indifferent to everything but his own selfish needs and desires.

"I promise you, Raffaello," she said, curling her fingers around his, "nothing's going to happen."

"I'm counting on you to keep to that, *cara mia.*"

Once upon a time, when her understanding of Italian had been limited to the most basic terms, she'd have bloomed under the endearment. Now, she knew it carried none of the intimate clout associated with *amore,* or *tesoro,* and amounted to little more than an avuncular "my dear." Nevertheless, the way his gaze rested on her, so warm and concerned, caused her stomach to flip in a funny little somersault. Was it possible he *did* care for her, just a little bit?

"We'll keep a close eye on her," his mother promised.

"And make sure she doesn't overdo," Leonora chimed in.

Holding his gaze, Corinne went one step further. "If it'll ease your mind any, and if your mother and aunt don't mind looking after the children, I'll even promise to put my feet up and not lift a finger while you're gone."

Nods of approval all around made it clear she'd said the right thing.

"*Si,* it will ease my mind," Raffaello admitted.

That night in bed, he pulled her close and spooned his long body around her. "Remember, you are to be a very good wife while I'm away," he reminded her, his breath ruffling her hair and stealing warm and sweet over her nape.

Drowsy and safe in his arms, she said, "I will," and fell asleep, lulled by the steady thump of his heart.

Uncommonly heavy rain fell over the next two days and what had started out as a novelty for the children soon became a burden. Matthew, especially, chafed at not being free to race around outside and complained bitterly about missing his beloved pony. So when the sky cleared in midafternoon on the third day, and Malvolia and Leonora offered to take them to the stables, Corinne was happy to agree.

She couldn't wait for Raffaello to come home that evening. Although neither had said or done anything specific, she'd felt closer to him, that last night before he left for Milan, than she'd felt at any other time in their marriage. In the days since, she'd known a hopefulness, a sort of expectancy, as if they were on the brink of breaking free from the constraints they'd imposed on their relationship.

His phone calls each night had done nothing to disabuse her of this. The timbre of his voice, deep and quiet and intimate, had clothed even as straightforward a question as "How are you, Corinne?" with a subtext that hinted at more than simple concern for her health. If she'd dared, she'd have replied, *Lonely...I miss you...hurry home. Our bed is too empty without you....*

But tonight, she decided, she *would* dare. She'd risk his turning away from her, and tell him everything: about her failed marriage to Joe, but more importantly, about all that lay in her heart now. What could it hurt?

As the afternoon slipped toward dusk, she took a leisurely bath, smoothed scented lotion over her body and put on her favorite maternity gown, the deep purple velvet with the empire waistline. Then, sure the children would be back from their ride by now, she went looking for them.

The house, though, was eerily silent, so much so that the sudden shrill sound of the telephone filled her with an uncanny sense of foreboding as compelling as it was irrational. A stealthy whisper of fear crept up her spine. She knew with prescient certainty that someone dear to her was in serious trouble. She knew it as surely as she knew her own name.

"Raffaello," she breathed, and as if answering, a vicious burst of rain lashed at the windows.

Trembling, she picked up the handset. *"Pronto?"*

"Corinna!"

Relief washed over her at the sound of her mother-in-law's voice. "Malvolia, where are you? It's pouring out."

"Corinna…oh my dear…the children…"

"What about the children?"

"They've disappeared."

God help her, she laughed. "Don't be silly, Malvolia. They can't have."

"They can—they have. We've looked everywhere and there's no sign of them. I'm so afraid they might have wandered away from the estate."

The children are safe as long as they stay on Orsini land.…

Corinne's blood turned to ice. Fear stabbed again, sharp as a thousand knives. Her sixth sense had been right on target, except that it wasn't Raffaello in trouble, but the daughter he'd entrusted to her care, and her son, her precious Matthew.

"How long have they been gone?" she asked dully.

"I can't say for sure." Malvolia's voice quivered; verged close to tears. "I wasn't really paying close attention. They were riding in the paddock, just as they always do, and having a good time. Leonora and I went into the stables to shelter from the wind. Suddenly we realized it was too quiet outside, and that's when we discovered…oh, Corinna, what—?"

Hearing the rising hysteria in Malvolia's voice, Corinne stepped in to take control. "Stay put. I'll be right there."

"Please hurry, *cara.*"

She severed the connection, grabbed her car keys and within seconds was backing the Cayenne out of the garage and racing along the paved road toward the paddocks at the north perimeter of the estate.

By then, dusk had settled and swathed the land in varying shades of gray, but light shone from the stables, spilling out into the cobblestoned yard where a number of Orsini employees conferred with Malvolia and Leonora.

Dread fused into anger as Corinne braked to a stop next to them. *Why are you standing around talking, instead of searching every nook and cranny for my children?* she wanted to shriek.

But one look at the women's haggard faces, and any censure she might have uttered died on her lips. Guilt and misery etched their features, leaving them looking closer to eighty than sixty. Lowering her window, she said, "It'll be all right. They can't have gone far."

"I'm afraid they might have, *figlia mia.*" Malvolia lifted a trembling hand to her mouth. "The ponies are missing, too, you see."

Leonora, normally the one more prone to panic, put a comforting arm around her sister's shoulders. "But already a dozen or more stable and farm hands have started to search, and they know the area very well. I'm sure we'll hear good news soon."

The problem, Corinne thought, scanning the darkening landscape, was that the Orsini lands covered hundreds of acres. The children could be anywhere.

Lorenzo, the head groom, approached the car. "My men will cover every kilometer of land between here and the village, and also along the beach, Signora Orsini. We will find the *bambini* and bring them safely home."

Swallowing the terror clogging her throat, she said, "Do you have any idea which direction they might have taken?"

"We've found an open gate at the end of the lane behind the mobile field shelters. It is likely they went that way and followed one of several paths leading to the village."

He answered with authority, but she picked up on something else; an unspoken hesitation that spelled a different kind of message. "And if they didn't?" she forced herself to ask.

Overhearing, Malvolia shuddered. "There is another path, very steep and rough, heading up into the mountains," she whimpered.

...the land beyond the northern fence is wild and dangerous country....

As clearly as if he stood beside her now, Raffaello's warning came back to haunt Corinne. "I'm checking it out," she said, and ignoring the clamor of objections that arose in response, jammed the Cayenne into gear and roared off.

Ignoring the wide sandy lane beyond the open gate, which she knew led to the shore and from there to the village, she headed the other way, to the north. Searching... searching. Repeating over and over, *Please, God, keep my children safe. Let me find them and bring them home safe again.* And suddenly spying a rutted path on her right. Barely wide enough to accommodate the Cayenne, it snaked up past a grove of ancient olive trees, and without hesitation, she followed it.

Almost immediately, the sandy soil gave way to rough gravel that spat and pinged against the side of the SUV as it jolted and plowed its way uphill. Soon enough, Corinne found herself in inhospitable, isolated territory. The rain had stopped by then, but mist swirled down the mountainside, too thick for her headlights to penetrate more than a few feet ahead.

...wild and dangerous... The words echoed repeatedly through her mind, filling her head with crazy, self-perpetuating fears: of bandits and wild animals poised to strike; of bottomless ravines and rain-flooded creeks that swept away everything lying in their path. And of two little children, lost and cold and afraid, with night closing in. Her beloved Matthew. Raffaello's adored Elisabetta. Lindsay's daughter....

Something scraped the passenger side of the SUV. An outcropping of rock. And looming out of the mist, more of the same. The track had petered out into nothing. She had not found the right path, after all. Worse yet, she was closed in on three sides by towering slabs of rock, in a space so narrow, her only choice was to reverse the SUV until she could turn the vehicle around. No easy task at the best of times. And these were far from that.

The shifting mist deceived her time and again. Loose rocks skidded from beneath her tires and rattled into nothingness. She tried opening her door and leaning out, the better to judge her position on the track, but the bulk of her pregnancy made it impossible. The best she could do was inch along with one foot on the brake.

In the end, her best wasn't good enough. The Cayenne crunched up against something hard, and the next moment tilted at a terrifying angle that left her plastered against the back of her seat. For one endless nanosecond, it rocked gently, hovering between solid ground and heaven only knew what else, its headlights spearing the night in search of the hidden stars. And then it settled precariously, its rear end hanging out in space.

She froze, afraid to move, afraid to breathe.

She and her unborn child were going to die.

She would leave Matthew an orphan, and rob Elisabetta of a mother for the second time.

She would never have the chance to tell Raffaello she loved him.

CHAPTER ELEVEN

LORENZO contacted him when he was one and a half hours out of Milano: Corinne was missing. By some cruel twist of fate, she'd gone looking for the children whom everyone feared were lost, but who'd since been found alive and safe.

Queasy suddenly, Raffaello bellowed, "How the devil could she have just disappeared? Who was the idiot that let her drive off alone? Who left the bloody gate open in the first place?"

But killing the messenger accomplished nothing, and crushing the upsurge of terror churning in his gut, he forced himself into automatic control mode. He knew as well as the next man that in situations like this, a cool head always triumphed over a desperate heart. And he intended to win this latest battle, even if it meant going toe to toe with God Himself.

Ten minutes later, he clicked off the phone and ran a mental check to be sure he'd covered all the bases.

Search party: rounded up.

One Jeep, and one heavy-duty truck equipped with

twelve million candlepower spotlight, towing winch and chains: standing by.

Flashlights, ropes, and two-way radios, emergency foil blankets, medical equipment and supplies: assembled.

By the time the jet landed, everything should be ready to go. Pitifully and agonizingly little though it was, he'd done all a man could do when he found himself captive in an aircraft, cruising at an altitude of twelve thousand meters and a speed in excess of eight hundred kilometers an hour, while all hell broke loose on his home turf.

What he couldn't do was turn back the clock and prevent the crisis from having taken place to begin with. No matter which way he looked at it, his wife was missing, and no amount of cursing or barking orders over the telephone changed that.

Being powerless did not sit well with him. Only once had he found himself its prisoner, and that was when he'd had to watch Lindsay die. He would not let himself be robbed that way again. He would not, *could not* lose Corinne.

He could, he admitted, use a drink; a hefty measure of single malt scotch. But he'd never been one to turn to alcohol when the going got tough, and if ever there was a time that he needed his wits sharp and his head clear, it was now. So he dismissed his steward and, resigning himself to remaining inactive at least for the present, stared out the window. Not that there was anything to see apart from the flashing red light at the tip of the port wing, but that was better than the images waiting to pounce if he dared close his eyes.

They pounced anyway, a bittersweet montage of memories flitting across the black sky in brilliant Technicolor.

The first time he'd seen Corinne, slender as a reed in her

classic black dinner dress and pearls, her eyes as blue as Sicily's summer skies, her hair pale as wheat. He'd noticed she had great legs, a tiny waist, full, firm breasts. And a face that would make any man stop and take a second look. Creamy skin, sweetly curved mouth, delicate cheekbones.

Only as the evening progressed had he taken stock of her other qualities. The pride that wouldn't let her admit she barely made ends meet. Her independent spirit. The stubborn streak a mile wide that had made him want to shake her for refusing to consider his proposal. Even then, instinct had warned him that letting her goad him into rash action would prove a costly mistake that had nothing to do with money. Yet before the evening was over, he'd offered to keep her bed warm, if that's what it would take to seal the deal.

A lousy idea, she'd informed him which, along with her earlier assertion that he was *a few bricks short of a full load* made him smile even at a time such as this. In retrospect, she'd been right. He'd been so sure his heart was safe. There'd been no thunderclap of awareness, no heavenly chorus, none of the dizzy euphoria that had afflicted him the first time he'd set eyes on Lindsay. Corinne's was a more subtle assault, one that infiltrated his complacence when he wasn't looking, and blew it to smithereens.

He'd fallen in love with her in increments. Because she was kind and compassionate and patient. Because she was sensitive to his mother's insecurity, and didn't try to usurp her matriarchal role within the family hierarchy.

Because she didn't force herself on Elisabetta, but waited for the child to come to her. Because she was fair in her dealings with both children, never favoring her own at the expense of his. Because she was never too tired to listen to them, to play with them.

She didn't know how often he'd watched at a distance as she chased them over the lawns, her hair blowing in the breeze, her laughter music to his ears. Or how many times he'd stood at the top of the cliff and spied on her as she played lifeguard, standing waist-deep in the sea as they practiced their swimming. She had no idea how often he lingered outside the nursery, listening as she told Elisabetta about her birth mother; lovely, warm, generous stories full of love and laughter that would keep Lindsay alive forever in her daughter's heart.

Only once had she caught his covert scrutiny, and that had been at dinner, a scant week ago. Even in advanced pregnancy, she was elegant, beautiful, her radiant skin untouched by the harsh Sicilian sun, her profile pure as a cameo, her hair a thick, shining fall of pure pale gold. But seeing him watching her, she'd glanced aside, keeping her thoughts, her inner self, secret from him, and he'd wondered if there'd ever come a time that they'd trust one another enough to share all that lay in their hearts.

He'd wanted to tell her he loved her because she was sexy and desirable. Because she was his, and being around her day-to-day brought him happiness in ways he'd never thought to know again. Because she dared to challenge his pathetic charade of indifference, and forced him to acknowledge his caveman behavior on their so-called honeymoon had been driven by jealousy.

Ever since that time, he'd been so hungry for her, it shamed him. Sleeping in the same bed for the last four months had been nothing short of sublime torture. He'd ached to put his mouth on her belly and kiss their baby through her skin. To touch her in places he knew would leave her sweet and hot and eager for him.

He'd taken enough cold showers to fill an ocean, all to no effect. He wanted her all the time. *All the time.* Wanted to breathe in the fragrance of her skin, and feel her climax when he was gloved deep inside her. And was so deathly afraid he might hurt her or the baby if he gave in to passion raging within him, that he schooled himself to a restraint that nearly killed him.

He didn't know how to kiss her or touch her, and let that be enough. And so he turned away from her, when what he most wanted in the world was to hold her so close that he could feel their baby stirring against *his* belly.

He lay awake for hours, wrestling with his unflagging desire. When fatigue finally claimed him and he fell asleep, he embarrassed himself with dreams he thought he'd outgrown when he was a teenager.

The regrets, the guilt, swamped him. Once, he'd said he had no secrets, that if there was something about him she wanted to know, she only had to ask. But he'd lied. He'd kept his love secret, always waiting for another, better time to share it.

What if he'd left it too late?

The pilot's voice came over the intercom, announcing their final approach to the airfield. Glancing down, Raffaello caught sight of the intermittent flash from the lighthouse on the point ten kilometers east of the village, and moments later, the line of lights marking the runway.

Adrenaline surged through his blood, powerful, stimu-lating. *Now,* he could wrestle fate to its knees if he had to, instead of hanging fire and depending on blind luck to guide him. He knew better than most that bad things could happen to good people. Look at Lindsay, whose life had been over at twenty-four. But he would not let the same happen to Corinne. Death would not cheat him a second time.

Wherever you are, my love, I will find you and bring you home, he vowed.

The jet touched down and screamed to a stop. At once, he was through the exit door and racing across the tarmac to where one of the Range Rovers idled, with Lorenzo at the wheel. Lorenzo, his head groom, his friend since childhood, and the man he trusted most in the world to cover his back, no matter what.

"Anything new?" he asked, hurling himself into the passenger seat.

Before he had the door closed, the vehicle was in motion, racing through the night to the stables. "Not yet," Lorenzo said.

"No signal from her phone?"

"She didn't take it with her. Your mother found it at the house."

"*Porca miseria!* How often have I told her…!"

"Calm yourself, *mio fratello.* One search party is already out looking for her. The other is ready to go when we join them. We will find her. She'll be home soon."

"She should be home now."

"At least the children are safe."

"For the present," he growled, through clenched teeth. "They might not see it that way when I'm finished with them. What the hell did they think they were doing, taking off like that?"

"They are children, Raffaello, and children don't always think. We both know that."

He scowled. "They will from now on. I'll see to it."

When they arrived in the stable yard, one look at the faces of the men waiting there told him all he needed to know, but he asked anyway. "What's the word from those who went ahead?"

"They've reached the high pastures, *signor,* but so far have found nothing."

Impotent rage rose up and almost choked him. "Then the damn fools have missed something!"

"These are your men, Raffaello," Lorenzo reminded him softly. "They would lay down their lives for you. If they haven't found her, it's not from want of trying, but in weather like this, they could easily miss her."

"Either that, or they're looking in the wrong place. You're sure she headed up the mountain?"

"She said as much."

"She's never had reason to go that way before. I wonder…" He chewed his lip, reconstructing the lay of the land in his mind's eye. Treacherous territory, even for those most familiar with it. For a woman unused to such terrain…

Dio, he couldn't think about that. He dared not. Better to refocus on the idea surfing the corners of his mind. "Remember the time we ran away, Lorenzo, and when we couldn't be found, everyone thought we must be at least halfway to Palermo?"

"And all the time, we were no more than five or six kilometers from home."

"Staked out in a cave at the head of a canyon only you and I knew about."

Lorenzo's gaze locked with his in sudden dread. "Surely you don't think…?"

"At this point, we can't afford to overlook any possibility."

Calling to the waiting men, he outlined the change in plan. No point in going over territory already covered. They would strike out in a new direction.

Within minutes, they were off, four to a vehicle, and followed the trail heading north to the mountains. About five kilometers along, they stopped, and with the aid of flashlights found the clue the first searchers had not thought to look for: tire tracks in the muddy ground, at the point where a rough goat track forked away from the main path.

"God help her, she did go this way," Lorenzo muttered.

The convoy set off again, Raffaello in the lead, following the route she'd taken and inching along at no more than ten kilometers an hour, with all but the drivers playing the beams of the flashlights to either side.

Night and mist turned the landscape into an alien place, one made up of shifting shadows that briefly raised hopes too soon dashed into disappointment.

To one side, the cliff rose steeply. To the other, it dropped thousands of meters to the valley floor. And in between, a track barely wide enough for two cars to pass, paved with loose, uneven rocks, some the size of watermelons. When the branch of a stunted shrub clinging to the upper slope scraped harshly against the side of the Range Rover, Lorenzo voiced what Raffaello had known for some time. "We've made it about as far as we can in these vehicles."

"Then we'll go the rest of the way on foot. Radio the others and tell them we're turning around while we still can."

No mean feat that, but with flashlights signaling the way

and shouted instructions from the rest of the team, the drivers managed, beginning with the heavy truck now leading the pack, and the Range Rover bringing up the rear.

Raffaello's primary concern during this delicate maneuver was safety. He knew well enough that one false move could cost him his life. So when a faint beam of light caught his eye, a few meters farther up the track, he paid little attention, assuming it was a trick of the mist throwing back at him the reflection of his own headlamps as they sliced slowly through the dark. Only after he'd completed the turn and glanced through his rearview mirror did he notice that other pale glow still hanging in the fog-shrouded night. And only then did he understand its significance.

The others had seen it, and they, too, understood. Without needing to be told, they began attaching chains to the truck's tow bar, throwing coiled ropes over their shoulders, debating the best course of action.

Raffaello didn't wait to find out what that might be. All he knew, all that mattered was ascertaining if they'd found Corinne's car and if she was still inside it, alive and unhurt.

Cursing his leather-soled loafers, which were never designed for mountain climbing, he slipped and slid his way over the scree until he reached the source of that painfully weak gleam of light. Then, he froze in his tracks, transfixed by the sight in front of him.

His heart almost seized up. The Cayenne sat perilously balanced on a slab of rock at a bend in the path, its back wheels suspended in space. Even as he broke out in a cold sweat of horror, the body of the car rocked slightly, like the pendulum of a stopped clock about to start marking time again.

Lorenzo, following close behind him, skidded to a halt. *"Dio santo!"* he whispered. "Is she in there?"

"I can't tell from here," he said, and started to edge forward, one careful step at a time.

But Lorenzo caught him by the arm and held him back. "Wait," he cautioned. "There are others here, better able than either of us, to deal with this."

"This," he ground out, the metallic taste of fear thick on his tongue, "happens to be my wife. Do not ask me to wait."

"And if, in your haste, you send her to her death, how will you live with yourself, Raffaello?" his friend inquired. "Step away, for the love of God, and let those who know how, do what has to be done."

The fight went out of him and numb with despair, he nodded. He'd once hauled an overturned tractor upright; carried an injured man half his weight again to a first-aid station on Etna. But not even his mighty strength was enough to lift the Cayenne to safety. For once, he had to stand back and rely on the expertise of others.

Two wiry mechanics who looked after his farm equipment—husbands and fathers just like him with every bit as much to lose as he had—conferred briefly, clipped themselves to safety lines strung from the Jeep, and approached the SUV, moving as lightly, as carefully, as if they stepped on eggs. One aimed a flashlight while the other took the end of the heavy chain attached to the truck and hooked it to the Cayenne's frame.

Raffaello's blood froze as the car shuddered and rocked wildly. Then, the most beautiful sound in the world rumbled through the canyon—that of the powerful electric winch grinding into action and hauling its precious cargo to safety. The chain grew tight. Slowly, one agonizing centimeter at a time and screaming objections at the damage to its undercarriage, the Cayenne tipped away from danger and toward solid ground.

A cheer went up, and died quickly as the truck spotlight settled on the other vehicle's windshield and pinpointed the unmoving figure in the driver's seat. For a moment, Raffaello stood rooted to the spot, afraid of what he was about to learn; afraid not to know. Then tearing free of Lorenzo's restraining hands, he rushed forward and wrenched open the door.

She leaned against the headrest, the seat belt tight across her hips but hidden by the bulk of her pregnancy. She looked pale as moonlight, was cold when he touched her at the corner of her jaw, but her pulse was strong, and when he laid his hand on her belly, he felt their baby playing football inside.

"Corinne, *dolce amore*," he breathed, bending over her and stroking her beautiful face.

He knew all about hell, but had never really believed in heaven until that moment, when she opened her eyes and said drowsily, "Before I die, there's something I must tell you. I love you, Raffaello."

"You're not going to die," he murmured thickly. "I won't let you. I'm taking you home and never letting you out of my sight again."

She blinked and almost smiled, then reared up in the seat and clutched frantically at his hands. "Oh, Raffaello, the children—!"

"Are safe," he soothed her. "Their ponies showed more sense than they did and brought them back where they belong."

"How…?"

"The hows and whys can wait. Right now, we need to get you out of here." Carefully he unbuckled her seat belt and eased her out of the car. "Does anything hurt, *tesoro?*"

"My legs," she said, slumping against him. "They've gone to sleep."

Overhearing, Lorenzo asked, "Do you need the stretcher?"

Raffaello lifted her into his arms. "No," he said, sounding more like himself, and another cheer, more sustained this time, went up from the waiting group. Someone came forward to wrap a blanket around her shoulders, someone else spread another over the backseat of the Range Rover.

He climbed in beside her, and rested her head in his lap. She was shivering, from shock probably, but Lorenzo was already behind the wheel, with the engine running and the heater blasting. "Straight to the villa?" he asked, over his shoulder. "Or should I head for the nearest hospital?"

"The hospital," Raffaello said.

"No," she said. "Home."

"You should be checked over by a doctor, just to be sure, *amore mio.*"

"I don't need a doctor, I need you." She sighed and reached for his hand. "There's so much I have to say, Raffaello—things I should have told you a long time ago."

"And I you," he said. "I could spend a month cataloging my failures and shortcomings as a husband, but at this moment, the only words that really matter are that I love you."

In some ways, their return reminded her of the first time she'd set foot in the villa's grand entrance hall. But she saw it all now with a fresh eye; with an appreciation less for its elegant frescoed ceilings and wonderful arched windows, and more for the people waiting to greet her. The household staff, their smiles warmer than anything a blanket could offer. The children, so angelic in their pajamas it was hard to believe them capable of mischief. And Malvolia and Leonora, their poor faces drawn with anxiety and remorse.

"Ah, *figlia mia.*" Her mother-in-law wept, folding Corinne in a hug and pressing kisses to her cheeks, "can you ever forgive me?"

Not to be outdone, Leonora shoehorned her way into the embrace. "Please believe that we would never deliberately hurt the children, Corinna."

"Of course I believe you," she said, hugging them back. "I know how much you love them."

"And you, *carissima!*" Malvolia cried. "You are my daughter, my child. I was so afraid I would never see you again. What can I do to prove it to you?"

"I'd love to soak in a hot bath and change into something comfortable," she said, hoping to avoid a sobfest of mammoth proportions. "Then, you could feed me, if you like. I'm starving."

The words were scarcely out of her mouth before the staff jumped into action, Gastone sending a maid scurrying upstairs to fill the tub, and Filomena herding her crew back to the kitchen.

"But first," Corinne amended, when it was just the six of them left in the hall, "I'd like to give my children a big kiss." She held out her arms. "Come here, you little monkeys, and tell me what happened this afternoon, that you put the entire household into such an uproar."

Matthew raced over and barreled into her so hard, she'd have toppled over if Raffaello hadn't kept a firm grip on her. "Poopy pony ran away," he said indignantly. "He's a bad boy."

But Elisabetta hung back, her lower lip trembling.

"Come here, honey," Corinne said gently, disentangling herself from her son who showed not the slightest remorse for his shenanigans. "Right now, I could really use a hug from my girl, as well."

At that, Elisabetta flew to her and buried her face against her swollen belly. "It was my fault, Mommy," she wailed. "I shouldn't have let us go. Now you won't love me anymore."

So much for avoiding a sobfest! Corinne had held it together pretty well until that point, too glad and relieved that everyone was safe, to dwell on how close they'd come to tragedy. But Elisabetta broke her heart with that telling remark.

Tears rolling down her face, she lowered herself to her knees and held the little thing close. "I'll never not love you, darling," she whispered, when she could catch her breath enough to be coherent. "You're my special girl, and nothing will ever change that."

"I'm not as inclined to be forgiving," Raffaello said sternly, helping her to feet. "You two haven't heard the last of this. Go to the nursery and wait there for me."

"Don't be so hard on them," Corinne begged, watching as they made their doleful way upstairs. "They've been through enough for one day."

"What about what they've put the rest of us through?"

"They made a mistake."

"They put you and our baby in danger."

"And you rescued us." She leaned into him, loving the solid feel of his body, the strength of his arm around her. "A happy ending, for a change, Raffaello. Let's not spoil it."

Tightening his hold, he guided her up the stairs. "Not an ending, but a beginning, *amore mio,*" he replied, the look in his eye making her blush. "And it's about to start now."

CHAPTER TWELVE

FIRST, THEY STOPPED BY the nursery. "Because," Corinne pointed out, when he would have made straight for the master suite, "it's unfair to send them to bed without letting them know they're forgiven."

"Forgiven, my left foot!" he retorted. "Elisabetta was right. She knew better than to leave the property. *Dio*, Corinne, it's not as if they don't have space enough here to roam around pretty much wherever they like."

"You're forgetting she didn't act alone. You heard Matthew. The little imp probably goaded her into breaking the rules."

"If he did, he came by it honestly. You do a pretty good job yourself of making a person forget the rules, and here's the proof of that." He stroked her belly, the tenderness in his voice putting paid to his annoyance.

"Some rules are meant to be broken."

Sobering again, he said, "Not by our children, my darling. At least, not until they're old enough to understand the consequences. You could have died this afternoon, and while I won't overemphasize that with them because I think they're already frightened enough by what they did.

I do intend to make it very clear I won't tolerate such behavior again. Are we together on this, Corinne, or do I go in there and deal with them by myself?"

"We're together," she said, slipping her arm through his. "Always and forever."

She thought she knew what intimacy was all about, but that evening, he brought new and deeper meaning to the word, one that combined tenderness with passion, and murmured words of love that broke down all the barriers she'd thrown up in her misguided attempts to remain heart-whole.

"Now that that's over with, I have a confession to make," she began, the minute they'd put their chastened children to bed and were alone in their own suite, supposedly dressing for dinner.

"Shut up, *angelo mio*," he said softly. "I have waited long enough to do this and won't be put off a minute longer." And to make sure she fell in with his wishes, he captured her mouth with his.

If all he ever did was kiss her, she would be a happy woman, she thought dizzily, surrendering herself to him. But he had more in mind and murmuring to her between kisses, he deftly stripped away her clothes until she stood before him as she never had before, with lamplight illuminating every lush curve and contour. Self-conscious suddenly, she tried to cover herself—an exercise in futility, considering how much of her there was—but he imprisoned her hands in one of his, and skimmed his other over her breasts and belly to her thighs, all the time subjecting her to a slow, unblinking inspection that left her skin puckering with heated delight.

She knew then that kisses would never be enough. Every part of her, every pore, every strand of hair, needed him as a flower needed water.

"Sei bella," he whispered. "You are beautiful, my Corinne."

"I'm huge," she said.

He shook his head, his eyes scouring the length of her a second time. "You are a goddess."

"Who's sort of lied to you about her past."

"You served time behind bars?" he inquired, lazily cupping one full breast in his palm.

A shiver of pure pleasure raced up her spine. "Nothing that extreme," she said breathlessly. "Just something I should have told you a long time ago."

He steered her into the bathroom and handed her into the sunken tub, which the maid had prepared. "Then whatever it is can wait a few minutes longer."

Wreathed in scented coils of steam, she watched, heavy-eyed, as he tossed aside his own clothes and joined her, sliding in behind her and pulling her against him so that her spine rested against his chest and the water lapped at her chin. *"Va bene,"* he said, the words grazing her ear like a caress, "I'm listening."

Now that the moment was finally at hand, all the reasonable explanations she'd rehearsed slipped from her mind. "I wasn't happily married to Joe," she said baldly. "In fact, I was almost relieved when it came to an end. Not that I was glad he died, you understand—he was much too young for that—but because I didn't have to keep trying to fix what I knew had been broken almost from the beginning."

"I see," he said. "And you couldn't tell me this before, because…?"

"I was jealous. You and Lindsay got it right the first time, and were so happy together. Just from the way you spoke, I knew that you had such reverence for marriage, and I was afraid if you knew about mine, you'd think less of me for not trying harder to make it work."

"You worried for nothing, *tesoro*. I'd never hold myself up as an expert on making a marriage work. I might have got it right, as you put it, with Lindsay, but look how close I've come to ruining ours because I was too blind to recognize a gem when one landed in my lap."

"You don't have to say that, Raffaello. I knew from the outset that you didn't marry me for love."

"No," he said, "I didn't. With you, the order was reversed. I married you first, then I fell in love with you. But Corinne, *angelo mio, anima mia,* that doesn't mean I love you less."

He rested his chin on her head and was silent a moment. When he spoke again, his voice trembled. "This afternoon, when I thought I might have lost you, I didn't know how I'd go on. Were it not for the children, I'm not sure I'd have wanted to. But you're here now, and I thank God for giving me a second chance to show you how much you mean to me."

Turning her head, she kissed his jaw. "You are my life, Raffaello. I am so honored to be your wife, so proud to be carrying your child."

"I would take you to bed now, if I could," he murmured. His flesh stirring urgently against the small of her back, "but I know my mother still hasn't forgiven herself for causing us so much distress, and if we don't put in an appearance for dinner, she'll worry all night long that we haven't forgiven her, either. But later, my love…"

"Later," she echoed, a thrill of anticipation streaming through her blood.

But later came sooner than either of them anticipated. Drying each other metamorphosed into an exploration that went far beyond the mundane, and somehow they were on the bed and he was kissing her all over and she was reaching for him and whimpering with need.

He took her breath away. She had never felt more loved. The entire universe narrowed until there was nothing but the feel of his skin against hers, the taste and scent of him filling her senses. And finally, the fierce strength of him inside her, smooth as marble, hot as fire.

"It is not safe," he muttered hoarsely, desperately trying to stem the passion coursing between them.

But safety was all about lying in his arms, with him buried so deeply inside her that they were as one. Safety came from hearing him say *I love you,* and for her daring to say, *I love you, too.* Safety was knowing that her heart had found a home at last.

Touching her finger to her tongue, she dipped it in the hollow of his throat. "I'm branding you," she whispered, echoes of passion lingering in her voice. "Now you're mine."

"I've been yours almost from the day I first saw you," he said. "I just didn't know it at the time."

Later, after they were dressed finally, she lifted her hair so that he could fasten her pearls around her neck. "This is the last time you wear these," he grumbled, struggling with the clasp. "I shall buy you the finest to be found, one for every second of happiness you have brought me, and all strung together with a diamond clasp that works as it should."

"I don't need diamonds or pearls," she said. "I have you and our children. Which reminds me. If the baby's a girl, I think we should call her Lindsay."

But he shook his head. "No, *amore mio*. This is our child. Yours and mine. I loved Lindsay, but I came to terms with her death before I even knew you. She is part of my past and I'll never forget her, but the future belongs to you and me."

His mother and aunt seemed to be of the same opinion, albeit for different reasons. "We have reached a decision," Malvolia announced over a fabulous dinner of crayfish bisque and poached fish. "You have been very tolerant of our meddling, Corinna, but you are the mistress of this house now, and it's time my sister and I moved to the dowager villa."

Once upon a time, she'd have welcomed such news, but that was before when her insecurity had left her vulnerable to the slightest hint of criticism. "I won't hear of it," she said. "You belong here. I need you, this baby needs you, and so do your other grandchildren."

"You're a sweet girl to say so," Malvolia said, sudden tears sparkling in her dark eyes, "but I think we proved today that we are not nearly as necessary to your happiness as we liked to think and are, in fact, more of a liability than an asset."

"Tell them they're wrong," Corinne said, appealing to Raffaello.

He shrugged. "They are wrong only if you say so, *tesoro*. Because my mother is right. You are the mistress of this house and you decide whom you want living under its roof."

"I want you," she said, encompassing both women in a steady gaze. "More than that, I need you. You've taught me what real family is all about and that's something I never knew until I came here. Please don't take it away from me now. And please don't cry," she added, as Leonora buried her face in her napkin and gave way to an emotional outburst of weeping. "This is a happy day, a wonderful day. We are all here, safe and well, with enough love to go around for everyone to get his and her fair share. So let there be no more talk of anyone moving out. We are a family and we belong together."

"You are right about one thing," Malvolia said, succumbing to tears herself. "There is more love here than I have known in years. I see it when my son looks at you, Corinna, and when you look at him. I hear it when you take my grandson on your lap and sing to him, when you fill my granddaughter's heart with stories of her birth mother. And I hope you feel it when my sister and I look at you because, *figlia mia,* you have become so very, very dear to our hearts."

Either the crying was contagious or her hormones were in more of an uproar than usual. "Well, it's settled, then," she said, surreptitiously wiping away a tear.

"I hope so, because Filomena has made cannoli, your favorite dessert, my darling, and it would be a crime to ruin it by drowning it," Raffaello said, raising his wineglass. "So let me propose a toast. To my wife, who has brought more joy to all our lives than any of us ever hoped for or had the right to expect."

Ten days later, Corinne went into labor, and as it turned out, the question of choosing a girl's name didn't arise because, early on the morning of December 15, she gave birth to a nine pound, four ounce boy.

Raffaello was at her side from the first, doing all the things that strong men do when they watch their wives struggle to bring a new life into the world. He wiped the sweat from her brow, spurred her on to fresh effort when exhaustion sapped her strength and uttered not a word of complaint when she gripped his hand so tightly that she almost crushed the bones in his fingers.

He told her she was brave and wonderful and beautiful. He turned pale when the baby's head presented, and cried unashamedly when their son made his lusty debut.

"He's perfect," she said, when he placed the baby in her arms.

"*Si,*" Raffaello whispered, showering her face with featherlight kisses. "Just like his mother."

She brought her new son home from the hospital that same evening, to find the house dressed up for Christmas, with twinkling lights and trees in every room, carols playing softly on the stereo, gifts for the baby piled high in the nursery and a huge bouquet of gorgeous red roses in the bedroom.

"A dozen for each child," Raffaello told her, when all the excitement had died down and they were at last alone in bed together. Then taking a black velvet box hidden among the blooms' soft, fragrant petals, he withdrew an engagement ring, a magnificent diamond solitaire.

"As usual, I'm doing things in reverse order," he said, sliding it next to the wedding band on the third finger of her left hand, "but even though it comes almost a year after I asked you to marry me, know that, just like my love for you, I give it to you now because a diamond is forever."

"I like that word, 'forever,'" she said, sinking into the warmth of his embrace.

"Why is that, *adorata?*"

"Because all my life I've searched and at last, here on your wild and beautiful island, my heart has found its home. With you. Forever."

Special Offers

Every month we put together collections and longer reads written by your favourite authors.

Here are some of next month's highlights— and don't miss our fabulous discount online!

On sale 19th August

On sale 19th August

Julie Miller & Maureen Child

On sale 2nd September

Save 20% on all Special Releases

Find out more at
www.millsandboon.co.uk/specialreleases

Visit us
Online

0911/ST/MB347